P9-CKL-983

A WILLIAM MARCH OMNIBUS

books by ***WILLIAM MARCH***

COMPANY K

THE LITTLE WIFE AND OTHER STORIES

COME IN AT THE DOOR

THE TALLONS

SOME LIKE THEM SHORT (*short stories*)

THE LOOKING GLASS

TRIAL BALANCE (*short stories*)

OCTOBER ISLAND

THE BAD SEED

* A WILLIAM MARCH OMNIBUS *

*

WITH AN INTRODUCTION BY

ALISTAIR COOKE

RINEHART & COMPANY New York · Toronto

Published simultaneously in Canada by
Clarke, Irwin & Company, Ltd., Toronto

Printed in the United States of America

Library of Congress Catalog Card Number: 56-5630

Introduction to William March

BY ALISTAIR COOKE

William March Campbell, an organizer and later vice-president of the Waterman Steamship Corporation, was born in Mobile, Alabama, on the eighteenth of September, 1893. William March, the writer, was born sometime after that, not in fact until he was in his middle thirties, when a long attack of hysterical blindness left him at the mercy of what he discovered to be a wry and melancholy imagination. He recalled over and over again the men and the exploits of his own company of Marines in the First World War. When he regained his sight, he wrote *Company K*, and thereafter his preoccupation with human character, and what he could do with it on paper, gradually absorbed him, so that about ten years later he shed his active interest in the shipping business. It gave him, however, a comfortable income. No one knew quite how much until, after his death in May, 1954, his collection of paintings, including enough Soutines to furnish an asylum, was valued at a quarter of a million dollars.

The picture that these few sentences evoke may well be that of a successful tycoon with a dilettante itch for writing. Nothing could be less like the familiar image of this small, gray, bemused bachelor. The modeling of his big head, and a handsome aquiline nose, were the only remarkable things about his appearance. Met on a street or coming into a room, he could have passed anywhere as a small-business man resigned to frequent losses, a dry-goods salesman perhaps, not unlike the man on the train in "The Little Wife." He had the soft pale skin of a Southerner who has tolerated intolerable summers; the bland glance of a retailer who has encountered rapacity in the unlikeliest people; and, when the last guest was gone, the weariness of a man well acquainted with grief. He had a ready chuckle, but always for the more sardonic aspects of the human situation. I remember the relish with which he once quoted a remark of Salvador Dali's: "The only difference between me and a schizophrenic is that I am not a schizophrenic." March could savor this rather horrible truth because he had the advantage here over Dali: he had been there and back. When he could let loose and tame his fantasies on paper, he remained a fairly contented social animal. When he could not, the abyss was never far away. In the late 1940's he vanished from New York and, it turned out, from nearly all human society. Down in the place where he was born he relapsed into the lonely sickness that had always offered him an inferno of tragic situations. His friends did not expect him to come out of it, but he did. He bought an agreeable house in the French Quarter of New Orleans, resumed his quiet orderly life, and there composed his last work, *The Bad Seed.* In the middle of the night of May 15, 1954, he died in his sleep of a heart attack.

He was the second of eleven children in a humble family of Scots-Irish origins. And if his memories of childhood are to be believed, the small sawmill towns of Alabama and Florida sprouted as much melancholia as any crossroads in Faulkner's Mississippi. Twice he went north, once in his teens to attend the University of Valparaiso, Indiana; again, after he studied some law at the State University of Alabama, to be a law clerk in New York City. He was not long there, for as soon as the United States declared war on Germany, he enlisted in the Marines and was overseas almost at once. He took part in most of the grisly action that the Marine Corps saw and along the way, in his inconsequential way, he picked up a Distinguished Service Cross, the Navy Cross and a Croix de guerre. The experience of living as an acceptable member of a body of men whose lives were held cheap was, he later maintained, a cheering thing to him. From his account, he came back to America in good shape and went down to Mobile and helped to organize his shipping company. It flourished through the 1920's and began to open branches both at home and abroad. He was made the vice-president in charge of traffic in 1932 and was running the Hamburg office when his first book was published. He moved on to London in the mid-1930's and it was here, after the success of *Company K,* that he turned to writing as a substitute profession. *The Tallons* is dedicated to the Scottish analyst, Dr. Edward Glover, who rescued him over a couple of years from another descent into the pit. In the late 30's he came home to New York City and lived there, through the Second War, a life as untouched by its frenzy as it is possible to imagine. As an old soldier of an introspective and skeptical turn of mind, he shared the poet's, and scorned the politician's, view of war. He took a daily afternoon walk in Central Park but otherwise abhorred all country excursions; threw occasional pleasant cocktail parties; saw all the Hollywood movies on view; and like a tidy accountant gave over his mornings to the composition of fables, short stories and his masterpiece, *The Looking Glass.* It is not represented here, and rightly. Robert Loomis, who has put together this collection, searched through *The Looking Glass* twice to see if there was some fine episode that might stand alone. But it is too well-knit to unravel into fragments, its several tragedies overlap like the leaves of an artichoke, and you must strip them away one by one to reveal the core.

William March lived and died without much acclaim, except for the two books he cared least about: his first and his last. He won a few prizes for short stories. He is not mentioned in the 2,239 pages of the Spiller-Thorp-Johnson-Canby *Literary History of the United States.* Among the professional critics who remembered him for anything later than *Company K,* he was thought of, but not for long, as a journeyman realist, a third-rate Sherwood Anderson. When he was singled out, it was as a minor connoisseur of morbidity. This last is the point to start an analysis of his work. For it is relevant, if only because it occurs to so many people who have tried to read him. It is, I think, a misinterpretation of the tradition he sprang from, which is that of the great Victorians. For he shared their conventional assumption, which in our later emancipation we have shelved, that the depths of human nature are tortured and unpleasant. The Victorians had pressing reasons to feel so, since the strict propriety of their public life could be preserved only at the cost of a rich, private turmoil. It is an odd commentary on the discrepancy between our critical insight and our creative timidity that the Victorians we now tend to glorify are just those writers who mined what Gissing called "the dark underside" of human nature, but who had to make it acceptable to the Victorian reading public under various disguises: Melville passing off the deep human conflict with the sea as a piece of popular adventure; Lewis Carroll marketing a nightmare by calling it child's play; most of all Dickens, who had a merciless sense of the unconscious roots of character, but took the curse off it by kidding it in exaggeration, who waved the wand of his comic imagination so wildly, and so generously popped the candy of his sentimental sermons into the gaping mouths of the audience he had charmed that his admirers were willingly blinded to the very raw material he was feeding them—the murders, seductions, thieveries, extortions; the sadism, miserliness, alcoholism, and ingrown virginity that were his meat.

March, too, is a preacher but he offers no sermons that deny, by sentimental contradiction, the ruthlessness of his observation. His imagination is boundless, and sometimes comic, but it is neither playful nor lusty. The shadows of dubious motives, of second thoughts, fall on even the scenes of gaiety. His world is indeed the wild, true and exquisitely felt world of the schizophrenic. It is now surely no indiscretion to recall a remark Dr. Glover once made about him: "He taught me more about schizophrenia, by his idle fantasies on his lazy days, than all the books and thirty years of analytic practice."

The standard objection to him, then, is about the pathology of his material, and it is one that is central, I believe, to an understanding of his great gifts, because it must go deeper than those who hold it would care to confess. Americans have not been too squeamish on this account toward native writers with a more direct, and even wilful, attraction to morbidity. The nineteenth century took with gusto to Poe and Bierce; and we do not resent, as such, the impotent heroes of Hemingway, the euphoric or embittered bums of Saroyan or Steinbeck, the flashy decadents of James M. Cain, not to mention the more unrelieved psychopaths of Faulkner and Caldwell. Why, then, should these men be so lavishly celebrated, while March lies buried as an occasional irritant in books of semi-popular fiction? One reason could be the marked distance that separates most clinical fiction from the reader's daily experience.

But March provides no such *cordon sanitaire*. Almost anyone can be a park-bench sitter, a nurse, a shoe salesman, a father in a badly paid job, a husband with a nagging wife. And March, with his guileless pedestrian style, is so easily able to enlist the sympathy of the reader in people as "ordinary" as himself that, when he proceeds to track down the secret springs of their behavior, it is too late for the reader to extricate himself or deny his now angry identification, which might after all land him in one of the pitiable crises that confront so many of March's characters. His art is so direct, so patently engaging, and its symbols so familiar, that the reader unwittingly recognizes his own world and gladly becomes part of it, until the line between it and the swarming pit of the unconscious is seen to be disturbingly thin. Not many people are grateful for being asked to sink themselves in a mess of human tragedy where but for the grace of God or the comforts of Mammon go they. The audience for tragedy, when its subjects are contemporary, is greatly overestimated.

This echo of the Greek prescription for tragedy is not accidental. March's writing is classic (some say dull) in its undistracted realism, its bareness, its lack of salable amenities. And this, too, may make it forbidding or negligible to the modern reader, for he is wholly free from the characteristics of contemporary American fiction that have come to be fashionable: from the tough, monosyllabic narrative style; from the vaguely liberal humanitarianism that is so often no more than a wish to be thought a man of goodwill; from the self-conscious regionalism that flourished in American writing and painting throughout the 1930's and 40's. Any notable indifference to Southern chauvinism is remarkable in a Southern writer, for all of them are weighed down by the pride of shabby-genteelism. And more than half of March's work is about the fictional town of Reedyville. Yet even a devoted reader might not gather for some time that it is in Alabama. Few American writers are so accurate in the sense of their region—its folkways, vegetation, food, dialects, social equations—and yet again no writer is less "regional." Small-town life of the Deep South is, almost incidentally, what he knows best, but I doubt that Alabama will throw up an equestrian statue in his honor, for Reedyville becomes in his work simply the handiest familiar habitation for many moods of the human spirit, and in *The Looking Glass* it is a microcosm of all communities everywhere. An Englishman, a Frenchman or a Dane might recognize in Reedyville the spiritual anatomies of his neighbors, where Faulkner's famous county or Steinbeck's Cannery Row would only appall or fascinate him as an exotic.

If March's work had borrowed some of these familiar pigments, it would have been more pretentious, highly colored and impure. And his international reputation, I have no doubt, would have been more dashing. As it is, we have a prose style rather old-fashioned in its grave, consequential way, describing in unhurried serenity life as he has known it since the late 1890's. Most of his characters, considered as historical types, appear to be Southerners of the years before and during the First World War.

Minding the warning of Longinus that "the judgment of contemporary work is the last and ripest fruit of much experience" (and, he might have added, is rarely confirmed by posterity), we can come to a rough conclusion, and one most apt if we pursue the most familiar of the charges brought against March: that he is too clinical. It is true, more often than I care to admit, and he occasionally mars promising work by guiding the reader toward a doctrinaire view of character, or motive, where the observation of life is larger than any theory that would try to enclose it. But his essential gift is a deep and tender understanding of what Fromm has somewhere called "the pathology of the normal." March has a steady perception of human character, a knowledge of why so many human relationships must end in unsought tragedy, which is still only a fitful insight in the age of which Freud is glibly assumed to be the pioneer moral naturalist. If he attributes an audacious emotional health so often to social outcasts (the two Shakespearean whores in *The Looking Glass*) and illiterate Negroes (Lula in "She Talks Good Now"), it comes from March's enjoyment of irony in contemplating those whom the educated and the superior tend to pity.

He can be protesting and inept, and sometimes his satire is heavy-handed. Yet his best work—at least half of the fifty-five stories in *Trial Balance* and the whole of the incomparable *Looking Glass*—reflects the alternate play of two qualities that Anatole France perceived in fiction that is to be classic: pity and irony. There is less of them around than we incline to suppose, though their twin impostors—sentimentality and cynicism—run riot. For those who value this prescription, William March will be not so much an American classic as a classic modern who happened to be an American and who, therefore, in a time when literary jingoism pads like a witless hound-dog at the heels of political nationalism, is understandably one of the most underrated of contemporary American writers of fiction.

CONTENTS

NOVELETTE

NOVEL

*

COMPANY K

ROSTER

PRIVATE JOSEPH DELANEY

We have had supper and my wife and I are sitting on our porch. It will not be dark for an hour yet and my wife has brought out some sewing. It is pink and full of lace and it is something she is making for a friend of hers who is going to be married soon.

All about us are our neighbors, sprinkling their lawns, or sitting on their porches, as we are doing. Occasionally my wife and I speak to some friend who passes, and bows, or stops to chat for a moment, but mostly we sit silent. . . .

I am still thinking of the book which I have just completed. I say to myself: "I have finished my book at last, but I wonder if I have done what I set out to do?"

Then I think: "This book started out to be a record of my own company, but I do not want it to be that, now. I want it to be a record of every company in every army. If its cast and its overtones are American, that is only because the American scene is the one that I know. With different names and different settings, the men of whom I have written could, as easily, be French, German, English or Russian for that matter."

I think: "I wish there were some way to take these stories and pin them to a huge wheel, each story hung on a different peg until the circle was completed. Then I would like to spin the wheel, faster and faster, until the things of which I have written took life and were recreated, and became part of the wheel, flowing toward each other, and into each other; blurring, and then blending together into a composite whole, an unending circle of pain. . . . That would be the picture of war. And the sound that the wheel made, and the sound that the men themselves made as they laughed, cried, cursed or prayed, would be, against the falling of walls, the rushing of bullets, the exploding of shells, the sound that war, itself, makes. . . ."

We had been silent for a long time, and then my wife spoke: "I'd take out the part about shooting prisoners."

"Why?" I asked.

"Because it is cruel and unjust to shoot defenseless men in cold blood. It may have been done a few times, I'm not denying that, but it isn't typical. It couldn't have happened often."

"Would a description of an air raid be better?" I asked. "Would that be more humane? Would that be more typical?"

"Yes," she said. "Yes. That happened many times, I understand."

"Is it crueler, then, for Captain Matlock to order prisoners shot, because he was merely stupid, and thought the circumstances warranted that, than for an aviator to bomb a town and kill harmless people who are not even fighting him?"

"That isn't as revolting as shooting prisoners," said my wife stubbornly. Then she added: "You see the aviator cannot see where his bomb strikes, or what it does, so he is not really responsible. But the men in your story had the prisoners actually before them. . . . It's not the same thing, at all."

I began to laugh with bitterness: "Possibly you are right, I said. "Possibly you have put into words something inescapable and true."

Then my wife reached out and took my hand. "You think I'm hard and unsympathetic," she said; "but I'm not, really, darling."

I sat silent after that, watching the Ellis children across the street shouting and laughing and playing on their lawn. It was early June and there was a faint breeze carrying with it the smell of spiced pinks and Cape jasmine. Gradually it got darker and my wife put away her sewing, yawned and rubbed her eyes. All about us were the green, well-kept lawns of our neighbors, with flowers in bloom and shrubs banked against walls and fences. The sight of this green, flowing smoothness made me think, somehow, of old battlefields which I have seen. . . .

You can always tell an old battlefield where many men have

lost their lives. The next Spring the grass comes up greener and more luxuriant than on the surrounding countryside; the poppies are redder, the corn-flowers more blue. They grow over the field and down the sides of the shell holes and lean, almost touching, across the abandoned trenches in a mass of color that ripples all day in the direction that the wind blows. They take the pits and scars out of the torn land and make it a sweet, sloping surface again. Take a wood, now, or a ravine: In a year's time you could never guess the things which had taken place there.

I repeated my thoughts to my wife, but she said it was not difficult to understand about battlefields: The blood of the men killed on the field, and the bodies buried there, fertilize the ground and stimulate the growth of vegetation. That was all quite natural, she said.

But I could not agree with this, too-simple, explanation: To me it has always seemed that God is so sickened with men, and their unending cruelty to each other, that he covers the places where they have been as quickly as possible.

PRIVATE ROWLAND GEERS

IT HAD snowed steadily, and the Virginia countryside was white and still; close-order drill was impossible that day, so Captain Matlock took us for a long hike across the hills. Coming back, our spirits were so high that we began to double time of our own accord, shouting at the tops of our voices and hitting each other with snowballs. We came to the top of the hill and looked down. It was almost dusk, and below us, in the valley, lights began to show in the barracks. Then Ted Irvine gave a shout and ran down the hill, and in a moment we had all broken ranks, rushing after him, pushing and laughing and piling into the bunk houses.

It was an hour before supper, so Walt Webster and I decided to have a bath, but when we got to the bath house, we found there was no hot water there, and for a minute we stood with our clothes off, shivering. Then, we held our breath and ran under the cold shower, jumping up and down and hitting each other on the chest, until a warm glow began to flow through our bodies. "This is great," I said. "This is great, Walt!"

But Walt who was singing senselessly, at the top of his lungs, merely because he was young and full of life, stopped suddenly, and picked me up in his powerful arms, carrying me to the bath house door, trying to throw me into a snow bank. But I locked my legs around him and held on, and we both went into the bank together. We floundered about in the snow wrestling and laughing. The other boys in the bunk house saw us and soon every man in the company was naked and wallowing in the snow, shouting with exhilaration.

Walt stood up, slapped his thighs, and began to crow like a cock. "Bring on the whole German army!" he shouted. "Bring them on all together, or one at a time. I can whip them all!"

CORPORAL JERRY BLANDFORD

Sitting next to me at the counter was a sweet-looking girl, or rather she was a grown woman, twenty-eight or thirty years old, and we got to talking. I reached over and took her check, but she put up a kick. "I think I ought to be the one to be paying the check," she said laughingly. Then we went out of the drug store and walked down the street. I told her how I had looked forward to my leave and how disappointed I was. It wasn't much fun when you didn't know anybody. I didn't have any place to go in particular, so I was walking in her direction, but finally she said she had to turn. "Well, good-by," she said, and held out her hand.

"Don't leave me," I said. "Come on to the hotel and stay with me. I'm not insulting you," I said. "I respect you. I'm not trying to insult you."

She thought a minute and then shook her head.

"I just want you to be with me," I said. "I want to smell

cologne on a woman and I want to see her with her hair down. I won't do anything that you don't want me to do. I won't even touch you, unless you say it's all right. . . ."

"You must have a very poor opinion of me, to think I'm the sort of woman you can pick up on the street."

"No," I said, "I respect you. If I didn't respect you, I wouldn't ask you to come. If I wanted a street-walker, I could get fifty, and you know it. I respect you," I said; "I really do."

She stood there, looking at me. Then she shook her head. "I'm sorry," she said.

"I'm going across next week," I said. "I may be killed in a month. I may never have a chance to be with a decent woman again. . . ."

Then suddenly she made up her mind. "Very well," she said, "I'll come. I'll stay with you every minute of the time until your leave is up. Go get your things and we'll go to another hotel and register as man and wife."

"I'll be careful not to embarrass you. I won't make any breaks, or let any of the boys know."

"I don't care," she said. "I don't care who knows. I wouldn't come at all if I cared about that." Then she slipped her arm through mine and we walked away.

CORPORAL PIERRE BROCKETT

We knew they wouldn't sell to soldiers in uniform as a rule, but this bar was out of the way, and we figured we might talk the bartender into it. So all three of us went in and lined up.

"Well, what will you gentlemen have?" asked the bartender in a polite voice.

"Give me a rye straight," I said.

"Give me rye with a beer chaser," said Bill Anderson.

"I'll take Scotch," said Barney Fathers.

The bartender picked up a bottle and then put it down again. "Are you boys in a big hurry?" he asked.

"No," we all said together, "oh, no, we got lots of time!"

"All right, then," said the bartender; "just stand there until war is over and I'll be glad to shake up them drinks."

PRIVATE ARCHIE LEMON

THE FOURTH day out was a Sunday, and that morning the Captain held services on deck. It was December, but the sun was shining on the surrounding water, its light reflected blindingly in the ship's brass. It was almost too warm, in the sunlight, for the heavy overcoats we wore. We stood there for a while, and then the services began. They were very simple: a hymn, a prayer and a short sermon. Then, at the end, a benediction in which the chaplain asked God to give our hearts courage, and our arms strength, to strike down our adversaries. He said we were not soldiers, in the accepted sense of the word: We were crusaders who had dedicated our lives and our souls to our country and to our God that the things we revere and hold sacred, might not perish.

When we got back to our quarters, we were all silent and thoughtful. We lay on our bunks thinking of the chaplain's words. Sylvester Keith, whose bunk was next to mine, gave me a cigarette, and lit one himself. "The chaplain has got the right dope," he said: "I mean about saving civilization and dedicating our lives to our country."

Bob Nalls had come up, and joined us. "I've been thinking over what he said about this being the war to end injustice. I don't mind getting killed to do a thing of that sort. I don't mind, since the people coming after me will live in happiness and peace. . . ."

Then we sat there smoking our cigarettes and thinking.

CORPORAL WALTER ROSE

GOING across in the transport, I was picked for a special submarine guard. Each man in our detail was given a pair of glasses and assigned a certain angle of water to watch, so that the entire horizon was constantly observed. My angle was 247 to 260 and in the tower with me was Les Yawfitz, whose angle joined mine. There was a telephone by each of us which communicated with the engine room below and the gun crews standing by on deck.

Late one afternoon, when it was cold and raining, I saw a tomato crate floating on the water. I looked at it for a long time, trying to make up my mind if it was moving with the tide. Then when I'd about decided that it was, I noticed it had moved backward a foot or two, contrary to the direction of the waves. I grabbed my 'phone and reported to the gunners, and the engineers, that there was a periscope concealed under the crate. The transport swung to one side quickly, and at the same moment the gunners began to fire. Immediately we saw a submarine come to the top, flounder, and turn sidewise in a burst of steam.

Everybody gave me the old glad-hand and wanted to know how I could tell that the tomato crate camouflaged a periscope. I didn't know, as a matter of fact, I just guessed right; that's all: So I was an intelligent hero, and got the Navy Cross. If I'd been wrong, and there'd been nothing under the crate, I would have been a dumb bastard, a disgrace to the outfit, and, like as not, would have been thrown into the brig. They're not fooling me any.

PRIVATE SAMUEL UPDIKE

IT FELT good to be on solid land again after fourteen days on a crowded transport. Our hobnailed boots clattered on the cobblestones, as we marched at ease down the main street of the town and up the hill that led to the barracks. It was cold, but the sun was out, and everybody was in high spirits, and full of fun. We laughed and shoved each other about. Then Rowland Geers passed his pack and rifle to Fred Willcoxen and began to turn handsprings, and clown. But the French people stood there looking at us, with their mouths open, a surprised expression on their faces. They weren't at all like an American crowd: We tried to joke and kid them, but they wouldn't answer. They just looked at us like we were crazy, and turned their heads away.

"What's the matter with these people?" asked Tom Stahl. "Where's their pep? Where's their spirit?"

"Everybody is wearing black," I said. "You'd think they'd just come from a funeral."

Then a woman in the crowd, standing near the curb, answered me in a broad, English voice: "The people wearing black are in mourning," she said, as if she were speaking to a child. "We're having a war, you know."

"Oh, I didn't realize!" I said. "I'm sorry, I really am!" But the English woman had turned and walked away.

I've thought many times afterwards what clowns we must have seemed.

SERGEANT MICHAEL RIGGIN

One thing that puzzles me about these new men is why they are always writing letters home, or getting packages from their mothers or sweethearts. You didn't see much of that in the old days, when I came into the service. Most of the boys then didn't have any people to write to, and the only letters they got were from strumpets they'd met while on liberty. But, as I said, these new men are always writing letters and sending letters off. I can't understand that.

I was raised in an orphan asylum, myself. No chance of anybody who was raised in an orphan asylum, under Mrs. McMallow's care being homesick. . . . I'll never forget the old Tartar. She had a long, bony face and yellow teeth. She pulled her hair back as tight as she could, and pinned it to her head. She talked in a sharp, worried voice. She wasn't very good to any of the kids, but she used to pick on me more than the others.—Well, I guess I gave her more trouble than the others. She said she'd break my stubbornness, and I guess she'd a-done it, too, if

I hadn't run away when I was fourteen, because I couldn't stand it any longer.

I don't mean she beat me. She never done that. (Unless I damned well deserved it, of course, and then it didn't hurt much.) She was just mean. . . . This'll give you an idea: When I was nine years old, I cut my foot on a piece of glass and the doctor had to sew it up. That night Mrs. McMallow came to the hospital to see how I was getting along. (Oh, she always done what she thought was her duty, all right.) She had made a bowl of soup with macaroni in it, knowing that I liked macaroni soup better than anything else. When I realized she had made the soup just for me, I put my arms out and pulled her down on the bed beside me. I wanted her to take me in her arms, and kiss me, but I didn't know how to ask her to do it, so I reached up and tried to kiss her, but she pulled her face away quickly and took my hands off her arm. "Michael Riggin," she said, "how many times have I told you to keep your finger nails clean!" Then I picked up the bowl of macaroni soup and threw it across the room. I wouldn't have eaten a spoonful of it to save my life. . . .

That's what I mean about these fellows writing home all the time. I can't understand it. That's all a bunch of hooey. Anybody who cares for anybody else is a God damned fool, if you ask me! I don't care a hoot for anything there is: Take all you can get, I say, and don't give anything in return, if you can help it.

SERGEANT THEODORE DONOHOE

If you worked for a grocer or a candy maker, or even an undertaker, and went around talking about what inferior groceries, or candy, your employer sold, or how unsatisfactory all funerals were, you would not, unless you were a fool, expect any advancement or honors in your chosen business or profession, would you? Then why in the name of heaven do otherwise intelligent men like Leslie Yawfitz or Walter Rose talk contemptuously about the mismanagement, waste and stupidity of war and then expect to receive promotions or decorations, becoming sullen and dissatisfied when those things fail to appear?

I tell you war is a business, like anything else, and if you get anywhere in it, you've got to adjust yourself to its peculiarities and play your cards the way they fall.

CAPTAIN TERENCE L. MATLOCK

WHEN my platoon sergeants had assembled, I read the order granting liberty to fifty men from each company. . . . "Trucks will pick up the liberty party at two o'clock, this afternoon, at Regimental Headquarters, and the same trucks will be waiting for the men in Celles-le-Cher in front of the Y.M.C.A. hut, until eight o'clock, Sunday night," I read. Then we went over the company roster, squad by squad, and picked the men who were to go. Sergeant Dunning looked at his watch. It was 11:10. "I guess the boys will have to hurry to make that two o'clock truck," he said. My other sergeants moved away also, but I stopped them.

"Before these men go on liberty, I want their equipment shined up; their rifles cleaned and oiled, and their extra clothes washed and hung on the line to dry." The sergeants saluted me and turned to go.

"Yes, sir," they said.

"Wait a minute," I continued. "Don't be so fast: I'll inspect the rifles and equipment of the liberty party at 12:30 in the billets. Then, at 1 P.M. have each man report to me, outside the office, with his extra clothes washed and wrung out. . . . And tell the men they'd better wash them clean! . . ."

Promptly at one o'clock the men began lining up outside the company office, their uniforms scraped and brushed, their faces shining. It had rained the night before and they picked their way across the muddy courtyard, so as not to soil their boots, which had been rubbed with a mixture of soot and dubbing. Across the arm of each man were the clothes he had washed out.

I sat at a table in the courtyard with Sergeant Boss, my top sergeant, and Corporal Waller, my clerk, who had the passes made out and ready for the men, beside me. Then the first man, Private Calhoun, came up and spread his clothes on the table. I opened them up, looking carefully at the seams.

"Is that your idea of a clean pair of drawers?" I asked.

"That's mildew," he said; "I tried, but I couldn't get it out, sir."

"Well, go back and try some more," I said.

Calhoun turned away, and as he did somebody at the rear of the line gave me the raspberry.

"Who did that?" I asked.

Nobody answered.

The second man had placed his clothes on the table. I picked them up and threw them in the mud without looking at them. Then as each man came up with his clothes, I took them from his arm and threw them into the mud-puddle. After that, I took the passes from Waller, tore them into tiny pieces and scattered them on a pile of manure. . . .

"When you men have learned to respect your commanding officer, things are going to be better all the way round," I said.

FIRST SERGEANT PATRICK BOSS

I've seen some pretty bad outfits in my time, but this one takes the cake. In the old days men knew how to soldier and how to take care of themselves. They were tough birds all right, but they knew discipline, and they respected the officers over them because the officers respected them, too. In the first place, you had to be an A No. 1 man to get in: They weren't taking just anything in those days.—Well, they've let the bars down now, all right! Look at the riffraff we get.—Half of them, right now, don't know the difference between the orders "right front into line" and "on right into line." Part of the company starts to execute one command, and a part another, while some of the men just stand still, looking about them helplessly. I've tried to beat it into their thick heads. I've tried and tried.—Christ, it's enough to make a man tear out his hair, I tell you! . . .

In the old days they used to say that a company with a good top sergeant didn't need a captain. I guess that's true. I don't want to throw any bouquets at myself, but if it wasn't true, I don't know what would become of *this* one. Nit-wit Terry—that ribbon-selling wonder! . . . How do men like him get a commission, anyway? It beats me. It's over my head. Well, anyway, I'm getting out of the outfit when this hitch is done. It's not like it was in the old days, when a man could really have some self-respect.

PRIVATE ROGER JONES

I NEVER saw the trenches so quiet as they were that time at Verdun. There wasn't a squarehead in sight, and except for the fact that they fired a machine gun every once in a while, and sent up a rocket, you wouldn't have known there was anybody ahead of us at all. Everything would be very quiet when suddenly the rocket would go whizzing up and the machine gun would splutter a time or two. Then a few minutes later another rocket would go off, farther down the trench, and there would be a dozen more machine gun bullets to go with it.

The boys made up a story that there wasn't anybody in front of us except an old man, who rode a bicycle, and his wooden legged wife. The old man would ride down the duckboards, with his wife running behind him carrying the machine gun. Then the man would stop and send up a rocket, while the old woman fired the gun. After that they started all over, and kept it up all night.

The boys talked about the old German, and his wife with the wooden leg, until, after a while, everybody began to believe they were actually there.

"It's just like a German to make his wife run behind him and carry the heavy gun," said Emil Ayres one night. "They all beat their wives, too, I've heard it said."

"That's a lie!" said Jakie Brauer whose mother and father were both born in Germany. "Germans are as good to their wives as Americans, or anybody else!"

"Then why don't he carry the gun sometime?" Emil asked; "why don't he carry the gun and let the old woman ride on the bicycle?"

PRIVATE CARTER ATLAS

For breakfast weak coffee, a thin slice of bread and a dipper full of watery soup; for dinner two soggy potatoes, with dirt still clinging to their jackets, a piece of meat the size of a man's thumb and a spoonful of jam; for supper more coffee, but weaker this time, and a pan full of unseasoned rice.—How can a man keep going on such rations? But try to get more? Try and see what happens to you!

I thought about food all the time: I remembered all the good meals I had ever eaten and thought of rare dishes, such as truffles or ortolans, which I had read about, but never tasted. I used to plan my first meal on the outside, but thinking about those things all the time made me so hungry, I was almost crazy. When I closed my eyes I could see a thick, luscious steak, broiled a deep brown, a lump of butter melting over it and becoming a part of its juices. I could see the steak, surrounded by tender, French fried potatoes, and smell its flavor as distinctly as if it were actually before me. I lay on my bunk with my eyes closed, gloating over the steak. . . . "In just a minute I'll cut into it, and begin to eat," I thought. . . .

Then the detail returned to the trenches, bringing our supper in a g.i. can. It was rice again, cold and clammy, and when Sergeant Donohoe gave me my part of it, I took it, hungry as I was, and dumped it in the mud. Then I went back to the dugout and lay on my bunk and cried like a baby. If they'd just give me a good meal every once in a while, I wouldn't mind this war so much!

PRIVATE LUCIEN JANOFF

My trouble went back to that pair of shoes the supply sergeant issued me at St. Aignan. They were three sizes too big for me and they felt like they were made out of cast-iron. My heels kept blistering every time I took a hike. They were sore all the time. After a while they got callused, and they didn't blister any more, but when they quit blistering, they hurt worse than ever. I couldn't even bear to touch them, they hurt so.

Finally Roy Winters said he thought there was pus under the calluses and that was why my heels ached so. He said I ought to go to the dressing station and have them opened up. "Nothing doing!" I said. "Fat chance of me doing that! I know well enough what *those* babies will do to me: They'll give me chloroform, and when I wake up my feet will be cut off at the ankles. . . . 'What the hell you kicking about?' they'll say to me; 'your *heels* don't hurt you no more, do they?' . . . That's what they'll say.—You can't fool me. . . ."

Then Roy said he would split my heels himself and get the pus out, if I thought I could stand it. Told him to go ahead. Told him I'd stand it, all right. A fellow named Rufe Yeomans and a fellow named Charlie Upson held my legs, so I wouldn't jerk away. I said I wouldn't make a sound. Didn't either, while Roy was cutting, but when he was scraping near the bone I hollered some. I couldn't help hollering a little, I guess.

PRIVATE THOMAS STAHL

In Merlaut, where we were billeted, Wilbur Halsey and I were drawing water from the well when the bucket came off and fell to the bottom with a splash. "Wait a minute," said Wilbur; "I'll go inside and tell the old lady, and get another bucket from her." A few minutes later the old lady came running out tearing her hair and beating her breasts, with Wilbur walking behind her, trying to explain what had happened. When the old lady reached the well, it was all Wilbur and I could do to keep her from jumping after the bucket. She got more and more excited every minute.

Allan Methot, who speaks good French, came out of the billet and explained to the woman that it had been an accident, and that Wilbur and I were willing to pay for the bucket, but she knocked the money out of his hand and threw herself on the ground. A crowd of French people had gathered. They stared over the wall, and the old woman pointed at us and began to talk excitedly. Then the French people all made clucking noises and each, in turn, went to the edge of the well and peered over, shaking their heads and spreading their arms out.

"That must have been an extra fine bucket," said Wilbur. "The way they act, you'd think it was made out of platinum."

By the next day everybody in town had come to look down the well and listen to the old woman's story, and to sympathize with her. That afternoon when we got orders to move, there was a crowd around the well looking down, as if they expected the bucket to jump up into their arms, of its own accord, while the old lady wiped her eyes on the bottom of her petticoat.

"This is getting on my nerves," said Wilbur . . . "I'll be glad to get out of this place. Everybody here is nuts."

SERGEANT JAMES DUNNING

Lieutenant Fairbrother had just been assigned to my platoon when he thought of a way to find machine gun nests at night. He said four or five men should fill their pockets with rocks and creep along the German lines until they came to a clump of bushes or a mound that looked suspicious. Then they were to throw in a couple of rocks. If there was a machine gun concealed, the throwing of the rocks would make the gunners mad at us, and they would begin to fire, thus exposing their position. Nobody cracked a smile while he was speaking to the platoon, but when he had gone out of the bunk house, we began to laugh.

"I think one of the men should carry a sky-rocket in his right hand," said Frank Halligan. "Then, when the machine gunners start firing, he can hold the rocket between his thumb and forefinger until it is struck by one of the passing bullets and ignited. Then the rocket will soar into the air and fall behind the German lines, where the Kaiser is pinning Iron Crosses on a regiment. As the rocket comes down, the Kaiser bends over, and the tip of the hot rocket catches him squarely on his military butt. The Kaiser jerks forward and rubs the place with his hands, thinking that somebody has kicked him, and that the men have mutinied. This frightens His Majesty, and he begins to run toward our lines. As he runs, the whole German army falls in behind him, trying to explain what had happened, but the Kaiser won't listen: He runs and runs until he reaches the Marne, which he tries to jump, falls short, and is drowned. Then the entire German army, out of politeness, jump in also, and are drowned, and the war is over and we all go back to the States."

Albert Nallett got up and closed the door. "Don't let anybody hear you talking like that, sarge," he said. "If they knew at Divisional about your fine military mind, they'd have bars on your shoulders and a Sam Browne buckled around your waist before you could say scat."

SERGEANT WILBUR TIETJEN

I would take up a position in the line, my rifle strapped to my shoulder, the barrel resting on the bank, and look through my telescopic sights at the German trenches, a thousand or more yards away. (A sniper must have patience; that is as important as ability to shoot good.) And so I would lie there for hours, studying the German line, which looked deserted. "There are men there, all right," I'd say to myself, "and one of them will get careless and show himself before long." Sure enough, sooner or later, a head would appear over the side of the trench or a man would crawl outside for a minute.

Then I would figure windage and elevation, line up my sights, slack my body, take a half-breath and squeeze the trigger very slow. More often than not the man I was aiming at would jump up and spin around a couple of times before falling. He looked very comical from where I was—like a toy soldier which somebody had whittled being upset by the wind.

I was the best rifleman in the regiment, so everybody said. One time, in July, I hit nine men out of a possible twelve. The colonel was in the line that afternoon and he and his adjutant were watching my shots with their strong field glasses. They made a lot over me when I plugged the ninth man and I grinned like a great fellow. You see, the men were so far away, it didn't seem like killing anybody, really. In fact I never thought of them as men, but as dolls, and it was hard to believe that anything as small as that could feel pain or sorrow. If there was a race of people no bigger, say, than your thumb, even the best hearted person in the world could step on one of them and not feel bad about it. When that thought came into my head, I told it to Allan Methot, but he said a fellow had already used it in a book. "Well, it's the truth, even if a book *has* been wrote about it," I said.

PRIVATE JESSE BOGAN

WE CAME to a long hill shaped like a semi-circle and dug in against the protected side. Below us the Germans were shelling Marigny, a small town. We could see people running out of the houses, making funny gestures, and down the narrow streets, until they joined the line that filled the highway. Then we dug in on the off side of the hill and waited.

It was late May and the whole countryside was green and beautiful. Below us, in the valley, fruit trees were in bloom, pink, white and red, running across the valley in strips of color, and spotting the side of the hill. Then a haze settled over the valley, and gradually it got dark.

The Germans had quit shelling the town. It lay demolished below us. Lieutenant Bartelstone came up: "All right, men! Get your things together. We're going in the wood when it gets dark." Then he spoke to Sergeant Dunning: "The orders are to stop the Germans and not let them advance an inch farther. . . ."

"Well, anyway," said Alex Marro, after the lieutenant had gone, "that's simple and to the point."

"What's the name of this place?" asked Art Crenshaw.

"I don't know," said Sergeant Dunning. "What difference does that make?"

"I asked a Frenchman on the road," said Allan Methot, "and he said it was called Belleau Wood."

"Come on! Come on!" said Sergeant Dunning. "Get your equipment together, and quit chewing the fat!"

PRIVATE PHILIP CALHOUN

AL DE CASTRO and I sat crouched in a small shell hole, excited, watching the German artillerymen destroy Marigny. A shell-shocked dog was huddled against the community wash house. His tail curved under him, and the hair on his back was stiff and erect. Water ran from his eyes and his mouth slavered. Occasionally he would spin rapidly in a circle, and attempt to bite his tail; then he would stop, exhausted, and snap weakly to right and left; or occasionally he thrust his muzzle to the sky, and his jaws opened widely, but the sound of his voice was lost in the sound of the shelling.

At last little remained standing in the town except one wall of white limestone. On this wall was a religious print, in a gilt frame, showing a crown of thorns and a bleeding heart from which flames ascended; while beside it, on a wooden peg, hung a peasant's shapeless coat. I lay on my belly and stared at the wall. . . . The shells fell faster and the frightened dog began again to spin and chase his tail. The white wall trembled and a few stones fell, and when I looked up again, the coat had slipped from its peg and lay in the dust like a sprawling, dead bat. . . . Then, suddenly, the shelling stopped, and the silence that followed was terrible. The dog sniffed the air. He lifted his voice and howled.

I got up, then, and put on my pack and a moment later Al stood beside me. For a moment we both looked at the white wall, still standing, and at the sacred picture untouched in its place.

Al walked over to the wall and stood regarding it curiously: "Why should that one wall remain?" he asked. "Why should it alone be spared? . . ."

Then as he stood there adjusting his pack, and fumbling with the rusty catch of his cartridge belt, there came a tearing sound, and a sharp report; and down fell the wall in a cloud of dust, smothering the heart from which flames were ascending, and crushing him to death with its weight.

PRIVATE EDWARD ROMANO

I WAS out on observation post near Hill 44 and it was raining. There was no wind and the rain fell straight down. To the north there were flashes, like heat lightning, along the horizon, and the low growling of distant batteries. As I crouched in the trench, wet to the skin and shivering with cold, I thought: "It's quiet here tonight, but up to the north terrible things are happening: There, at this instant, men are being torn to pieces, or stabbed to death with bayonets."

A Very light went up suddenly, to break in the sky with a faint kiss, and against its flare I saw the intricate intrenchments of rusting barbed wire. I saw, too, the slow rain, gleaming like a crystal against the light, and falling in dead, unslanted lines to the field. I lay huddled and trembling in the shallow trench, my rifle pressed against my body. . . . The rain was washing up bodies of men buried hastily; there was an odor of decay in the air. . . .

I saw a man walking toward me, upright and unafraid. His feet were bare and his beautiful hair was long. I raised my rifle to kill him, but when I saw it was Christ, I lowered it again. "Would you have hurt me?" he asked sadly. I said yes, and began to curse: "You ought to be ashamed of yourself to let this go on! —You ought to be ashamed! . . ."

But he lifted his arms to the sodden field, to the tangled wire, to the charred trees like teeth in a fleshless jaw. "Tell me what to do," he said. "Tell me what to do, if you know! . . ." It was then that I began to cry, and Christ cried, too, our tears flowing with the slow rain.

At twelve o'clock my relief came. It was Ollie Teclaw, and I wanted to tell him what I had seen, but I knew that he would only laugh at me.

LIEUTENANT EDWARD BARTELSTONE

I came off watch cold and sick—shivering; wet to my miserable skin. I could feel vermin itching my back and crawling over my chest. I had not bathed for weeks and my feet had blistered offensively. There was a sour, overpowering smell in the dugout, and it turned my stomach and made me want to vomit. . . . I lighted my candle and looked for a long time at my dirty hands, and my finger nails, caked with muck. A feeling of revulsion came over me. "I'll stand anything else," I said, "but I won't stand this filth any longer. . . ." I cocked my pistol and placed it on the shelf beside the candle. . . . "When it's exactly midnight, I'm going to kill myself. . . ."

On my bed were some magazines which Archie Smith had read and passed on to me. I picked one up at random, and opened it; and there looking at me with sad, pitying eyes was Lillian Gish. Never in my life have I seen anything so pure or so clean as her face. I kept wrinkling my eyes, as if unable to believe what I saw. Then I touched her cheeks with my finger, but very gently. . . . "Why, you're clean and lovely," I said in surprise. . . . "You're pure and lovely and sweet! . . ."

I cut out the picture and made a leather case for it, and I carried it with me as long as war lasted. I used to look at it every night before I went to bed, and every morning when I awoke. It took me safely through those terrible months and it brought me out, in the end, calm and undisturbed.

PRIVATE JACOB GELLER

One day a fellow named Harry Waddell and myself came upon a dead German who had fallen across a log and rested on his shoulders. He still had his light knapsack strapped to his back. (The knapsack was made of cowhide with some of the hair still on it. The hair was dark brown, with white markings, and I remember saying to Harry, at the time, it must have come off a Holstein.)

When Harry and I looked at the man good we saw that he had been killed by a piece of h.e. There was a hole in his chest as big as your fist. Harry and I went through him for souvenirs, but he didn't have anything except a few photographs of his family, and some letters, which we put back in his pocket, in accordance with regulations. Then we turned him over on his belly to see what he had in his knapsack. There was blood all over the knapsack, too, and there was nothing in it except a pair of winter drawers, and a half loaf of brown German bread.

"That's luck," said Harry, "we can eat the bread!"

My mouth commenced to water and I could feel my stomach growling, but when we looked at the bread close we saw that it was covered with blood. (The bread was what the Heinies called pumpernickel, and it was still a little soggy on the inside where the blood hadn't dried out.)

I took out my knife and tried to scrape off the blood, but when I saw that it went all the way through, I gave up that idea.

"Don't waste the bread that way!" said Harry. So I cut it in two equal parts and Harry Waddell and me ate every crumb of it.

PRIVATE WALTER LANDT

It was only a small flesh wound, but Lieutenant Bartelstone thought I'd better go back to the dressing station and take a shot of anti-tetanus anyway. When I got there, the two doctors couldn't decide which was the best way to give it to me. The tall doctor thought it should be injected directly into the stomach, and so I pulled up my shirt while he jabbed me, but the glass tube broke, and most of the fluid spilled down my leg. Then the fat doctor said his partner was doing it all wrong, and I took down my pants while he jabbed me in the stern. But his tube broke, too, and then it was the tall doctor's turn to laugh and make humorous remarks. They kept me there, pulling up my shirt, and taking down my pants, for about an hour, while each argued the merits of his method, and tried to get a full shot into me without breaking the tube. The fourth time the tall doctor punctured my belly, my arms and legs were beginning to swell. Then I remember the other doctor saying: "All right, soldier, take down your pants again and we'll show him how it really ought to be done!" After that everything got black, and the room started whirling.

That's all I remember, but they tell me I hollered without stopping, for two days and two nights, and that I swelled up bigger than a dead soldier who has been lying in a shell hole for a week. Next time I get wounded, I'll have lockjaw and enjoy it.

PRIVATE GRALEY BORDEN

We were detached temporarily from our division and assigned to the French, and for six days and nights we were fighting without sleep and without rest. Since we were fighting under French orders, we drew supplies and food with them also. When the first food arrived, there was red wine and a small ration of cognac for each of us. We were hungry, cold, and very tired, and the cognac warmed our blood, and made the long nights bearable.

But on the second day, when rations were delivered again, the wine and the cognac were missing from the allowance of the American soldiers. The religious organizations in France had protested against rationing intoxicants to us: It was feared the news would get back to the United States, and that the Woman's Christian Temperance Union and the Methodist Board of Temperance and Public Morals would hear of it and would not be pleased.

LIEUTENANT THOMAS JEWETT

SERGEANT PRADO and I were examining our position that June morning. To our left, and about half a kilometer in advance of our line, was an isolated clump of small trees. "That grove should be a good place for a squad of machine gunners, if the Germans should attack," I said.

Sergeant Prado looked up. "I don't think so," he said; "I don't think that at all." He stood there stubbornly, shaking his head. I did not answer him immediately, as if I had not heard. "I think you'd better take several men to those trees and dig a line of trenches there," I said finally.

"I wouldn't do that, Lieutenant," he said. "That clump stands out like a sore thumb. The Germans are sure to figure we'll put men there, and shell hell out of it,—I been expecting that all morning."

"I'm sorry," I said; "but I think you understand my orders."

"Yes, sir," he said.

A few minutes later Prado and his men had wormed their way through the wheat, and with my field glasses I saw them enter the trees. Then, as I lowered my glasses, and was walking away, I heard one shell in the quiet air. I stopped, turned, and saw it strike short of the clump by ten yards. There was silence while I held my breath, and the German artillerymen recalculated their range. Then there came innumerable shells which twisted and whined in the air and exploded with terrific blasts among the trees. Geysers of dirt, leaves and broken branches sprang upward, and the trunks of the lashed trees bent this way and that, as if a hurricane were lost among them, and could not find its way out.

The shelling lasted for twenty minutes and then lifted as suddenly as it had begun. I ran through the wheat, terrified, regretting what my vanity had made me do; and when I reached the clump, the first objects I saw were the bodies of Alden, Geers and Carroll huddled together, their faces torn away, the tops of their skulls caved in. Lying across a fallen tree, his body ripped from belly to chin, was Sergeant Prado, while Leslie Jourdan stood upright looking down at his hand, from which the fingers had been shot away.

I leaned against a tree to keep from falling. "I didn't mean to do it," I said; "I didn't mean to . . ."

PRIVATE STEPHEN CARROLL

When we reached the clump of trees, Sergeant Prado told us to dig in at once.

"I never heard anything so dumb," said Rowland Geers. "What's his idea in sending us out here?"

"Don't ask questions," said Sergeant Prado. "The government pays you your thirty bucks a month for doing what you're told, not for asking questions."

"Doesn't he know the Germans saw us crawling out here?" asked Les Jourdan. "Does he think the Germans are nit-wits?"

"You'd better start digging," said Sergeant Prado, "and save your conversation.—Write me a letter about it."

Then the first shell hit to the right of the clump, and we flattened against the earth. We lay there for a moment, hoping the shell had been a chance one, but in a few minutes the clump was full of shells. The young saplings swayed back and forth, while broken branches and leaves rained down on us. The ground seemed to explode under us, and the bursting shells and the whirling shrapnel made a noise like men playing different instruments in different keys.

Bob Alden was lying in the hollow with me. His eyes were turned so that only the whites showed. His lids kept fluttering down, and his lips puckered out. Then Rowland Geers crawled in the hollow with us. Bob turned and tried to speak to him and Geers leaned forward, his ear close to Bob's mouth, to catch the words, just as a shell landed squarely in the hole with us.

PRIVATE CARROLL HART

SERGEANT TIETJEN was with me that day we took the machine gun nest in Veuilly Wood. We found the crew all killed except one heavyset, bearded man, and he was badly wounded. Just as we came up, the bearded man reached inside his coat and fumbled. I thought he was going to throw a grenade, so I emptied my pistol into him. His arm came away from his coat with a jerking, irregular motion and his palm rested for a moment against his lips. Then the blood in his throat began to strangle him, and he made a gurgling, sighing sound. His eyes rolled back and his jaw fell open.

I went over and opened his palm to see what he had in it. It was the photograph of a little German girl. She was round-faced, and freckled, and her hair was curled, for the occasion, over her shoulders. "That must have been his daughter," said Sergeant Tietjen.

That night I couldn't sleep for thinking of that German soldier. I rolled and pitched about and toward daybreak Tietjen came over and lay down by me. "It's no use blaming yourself that way, fellow," he said; "anybody in the world would have thought he was going to throw a grenade."

PRIVATE WILLIAM ANDERSON

There I was, with my foot split open from heel to toe, and that doctor at the dressing station thought I'd stand for him sewing it up again without given me anything to deaden the pain, except a couple of drinks of cognac. "I want some sort of an anesthetic!" I said, and I didn't say it in any uncertain voice, either.

A hospital corpsman tried to tell me that they were almost out of morphine, and that they were saving the little they had for officers. Did you ever hear anything so God damned silly? "What the hell!" I said. "Do you think officers are more delicate than anybody else? Why don't you let everybody draw straws for the morphine? Or make a rule that nobody except blue-eyed men over five feet eight inches are to get it?—Why don't you make some reasonable rule about it?"

Then the doctor said, "Take that man out and let him lay in the snow for a while. That'll deaden him up some."

"By God, I'd like to see you try that once!" I said; "I'd just like to see you try that!—I'll write a letter to the Major General Commandant; I'll write a letter to President Wilson—!"

Another doctor whose arms were bloody to his elbows said: "For Christ sake, give him a shot, if that will keep his mouth shut." Just when I was feeling numb I raised up and said to the first doctor: "And by God! you'd better do a first class job on it, too!" The bloody doctor laughed. "Are you still with us, 'Gentle Annie'?" he asked.

"——— Jack!" I said.

PRIVATE MARTIN DAILEY

I awoke in a hospital train. My eyes burned and chest ached and I could feel my leg throbbing with pain. From where I lay, I could catch a glimpse, occasionally, of the French countryside covered with poppies and mustard plants in bloom. I could hear the hum of voices and the clanging of engines when we stopped, for a while, at some station along the way. I lay back and closed my eyes again. There was a stench of disinfectant and dried blood in the coach, and that smell which comes from many men caged together.

Above me a man talked ceaselessly of Nebraska. His hand, hanging over his bunk, was grayish white and his nails were turning blue. He talked softly, in a slow voice. He wanted to talk a great deal, because he knew he was going to die before we reached the hospital. But there was nobody to listen to him. We lay there, mostly in silence, and thought of our own misery, like newly castrated sheep, too tired to find comfort in curses. We stared at the ceiling dumbly, or glanced out of the doors at the lovely countryside, now in full bloom.

PRIVATE HENRY DEMAREST

When I arrived at the hospital, they gave me a hot bath and put a clean night shirt on me. Then an attendant wheeled me into the operating room, where the doctors worked night and day in shifts. I woke up, sometime later, between cool sheets that smelled of lavender.

The hospital had been a fine, private residence, in its time, and the room where my bed was placed had been the conservatory. Outside, I could see the park, with trees bending this way and that against the wind, like old women with capes spread out. I watched the trees and the rain for a long time. Then I understood for the first time those lines of Verlaine: "Tears fall in my heart like rain upon the town. . . ." I kept repeating them under my breath.

A long time afterward a doctor came by to look at me. I was crying, without making any sound. I knew what I was doing, but I didn't want to stop. "What's the matter with you, sonny?" he asked. "You haven't got anything to worry about. They'll make you another leg so good that nobody can tell it."

"I feel so grateful for being here," I said. "You see, I was on the line for six months, and I expected to be killed every minute of that time. . . . I never expected to come out alive. And now to be here between clean sheets, with everybody so nice to me. . . ." I tried to stop crying, but I couldn't. . . . "This isn't very dignified," I said, "but I feel so happy, I'd like to go about licking people's hands . . ."

"All right," said the doctor, patting my head. "You go to sleep now. You tell me all about it when I come around to-morrow morning."

CORPORAL LLOYD SOMERVILLE

All the men in our ward were gas patients, and all of us were going to die. The nurses knew there was nothing that could be done for us, and most of the men realized it too. . . . Across the room, a man lay straining, and trying to breathe. Sweat rolled from his face and he caught his breath with a high, sucking sound. After each spell had passed he would lie back, exhausted, and make a bubbling noise with his lips, as if apologizing for disturbing the ward; because each time the man strained for his breath the other men unconsciously struggled with him; and when he lay back exhausted, we unclenched our fists, and relaxed a little ourselves. I thought, "That fellow reminds me of a broken-down soprano practicing her scales. . . ."

A man whose face was turning the color of wet cement leaned over his cot and began vomiting into a tin bucket. . . . Then the soprano tried again for a high note, and I knew that I couldn't stand it any longer. I beat the mattress with my fists, and my heart began racing, and I remembered the doctors had said my only chance lay in keeping calm and unexcited. . . .

The night nurse came over to me. She was fat and old, and she walked on the sides of her feet like a tame bear. There was a purple birth-mark on her chin. She stood looking down at me helplessly.

"This is pretty amusing for you, isn't it?" I said. She didn't answer me, and I commenced laughing and crying and saying every filthy thing I had ever heard, but she bent over me quietly, and kissed me on the mouth. . . . "A big boy like you!" she said scornfully.—"Oh, I'd be ashamed: I really would! . . ." I took hold of her hand and held it tightly. I could feel my heart slowing down again. My toes uncurled and my legs began to relax. My legs were stiff and numb. They felt as if they had been beaten with a stick.

And so she stood above my bed trying to think of something to do for me. I turned my head and pressed my lips against her palm. I wanted her to know that I was not frightened any more. I looked into her eyes steadily, and smiled, and she smiled back at me. . . . "I know what will help you," she said, "and that's a good stiff shot of cognac." I said yes, I thought so too.

"You've drunk cognac before, haven't you?" she asked anxiously. "I don't want to be the one to give you your first drink. . . ."

PRIVATE LAWRENCE DICKSON

EARLY in June we took over a position in Belleau Wood just evacuated by the Sixth Regiment, who had made an attack that morning. There was a lot of salvage around and a number of letters which had been torn up and thrown away. I pieced a part of one letter together and read it, but I could never find the last pages. It was addressed to a man named Francis R. Toleman and it was the most interesting letter I ever read. I carried it around with me for a long time hoping that some day I'd meet this fellow Toleman, but I never did.

If he's alive to-day and reads this, I'd appreciate it if he would write and tell me if Jim and Milly ever made it up. I'd also like to know what in the world Alice Wilson did to make her own people turn against her that way.

PRIVATE NATHAN MOUNTAIN

We could hear the motors droning above us, like a planing mill a long way off. Then there would be silence before the bomb came hissing down. At the first rush of the bomb, the column stopped in fright and the men braced themselves, hoping the aviator would miss the road that time. Then there would be a flash of light and an explosion, and we would walk around the shell hole, still smoking, and the dead men lying in it. The men would double time to catch up with the advance column, quarreling and jostling each other, carrying light packs only, their rifles slung over their shoulders.

Then Mamie, the galley mule, went nuts. She kicked and jumped forward and brayed steadily with a rasping sound. When Pig Iron Riggin tried to quiet her, she flattened her ears and snapped at his hand, her eyes rolling wildly. Finally she freed herself from her harness and came kicking and screaming down the road, the broken trace chain rattling behind her. She kicked furiously in circles for a minute and then she leaped the road and ran through the woods.

Afterward the planes, bolder now, came close to the road and sprayed us with machine guns. We could see the flash of the guns, and the red tracer bullets looked like fireflies against the sky. . . . We lay flat in the road, hugging it, striving to become a part of the earth, while the bullets splattered around us.

"Old Mamie's having a spell of nerves," shouted Albert Hayes, laughingly.

"Yes," I said.

At daybreak we reached Soissons and began the attack.

PRIVATE CHRISTIAN GEILS

"Come out of that shell hole!" said Sergeant Donohoe. "Come out.—Get going!"

"No," I said. "No." My body was jerking like a man with Saint Vitus's dance. My hands were trembling and my teeth kept clicking together.

"You bastard you!—You yellow bastard!" said Donohoe.

He began to jab at me with the barrel of his rifle. "Come out of there!" he said again.

"I'm not going any farther," I said. "I can't stand it any longer."

"You yellow bastard!" he repeated.

Lieutenant Fairbrother came up. "What's the matter here?" he asked.

I crawled out of the shell hole and stood facing them. I wanted to say something, but I couldn't. I began to back away slowly. "Stand still!" said the lieutenant, but I continued to back away.

"You yellow bastard!" said Sergeant Donohoe.

Then he raised his pistol and took aim at my head.

"Stand still!" said Lieutenant Fairbrother.

I wanted to stand still.—I tried to stand still.—I kept saying to myself: "If I don't stand still he'll shoot me as sure as the world! . . ." But I couldn't: I kept backing away. There was a silence for a moment. I could hear my teeth clicking together, playing a tune. "Stand still!" I said to myself. "Stand still, for Christ sake . . . he'll shoot you!" Then I turned and began to run, and at that instant I heard the crack of Sergeant Donohoe's pistol, and I fell in the mud, blood gushing out of my mouth.

PRIVATE MARK MUMFORD

WHEN Bernie Glass, Jakie Brauer and I jumped into the trench we didn't see anybody except a fat little German boy who was scared to death. He had been asleep in a dugout, and when we jumped down, with bayonets fixed, he ran out of the dugout and tried to climb over the side of the trench. Jakie caught him by the slack of the pants, and pulled him back and Bernie made a couple of passes at him with his bayonet, just to frighten him, and I'll say he did it! But when Jakie started talking to him in German, he calmed down a little.

He begged us to let him go free, but we told him we couldn't do that, as we had to take him prisoner, according to instructions from Captain Matlock. Then he said he'd rather be killed outright than taken prisoner, because the Americans chopped off the hands and feet of all their prisoners. Did you ever hear anything as foolish as that in your life? When Jakie told us what he had said, Bernie got sore for a minute. "Ask him where he got his dope," said Bernie. "Ask him who's been telling him such lies."

After Jakie had spoken to him again, he turned to us and repeated his answer in English: "He says they told him that in training camp. He says everybody knows it. It's even in the newspapers."

"Well, the dirty little louse," said Bernie, "to say a thing like that when everybody knows it's the *Germans,* and not ourselves who do those things. Christ Almighty, that's what I call crust!"

Then he began to laugh: "I'll tell you what: Let's have some fun with him. Tell him, regulations say that when a man takes a prisoner, he's got to cut his initials on the prisoner's belly with a trench knife!"

"All right," said Jakie, and began to laugh.

When he got his face straight again, he told the German boy what Bernie had said, and I thought the boy was going to faint. He turned pale and lay with his cheek against the side of the trench, groaning. Then he unbuttoned his blouse and we saw that he was wearing a fine *Gott Mit Uns* belt. Jakie wanted it for a souvenir. He showed it to Bernie and told him he was going to take it, if one of us didn't want it, but Bernie said: "You can't do that: that would be stealing!"

Jakie said, "All right, then, I'll buy the belt offen him."

So he told the German boy he wanted his belt, and that he'd give him ten francs for it.

The German boy didn't answer him. I don't think he even heard Jakie, he was crying so and wringing his hands, thinking about how we were going to slice up his belly.

"Go on and take it, then!" said Bernie; "take it, if you want it!"

But when Jakie reached forward to unbuckle the belt, the little German boy screamed and cut his throat from ear to ear with a knife, which he had hidden under his tunic!

PRIVATE BERNARD GLASS

WHEN I saw Jakie Brauer fall, his arteries spouting blood against the side of the trench, like a chicken whose neck has been twisted off, I was so surprised that I stood like a fool while the German boy climbed over the side of the trench and started running. Then I came to myself and ran after him. I could have shot him easy, but that was too good for the bastard. . . . After the decent way we'd treated him: offering to *buy* his belt instead of taking it away from him, as we could have done without any trouble! He almost had me winded, but finally I caught him. I stuck my bayonet into him time after time. Then I hit him on the head with the butt of my rifle.

It was a treacherous, dirty trick to cut Jakie's throat that way. Jakie was the straightest man I ever knew and he wouldn't hurt a fly, if he could get out of it.—And to see him with his head almost cut off, and his eyes . . . It all goes to show that you can't trust a German. I know I never gave one an even break after that.

PRIVATE JOHN TOWNSEND

I WAS gassed about dusk, too late to be sent back to the dressing station, so Lieutenant Bartelstone told me to go into the deep dugout and get some sleep. He said he would have me sent to the rear the first thing in the morning.

Sometime in the night I was awakened by the sound of automatic rifles, and I heard shouting and cursing all down the line. I knew there was a raid coming off. I sat up and tried to open my eyes, but they had festered and stuck together. My chest felt tight and I was sick at my stomach. The firing increased and the shouting got nearer. I thought: "They're going to take these trenches! I'd better get out now, while I can!" I got up from the wire bunk and tried to grope my way out, but I kept stumbling over things and bumping my head; and at last I was so confused I didn't remember where the stairs were any more. I became frightened. I stood with my palms pressed against the wall and called softly: "Romano! . . . Halsey! . . ." But even as I called I knew that I was alone in the dugout.

There was shouting and firing directly over my head, and after that I heard running on the duckboards outside, and excited guttural words which I could not understand. The door of the dugout was opened and some one threw in a grenade. "Don't," I said, "don't. . . ."

I found the stairs at last and commenced climbing them carefully on my hands and knees until I reached the top step, and felt cold air in my face. I stood upright and raised my hands to show that I was not armed. I could not see, but I had a feeling that many men stood in front of me. . . . "I'm blind and helpless," I said; "please don't hurt me. . . ." There was silence, while I stood there waiting, my hands raised above my head; and then somebody jabbed a bayonet through my body and somebody clubbed me with the butt of a rifle and I fell down the stairs and into the dugout again.

PRIVATE WILBUR HALSEY

THE head nurse told us it was all right to go anywhere else in town, but to keep away from the Rue Serpentine: If we went there our passes would be revoked, and we wouldn't get liberty again as long as we remained in the hospital.

When we were outside in the sunshine, the first thing Herb Merriam said to me was: "Where the hell is this Rue Serpentine?" I laughed. "I don't know," I said; "but let's go find it."

We looked around, but we couldn't locate it. Finally we

crossed the canal and went into a little café. We ordered cognac. "Ask the waiter where it is," said Herb Merriam. "Oh, I don't like to do that," I said. "Go on!" said Herb. "Go on and ask him!"

When the waiter came around again, I spoke to him in my best French: "Will you direct us, please, to the—"

But the waiter didn't hear me out. "Walk four blocks east and turn to your right for the Rue Serpentine," he said in a bored voice, without even raising his eyes from the table.

Herb and I began to laugh. "Hurry up and finish your drink," he said, "and let's get going."

We got back to the hospital an hour before supper time. Miss Mattson, the day nurse, was just going off duty. "Well, how did you boys like the Rue Serpentine?" she asked.

Herb began to blush, and so did I, both of us looking down at our feet.

"You better go downstairs and take a prophylactic," she said in a matter-of-fact voice. "Take the corridor to the right and knock on the first door."

PRIVATE HARRY WADDELL

THIS is the way it really happened: We were lying in a wood near Boissy, having just returned from the front where we had been in the line for ten days. Most of the men got soap and washed their clothes that afternoon, or wrote letters home, but one or two of us decided to go A.W.O.L. and see what the country looked like.

On the road, between two fields, I saw a girl watching a cow, brushing flies off its back with a willow stick. When she smiled at me, and made a sound with her mouth, I leaped the fence and came over to her. She looked at me, closing her eyes halfway, and laughed. Then she put her arms over her head and yawned, and as she did her breasts jumped at me like young rabbits. I walked over to her and put my hands on her thighs, and she came up to me with her hips and started to grind coffee. Then she pulled my head down against her breast, her eyes rolled back and we began to kiss. It was a hot day and her hair was plastered to her skull. Beads of perspiration were on her throat and lips and there was a smell of sweat and clover hay about her.

Then suddenly she shoved me away like she was scared of something, and at the same moment I saw a man watching us over the hedge. The girl began to scream and hit me with the branch. I leaped the hedge and ran down the road, but the man came after me, shouting as he ran and waving a spade. Then other people joined in the chase, men and women armed with sticks and pitchforks. Finally they had me cornered in a pocket, and I stood still.

That was the way it really happened. So help me, God.

PRIVATE BENJAMIN HUNZINGER

I didn't have the faintest idea of deserting: Nothing was farther from my thoughts, that night. But you see I'd met a barmaid in a café that afternoon, while on liberty in the village, and she had promised to meet me later down by the canal. Sergeant Howie was with me when I made the date, and testified for me at the trial, but it didn't do much good.

Well, after taps had sounded that night, I slipped out of camp and past the sentry on guard at the road. Annette (her name sounded something like that: I never did catch it exactly) was waiting for me, like she said she would. We walked arm in arm along the bank of the canal and sat down on the grass behind a thorn hedge in full bloom. I didn't know what to say, and she didn't know what to say, and neither would have understood the other, anyway. So we sat with our arms around each other, smelling the thorn flowers and listening to the canal swishing against reeds.

Then a moon came up and we stretched out on the grass. Later, we rolled under the hedge, and she let me get at her. We lay in each other's arms all night, but just before daybreak we parted, I going back to my company, and she standing with her back to the hedge, waving.

I cut across fields, hurrying to reach the bunk house before roll-call, but when I reached camp, my company was gone. I rolled my pack and hurried after them, trying to overtake them. When I did, ten days later, they were in action at St. Mihiel. My rifle was taken away and I was put under arrest, charged with desertion in face of the enemy. "You can't say that about me, by God!" I kept repeating. "I'm not a deserter. I didn't have any idea of deserting."

PRIVATE PLEZ YANCEY

WE WERE DUE a quiet sector for a change, and I'll say we got one. Behind us was the town of Pont-à-Mousson, in front of us the Moselle flowed, and on the other side of the river the Germans were dug in. The night we took over the trenches, the French told use the club rules and asked us not to violate them: In the morning the Germans could come down to the stream to swim, wash clothes, or gather fruit from the trees on their side of the river. In the afternoon they had to disappear and we were free to swim in the river, play games, or eat plums on *our* side. It worked nicely.

One morning the Germans left a note of apology telling us that we were going to be shelled that night at ten o'clock, and that the barrage would last for twenty minutes. Sure enough the barrage really came, but everybody had dropped back a thousand yards and turned in for the night, and no harm was done. We stayed there by the Moselle for twelve lovely days and then to our regret, we shoved on. But we had all learned one thing: If the common soldiers of each army could just get together by a river bank and talk things over calmly, no war could possibly last as long as a week.

LIEUTENANT ARCHIBALD SMITH

When I entered the communication trench, I heard a pattering noise behind me, like somebody walking in his stocking feet. I turned quickly and Private Carter stood there, his rifle raised, with bayonet fixed, its point almost touching my breast. There was a strange, doped glitter in his eyes. His face was working and he made a piglike grunting noise in his throat. He pressed the bayonet against my belly and backed me to the wall of the trench. I looked about me, but there was nobody in sight; I listened with strained ears, but there was no sound on the duckboards.

"What do you want, Carter?" I asked as quietly as I could.

"You know!" he said. "You know you got it in for me!"

I shook my head. "You're mistaken," I answered. "You're very much mistaken, indeed, if you think that."

"Why don't you leave me alone?" he asked. "Why don't you take somebody else on patrol.—Why don't you let me go to sleep?"

Suddenly he began to yawn and a tired look came into his eyes. He swayed back and forth on his feet. I started to lower my hands and grasp the rifle, but he recovered, pressing me warningly with the bayonet, and my hands went up again. . . . Suddenly the whole thing struck me as absurd. I began to laugh. "Don't you see," I said, "I wanted to take you with me on patrol because I trust you, and consider you the best man in my platoon. That's all there is to it. I'm not trying to ride you. . . ."

He shook his head. "You got it in for me," he repeated.

"No!" I said. "No: you're wrong about that.—You're mistaken!"

"I got to get some sleep," he said. "I'm tired. I got to get some sleep. . . ."

"All right," I said. "Go back to the dugout and turn in. I'll see that you're not disturbed for twenty-four hours.—Go on back to the dugout and turn in, and we'll both forget this ever happened."

He shook his head again. His eyes blinked and almost closed. "You got it in for me," he repeated, as if he were reading from a book. Then, without haste, he pressed on the butt of his rifle and the bayonet entered my body slowly. Then he withdrew the bayonet and struck me quickly again and again. I fell to the duckboards and lay there in the mud. Above me Carter stood cleaning the blade with blue clay which he dug from the side of the trench.

PRIVATE EDWARD CARTER

On Sunday night I was on a wiring party with Sergeant Mooney. It was not my turn, but Lieutenant Smith said he wanted Mooney to take me along. Monday morning I caught galley police, finishing up just in time to go on patrol with Lieutenant Smith, who had asked for me again. Tuesday morning was my regular turn for guard duty, and Tuesday night I was gas sentry at the dugout. Early Wednesday morning a detail went to the rear to bring up rations, and Lieutenant Smith said I'd better go along because I knew the roads. I had just got back and closed my eyes when Sergeant Tietjen woke me up. "For Christ sake," I said. "Get somebody else. I'm not the only man in this platoon. I haven't had any sleep for a week."

"I can't help it," said Tietjen. "I know it looks lousy, but Lieutenant Smith said I was to take you along."

"That bastard!" I said.—"Why has he got it in for me? Why does he want to ride me all the time?"

"I don't know," said Tietjen. "I'm just telling you what he said."

I got up again and went with the working party. Coming back I was so tired and sleepy I could scarcely hold my eyes open. I didn't wait for supper. I turned in, like I was, and was asleep before I got on the bunk good. . . . Then, almost immediately, somebody was standing over me, shaking me. I was not entirely awake, but I heard Corporal Brockett's voice coming from a long way off. "Eddie's pretty tired, Mr. Smith. He's been on a working party all day. Maybe you'd better take somebody else . . ." And Lieutenant Smith's voice: "He'll be all right when he gets on his feet."

I opened my eyes and sat up, and Lieutenant Smith stood before me looking fresh and rested. "You bastard!" I thought. "You dirty bastard! . . ." I looked down at the floor and covered my face with my hands so that he couldn't see how much I hated him.

"We start at ten o'clock," he said. "We'll be out all night." Then he looked at his watch. "I've just got time to go to Headquarters and write a few letters before we start," he said. Then he laughed, patted me on the shoulder and went out. . . . "You bastard!" I thought.—"Why do you keep riding me?"

After he had gone, I sat there for a minute before making up my mind. Then I slipped out of the dugout and ran down the old communication trench which the French had abandoned, and which was partially filled up. I was waiting for him at the supply trench when he passed humming "La Paloma" under his breath. I had taken off my shoes, so as not to make a sound on the duckboards. I followed him for about three hundred yards, still undecided what to do, and then he turned and saw me. He tried to talk me out of it, but I pinned him to the side of the trench and stuck my bayonet in him until he quit breathing. After that I ran back as quickly as I could and was in the dugout, and asleep again, before the guard had completed his round, or before anybody had missed me.

PRIVATE EMIL AYRES

At first I used to listen to Les Yawfitz and that fellow Nallett argue in the bunk house. They'd been to college, and they could talk on any subject that came up. But mostly they talked about war and how it was brought about by moneyed interests for its own selfish ends. They laugh at the idea that idealism or love of country had anything to do with war. It is brutal and degrading, they say, and fools who fight are pawns shoved about to serve the interest of others.

For a while I listened to them, and tried to argue the things out in my mind. Then I quit thinking about it. If the things they say are really true, I don't want to know it. I'd go crazy and shoot myself, if I thought those things were true. . . . Unless a man does feel like that, I can't understand how he would be willing—how he would permit himself to—

So when they start talking now, I get up and leave the bunk house, or turn over to the wall and cover up my ears.

PRIVATE MARTIN APPLETON

DID you ever stand alone on a quiet night while the world trembled to the vibration of guns, and watch soundless light touch the horizon in unexpected places? Did you see a moon rise behind poplars and watch it climb upward, limb by laced limb, until it swung clear of the dead branches and into a quiet sky? . . . I have seen these things, and I tell you they are beautiful.

Then there are rockets, Very lights and flares (white, golden or green) that rise indolently to the air in long curves. Sometimes the rockets puff softly before your eyes into impersonal light that drifts down the wind; and sometimes they become stars of warm and beautiful coloring that burn purely for a moment, and expire before you can mark the instant of their annihilation.

I never see flares of Very lights floating over the trenches that I do not think of time and infinity, and the Creator of the universe; and that this war, and my despair, are, in His sight, as meaningless, and, no doubt, as remote as are the ascending and falling rockets to my finite mind.

PRIVATE LESLIE WESTMORE

Something kept saying to me, "If your gun should go off by accident and shoot you in the knee, your leg would become stiff, and the war would be over for you.—You would be lucky to get off that lightly."

I wouldn't listen to the voice whispering to me. "That would be a cowardly thing to do.—I'd never be able to hold my head up again.—I'd never be able to look people in the eyes," I thought. . . .

"If you were *blind,* now," the voice said again; "surely nobody could blame you if you went blind!—Think! Your uncle Frederick went blind and your grandmother lost her sight before she died. It runs in your family."

"That's very true," I said, "but Uncle Fred had cataracts, which could have been removed, and grandmother had good sight until she was past seventy-five."

"All right," said the voice. "Go ahead, then, if you'd rather be killed. . . . But you're a fool, that's all I can say!"

"I'd rather be killed than go blind," I said. "I'll take my chance on getting killed."

"You're lying," the voice said. "You know very well that you're lying. . . ."

I turned over on my bunk, thinking how comfortable this rest billet was compared with the dugouts in the line. In a few days we would be back at the front again. . . . "Try it!" said the voice.—"It isn't so bad. Your Uncle Fred was happy afterward, wasn't he? Think what a fuss everybody made over your grandmother, waiting on her hand and foot! . . . Shut your eyes and try it for a while! You'll see it isn't so bad. . . ."

"All right," I said, "but it's just for a minute."

I closed my eyes and said to myself: "Now I am blind." Then I opened them again, but when I did so, I couldn't see anything. . . . "This is ridiculous," I said. "There's nothing the matter with my eyes.—This is absurd." . . . "How do you know?" asked the voice. "Remember your grandmother and your Uncle Fred."

I jumped up, frightened. Everything was black in front of me as I walked forward and stumbled over some men playing black jack on the floor. "Look where you're going!" said Sergeant Howie. "Where the hell do you think you are?"

I stood there not moving. Then I felt Walt Rose standing up. I could hear his breathing and I knew he was peering at my face. . . . "Say, come here quick!" he said in an excited voice. I heard the squeak of Carter Atlas' bunk as he got up quickly. I heard the voices of Walter Landt and Larry Dickson. I felt them closing in around me, but I stood there without saying anything.

"Can't you see us?" asked Walt Rose. "Can't you see us at all, Les?"

"No," I said. . . . "I'm totally blind." Then a feeling of relief came over me. I felt happier than I had in months. "The war is over for me," I said.

PRIVATE SYLVESTER WENDELL

CAPTAIN MATLOCK was receiving a number of letters from the parents of men killed in action, so he decided to write to the next of kin of each dead man, as shown by his service record book, and he detailed me to gather the facts in each case and to write appropriate letters of condolence.

I sat there in the company office writing my letters while Steve Waller, the company clerk, made up his payroll. I gave every man a glorious, romantic death with appropriate last words, but after about the thirtieth letter, the lies I was telling began to gag me. I decided I'd tell the truth in at least one of the letters, and this is what I wrote:

"DEAR MADAM:

"Your son, Francis, died needlessly in Belleau Wood. You will be interested to hear that at the time of his death he was crawling with vermin and weak from diarrhea. His feet were swollen and rotten and they stank. He lived like a frightened animal, cold and hungry. Then, on June 6th, a piece of shrapnel hit him and he died in agony, slowly. You'd never believe that he could live three hours, but he did. He lived three full hours screaming and cursing by turns. He had nothing to hold on to, you see: He had learned long ago that what he had been taught to believe by you, his mother, who loved him, under the meaningless names of honor, courage and patriotism, were all lies . . ."

I read that much of the letter to Steve Waller. He listened until I finished, his face without expression. Then he stretched himself a couple of times. "Let's go to the billet and see if we can talk the old woman into frying up a batch of eggs," he said.

I didn't say anything. I just sat there at the typewriter. "These frogs can beat the whole world when it comes to frying eggs," he said. . . . "Christ knows how they do it, but they're the nuts when it comes to cooking."

I got up then, and began to laugh, tearing into fragments the letter I had written.

"All right, Steve," I said; "all right; just as you say!"

PRIVATE RALPH BRUCKER

If you boys want the real low-down on Fishmouth Terry, here it is: He's thirty-five years old and before war times he was a floor walker in a department store. His wife weighs two hundred pounds and in the picture I saw, she was wearing a low-cut dress and was smelling a rose. Fishmouth calls her "Poochy," and she calls him "Terry-boy" and they write baby talk to each other in letters.

But wait, you haven't heard the worst about him. At night back of the line, he sits around in his underwear scratching his feet and eating Fig Newtons, and reads a book called "East Indian Love Lyrics." . . . But he's not a bad guy, really. Terry means well, but he hasn't got a whole lot of sense and when they begin to ride him at Divisional, it gets him excited and he takes it out on the company. He's always treated me right, and he's not a bad guy, no matter what you fellows think.—I guess I ought to know: I've been his orderly for eight months.

PRIVATE BYRON LONG

We camped near Belleville that night and the next morning we had orders to go through a delousing plant situated in an open field. We took our clothes off outside the building, tied them together in a bundle with our identification cords, and the attendant put them in an oven to bake for an hour or so. Then we went through the plant in groups of fifty. It took all morning to run the battalion through and we had to stand around the field naked during that time, waiting to get our clothes back from the ovens.

After a while the sides of the field were lined with spectators, mostly women, who sat on the grass and watched, or ate their lunches, completely unconcerned. One old lady had brought a chair and some sewing with her. I walked over to where she was sitting, as naked as the day I entered this world. "They're going to delouse the First Battalion this afternoon," I said, "but if I were you ladies, I wouldn't wait. When you've seen a thousand naked men you've about seen them all."

"Comment?" said the old lady, smiling sweetly.

PRIVATE PHILIP WADSWORTH

My chastity was one of the stock jokes in our company: replacement troops heard of it before they learned the names of their platoon commanders. I let them laugh, and minded my own business. It was useless, I knew, to try to make them see my viewpoint. I mention it now, merely because it accentuates the drollery of my ultimate fate.

Here's the way it came about: We were billeted in a French

town to reorganize and replace equipment, and we were allowed considerable liberty during that time. Jesse Bogan, who was in my squad, suggested, one night, that we go to the Café de la Poste and split a bottle of wine. I had some letters to write; I wasn't keen about going; but he made such a point of it, I consented.

When we reached the café, it was full of soldiers, and there were a number of women sitting at the tables with them. As soon as Jesse and I came in, one of the women left the group she was with and joined us at our table. Sergeant Halligan and Hyman White and one or two others followed her, and tried to make her come back, but she put her arms around my neck and said, "No! No! This is my baby!" (I found out later the whole thing was arranged. Even Jesse Bogan, whom I trusted, was in on the joke.)

At last the men pretended to be sore with the woman, and went back to their table to enjoy the fun. Then Bogan got up and left, after a time, and the woman and I were alone at the table.

She asked me to go with her to her room, but I refused as politely as I could. I explained about Lucy Walters and how we had promised to remain pure, for each other, until we were married. The woman sat listening to me sympathetically. She said I was right. She said a girl rarely met a man with such a fine viewpoint. Then she commenced talking about the farm, near Tours, where she had been born, and how happy she had been there. She told me of her sweetheart, a boy from her village; how they, too, had loved each other, and planned marriage, and how he had been killed at the first battle of the Marne. She thought of him constantly, she said: She regretted, always, that he had died before he had consummated their love, or learned how rich and beautiful life could be. . . .

As she talked, I kept thinking: "My morals are absurd. I may be killed next week. I may never see Lucy again." The girl took my hand, and tears came into her eyes. "Everything is sad and a little mixed-up," I thought. "What difference can it make, one way or the other, if I go with this woman?"

Afterward I was ashamed of myself. I offered her twenty francs (I had no idea what the proper fee was in such cases), but she refused it. She clung to me and kissed me. She said I reminded her of the boy who had been killed at the Marne: he, too, had been very innocent. . . . And all the time she knew that she had diseased me.

Later I became alarmed and went to the dressing station. The doctor looked me over, laughed, and beckoned to the hospital corpsmen. I was courtmartialed for failing to report for a prophylactic and sent to this labor battalion. I have thought the matter over a thousand times, but I cannot understand, even yet, what there is about male chastity that is humorous, or why it repels and offends. The woman in the café got two hundred francs from my friends for seducing me. She reënacted the entire scene for them when she returned to the café: I was very clumsy and funny, I understand.

PRIVATE ALEX MARRO

We were camped in a wood about ten kilometers from Nancy, and that afternoon Gene Merriam, our regimental runner, dropped by to see his brother, Herb. He had just been to Nancy with a message, and he was telling us all about it. "There's a house running wide open there," he said; "and you never saw such good-looking girls in your life. They've all got blonde hair, and they sit around on their big, fat cans dressed in lace kimonos, fanning themselves and eating pears. . . ."

After he had gone, Nate Mountain, Mart Passy and I kept talking of the various women we had known in our lives and wondering if we could get away with going A.W.O.L. that night. We put our money together, and it came to seventy-eight francs. We figured that should be enough for the three of us, even if it was a first-class house, so after roll-call had been taken, we slipped out.

Gene Merriam had given us exact directions. We didn't have much trouble in finding the place. Nate went up to the door and rang the bell and presently a big, raw-boned woman with a gray streak in her hair, opened it. But when she got a look at our dirty uniforms, she made motions for us to go away. Then she tried to shut the door again, but Nate was too quick for her. He got his foot in the crack and held it there. The woman began to chatter in a shrill voice, and to curse us in English.

Then an M.P., attracted by the noise, came up to see what it was all about. At first he said he was going to put us under arrest for being A.W.O.L., but Mart gave him fifty francs, and that put him in a good humor. "Who do you think you are?" he asked. "That house is for officers only: You got to wear captain's bars or better to get in there. . . ." Then he began to laugh. "Those whores are refined, sensitive girls. They wouldn't even unbutton their drawers for a bunch of grease-balls like you." Then the M.P. stopped laughing and began to scowl. "Say, you get back to your outfit!" he said.—"You get the hell back before I change my mind and run you all in!"

PRIVATE JOHN McGILL

I went out on raiding parties time after time where every man except myself was killed or wounded. I have had my rifle splintered in my hands and twice my helmet was ripped through by shrapnel. I've had the buttons shot off my tunic and one time even the tape holding my identification discs was cut by machine gun bullets. And yet I never received a scratch, although I participated in all action with my company. I could go on citing you innumerable instances to show how lucky I am, but the strangest thing of all happened just after the battle of Soissons.

We were back in a wood reorganizing and waiting for stragglers to catch up. I needed a new mess-gear, my own having been destroyed with my pack, while strapped to my back during the fighting. (Another close shave, you see!) So I walked to a salvage pile and picked up a new mess-gear at random. When I got back to my tent and looked at it closely, I saw that it had my name, John McGill, cut into the metal with beautiful old English letters. That really was remarkable, wasn't it? . . . You can call it coincidence, if you like, but I know better. There are many things we cannot account for with all our laws of average and rules of chance. There are many strange forces working around us which we cannot understand. . . . The men in my company marveled at my luck. Before going over the top many of them would put their hands on my forehead, hoping thereby to become lucky themselves, but whatever the power that protected me, it never worked for any one else.

PRIVATE SIDNEY BORGSTEAD

WHEN Captain Matlock saw from my service record book that I had been a *couturier,* he, with his penchant for doing the inappropriate thing superbly, decided to transfer me to the galley and make a cook out of me. To him it seemed entirely logical that a man who had handled chiffons and lovely taffetas would be equally deft in the medium of beef carcasses and dehydrated potatoes.

At first I tried to prepare the rations as attractively as possible, but I soon found out nobody cared how the food was cooked. All they wanted was quantity, I mean, and positively hours before a meal was ready the men stood in line waiting hungrily and watching my every move. Of course it made me nervous and irritable! But the worst time of all was when we were dishing up the food, the men would stare at their rations and growl: not because of its quality, mind you (I could have understood and condoned that!), but merely because there wasn't *more* of it. (Heaven knows I couldn't cook any more food than Headquarters issued me: I'm not a magician, after all!) Then they would gobble it down like swine and get in line hoping for seconds.

One day in Courcelles I was making a stew in a g.i. can, it was an hour before supper time but as I looked up I saw a line of men already forming. I became slightly hysterical, I'm afraid. I wanted to say to them, "Don't worry, little piglets, mamma pig will soon have supper ready!"

On a shelf to one side of the kitchen were some medicines and salves which Mike Olmstead, the mess sergeant, carried around with him for emergencies. I had a sudden idea and it set me to giggling. I opened the lid of the g.i. can and stirred it all into the stew.

When I was in bed that night, I thought, "Well, anyway, nobody will show up for breakfast and *that* will be a relief!" but when the guard woke me at five o'clock the next morning, the first thing I heard was somebody scraping his dirty mess-gear with a spoon. Then I heard men running and coughing and jostling for places in the line. When I came into the kitchen and started my fires, the line extended half a block. If there was anybody absent, you'd never be able to tell it with the naked eye.

I turned and ran. I didn't know where I was going, but I knew that I must get away. I bumped into Sergeant Olmstead in the doorway. He saw that I was profoundly upset and nervous. I stood beating him on the chest. "Let me pass!" I demanded, "Captain Matlock can get another cook, because I'm through. They can put me in jail—they can shoot me, if they want to, but I'm through for good!"

Sergeant Olmstead—he's really a good sort, but terribly dull—put his arm over my shoulder and stood patting my back. "Now, Cookie, don't get your bowels in an uproar," he said soothingly.

"Let me pass, please!" I said firmly.

"You wouldn't leave me flat, that way, would you?" he asked.

"Yes," I said.

He didn't try to detain me any longer. "Well, before you go, I want you to make some more of those apple turnovers. I never ate anything better in my life."

I looked at the man incredulously. "Did you think they were better than those peach pies I made for you in St. Aignan?"

Sergeant Olmstead thought it over carefully and then decided to be diplomatic. "They were both so good that it's mighty hard to say which *was* the best," he said. I stood there uncertain and

Sergeant Olmstead followed up his advantage. "How would the boys get along if they didn't have you to take care of them when they come back from the trenches?" he asked.

I laughed derisively. "They would be delighted!" I said. "They all hate my cooking."

Sergeant Olmstead shook his head seriously. "Don't you ever believe that," he said, "because you'll be wrong, if you do." Then he continued, "I heard some of our boys boasting in the café that we fed better than any company in the regiment. They said they sure felt sorry for those other companies."

"Are you really telling me the truth?" I asked.

"Sure. I'm telling it to you straight."

And because I'm a "dee" fool and haven't two brains to knock together, I let him exploit the better side of my nature, and I went back into the kitchen and started breakfast again.

PRIVATE ALLAN METHOT

My poetry was beginning to attract attention when I enlisted, convinced of the beauty of war by the beauty of my own sonnets. Then months of training, drudgery and pain. But I could have stood the humiliation and the long hours of senseless work. I grew accustomed to those things and I could shake them off. It was the spiritual isolation that was unbearable.—Who was there to talk to? Who was there to understand me?—There was no one. . . . No one at all.

That sense of strangeness, of being alone! It closed around me more and more. I looked at my comrades with their dull, sheeplike faces. They asked nothing of life except sleep and food, or a drunken night in a brothel. A sense of revulsion came over me. Sodden, emotionless creatures, insensitive to beauty . . .

Then those nights on watch with Danny O'Leary, his eyes unlit by intelligence. He would stand there stupidly and stare at me, his heavy brows drawn together, his thick lips opened like an idiot's. I tried to talk to him, but it was useless. He lowered his eyes, as if ashamed of me, and stared at the duckboards, fumbling at his rifle. . . . "I wonder if we get paid when we get back this time?" he said.

I began to laugh. I walked to the end of the trench and stood looking at a gas flare burning with a green light in the north.—That sense of isolation! That sense of being alone among aliens! I climbed out of the trench and walked toward the German lines. I walked slowly, watching the flares and whispering the words of my poems, pausing and walking forward again.

"Soon a hand will stretch out and jerk me off my feet," I thought, "and I shall lie broken against this broken earth. . . . Soon a foot, shaped like infinity, will step upon my frail skull, and crush it!"

PRIVATE DANNY O'LEARY

I WOULD LIKE you to see me now, Allan Methot: I would like you to see what you have created!—For you did create me more completely than the drunken longshoreman from whose loins I once issued.

I was so gross, so stupid; and then you came along.—How did you know? How could you look through layer upon layer until you saw the faint spark that was hidden in me? . . . Do you remember the nights on watch together when you recited Shelley and Wordsworth?—Your voice cadencing the words was the most beautiful thing I had ever heard. I wanted to speak to you, to tell you that I understood, to let you know your faith in me would not be wasted, but I dared not.—I could not think of you as a human being like myself, or the other men of the company. . . . I thought of you as some one so much finer than we that I would stand dumb in your presence, wishing that a German would jump into the trench to kill you, so that I might put my body between you and the bullet. . . . I would stand there fumbling my rifle, hoping that you would speak the beautiful lines forever. . . . "I will learn to read!" I thought. "When war is over, I will learn to read! . . ."

Where are you now, Allan? I want you to see me.—Your friendship was not wasted; your faith has been justified. . . . Where are you, great heart? . . . Why don't you answer me?

PRIVATE JEREMIAH EASTON

After we had taken over our position, Captain Matlock sent me back to the cross-roads, a kilometer to the rear, to guide in the wagon train. The woods were filled with artillery and troops were moving up all along the line. "This is going to be something big," I thought. "It's no little trench raid, this time!"

Then, at dusk, the German planes came over and began bombing the roads and wood. They would swoop down suddenly and open up with machine guns and then dart up again out of range. At nine o'clock it was pitch dark, and at ten it began to rain. The rain fell in torrents and a cold wind swirled it about, but still the men came on, thousands and thousands of them. When it lightened I could see them distinctly, their heads lowered to the blinding rain, pushing forward slowly down the roads and through the woods, disappearing like giant snakes into the communication trenches that emptied into the line. . . . "This is really going to be something big," I said. "No little penny fight this time."

Then toward morning the rain stopped and the first of the guns opened. Instantly a thousand guns were firing in a roaring, flashing semi-circle, and a thousand shells were flying through the air and exploding in the German lines. The barrage lasted for three hours and then, just at daybreak, it lifted. From where I was, I could see our men going over, the early light gleaming against fixed bayonets. But there was little for them to do, for there was nothing left of the German trenches or the surrounding terrain: Not a tree, not a blade of grass. Nothing living. Nothing at all. The dead lay thick in the trenches, in strange and twisted groups. . . . "There's nothing living left," I thought; "nothing at all!"

And then from a demolished pill-box a man crawled out of wreckage. His jaw was partially shot away, and hung down, but he held up the pendulous bone with his hand, when he saw us, and made a frightened, conciliatory sound.

PRIVATE WILLIAM MULCAHEY

WE CREPT toward the machine gun nest, each man with a grenade in his hand ready to throw, crawling slowly, hugging the earth, trying not to ripple the dense weeds. Then the Germans discovered us and opened fire, shouting excitedly.

We jumped up from the ground and hurled our grenades and ran forward firing our rifles, our bayonets fixed for action. . . . Then something hit me squarely and I fell into the weeds again. Excited firing broke out all along the line. There were curses and shouts and then, a few minutes later, everything was quiet except Pete Stafford dragging himself back toward our line on his elbows and saying over and over: "My leg's broke!—My leg's broke! . . ."

I raised my head and tried to speak to Pete, but the ground tilted up and then began spinning around like a roulette wheel. I lay back in the weeds again.—"I'll never know how the war comes out," I thought. "I'll never know, now, whether the Germans win or not."

SERGEANT JULIUS PELTON

ON THE afternoon of the fourth day we fell back to the edge of the wood and dug in, and the First Battalion passed over our heads and continued the attack. In front of us stretched a wheat field and a wrecked farmhouse, and beyond that the wood started again. The wood before us seemed intact and unhurt, but the wood in which we lay was littered with toppling trees and torn branches, still green. To our left was a gravel pit, long abandoned, with one narrow opening; and back of that a ravine ran straight for a hundred yards and stopped blindly against a bank of clay.

From where I was lying I could see the gravel pit, with Johnny Citron on guard at the gap, watching the twenty-two prisoners we had taken that day. Then Captain Matlock came over to me. "What'll we do with them, sergeant?" he asked.

"I don't know, sir," I said.

"The easiest thing would be to train a machine gun on the gravel pit," he added; "that would be the simplest way."

"Yes, sir," I answered, and laughed, not taking him seriously.

"No," he said after a minute's thought; "the gap is too narrow and the sides are dug in so it would be pretty hard for the gunners. . . ."

I seen then that he was not joking.

"We'd better take them into the ravine and do it there," he said. . . .

I listened to what he was saying, keeping my mouth shut, but while he was talking I kept thinking: "I've been in the service since I was a kid eighteen years old. I've seen a lot of things that would turn an ordinary man's stomach. I guess I shouldn't be particular now. . . . But this is raw!—This is the rawest thing I ever heard of!"

When Captain Matlock stopped talking, I saluted him. "Yes, sir," I said.

"You'd better take Corporal Foster and his automatic rifle squad. I think Foster is the right man to do it."

"Yes, sir," I said; "yes, sir; I think he is."

"You'd better tell Foster to get it over with before dark."

"Yes, sir," I said.

Later, when I was talking to Foster, I felt ashamed. . . . "Christ! but this is raw," I thought. . . . "Christ! but this is the rawest thing I ever heard of!" . . . Then I remembered what my old drill sergeant had told me in boot camp, twenty years before. "Soldiers ain't supposed to think," he said; "the theory is, if they could think, they wouldn't be soldiers. Soldiers are supposed to do what they are told, and leave thinking to their superior officers."

"Well," I said to myself, "I guess it's none of my business. I guess I'm here to carry out instructions." Then I walked to where Foster was and repeated Captain Matlock's orders.

CORPORAL CLARENCE FOSTER

"THAT's an old trick," I said. "I remember reading about it in the papers back home before I enlisted: The Germans send men over in droves, to give themselves up, and after a while there are more prisoners back of the line than soldiers. Then the Germans make an attack, which is a signal for the prisoners to overpower their guards and come up from the rear.—It's an old gag!" I said; "and it generally works. Those Prussians are smart babies, don't ever forget that!—They've pulled that trick on the French time and time again. . . . I'm surprised you never heard about it, sergeant," I said.

"I've heard a lot of hooey in my time," he answered.

"Well, this is straight dope," I said. "I've seen it all written up in the newspapers."

"Do you believe all the tripe you read in newspapers?" asked Sergeant Pelton.

"Well, I believe *that!*" I said; "I wouldn't put anything dirty past a German."

Sergeant Pelton began to laugh. "Captain Matlock said you were the right man for the job."

"I take his confidence in me as a compliment," I answered. . . . "Christ almighty!—This is *war!* . . . What did you think it was? A Sunday-school picnic? . . . Take these Germans now.—Burning churches and dashing out the brains of innocent babies. —You've got to fight fire with fire," I said. "This is the only sort of treatment a German can understand . . ."

Sergeant Pelton walked away. "All right. Be ready in half an hour," he said. "Let's get it over quick." Then I walked back to the trench where my squad was and told them Captain Matlock's orders. I realized a great many people, who did not understand the necessity for such an act, would censure Captain

Matlock for shooting prisoners, but under the circumstances, there was no other way out. I expected an argument from Walt Drury and that sea-lawyer, Bill Nugent, and I got it. "Don't tell me," I said; "if the arrangement don't suit you, tell your troubles to Captain Matlock!"

"He wouldn't dare do a thing like that," repeated Nugent; "not a dirty thing like that . . ."

"What do you birds think this is?" I asked. "This is war! . . . Why didn't you bring along your dolls and dishes to play with! . . ."

PRIVATE WALTER DRURY

CORPORAL FOSTER told us to load our rifles and go to the gravel pit. There were some prisoners there, and Captain Matlock had ordered us to take them into the ravine, and shoot them. . . . "I won't do it!" I said.—"I might kill a man defending my own life, but to shoot a human being in cold blood . . . I won't do that!—I won't do it!" I said. . . .

"You'll do what the Captain says or you'll get a courtmartial. Then they'll stand you up and shoot you too.—Maybe you'd like that!"

"I won't do it!" I said.

"All right," said Corporal Foster. "Use your own judgment, but don't say I didn't warn you."

Then we took our rifles and walked to the gravel pit. There were about two dozen prisoners, mostly young boys with fine, yellow fuzz on their faces. They huddled together in the center of the pit, their eyes rolling nervously, and spoke to one another in soft, frightened voices, their necks bending forward, as if too frail to support the heavy helmets they wore. They looked sick and hungry. Their uniforms were threadbare and torn, and caked with mud, and their bare toes protruded through crevices in their boots. Some were already wounded and weak from loss of blood, and could hardly stand alone, swaying back and forth unsteadily.

Then suddenly my own knees got weak. "No," I said; "no.—I won't do it. . . ." Corporal Foster was getting the prisoners lined up in single file, swearing angrily and waving his hands about. . . . "Why don't I refuse to do this?" I thought. "Why don't all of us refuse? If enough of us refuse, what can they do about it? . . ." Then I saw the truth clearly: "We're prisoners too: We're all prisoners . . . No!" I said. "I won't do it!"

Then I threw my rifle away, turned and ran stumbling through the woods. I heard Corporal Foster calling to me to come back; I heard Dick Mundy and Bill Nugent shouting, but I ran on and on, dodging behind trees and falling into shell holes, hiding and trembling and then running forward again. Finally I came to an old barn and hid there behind a pile of refuse and tried to think of what I had done. I had no friends to shield me. I could not speak French. I didn't have a chance. I would be picked up by the military police sooner or later and tried as a deserter. That was inevitable, I knew. . . . "Better give myself up and get it over with," I decided; "maybe I'll get off with twenty years.—Twenty years isn't such a long time." I thought, "I'll only be forty-two, when I come out, and I can start life all over again. . . ."

PRIVATE CHARLES GORDON

When we got the prisoners lined up, and had started them out of the pit, Walt Drury made a funny noise, threw his rifle away and ran through the woods. . . . "Walt!" I called.—"Walt!"

"Let him alone," said Corporal Foster, "he'll get his later."

Then the prisoners came out of the pit stolidly with their heads lowered, neither looking to the right nor the left. The wood had been raked by artillery fire but recently, and the leaves that clung to the shattered trees and the pendent branches were still green. In places the trunks of the trees had been scored by shrapnel, leaving strips of bark, gnawed-at and limp, dangling in the wind; leaving the whitish skin of the trees exposed, with sap draining slowly . . .

"Come on," said Foster. "Come on. Let's get going before dark."

We picked our way through the wrecked wood, lifting aside the trailing branches, kicking with our boots the leaves that had rained down and made a green carpet. When we reached the entrance to the ravine, the prisoners drew back, frightened, and began to talk excitedly amongst themselves, then, glancing apprehensively over their shoulders, they entered, one by one, and huddled against the far bank.

One of the prisoners had very blue eyes and didn't seem frightened at all. He began to talk to his comrades, smiling and shaking his head. I couldn't understand what he was saying, but I had an idea he was telling them not to worry because there was nothing to fear. . . . "These men are wearing different uniforms and they speak a different language, but they are made out of the same flesh and blood that we are," I imagined him saying. "There's nothing to fear. They aren't going to hurt us."

Suddenly the blue-eyed man looked at me and smiled, and before I knew what I was doing, I smiled back at him. Then Sergeant Pelton gave the signal to fire and the rifles began cracking and spraying bullets from side to side. I took steady aim at the blue-eyed man. For some reason I wanted him to be killed instantly. He bent double, clutched his belly with his hands and said, "Oh! . . . Oh!" like a boy who has eaten green plums. Then he raised his hands in the air, and I saw that most of his fingers were shot away and were dripping blood like water running out of a leaky faucet. "Oh! . . . Oh!" he kept saying in an amazed voice. . . . "Oh! Oh! Oh!" Then he turned around three times and fell on his back, his head lower than his feet, blood flowing from his belly, insistently, like a tide, across his mud-caked tunic: staining his throat and his face. Twice more he jerked his hands upward and twice he made that soft, shocked sound. Then his hand and his eyelids quit twitching.

I stood there spraying the bullets from side to side in accordance with instructions. . . . "Everything I was ever taught to believe about mercy, justice and virtue is a lie," I thought. . . .

"But the biggest lie of all are the words 'God is Love.' That is really the most terrible lie that man ever thought of."

PRIVATE ROGER INABINETT

WHEN the last prisoner quit kicking, my squad went out of the ravine and back to their trench. I stepped behind a fallen tree, and they passed on ahead without missing me. For a while I could hear them moving through the wood, rustling the leaves with their feet, but after a time everything was quiet again. Then I went back and began going through the pockets of the dead men, but it was hardly worth the trouble. Most of them had paper marks and a few metal coins with square holes punched in them. I put these in my pocket. They might have some value: I didn't know. Then there were a lot of letters and photographs which I tore up and threw on a pile. Some of the men were wearing regimental rings which I took off their fingers—they're worth three or four francs each—and one had a fine, hand-carved cigarette lighter, shaped like a canteen, but there wasn't much of anything else.

What I was really looking for were Iron Crosses. They're worth real money back in the S.O.S. They make fine souvenirs and the boys buy them to send back to their sweethearts. Sometimes they bring as much as 150 francs each. The squareheads generally wear them pinned to their undershirts, under their tunics, where they won't show. I looked over every man carefully, but if there was a single decoration among those prisoners, I couldn't find it.

When I was almost through, I looked up and saw Sergeant Pelton watching me steadily, without moving his eyes.

"I'm looking for Iron Crosses," I said.

Then he caught me by the collar and pulled me up. "Put that stuff back," he said.

"What's the sense in that, sarge?" I asked. "We got more right to it than anybody else. If we don't get it, somebody else will."

Then I took the cigarette lighter and offered it to him. "Here, you can have this, if you want it," I said.

For a moment I thought he was going to hit me, but he thought better of it. He turned me loose suddenly and walked away. "Get on back to your squad," he said.

"All right," I said; "if that's the way you feel about it, it's all right by me.—But there's no use your getting sore."

"Get on back to your squad!" he said.

PRIVATE RICHARD MUNDY

I DECIDED to take my rifle apart and clean it thoroughly. I didn't want to think about those prisoners any more, but as I sat there with my squad in the shallow trench, with the rifle parts scattered about me, I couldn't help thinking about them. Corporal Foster was opening cans of monkey meat with a bayonet and Roger Inabinett divided the meat and the hardtack into eight equal parts.

Charlie Gordon got out his harmonica and began to play a lively tune, but Everett Qualls stopped him. Then Foster passed out the rations and each man took his share. At sight of the food, Bill Nugent took sick. He went to the edge of the trench and vomited. When he came back his face was white. Jimmy Wade had a canteen of cognac which he passed over to him and Bill took a big swig of it, but immediately he got up and vomited again. Then he lay stretched out and trembled.

"What's the matter with you, Bill?" asked Foster.

"Nothing," he said.

"They've pulled that trick on the French a thousand times, and got away with it, too!" said Foster. "These Germans are smart hombres. You got to watch them all the time."

Ahead of us in the wheat field, the rays of the late sun lay flat on the trampled grain, but in the wood it was almost dark. Inabinett was playing with a cigarette lighter he had found in the wood. He kept snapping it with a clicking sound. "All it needs is a new flint," he said. "It'll be as good as new with another flint."

I put my rifle back together and rubbed the butt with oil. I kept seeing those prisoners falling and rising to their knees and falling again. I walked to the end of the trench and looked over the top. A long way ahead was the sound of rifle fire and to the west there was intermittent shelling, but here, in the wood, everything was calm and peaceful. "You wouldn't know we were in the war at all," I thought.

Then I had an irresistible desire to go to the ravine and look at the prisoners again. I climbed out of the trench quickly, before anybody knew what I was going to do. . . .

The prisoners lay where we had left them, face upward mostly, twisted in grotesque knots like angleworms in a can, their pockets turned outward and rifled, their tunics unbuttoned and flung wide. I stood looking at them for a while, silent, feeling no emotion at all. Then the limb of a tree that grew at the edge of the ravine swayed forward and fell, and a wedge of late sunlight filtered through the trees and across the faces of the dead men. . . . Deep in the wood a bird uttered one frightened note and stopped suddenly, remembering. A peculiar feeling that I could not understand came over me. I fell to the ground and pressed my face into the fallen leaves. . . . "I'll never hurt anything again as long as I live," I said. . . . "Never again, as long as I live. . . . Never! . . . Never! . . . Never! . . ."

PRIVATE HOWARD NETTLETON

"I DON'T want to hear any more out of you," said Sergeant Dunning. "Captain Matlock has passed an order that everybody, except the men detailed to repair roads, are to go to church, and like it, and by God! you'd better do it, if you know what's good for you!—Don't think you can get away with anything, either, because Pig Iron Riggin is going to be there with a roster, and check every man off." Well, that broke up the black jack game. "It looks like they could leave a man alone on Sunday morning back of the line," said Archie Lemon; "it looks like they could, at least, do that."

"Come on, let's get it over with," said Vester Wendell. "Once more won't hurt anybody."

Bob Nalls spoke up: "If I have to listen again to that chaplain praying to God to spare all the American Galahads and destroy their ungodly enemies, I'm going to get up and say: 'Who was telling you? Where do you get all this inside information? . . .' If he does that again, I'm going to ask him if he doesn't know that the Germans are praying too.—'Let's be logical about this thing,' I'm going to say; 'Let's pick out different Gods to pray to. It seems silly for both sides to be praying to the same one! . . .' "

"Come on! Come on!" said Sergeant Dunning. "You birds give me a pain.—You're not going to say anything at all: You're going to do just what you're told, and you're going to pray and sing hymns and like it!—Come on," he said, "let's get going."

PRIVATE HARLAND PERRY

A MAN from the Fifteenth Field Artillery named Charlie Cantwell told me this story. It seems he had been gassed, and was lying with his eyes bandaged, when the man next him reached over and woke him. He thought, at the time, that it was about three o'clock in the morning, but he didn't know for sure.

Then, according to Charlie's story, his neighbor said that he was going to die. Charlie couldn't see him, of course, because of his bandaged eyes, but he had a feeling that the man was about twenty-five years old, with brown eyes, black curly hair and a cleft in his chin. Charlie scoffed at the idea of the other man dying, but the man insisted that he was. Then he asked Charlie if he thought he, Charlie, was going to get well, and Charlie said yes, he was pretty sure of it. So the man reached under his pillow (I don't know how Charlie knew all this, if he had his eyes bandaged like he said) and pulled out a roll of bills that would choke a cow. "Here are ten thousand francs," the man said. "Spend it all for a good time." Charlie took the money and slipped it under his mattress. "Spend it foolishly," the man said; "spend as much of it on women as possible." Charlie promised to do that, and toward morning the man died. . . .

Well, that's the way Charlie told me the story, and personally I don't give one good God damn whether you believe it or not! It's no skin off my back-side.—All I know is what Charlie told me, and that he did have ten thousand francs, and that we spent hell out of the money after we got well enough to go on liberty into the town.

PRIVATE ALBERT NALLETT

Before the company came to France, they were stationed in the tropics and while there they picked up Tommy, the company mascot. I don't know exactly what he was, but he looked more like a 'coon than anything else. Sergeant Halligan said the natives of Honduras called them ant bears. I don't know about that, but I do know Tommy had more sense than Captain Matlock and all his officers put together. We'd all be asleep in a dugout and some sentinel would sniff the air, get excited and turn in the gas alarm. Then the men would sit around with their gas masks on until their heads ached with the strain. Finally I tumbled to the fact that Tommy would lie curled up asleep through the excitement, if the alarm was false, but if there really was gas about, he didn't need a sentinel to tell him: He'd go dig a hole in the ground and pile dirt up around his snout. After I found that out, I never paid any attention to the alarms unless Tommy said it was all right. I never got gassed, either.

Tommy was very fond of condensed milk and Mike Olmstead, the mess sergeant, used to feed it to him. One time after St. Mihiel, the rolling kitchen got lost from the company for two days. Captain Matlock sent out a dozen runners to try to locate it, but none of them could. Then I unchained Tommy and said to him: "Listen, Tommy!—Find Mike!—Condensed milk! . . .

Mike's got condensed milk for you!" Tommy jumped off my shoulder and took out through the woods, straight ahead, his tail twitching with excitement. I thought he was wrong that time, myself, but I followed him, anyway, and in fifteen minutes he had located the kitchen and was climbing up Mike's leg and nuzzling his cheek. It turned out that Mike and his kitchen had passed us in the night, on the road, and was several kilometers in *advance* of our line, but Captain Matlock hadn't sent any runners in that direction. When Mike came back with his kitchen and reported where he had been, Captain Matlock said that that was impossible. He said Mike couldn't possibly have passed us in the night without somebody hearing him.

I scratched Tommy's belly, which was full of condensed milk, and winked and Tommy drew back his lips and rubbed his snout, which is as close as he can come to giving anybody the horse-laugh.

PRIVATE ROBERT NALLS

FOLLOWING the fighting at St. Mihiel, we were billeted in Blenod-les-Toul with an old French couple. They had had an only son, a boy named René, who had been killed early in the war, and they were constantly finding points in common between us and him. I had brown eyes, and René's eyes had also been brown; René had had long, slender fingers, and Sam Quillin's fingers were also long and slender. They found resemblances to René in every one: Jerry Blandford because his teeth were even and white; Roger Jones for his thick, curling hair and Frank Halligan because of the trick he had of closing his eyes and throwing back his head when he laughed. Their lives centered around their dead son. They talked about him constantly; they thought of nothing else.

After his death, the French government had sent them a small copper plaque showing in bas-relief the heroic face of a woman surrounded by a wreath of laurel, and under the woman's face were the words, "Slain on the Field of Honor." It was not an unusual decoration. It was the sort of thing that a Government would send to the next of kin of all men killed in action, but the old couple attached great importance to it. In one corner of the room they had built a tiny shelf for the medal and its case, and underneath it the old woman had fixed up an altar with two candles that burned day and night. Often the old woman would sit for a long time silent before the altar, her hands twisted and old, resting her knees. Then she would go back and scrub her pans, or walk outside to the barn and look at her cow.

We remained in Blenod for five days, and then one night we got orders to move. The old couple had become very friendly with us by that time. They walked with us to the place of assembly, offering to carry our rifles or our packs. Then they stood in the muddy road, the September wind blowing against them strongly, crossing themselves and asking God to bring us all safely back.

A few weeks later, when we were miles away from Blenod, I saw the copper plaque again: It rolled out of Bernie Glass's kit bag while he was shaving one day. He picked it up quickly, but he knew that I had seen it.

"How could you do it, Bernie?" I asked; "how could you do a thing like that?"

"I don't know that it's any of your business," said Bernie, "but I thought it would make a good souvenir to take home."

I never returned to Blenod, and I never saw that old couple again, but somehow I wish they knew that I am ashamed of the whole human race.

PRIVATE OSWALD POLLARD

Here's a funny thing: In September a fellow named Fallon out of the fourth platoon went off his nut. He got up on the parapet of the trench, during a barrage, and nobody could coax him in. We tried to talk to him, to make him come back, but he wouldn't do it. "I want to get shot," he kept saying; "I know perfectly well what I'm doing. I want to get shot—I'm committing suicide, you see!"

Then Pig Iron Riggin took out his pistol and leveled it at this fellow Fallon's head. "If you don't quit committing suicide, I'll kill you as sure as I'm a foot high!" he said. Instantly Fallon turned white and began to whimper. He jumped into the trench and got down upon his knees. "Don't!" he said. "Don't kill me—please . . ."

PRIVATE MARTIN PASSY

THE boys all wondered about my lack of fear. I didn't let on, but deep in my heart I knew I didn't deserve any credit like Harold Dresser or Sergeant Tietjen for the things I did. At first I used to worry about the war and getting killed, and then that day in Baltimore, while on leave, I saw a sign on a door:

MADAME BONATURA
THE SEERESS OF THE EAST
Tells Your Past, Present and Future

I went into her parlor and we sat there talking for a time. Then she lowered the blinds and lighted a tiny lamp that shone on her face, and looked into a crystal ball. A funny expression came into her eyes and she began to twitch. Then she started talking in a sleepy voice, telling me the names of my two brothers, the number of my company and many other things. Finally she seemed to get excited: she began to talk hoarsely. "Ask me a question, and I will answer it," she said.

"Well," I thought, "I might as well know once and for all and get it off my mind. . . ."

"Ask me a question—any question you want," she said.

"Will you really tell me the truth, even if the answer is bad?" I asked.

"Yes," she said.

"Then tell me if I will be killed in the war."

Madame Bonatura looked into the crystal ball for a long time before answering. I wanted to say, "No!—Don't tell me! Don't answer!" but I wouldn't do it. "I might as well know the truth now, as any time," I thought. Finally the Madame began to speak, and I caught my breath again. "You will not be killed, or even wounded," she said. "You will be returned to those you love, will marry the girl of your choice and live happily ever after."

So you see I didn't really deserve all the credit I got. I wasn't any braver than anybody else and besides that I knew all the time that nothing could possibly happen to me, no matter what I did.

PRIVATE LEO HASTINGS

ALL THAT morning the German sniper shot at me. I would stick my head up, or walk across the open space, and there would come a faint ping and a bullet would pass harmlessly over my head. Then I would stop in my tracks and stand there a full two seconds, or suddenly take a step backwards and a step to the side. I would walk that way up and down the parapet of the trench laughing at the sniper. I knew I had him so sore at me that he was almost ready to break down and cry. I'd shot with telescopic sights myself and I knew no sniper in the world could hit a man who varied his stride as I did, unless the sniper could figure out in advance the man's system and he's got about as much chance of doing that as he has of breaking the bank at Monte Carlo.

"I'll stand here and let him take pot shots at me all day," I said; "he can't hit me in a thousand years.—See, as I stand now, he's got me covered. But wait! He's got to figure his distance, taking an angle between that dead tree and the farmhouse, probably. Now he's got it all doped out. He's taking his windage and calculating elevation. Now he's already to plug me, but by stepping one pace to the right, or doing this clog step, I upset all his calculations. See," I said, "there goes his bullet two feet to the right. He can't hit me to save his neck," I said.

PRIVATE SILAS PULLMAN

ONLY a few minutes more and we'll be going over. I can hear my watch ticking—ticking. This silence is worse than shelling. . . . I've never been under fire before: I don't know whether I can stand it or not.—This isn't the way I thought it was going to be.—I want to turn and run. I'm yellow, I guess. . . . The other men aren't frightened at all. They just stand there holding their rifles, cracking jokes. . . . Maybe they're as frightened as I am. How do I know? How can I tell what's going on in their minds. . . . Sergeant Mooney is speaking to me: "See that your bayonet is fastened tight," he says.—I nod my head.—I don't dare speak. . . . Oh, Christ! don't let anybody see how frightened I am.—Don't let them see, please! . . . I won't think about it any more. I'll think about something else.

Lieutenant Jewett has given the signal. Sergeant Mooney is climbing out of the trench. "All right, over you go!" he says. We're all climbing out. Now we're walking forward slowly.—Why don't the Germans open fire? They know we're coming over. They can see us.—For Christ sake, start firing! We're not fooling you! Go ahead: shoot at us! . . .

Down! Down!—Down on your belly, you fool! Do you want to be bumped off?—The Germans have opened up. We're down close to the ground, crawling; crawling inch by inch. They haven't got our range yet. . . . "Our orders are to crawl until we're fifty yards from their trenches, and then dash forward and attack."—Just dash forward, and attack.—That's very simple. —Just attack. . . .

They've got our range now. Corporal Brockett is hit in the shoulder. He's crawling for a shell hole.—Now he's in it. He's safe from the machine guns' bullets there. . . . Why doesn't he stop twisting about? That won't help matters.—That won't do any good. . . .

The bullets are plowing the dirt a foot from my head. Down closer! Hug the ground closer, you fool! . . . Mart Appleton and

Luke Janoff are hit now. They fell at the same instant, almost. They lay there quietly, neither of them moving. . . . Now the man next to me is hit. Who is he? . . . His name is Les Yawfitz, I think. He stands up and then falls down. He's shot in the face. Blood is running down his face and into his mouth. He's making a choking sound and is crawling about like an ant. He can't see where he's going. Why don't you lie still. . . . That seems the sensible thing to do: You can't see where you're going, you know.

We're closer to the trenches. . . . Get up! Get up!—It's time to rush forward and throw grenades. It's time to take the trenches.—We're fighting with bayonets. We're in the German trenches. We're fighting with clubbed rifles and trench knives. There are screams and men running about in confusion. . . . Now everything is quiet again. We've started back with our prisoners.—Sergeant Dockdorf is lying with his throat cut, half in the trench and half out. . . . Jerry Easton is stretched on the German duckboards, his eyelids still fluttering. . . .

PRIVATE SAMUEL QUILLIN

It was partly a dugout, and partly a dwelling, and it had been an officers' casino before we had taken the territory from the Germans, the day before. It faced the Somme-Py road, and immediately we turned it into an evacuation station. When I went up that night, to check the casualties in my battalion, the place was full of wounded men awaiting ambulances. It was in October, I remember, and the air was crisp, with a feeling of frost. For a few minutes I was busy going from man to man, looking at identification tags. Then I heard a whine and a rushing sound in the air. I covered my ears, and braced myself, because I knew by instinct that the shell was going to register a direct hit. The sound increased to a shriek. Then a flash of light and a thundering explosion that blew the walls outward, and I fell swiftly into a lake of ink and lay prone on the bottom and at peace, for a long time, not breathing . . . and then climbed out of the ink slowly, inch by inch, and began to groan. . . .

"There's a man alive down there," I heard somebody say. Nobody answered the voice for a moment. Then finally there came another voice: "Nobody could be alive with all that weight on him. . . ." Then I remembered where I was. I was lying on my back and through the beams, iron sheets and tons of earth, I could see one star, tired and faint in the sky. I became frightened and began to shout. . . .

"Lie quiet!" said the first voice sharply. "You've got to keep your head. . . . Lie quiet! and listen to what I say: There are hundreds of tons balanced over you. If you move about you'll bring it down." Then I became quiet. Above me I could see the men moving beams, but very cautiously, taking out the bodies as they came to them. The first man spoke to me again. "Are you hurt?" he asked.

"I suppose so," I said.

Then after a while I spoke again. "I'm going to start hollering: I'm thinking about those beams mashing me."

"You're a fool, if you do," he said.

I shut my eyes and began to compose a letter, in my mind, to a girl back home named Hazel Green, making each line rhyme. When I opened them, I could see a whole patch of sky. The patch got bigger and bigger until the last beam was lifted off my chest, and the men helped me out. I stood up, feeling my legs. I walked alone to the dressing station, and the doctor examined me, but there wasn't a scratch on me anywhere.

"Twenty-six men were taken out of that dugout, and you're the only one that came out alive," said the doctor. "You've had a lucky escape."

"Yes, sir, I sure did," I said.

PRIVATE ABRAHAM RICKEY

I WAS LYING in the wheat near Captain Matlock when he got hit and I was the first man to reach him. One machine gun bullet had hit him squarely between the eyes, plowing through his head and coming out at the base of his skull.

A boy out of the third platoon, named Mart Passy, came up when I called, and together we lifted the Captain and carried him to a trench where stretcher bearers picked him up and took him to the rear.

After the fighting was over and we were back at Fly Farm getting a batch of replacements, I was telling some of the boys about how Fishmouth Terry got hit. "He fell down without making any noise," I said. "He just fell down in the wheat and doubled up. I thought he was dead, sure, but he was breathing all right when the stretcher bearers took him. It was just one bullet, but it went all the way through his head. When I turned him on his face, I saw a teaspoonful of brains had run out on the ground."

"Wait a minute now . . . take it easy, sailor!" said Sergeant Dunning. "How much brains did you say ran out of Fishmouth Terry's head? . . ."

"About a teaspoonful," I said.

Everybody shook their heads and shrugged their shoulders.

"Are you sure it was Captain Matlock you picked up?" the sergeant asked again.

"Why, yes," I said. "Sure it was."

Everybody began to laugh. . . . "Be reasonable!" said Vester Keith. "Be reasonable!—If that many brains ran out, it couldn't possibly have been *our* Terry!"

PRIVATE WILBUR BOWDEN

IT WAS pitch dark, not even a star shining, when I crawled into a deep shell hole, and lay there listening. I knew, at once, there was a wounded man with me in the shell hole: I don't know how I knew it: I couldn't see him, certainly, but I did know it. Then I drew my trench knife and braced myself, but he spoke to me in English. He was an outpost sentry from the First Battalion who had run into a German patrol, and been wounded.

He whispered all this, his mouth close to my ear. The German trenches were only a short distance away, and we didn't dare make a sound that might be overheard.

"Where did they get you?" I whispered back.

He waited a long time to answer. "In the leg," he said.

I took off his first aid packet and straightened out the bandage as best I could. I didn't have a match, and I wouldn't have dared strike it, if I had. I unfastened his belt and pulled his breeches down. Then I slit his drawers with my knife.

"Which leg is it?" I asked.

"I'm not sure," he said slowly.

"I'll run my hand over your leg," I whispered, "and when I come to the wounded place, let me know, and I'll put on a bandage."

"All right," he said finally.

I ran my hand slowly down his left leg from thigh to knee, but he didn't flinch or give any sign of pain. Then I started on his right thigh, feeling cautiously. Suddenly he winced a little. "Is that the place?" I asked. . . . "Yes," he said.

His uniform was soaked with blood and my fingers were sticky from touching his legs. I put the bandage on the spot he had indicated and tied it tightly.

"Am I still bleeding?" he asked.

"No," I said, "you're not bleeding now." Then I added: "The wound must be pretty small, after all, because I couldn't even feel it."

"It's deep, I guess," he said.

When I got the bandage on, he said he felt sleepy, and would take a nap. "That's the ticket," I said. "You take a nap now, and as soon as I get back to the company, I'll send out a couple of stretcher bearers for you." He didn't answer me. He'd gone to sleep while I was talking to him.

When I got back to the line, an hour later, I told Sergeant Boss about the wounded man and he sent out for him, but the man was dead when they found him. We took him into the dug-out, and looked at him by candle light: The first thing we saw was a wound in his side that you could lay your fist in. I stood there puzzled, while the men kidded me. Then I took off the bandage I had put on his leg: The skin was unbroken. In fact there wasn't a scratch on his whole body except the one place in his side, from which he had bled to death.

I've thought about that man a good many times, but I can't make heads or tails of it. Why did he flinch, and say he was wounded in the leg, when he wasn't? Did he really know where he was wounded? Or was it because he knew he was going to die, and my questions bothered him? Did he think it would be easier to let me have my way, and put on a bandage, since I insisted on it? I've thought it over a good many times, without coming to any conclusion.

PRIVATE EUGENE MERRIAM

I DELIVERED the message to Lieutenant Bartelstone and turned to go, but the Germans had started shelling the wood again, and the Somme-Py road.

"You'd better wait until the barrage lifts," said Lieutenant Bartelstone.

"No, sir," I said; "I guess I'd better get on back to Regimental. —I'll get through, all right."

"That's a pretty heavy barrage," he said; "you'd better wait awhile."

"I'll be all right," I said; "I've been through a hundred worse than that. If I waited for every barrage to lift, I wouldn't get many messages delivered."

"Yes, I guess that's right," said the lieutenant laughing.

I turned up my coat collar, like it was a rain storm I was going through, and began loping through the woods. There were shells exploding in the tree-tops and the wood was filled with red hot shrapnel. The shrapnel swirled around and whimpered and sounded like horses biting at each other's flanks. It was autumn and the leaves of the trees were red and yellow and brown. They kept raining down before my eyes like dead birds falling to earth. The shelling seemed to get heavier, but I ran on and on. I knew it was useless to duck. . . . Then the woods opened and I saw the road.

"In just a minute now, I'll be out of the barrage and safe," I thought.

PRIVATE HERBERT MERRIAM

WHEN I got back from the hospital it was late September and the Company was billeted in a wood near Manorville. I asked Sergeant Boss about my brother, Gene, our regimental runner.

"Well, no, I haven't seen him lately," he answered, "but then we've been on the move most of the time and I haven't seen anybody from Headquarters hardly."

"I'll go over to Regimental to-night and surprise Gene," I said.

I threw my equipment down on an empty bunk but Byron Long picked it up. "Why don't you take my bunk, Herbie," he asked. "That one's broke.—You come over here and swap with me."

"Well, for Christ sake!" I said laughing. "What's come over you boys, anyway? Are you practicing up to be boy scouts?"

Byron didn't say anything, but he looked away.

"I wouldn't go over to Regimental to see Gene," said Sergeant Halligan.

"Why not?" I asked; "there aren't any regulations against it, are there?"

"I just wouldn't go, that's all."

I stood there thinking for a minute; then my heart began to beat too fast. My knees seemed to get weak, and for a minute I thought I was going to fall down.

"Oh," I said . . . "Oh, I see!"

"Why don't you lie down on Byron's bunk for a while," said Frank Halligan. "It's over against the wall, out of the way, where nobody will be stepping over you.—Why don't you lie down and take a little nap? . . . You must be tired, after that trip from the hospital."

"All right," I said. "I think I will take a nap."

"Stretch out all the way," said Byron. "Here—I'll put my blankets over you, so you won't get cold."

Then each man thought up some reason for going outside. They went out, one by one, and stood in the cold until finally I was alone in the bunk house.

PRIVATE PETER STAFFORD

WHEN I came out from the ether, I didn't know, at first, where I was, but after a while my mind cleared up and I remembered I was in a hospital, and that they had just cut off my leg. Then the nurse gave me some medicine to swallow and the pain stopped. Everything seemed to get all mixed up. For a little while I would know where I was, and what had happened to me, and then I would doze off and think I was back home again.

I don't know what time it was when I heard people whispering above my bed. I opened my eyes and looked up and all I saw at first was an elderly lady, with a sweet face, looking down at me. For some reason I thought I was back in Little Rock and that the lady was one of our neighbors, a Mrs. Sellers, come to call on Mamma.

"Hello, Mrs. Sellers!" I said: "what in the world are you doing up here in *my* room?"

Then I seen the doctors and the nurse standing there beside the lady, and I knew where I was. The lady didn't say anything, but she smiled in a friendly way. When I seen my mistake, I spoke to the lady more politely. "I beg your pardon, ma'am," I said, "but at first I taken you for a lady who runs a boarding-house across the street from where I live."

The lady spoke in a very cultured voice: "Do I resemble her a great deal?"

"Yes, ma'am," I said; "you sure do!—Why if you had on a dust-apron and a boudoir cap, nobody could ever tell you two apart."

Then I knew by the look on the nurse's face that I had made a break. Later I learned that I had been addressing her Majesty, the Queen of England. When I discovered that, I asked the nurse to be sure and tell the queen that Mrs. Sellers was a respectable woman who enjoyed the good opinion of everybody in Little Rock and she needn't feel ashamed of resembling her. The nurse said she and the queen were good friends and that she'd be sure and tell her the next time they had a visit together.

I never heard any more about it, but the mistake was unintentional on my part, and it was evidently regarded in that light by the queen. . . . I'll bet, though, she still remembers my error, and that she has had many a good laugh at my expense since that time.

PRIVATE SIDNEY BELMONT

THEY tell this story on the colonel of my regiment. He had come up to the line one afternoon, in a private's uniform, after having taken off his eagles, his belt and all other insignia of rank. While standing there inspecting the line, Gene Merriam came up with a message. When he saw the colonel, he stopped and saluted, in plain view. That made the colonel sore.

"Say, you stupid little so-and-so," he shouted, "haven't you got sense enough not to salute an officer on the line? Do you want every sniper in the German army to try to pick me off?" For a time he stood swearing and shaking his fist and then he began to feel sorry for Gene, who was blushing and looking down under the bawling out he was getting. . . .

"Listen," the colonel said, "in the future when you want to attract my attention on the line, don't salute me. Come up, instead, and kick me a couple of times and say: 'Listen to me, you dopey old son of a bitch!' That's the way to speak to me, when I'm on the line," said the colonel.

Later I heard that story told on the colonel of every regiment in France, but it really happened in my outfit.

PRIVATE RICHARD STARNES

AFTER the raid that night, we became confused, and unable to find the gap in our wire. There were five of us. Six, if you count the prisoner we had taken for questioning. While we stood there disputing, the Germans began throwing over gas shells. We took out our masks and put them on at once, but the prisoner didn't have a mask, and when the gas started choking him, he dropped down in terror and begged for his life. He cried and wrung his hands and talked about his mother and his home. We paid no attention to him. We wouldn't listen to what he was saying. Then he threw his arms around my knees and clung to me. I have never seen such cowardice. . . . I kept shoving him away with my foot, but he came back, time after time, crying and clinging to my legs. He was beginning to cough by that time, and water was coming out of his eyes.

Now here's the funny part of the story: As the little swine hugged my knees and cried, a curious feeling of pity came over me, and before I realized what I was doing, I had got down on my knees beside him. I put my arms around him. . . . "Take my mask, brother," I said gently.—I don't know why I did it. I've never been able to tell why I did it!—I must have been crazy. Certainly no man in his right mind would do a thing like that. . . .

If he'd had the slightest sense of decency, he'd have refused the mask, but he took it out of my hand and put it on. I hadn't really meant to give the mask to him. Why should I do a thing of that sort? . . . As soon as I realized what I'd done, I wanted to take the mask away from him, but I couldn't do that with the other men looking on.—You see what an impossible position I was in? . . .

"Yes," said the doctor, "I can see that."

"What right did he have to take the mask, when I didn't know what I was doing?—What right had he—"

"It was a fine thing to do," said the doctor.

"I tell you I was crazy," I shouted. "I was sorry the moment I had done it."

"Be quiet," said the doctor, "or you'll start bleeding again."

CORPORAL FREDERICK WILLCOXEN

IT WAS late October, the Germans were falling back all along the line, releasing towns which they had occupied for four years, and all day we saw French civilians, mostly old men and women, trudging to the rear, loaded down with their personal property. When we fell out for a ten-minute rest, we saw an old woman sitting against the side of a steep hill. Strapped to her back was a huge wicker basket filled with pots and pans and such things. Her face was wrinkled, and she seemed weak and all in. "Christ Almighty!" said Sergeant Halligan, "how can that poor old soul manage to lift such a load?"

"I don't know," I said, "but I'm going over and help her carry her stuff up the hill." I turned and walked toward her, and as I did so, she started shaking her fist at me. I stopped in surprise and spoke to her gently: "Don't be scared, Granny," I said; "I'm not going to hurt you." Then I smiled and walked toward her again, but she jumped up, at my approach, making a squeaking noise, and scurried up the side of the hill, basket and all, as quick as a lizard running up a wall. She went up so fast, I stood there with my mouth open. When she got to the top, she spat at me and called me a pig.

Everybody laughed and tried to kid me. Mart Passy lay on the ground and roared. "Say, Fred," he called, "ask your girl friend to come down again and carry up the rolling kitchen for us."

SERGEANT MARVIN MOONEY

ONE DAY in the Argonne Forest we came on a wounded German soldier. It was early in the morning and frost had fallen the night before. The German lay huddled on his belly, and he must have been there all night, because when I turned him over, there was no frost on the place where he had been lying. His face was white and he was shivering. He wore eye-glasses with thick, dirty lenses.

When he saw me, he begged for a drink of water. I said: "It was different when you were raping Red Cross Nurses and cutting off the legs of children in Belgium, wasn't it? The shoe's on the other foot, now.—Here's some of your own medicine!" Then I straightened out his head with my foot and pounded his face with the butt of my rifle until it was like jelly. After that I opened my canteen and poured all the water I had on the ground, as I didn't want anybody to think it was giving him the water I minded. "Here's a drink of water for you," I said. . . .

If you think I'm lying, just ask Fred Terwilliger or Harry Althouse. They were with me at the time. . . . He was a crummy little fellow and his eye-glasses were tied around his ears with two pieces of common twine. His face was white and he kept shivering and rattling his teeth together. He was about five feet six, I should say, although he might have been an inch or so taller than that. Every time I hit him his knees jerked up a little.

PRIVATE OLIVER TECLAW

WE WERE GOING up to the front line one morning when somebody began calling my name excitedly. "Ollie," he shouted, "Ollie Teclaw!"

It was Sergeant Ernest, my old drill sergeant. He used to say I was the worst soldier he ever tried to train, in all of his years of service.

"Hello," I said.

"Say, did you ever learn to hold a bayonet proper?" he asked.

"Nope," I said; "never did."

"Did you get so you could qualify with a rifle?"

"Never could shoot a rifle, Sarge," I said; "never could do that."

We were getting farther apart and Sergeant Ernest cupped his mouth with his hands and began to shout: "How about grenades? Can you throw grenades?"

"No better than I could in training camp," I said.

Ernest shook his head and groaned. "For Christ sake! Hasn't nobody killed you yet?" he shouted.

"Uh-uh," I said. . . . "Not so far."

PRIVATE FRANKLIN GOOD

It was November. The nights were cold and there was frost on the ground in the mornings. The roads were frozen, and hard as iron. The trees were all bare of leaves and their branches made a whispering sound in the wind like sandpaper. In the forest before us, the Germans were retreating steadily, their ammunition and equipment littering their trenches, their wounded abandoned on the ground. We came through the forest cautiously, watching out for mines.

We came on all that day, steadily. Then, toward dark, we saw the Meuse flowing before us. We hurried, at sight of the river, anxious to cross the bridge and dig in before night fell, but before we reached the bank, there came three explosions and the bridge flung upward before our eyes and slid into the swift current. We stood there looking at the wrecked bridge, blowing on our hands, our breath congealing into steam.

Then the engineers came up from the rear to construct a pontoon. We began digging in, by the bank, in anticipation of the barrage the Germans were certain to lay down on us. The engineers worked rapidly and the bridge was ready before the barrage began. But somebody had to swim the river and anchor the bridge to the opposite bank. Jerry Blandford volunteered to do this. He took off his clothes and plunged into the icy water, towing the frail pontoon behind him. When he reached the opposite bank, the barrage started. Then he tied the rope around a tree stump and the first man came over. The shells were striking all about us, throwing up spouts of water and clots of mud bigger than a man's body. Then, one by one, we ran quickly across the bridge and took up a position on the other side. At daybreak we were all over. Nine men had been killed crossing and the bridge partially destroyed and repaired three times. When the last man was over, the platoons were reorganized and the attack continued. We turned and looked back at the river and saw the engineers, as busy as ants, building another bridge which would be strong enough to bear the weight of our artillery.

THE UNKNOWN SOLDIER

We were returning from a wiring party that quiet night and the men were in high spirits. Then two Maxims opened a deadly, enfilading fire, and one of my companions threw his hands up and fell without a sound. I stood there confused at the sudden attack, not knowing which way to turn. Then I heard some one shout: "Look out! Look out for the wire!" and I saw my companions, flat on their frightened bellies, scattering in all directions. I started to run, but at that moment something shoved me, and something took my breath away, and I toppled backward, and the wire caught me.

At first I did not realize that I was wounded. I lay there on the wire, breathing heavily. "I must keep perfectly calm," I thought. "If I move about, I'll entangle myself so badly that I'll never get out." Then a white flare went up and in the light that followed I saw my belly was ripped open and that my entrails hung down like a badly arranged bouquet of blue roses. The sight frightened me and I began to struggle, but the more I twisted about, the deeper the barbs sank in. Finally I could not move my legs any more and I knew, then, that I was going to die. So I lay stretched quietly, moaning and spitting blood.

I could not forget the faces of the men and the way they had scurried off when the machine guns opened up. I remembered a time when I was a little boy and had gone to visit my grandfather, who lived on a farm. Rabbits were eating his cabbages that year, so grandfather had closed all the entrances to his field except one, and he baited that one with lettuce leaves and young carrots. When the field was full of rabbits, the fun began. Grandfather opened the gate and let in the dog, and the hired man stood at the gap, a broomstick in his hand, breaking the necks of the rabbits as they leaped out. I had stood to one side, I remembered, pitying the rabbits and thinking how stupid they were to let themselves be caught in such an obvious trap.—And now as I lay on the wire, the scene came back to me vividly. . . . *I* had pitied the rabbits!—I, of all people . . .

I lay back, my eyes closed, thinking of that. Then I heard the mayor of our town making his annual address in the Soldiers' Cemetery at home. Fragments of his speech kept floating through my mind: "These men died gloriously on the Field of Honor! . . . Gave their lives gladly in a Noble Cause! . . . What a feeling of exaltation was theirs when Death kissed their mouths and closed their eyes for an Immortal Eternity! . . ." Suddenly I saw myself, too, a boy in the crowd, my throat tight to keep back the tears, listening enraptured to the speech and believing every word of it; and at that instant I understood clearly why I now lay dying on the wire. . . .

The first shock had passed and my wounds began to pain me. I had seen other men die on the wire and I had said if it happened to me, I would make no sound, but after a while I couldn't stand the pain any longer and I began to make a shrill, wavering noise. I cried like that for a long time. I couldn't help it. . . .

Towards daybreak a German sentry crawled out from his post and came to where I lay. "Hush!" he said in a soft voice. "Hush, please!"

He sat on his haunches and stared at me, a compassionate look in his eyes. Then I began to talk to him: "It's all a lie that people tell each other, and nobody really believes," I said. . . . "And I'm a part of it, whether I want to be or not.—I'm more a part of it now than ever before: In a few years, when war is over, they'll move my body back home to the Soldiers' Cemetery, just as they moved the bodies of the soldiers killed before I was born. There will be a brass band and speech making and a beautiful marble shaft with my name chiseled on its base. . . . The mayor will be there also, pointing to my name with his thick, trembling forefinger and shouting meaningless words about glorious deaths and fields of honor. . . . And there will be other little boys in that crowd to listen and believe him, just as I listened and believed!"

"Hush," said the German softly. "Hush! . . . Hush!"

I began to twist about on the wire and to cry again.

"I can't stand the thought of that! I can't stand it! . . . I never want to hear military music or high sounding words again: I want to be buried where nobody will ever find me.—I want to be wiped out completely . . ."

Then, suddenly, I became silent, for I had seen a way out. I took off my identification tags and threw them into the wire, as far as I could. I tore to pieces the letters and the photographs I carried and scattered the fragments. I threw my helmet away, so that no one could guess my identity from the serial number stamped on the sweatband. Then I lay back exultant!

The German had risen and stood looking at me, as if puzzled. . . . "I've beaten the orators and the wreath layers at their own game!" I said. . . . "I've beaten them all!—Nobody will ever use me as a symbol. Nobody will ever tell lies over my dead body now! . . ."

"Hush," said the German softly. "Hush! . . . Hush!"

Then my pain became so unbearable that I began to choke and bite at the wire with my teeth. The German came closer to me, touching my head with his hand. . . .

"Hush," he said. . . "Hush, please. . . ."

But I could not stop. I thrashed about on the wire and cried in a shrill voice. The German took out his pistol and stood twisting it in his hand, not looking at me. Then he put his arm under my head, lifting me up, and kissed me softly on my cheek, repeating phrases which I could not understand. I saw, then, that he too, had been crying for a long time. . . .

"Do it quickly!" I said. "Quickly! . . . Quickly!"

He stood with trembling hands for a moment before he placed

the barrel of his pistol against my temple, turned his head away, and fired. My eyes fluttered twice and then closed; my hands clutched and relaxed slowly.

"I have broken the chain," I whispered. "I have defeated the inherent stupidity of life."

"Hush," he said. "Hush! . . . Hush! . . . Hush! . . ."

PRIVATE CHARLES UPSON

THE first thing we noticed was the silence of the German artillery. Then our own artillery quit firing. We looked at each other, surprised at the sudden quietness and wondered what was the matter. A runner came up, out of breath, with a message from Divisional. Lieutenant Bartelstone, in command of our company, read it slowly and called his platoon sergeants together. "Pass word to the men to cease firing, the war is over," he said.

CORPORAL STEPHEN WALLER

COMPANY K went into action at 10:15 P.M. December 12th, 1917, at Verdun, France, and ceased fighting on the morning of November 11th, 1918, near Bourmont, having crossed the Meuse River the night before under shell fire; participating, during the period set out above, in the following major operations: Aisne, Aisne-Marne, St. Mihiel and Meuse-Argonne.

A number of men were cited for bravery, the following decorations having been actually awarded for meritorious service under fire: 10 Croix de Guerre (four of them with palms); 6 Distinguished Service Crosses; 2 Medals Militaire and 1 Congressional Medal of Honor, the latter being awarded to Private Harold Dresser, a man of amazing personal courage.

The percentage of casualties in killed, wounded in action, missing or evacuated to hospital suffering from disease, was considerably higher than average (332.8) percent.

Our commanding officer, Terence L. Matlock, Captain, was able and efficient and retained throughout the respect and the admiration of the men who served under him.

PRIVATE LEO BROGAN

The Armistice had been signed, and for three days we had been moving across France, a short day's march behind the evacuating German army. It was raining: a thin, misty rain which fell straight down and penetrated to our shivering skin as we plowed raggedly down the muddy country roads. Seen through the slow rain, the country-side, with its barren brown fields and leafless woods, seemed very desolate, and the ruined villages were lonely against a sky as gray as pewter.

Occasionally we passed through a village which had been partially rebuilt, or only imperfectly destroyed, in which people still lived, and at such times the inhabitants stood in their doorways, silent, and a little frightened, and watched us go past; or occasionally we passed some splendid country estate which had, by its isolation, escaped any systematic shelling, and stood now, incongruously intact, beside the road, with its brick walls and its iron gates and its untrimmed hedges. It was near such a chateau that we received orders to fall-out for our noon meal. We drew to one side of the road and waited. Presently the company's rolling-kitchen, drawn by old Mamie the galley mule, lumbered up to the head of the column and pulled out from the road into an uncultivated field.

Hymie White of the Second Platoon slipped out of his pack and stretched his shoulders. When he had got the kinks out of his shoulders and had assembled his mess-gear, the kitchen had been set up and a circle had already formed around it. A boiler of steaming soup was being lifted to the ground by Sidney Borgstead and his assistant cook. Sergeant Mike Olmstead, the company mess-sergeant, who was loudly supervising the preparations for the meal, turned suddenly, and spoke to us: "What are you birds trying to pull off? You get in line, or you don't get no chow, see?" Long association with hungry men had made Mike suspicious of everything. Mike had a lumpy, badly molded face, and a ragged mouth which resembled a small shell hole.

A line quickly formed and Sid Borgstead commenced dishing out the food. Sergeant Olmstead stood by to see that each man got his fair share. When Hymie White's turn came, he was served with a dipper full of thin soup and a small slice of bread over which a spoonful of corn syrup had been poured. He looked at the scant rations and was furious all of a sudden.

"That's a hell of a meal to offer a man!" he said. The friendly look was gone from his eyes; his face was flushed and his nostrils dilated. "That's a fine God damned meal to offer a man!"

"If you don't like it, put it back in the pot," said Sergeant Olmstead.

"I haven't had enough to eat since I joined this bastardly outfit!"

"Don't tell me your troubles, sonny!"

"What this company needs most is a new mess-sergeant!"

"Yeah?" said Sergeant Olmstead. "Well, let me tell you something. I cook what Headquarters issues me, see?"

It was then that Hymie realized the futility of further argument. He walked back to the roadside where he had left his pack and sat down upon it to eat his meal. He noticed that several very old men and very young children had, in his absence, gathered by the iron gate of the château. They gazed steadily at the soldiers eating their food, following with slow eyes the rhythmic rise and fall of a hundred dirty spoons.

Presently an old lady, wrapped in a waterproof coat, came hobbling down the long, flag-paved walk that ran from the iron gate to the château. With her was a girl about eight years old: a homely child with tight pigtails and bangs and fat, clumsy legs. Beside the child there walked, sedately, a young fawn, with dappled gray sides and soft brown eyes.

When the party reached the gate the old lady dramatically placed one bony hand upon her heart and with a wide, inclusive gesture she blew a kiss to the reclining soldiers. Then she began to speak rapidly in French, clutching her heart, or her throat, at intervals, and at intervals pointing to the dull sky. Hymie turned and spoke to Pierre Brockett: "What the hell is the old bag making a speech about?" Brockett, who had been sopping his pan with a morsel of bread to get the last drop of soup, looked up and listened for a moment: "She's thanking the brave soldiers for saving her stricken France, and so on, and so on." "Oh, is that what it's all about?" said Hymie.

Then he noticed that the fawn had thrust its head between the iron bars of the gate and was regarding him, across the muddy road, with eager, infatuated eyes. Hymie whistled softly —ingratiatingly. Instantly the little fawn lunged against the gate, a ripple of excitement passing over its nervous body. It stood there trembling for a moment, then it withdrew from the gate and minced across the lawn, switching its fluff of a tail and running in sudden, clowning circles. Finally it stopped and looked at Hyman White to see if its efforts had been appreciated.

The soldiers laughed loudly at its antics. At the sound of their laughter the old lady paused in her speech, her right hand pointing straight up to the spot in the sky that she considered the abode of God, and the other resting on the black head of the little girl, who had turned and was clapping her hands in delight. The old lady smiled indulgently, stroked the cheek of the little girl, and, with another blown kiss and a low bow, brought to an end her speech. A dozen soldiers crowded in front of the gate, snapping their fingers and whistling to attract the attention of the fawn, but it ignored them: it gazed with fascinated eyes at Hyman White, alone.

"Try it again, Hymie!" said Graley Borden.

Again Hymie gave his long, soft whistle and, as if awaiting that signal, the little fawn ran crazily up the walk, kicking its heels in the air and showing the creamy softness of its belly. It made sudden, idiotic rushes at flower-beds and leafless shrubs, bracing itself quickly in time to avoid a collision, only to dash off, crazily, at another angle. At length it ran toward the iron gate and again hurled itself against the bars. Unable to escape as it wished, it stood looking at the old lady, its dappled hide twitching with nervous excitement.

The men who had gathered in front of the gate were delighted with the diversion. They laughed loudly and made ribald remarks about the power of love at first sight and Hyman White's unsuspected prowess as a charmer. There was a tender smile on the old lady's face, and suddenly she unfastened the great catch on the iron gate. There came a sharp cry and a quick sentence from the little girl, but the old lady patted her cheek and spoke a dozen soft, reassuring words in reply. For a moment there was silence, then the little girl nodded her head and stood stolidly regarding her boots. At the child's nod, the old lady swung wide the gate and the little fawn instantly leaped out and ran across the muddy road, hurling itself into the arms of Hyman White.

The soldiers crowded around him, trying to attract the fawn's attention, but it would not notice them: It would not move from the arms of Hyman White where it lay licking his cheek with its soft tongue, and gazing at him with loving, humid eyes.

I stood with John McGill watching the picture. John was considerably affected. He turned to me and spoke softly: "How surer than our human reason is the simple instinct of the fawn. . . . There must be a beauty of soul in Hyman White, instantly apparent and compelling to the fawn, that escapes our duller senses."

I looked at Hymie White for a minute and saw a stocky, stolid lad, with heavy features and reddened face. His mouth was stained with grease from the soup which he had just eaten, and his nose dripped a little.

"Maybe so, John," I said. "Maybe so."

After a while word came down the line for us to stand by. We rose and collected our packs and our scattered mess-gear.

Hyman White was still holding the little fawn in his arms, passing his hands lovingly over its soft, fat flanks. Finally he turned to Pierre Brockett, who was struggling into his marching-order.

"Ask the old girl what she'll take for the fawn," he said.

Brockett stated the question and again there came a quick, terrified cry from the little girl, but the old lady smiled and shook her head.

"Won't sell it," said Pierre.

Hymie walked regretfully across the road and put down the fawn beside the little girl. The fawn struggled and tried to free itself, but the little girl held it tightly in her arms. When Hymie had reached his place, and had thrown his rifle across his shoulder, the little girl burst into tears and spoke rapidly to the old lady. A moment later she released the fawn and it ran quickly to Hymie, again nuzzling his hand, and dancing around him.

The old lady held up her arm for attention. The troops turned to regard her. She spoke rapidly for a few moments, and Brockett translated to the troops, who were already moving off. "She says that she would never sell the fawn—no, no! not for any amount of money! But since the brave soldier and the fawn love each other so dearly, her granddaughter gives it to him gladly!"

The little girl took a step forward and spoke in a shrill treble. Then she stopped quickly, as if reproved, and looked at the muddy earth.

"Take care of him! Take care of him!" said Pierre Brockett. Then he added: "She says the fawn is very gentle."

Hymie looked back for an instant and waved his hand to the old lady, and the little girl, but the old lady did not see him; she had commenced speaking again, with sweeping gestures that included, impartially, the soldiers, the rain soaked country-side and the dull sky. There were still tears in the eyes of the little girl, and she gazed longingly at the fawn. In her heart there was a hope that the fawn, at last, would come to its senses and return to her, but the fascinated creature skipped up and down the side of the muddy road, and did not once look back.

The thin rain continued to fall. We walked in silence except for the occasional tinkle of a canteen and the monotonous sucking sound of many feet sinking and being withdrawn from the soft mud. Gradually the dark set in. Then Hymie lifted the fawn into his arms where it lay with its muzzle resting in the harness of his pack. When it was almost dark we reached the town where we were to sleep for the night. Roy Winters, our billeting sergeant, who had gone on before us, was waiting, and directed the company to its assigned space. When Hymie had got his squad all settled and had laid out his pack on the dry straw, he whistled to his fawn and went outside. I got up and followed him, and in the road in front of the billet, he spoke to me:

"Where has Mike set up his galley?" he asked.

"I don't know," I said.

He turned away and walked off, but I followed him at a short distance, dodging out of sight when he turned his head.

He found Mike, in an old stable, his kitchen set up and a great fire roaring. Sidney Borgstead was peeling potatoes and dropping them into a dirty, smoke-encrusted bucket at his side.

Hymie and the fawn entered the stable and I stood by the door, peering in, and listening to what they said.

"Get out of here!" said Sergeant Olmstead irritably; "supper ain't ready for an hour yet."

"Sergeant," said Hymie in a wheedling, placating voice, "I've got a proposition for you—just you and me."

"Yeah? What is it?" replied Mike, still suspicious.

Hymie hesitated for a moment, somewhat embarrassed. The dappled fawn was exploring the dark recesses of the stable, stepping daintily back and forth in the red light from the fire, and pretending to be frightened at a brown leaf blowing slowly across the uneven floor.

"Did you ever eat venison steaks?" he asked at last.

Mike's ragged, slack mouth opened a little in surprise. "Hell, man— You don't mean you're going to—!" . . . He paused, slightly shocked at the idea.

"I'm hungry," said Hymie. Then he added: "It'll be just me and you, sergeant; what do you say?"

"But say, you couldn't do that; not after the way the fawn took to you, and all. . . ."

"Sure I could. Why not?"

Mike rubbed his lumpy nose for a time. Finally he said: "A stew would be better—a stew with onions and potatoes in it."

"That's up to you, Mike; whatever you say is all right with me."

Then Mike laughed, as if ashamed, and nodded his head.

At Hymie's whistle the fawn turned quickly, and faced him. . . . The firelight gilded the soft cream of its throat and turned to dark copper the gray markings on its flanks. Its sweet brown eyes were bright with love as it ran quickly to Hymie White, and rubbed its nose against his knee, dancing about him.

"Pass me that breadknife!" said Hymie to Mike Olmstead.

PRIVATE ROBERT ARMSTRONG

The curtains parted and a secretary in a tailor-made uniform came onto the stage. Behind him we could see the orchestra, seated in a semi-circle, tuning their instruments. The secretary bowed to us and smiled. "Oh, I know soldiers hate speech making," he said, "but I have been delegated to make you an address of welcome, so I suppose I must go ahead and do my *darnedest!*" He laughed delicately and the men, after looking at each other, laughed too. There was an irregular clapping of hands. When it died, the secretary continued.

"I'm sure you will agree that this is the strangest dance you ever attended. At first we wondered how to give a dance at all without members of the fair sex present. Some of the organization were in favor of inviting local girls, but I'm glad to say that idea was overruled: We felt that was not fair to you fine young men." The secretary's voice became grave. "I'm sure you know what I mean . . . fellows!" There was silence for a moment, and then the secretary shook his head a couple of times and went on.

"Finally somebody had a happy thought and suggested that we invite boys from the various church homes and dress them up in women's costumes, thus preserving the element of exercise, and at the same time eliminating the more objectionable features of the dance."

The men looked at each other sheepishly. A few of us began to move toward the door, but the secretary stopped us. "But wait!" he said, holding up his hand for silence. "We have *another* surprise for you!—Two of the 'girls' present will really *be* girls! They have come all the way from the canteen in Coblenz, and their presence lends an added charm to the occasion."

Again the secretary smiled and showed his gleaming teeth. Then the folding doors to the right opened and the female impersonators entered. They were dressed in a variety of fancy costumes, but Pierrettes and Highland Lassies predominated. They stood in the center of the room and stared at the soldiers who lined the walls, and who, in turn, stared at them.

The secretary came back upon the stage and clapped his hands. "Fellows!—Fellows! Get into the spirit of the occasion, please!—No introductions are necessary, I assure you!"

Coming back that night Jim Dunning spoke suddenly, as if something had just occurred to him. "Say, did any of you guys run across the canteen dames the secretary mentioned?"

Frank Halligan spoke up. "I didn't dance with them, but they were those two who sat over by the palms all evening."

"Is that who they were?" asked Jim in surprise. "Well, that's rich; that sure is a good one on me.—I thought those two were a couple of mule skinners from Headquarters company!"

PRIVATE CHRISTIAN VAN OSTEN

IT WAS the Fourth of July following the Armistice, and early that morning Mrs. Steiner called at the hospital. She and her husband were in Paris buying for their chain of department stores and they wanted to entertain three American soldiers in honor of the day. . . . "We want you to send soldiers wounded in action," she kept repeating to the head nurse, "but nothing gruesome, you understand: nothing really revolting or gruesome! . . ." So the nurse selected a fellow from the First Engineers called "Bunny," a man from the Rainbow Division named Towner, and myself.

We were ready when the automobile came by for us, and a little later we were in Mr. Steiner's suite at the Ritz. He was a nervous, bald-headed little man and he kept hopping about like a bird. "We were afraid you boys might be timid about ordering expensive dishes, and try to let us off too easy, so dinner has already been ordered," he said. Nobody answered, so Mr. Steiner continued, rubbing his hands together. "Soak me good, boys!—I may not be the richest man in the United States, but I can stand a little gouging, I guess!"

"Adolph!" said Mrs. Steiner laughing and shaking her head; "Adolph! Don't be always talking about money."

"Well, it's true, ain't it?" asked Mr. Steiner. "I'm a rich man; why should I try to hide it?"

A little later two waiters brought up the dinner and began to serve it. "Lift up your plates," said Mr. Steiner, "and see what Santa Claus put in your stocking."

There was a fifty dollar bill under each plate. "Oh, say, now," said Bunny. "I can't really take this! . . ." "Take it and put it in your pocket quick," said Mrs. Steiner, winking; "there's plenty more where that came from!"

The dinner was excellent, and as each course was served Mr. Steiner told us what that individual item had cost him. "I don't begrudge it, though," he repeated; "I want you boys to have the very best of everything to-day. You've been through hell for us folks back home, and I say there's nothing too good for you now!"

At last dinner was over and we were having liqueurs. "How about a cigar?" asked Mr. Steiner. Bunny and I said we'd rather smoke a cigarette, but Towner accepted. Mr. Steiner called the waiter and told him to go to the adjoining room and fetch the box of cigars he would find on the writing desk. The waiter did so, and a moment later he was offering the box to Towner. Towner took one, and was just about to bite off the end, when Mr. Steiner stopped him excitedly. "No!—No!" he shouted angrily at the waiter.—"That's the wrong box!" Towner returned the cigar and Mr. Steiner came over and took the box from the waiter. "Get the other box," he said; "the one on the writing desk, like I told you!"

Then he turned to Towner, tapping the box against his palm.

"These cigars are made especially for me," he said in explanation. "You can't buy them in a shop."

"Adolph!" said Mrs. Steiner quickly. "Why, Adolph!"

Mr. Steiner began to look ashamed. "It's not the fact that those cigars retail for a dollar and fifty cents each," he said apologetically; "that's got nothing to do with it at all. But you see I've got so I can't smoke anything else, and I only got three boxes left to last me until I get back to the States. . . ." He put his hand on Towner's shoulder. "You understand my position in the matter, don't you?"

Towner said sure, he understood perfectly, and that he'd just as soon have a cigar out of the other box. He said it didn't make a particle of difference to him one way or the other.

PRIVATE ALBERT HAYES

In addition to the chocolate and cigarettes which were sold to us at three times their regular value, the canteen put in a line of sweaters and knitted socks. It was cold in the trenches and I wanted one of the sweaters to wear next to my skin to keep me warm at nights. I picked out a yellow one because it looked comfortable, and paid the canteen ten dollars for it. After I got back to my billet, and was examining it closely, I discovered there was a tiny pocket knitted in the bottom of the sweater and that a piece of paper had been tucked into it. Here's what I read:

"I am a poor old woman, seventy-two years old, who lives at the poor farm, but I want to do something for the soldier boys, like everybody else, so I made this sweater and I am turning it over to the Ladies Aid to be sent to some soldier who takes cold easy. Please excuse bad knitting and bad writing. If you get a cold on your chest take a dose of cooking soda and rub it with mutton suet and turpentine mixed and don't get your feet wet if you can help it. I used to be a great hand to knit but now I am almost blind. I hope a poor boy gets this sweater. It's not a very good one but I have put my love in every stitch and that's something that can't be bought or sold.

"Your obedient servant,

"(Mrs.) MARY L. SAMFORD.

"P.S. Don't forget to say your prayers at night and please write regularly to your dear mother."

PRIVATE ANDREW LURTON

THEY SAW from my service record book that I had been a court reporter on the outside, so they ordered me up to Regimental where Lieutenant Fairbrother, acting as Judge Advocate, was prosecuting General Courts.

On Monday a kid from my company named Ben Hunzinger got fifteen years hard labor for deserting in the face of the enemy, and a long talk from Mr. Fairbrother about justice tempered with mercy. On Tuesday a man from the First Battalion was awarded five years for leaving his post, thirty kilometers behind the lines, in order to warm his feet in the bunk house. On Wednesday it was a man named Pinckney who had gone nuts, after Soissons, and shot himself in the foot. He got eight and one-half years. . . . Why exactly eight years and six months?—I've never been able to figure that out. . . .

Then, on Thursday and Friday we had a big, front-page case. A sergeant named Vindt and a private named Neidlinger were accused of certain acts together and were sentenced, on the unsupported word of a sergeant, getting the limit that the court martial manual permitted. Fairbrother made another long speech—that lad will speak at the drop of a hat—about how Vindt and Neidlinger were blots on American citizenship, the flag, the home, etc., etc. He regretted he could not, by law, order them shot like dogs. I took it all down. . . . "I had no idea that such things actually existed!" he kept repeating in his fine, mellow voice. . . . (Well, you'd better go see your old nursie when you get home and ask her a few questions, I thought.)

But the funniest case of all was reserved for Saturday. The man on trial was named Louis de Lessio. He had been sent back to an officers' training school, in the rear, but he hadn't got his bars, and for some reason or other he was returned to the company. Sergeant Donohoe, it seemed, had ordered him to go on a working party to repair roads, and reported later to Captain Matlock that de Lessio had refused to go, saying: "To hell with you and Fishmouth Terry!—I don't intend soldiering until they send me my commission."

De Lessio denied saying this. He stated that what he had really said was: "Very well, Sergeant Donohoe; I shall be extremely glad to go on your working party, because I realize that I shall have to soldier harder than ever now, if I expect to receive my commission. . . ." Sergeant Donohoe had thirty-two witnesses to prove his story, but de Lessio found thirty-five men who had understood him to say what he claimed. It went back and forth that way all day, and half the night.

I wish the lads who talk about the nobility and comradeship of war could listen to a few general courts. They'd soon change their minds, for war is as mean as poor-farm soup and as petty as an old maid's gossip.

PRIVATE HOWARD BARTOW

After that first trip to the trenches, I made up my mind that I would not go back again. Of course I had no idea of deserting like Chris Geils or Ben Hunzinger: That, obviously, was as stupid as going to the line and getting shot. I determined to keep my eyes open and use my head.

I knew, in May, from what the French told us, that something was coming off, so when an order came around asking for one man from each company to attend grenade school, I put in for the place. There were no other applicants. As our company went to the front in crowded camions, I passed to the rear seated comfortably in a truck. When I rejoined my company, the fighting at Belleau Wood was over, and the handful of men who had survived were behind the lines again.

Then, in July, any idiot could have seen the obvious preparations for another drive. So I managed, while on a working party, to let one end of the field desk fall on my foot. The three weeks in the hospital that followed were really delightful, and when I got back, Soissons was a thing of the past. It amused me to hear that that ass, Matlock, had instructed Steve Waller, his clerk, to prepare court martials for several men, because of self-inflicted wounds. Waller didn't quite know how to do it, so I helped him with his forms, making them all air-tight. It was most amusing.

In September I went back to Divisional Headquarters as an interpreter. They soon found out that my French was the elementary French of a school-boy, and that I knew no word of German. But I was so contrite and so anxious to please, that the staff officers hated to return me to my company. "You've seen a lot of service," they said; "and a little rest won't do you any harm. You'd better stick around for a few days, anyway, and join your company when it comes out. . . ."

I thought, though, they had me in November, when we were entering the Argonne, but I volunteered to take a message back to Regimental Headquarters. On my way to the rear, I decided to take a chance. I lay hidden in a cellar in Les Eyelettes for six days, and when I joined my company at Pouilly, the day after the Armistice was signed, I told a story of having been captured by Germans. Nobody doubted the story, because I was careful to make my part in it unheroic and ridiculous.

During my entire enlistment I was in only one barrage. I never fired my rifle a single time. I never even saw a German soldier except a few prisoners at Brest, in a detention camp. But when we paraded in New York, nobody knew I had not been through as much as any man in the company. Just as many silly old women cried over me and I had just as many roses thrown at my head as were thrown at the heads of Harold Dresser, Mart Passy or Jack Howie. You've got to use your brains in the army, if you expect to survive!

PRIVATE WILLIAM NUGENT

THE WARDEN asked me again if I wouldn't see the chaplain. "What the hell do I want to see him for?" I asked. "Say, listen to me—you'd better keep that bird out of here, if you don't want to get him told! If there's anything I hate worse than cops, it's preachers!" I said.

Everybody in the House was listening to me telling the warden. "I'm a tough baby," I said. "I bumped that cop off. Sure I did. I never denied that at the trial, did I? . . . It wasn't the first one, either. I'd bump off a dozen more, right now, if I had a chance. . . . Tell the chaplain that for me, will you? . . ."

Then the warden went away and after a while my cell door opened and the chaplain come in. He had a Bible in his hand with a purple ribbon to mark the place. He come in softly and closed the door behind him, a couple of guards standing outside to see I didn't harm him none.

"Repent, my son, and give your soul to God! Repent and be saved before it is too late!"

"Get out of here!" I said. "Get out! I don't want to have nothing to do with you!"

"You have sinned, my son," he said. "You have sinned in the sight of Almighty God. . . . 'Thou shalt not kill!'—Those are the words of our blessed Lord. . . ."

"Listen," I said. "Don't pull that stuff on me, or I'll laugh in your face. I'm wise to how things are done. . . . Sure I killed that cop," I said. "I hate cops! Something burns me up and I get dizzy every time I see one. I bumped that cop, all right. Why not? . . . Who the hell are cops to make a man do things he don't want to do? . . . Say, let me tell you something about a big job I pulled once when I was in the army. I was a young fellow then, and I believed all the baloney you're talking now. I believed all that. . . . Well, anyway, we took a bunch of prisoners one day. It was too much trouble to send 'em back to the rear, so the cop of my outfit made us take 'em into a ditch, line 'em up and shoot 'em. Then, a week later when we were back in rest billets, he lined the company up and made us all go to church to listen to a bird like you talk baloney. . . ."

"My son," said the chaplain, "this is the last day of your life. Can't you realize that? Won't you let me help you? . . ."

"Get out of here," I said, and began to curse the chaplain with every word I knew. "You get out of here! If there's anything I hate worse than cops, it's preachers! . . . You get out!"

The preacher closed his Bible, and the guards opened the door. "I guess I got that bastard told!" I said; "I guess I blew his ears down for him!"

The other boys in the House began to beat on the sides of their cells. "That's telling him, kid!" they said; "that's telling him!" Then I sat down on the side of my bunk and waited for them to come in and slit my pants and shave my head.

PRIVATE RALPH NERION

WHY DIDN'T they make me a non-commissioned officer? I knew the I.D.R. backwards and forwards. I'm intelligent, and I have natural executive ability: I could command a squad, a platoon, or a company, for that matter. Did you ever stop to think about that? Do you realize I participated in all the action my company saw? I was with Wilbur Tietjen and Mart Passy on most of their exploits. They received fame and decorations and French generals kissed them and commended them before the Regiment. But did I get any recognition for what I did? Ha, ha, ha! Please don't be ridiculous! . . .

They had it in for me from the very beginning: Sergeant Olmstead instructed his cooks to give me the worst ration of beef and the smallest and dirtiest of the potatoes. Even the supply sergeant had it in for me: When he got in new shoes, or new uniforms, he could never find the sizes I wore. Oh, no! Not *my* size: but he could find the *same* sizes for Archie Lemon or Wilbur Halsey! . . . So I went into the service a private and came out a private. I went in unknown and was discharged the same way, without recognition. I know why, of course: in fact I didn't expect anything else. . . .

Those remarks I made about the United States Government and President Wilson were overheard and repeated in Washington, and secret service men have trailed me ever since. Do they think I did not know that Pig Iron Riggin is in the secret service? Or that he watched me like a hawk, hoping that I would betray myself? . . . I didn't mind it in the army so much, but now that war is over why can't they let me alone? Why don't they stop following me home and calling me on the telephone, only to hang up when I have answered? Why do they write letters to my employer, trying to get me discharged? Who is that mysterious person my wife talks to down the air-shaft? . . . I tell you I can't stand this continual persecution much longer. . . .

PRIVATE PAUL WAITE

I ENLISTED the day after war was declared, but my brother, Rodger, sat around talking about the barbarity of the Germans, selling Liberty Bonds and making speeches. Then, finally, the draft got him and he came to France, just in time to get into action for two days in the Argonne before the Armistice was signed. (I'd been in the service a year and a half by that time, and on the line constantly for almost eight months.)

On the last day of the fighting Rodger got his shoulder nicked by a piece of shrapnel, or at least that's what he said; anyway, it was so small you couldn't even see the scar when I got back home, almost a year later. So Rodger was sent to a hospital and returned to the United States. They made a hell of a lot over him when he got home, the first of the returning soldiers, and all that sort of thing. He sat in an arm chair on the front porch impersonating a wounded war hero, talking to old ladies and admiring young girls.

It was pretty soft for Rodger, but when I got home everybody was sick of the war. "Now, dear," said my mother, "Rodger has told us all about it. I know it must be painful to think about those things, so you don't have to talk about them. Rodger has told us everything. . . ."

"Is that so?" I asked. "Well, I wonder who told Rodger about it?"

"Now, Paul," said my mother, "you're not being fair to your brother."

But I wanted to talk anyhow. At the supper table that night I was telling about a gas attack, when Rodger stopped me. "No," he said, "that wasn't the way it was done." Then I spoke of airplanes coming down close to the road and spraying troops with machine guns.

"That's really absurd," said Rodger; "I never saw anything like that when I was in France."

"How the hell could you," I said. "Your excursion ticket was only good for three days. How could you see anything in that time! . . ."

Rodger turned his head away and lay back in his chair. "Please . . ." he said in a gasping voice. Then Mamma ran over and put her arms around him, and my sisters looked at me angrily. "I guess you're satisfied, now that you've made poor Rodger sick again!" they said.

I turned and walked to my room. A little later my mother stood in the door. "You shouldn't treat your brother so unsympathetically," she said. "After all, Rodger *was* wounded, dear!"

SERGEANT JACK HOWIE

The people in Savannah treated us fine. They gave us a party that night and all the girls in town were there to dance with us. One of them took a shine to me right off the reel. She was the prettiest girl at the party, too. She had dark eyes, and dark curly hair, and her skin was as white as milk. On her left cheek, almost up to her eyebrows, were three brown moles that formed a triangle. The one at the top was a little larger than the other two, but not much. When she saw me she came straight past all the other men, and asked me to dance with her. Gee! I thought I'd fall over backwards.

When I had her in my arms I kept thinking: "Good Lord! If I gave you a good squeeze you'd break right in two! . . ." I kept stepping on her feet and bumping into her knees, but this little girl said I danced fine. My hands felt as big as skinned pork loins and my uniform seemed too tight for me. Then we went outside and sat in the moonlight. Say, this was the most beautiful girl I ever saw. I thought her eyes were brown at first, but they weren't brown at all: they were dark blue. Her hair smelled like violets. I wanted to put my arms around her, but I didn't dare make a break. I kept thinking: "Gee, what a help you'd be to a man on a farm! . . ."

I don't like to tell this part of it, but after a while she said: "You are the handsomest man I have ever seen." I giggled like a fool. "Say, what are you trying to hand me, sister?" I asked. Then I wanted to kick myself for saying that. "I sounded just like a village yokel that time!" I thought.

But the little girl didn't seem to hear me. She touched my cheek with her fingers. "Will you be my perfect knight, without fear and without reproach? . . ." I didn't say anything, but this thought crossed my mind: "She's talking like that because I've got on a uniform. If she'd seen me first in dirty overalls working on a farm, she wouldn't so much as speak to me." I turned away from her and sat up straight. . . . "The fine lady of the castle sending one of the peasant boys off to war!" I thought. . . . Then I stood up and yawned. "Don't talk silly," I said. . . .

But this little girl I'm telling you about got up too. She put her arms around my neck and kissed me on the mouth. "Never forget me!" she whispered; "never forget me as long as you live!" I took her arms away and began to laugh. "Don't be a fool," I said; "I won't even remember you to-morrow! . . ."

But all during war times I thought about her, and I pictured, a thousand times, my return to Savannah to show her my medal, and to tell her that I'd been her knight as well as I knew how, not talking dirty or having anything to do with street walkers, or anything like that. But when war was really over I went straight back home and took over the farm. (A swell help *she'd* have been to a man on a farm!) Then I got to going with Lois Shelling and we married soon after that. Lois and me get along fine together. So the girl in Savannah was wrong about my not forgetting her: I can't even remember now what she looked like.

PRIVATE ARTHUR CRENSHAW

When I came home the people in my town declared "Crenshaw Day." They decorated the stores and the streets with bunting and flags; there was a parade in the morning with speeches afterwards, and a barbecue at Oak Grove in the afternoon.

Ralph R. Hawley, President of the First National Bank and Trust Company, acted as toastmaster. He recited my war record and everybody cheered. Then he pointed to my twisted back and my scarred face and his voice broke with emotion. I sat there amused and uncomfortable. I wasn't fooled in the slightest. There is an expressive vulgar phrase which soldiers use on such occasions and I repeated it under my breath.

At last the ceremonies were over and Mayor Couzens, himself, drove me in his new automobile to my father's farm beyond the town. The place had gone to ruin in my absence. We Crenshaws are a shiftless lot, and the town knows it. The floors were filthy, and there was a pile of unwashed dishes in the sink, while my sister Maude sat on the step eating an apple, and gazing, half asleep, at a bank of clouds. I began to wonder what I could do for a living, now that heavy farm work was impossible for me any more. All that afternoon I thought and at last I hit on the idea of starting a chicken farm. I got pencil and paper and figured the thing out. I decided that I could start in a small way if I had five hundred dollars with which to buy the necessary stock and equipment.

That night as I lay awake and wondered how I could raise the money, I thought of Mr. Hawley's speech in which he had declared that the town owed me a debt of gratitude for the things I had done which it could never hope to repay. So the next morning I called on him at his bank and told him of my plans, and asked him to lend me the money. He was very courteous and pleasant about it; but if you think he lent me the five hundred dollars you are as big a fool as I was.

PRIVATE EVERETT QUALLS

ONE BY ONE my cattle got sick and fell down, a bloody foam dripping from their jaws and nostrils. The veterinarians scratched their heads and said they had never seen anything like it. I knew what was the matter, but I didn't say anything, and at last my stock was all dead. I breathed with relief then. "I have paid for what I did," I thought; "now I can start all over." But about that time a blight came upon my corn, which was well up and beginning to tassel: the joints secreted a fluid which turned red over night. The green blades fell off and the stalks withered and bent to the ground. . . . "This, too!" I thought; "this, too, is required of me!"

My crops were ruined, my cattle dead. I talked it over with my young wife. She kissed me and begged me not to worry so. "We can live some way this winter," she said. "We'll start again in the Spring. Everything will be all right."

I wanted to tell her then, but I didn't dare do it. I couldn't tell her a thing of that sort. And so I went about hoping that He had forgotten and that my punishment was lifted. Then my baby, who had been so strong and healthy, took sick. I saw him wasting away before my eyes, his legs and arms turning purple, his eyes glazed and dead with the fever, his breathing sharp and strained.

I had not prayed for a long time, but I prayed now. "Oh, God, don't do this," I pleaded. "It's not his fault; it's not the baby's fault. I, I alone am guilty. Punish me, if You will—but not this way! . . . Not this way, God! . . . Please! . . ." I could hear my baby's breath rattling in the next room; I could hear the hum of the doctor's voice, the clink of an instrument against glass and the worried words of my wife. Then the baby's breathing stopped altogether and there was my wife's intaken wail of despair.

I beat my breast and flung myself to the floor and that scene I had tried to crush from my mind came back again. I could hear Sergeant Pelton giving the signal to fire and I could see those prisoners falling and rising and falling again. Blood poured from their wounds and they twisted on the ground, as I was twisting now on the floor. . . . One of the prisoners had a brown beard and clear, sunburned skin. I recognized him to be a farmer, like myself, and as I stood above him, I imagined his life. He, too, had a wife that he loved who waited for him somewhere. He had a comfortable farm and on holidays, at home, he used to drink beer and dance. . . .

My wife was knocking on the door, but I would not let her in. Then I knew what I must do. I took my service revolver, climbed out of my window and ran to the grove of scrub oaks that divided my land. When I reached the grove, I put the barrel in my mouth and pulled the trigger twice. There came blinding pain and waves of light that washed outward, in a golden flood, and widened to infinity. . . . I lifted from the ground and lurched forward, feet first, borne on the golden light, rocking gently from side to side. Then wild buffaloes rushed past me on thundering hooves, and receded, and I toppled suddenly into blackness without dimension and without sound.

PRIVATE HAROLD DRESSER

THE French Government gave me a Croix de Guerre with palm for crawling out in a barrage and rescuing a wounded French captain and his orderly. That was in April, 1918. Then, in July, I destroyed, single handed, a machine gun nest that was holding up our advance and killing many of our men, and I got both the Medal Militaire and the D.S.C. for that. I got the Medal of Honor in October and this is the way it came about: We were advancing behind our own barrage when the shells commenced falling short, killing some of our men and wounding others. There was no communication by telephone with the batteries, so I volunteered to go back to Regimental and report what the artillerymen were doing.

The German line made a deep pocket to our left, so the shortest route to Regimental lay across an open field and straight through the German lines. Captain Matlock said I'd never be able to make it through alive, but I thought I could do it, all right, and in ten minutes after I had started, I was at Regimental Headquarters giving them the dope.

After war was over I returned to my old job with the General Hardware Company and I've been there ever since. In my home town people point me out to strangers and say, "You'd never believe that fellow had a hat full of medals, would you?" And the strangers always say no, they never would.

PRIVATE WALTER WEBSTER

"It was different when war was declared, and the band was playing in Jackson Park and there were pretty girls dressed in nurses' uniforms urging the men to enlist and fight for their country: it was all different then, and all very romantic. . . ." That's what I said to Effie's mother when she came to me about breaking the engagement.

"Effie will marry you, if you insist on it," her mother said. "She knows what you have suffered. We all know that. She'll go through with the wedding, if you want her to."

"All right—I want her to!" I said. "We made a bargain: she promised to marry me if I enlisted. I carried out my part of the contract. She's got to carry out hers."

Effie's mother spoke slowly, trying to pick words that wouldn't hurt my feelings. "Probably you don't quite realize how—how—you have changed," she said. "Effie is a high-strung, sensitive girl, and while we all realize you have been unfortunate, and cannot help your—your present appearance, still . . ."

"Go ahead and say it!" I said. "I've got a looking-glass. I know how I look with my face burned and twisted to one side. Don't worry," I said; "I know how I look, all right!"

"It isn't that at all, Walter," her mother said. . . . "We just want you to come to Effie, of your own accord, and release her from her promise."

"I won't do it," I said. "Not as long as I live."

Mrs. Williams got up and walked to the door. "You are very selfish, and very inconsiderate," she said.

I put my hand on her arm. "She'll get used to me after a while. She'll get so she won't even notice my face. I'll be so good to her, she'll have to love me again."

What a fool I was. I should have known Mrs. Williams was right. I shouldn't have gone through with it. I can see Effie's face now. I can see her face that night when we were alone in our room for the first time in that hotel in Cincinnati. How she trembled and covered her face with her hands because she couldn't bear to look at me. "I must get used to that," I kept thinking. "I must get used to it. . . ."

Then I came over to her, but I did not touch her. I got down on my knees and rested my face in her lap. . . . If she had only touched my head with her hand! If she had only spoken one word of understanding! . . . But she didn't. She closed her eyes and pulled away. I could feel the muscles in her legs rigid with disgust.

"If you touch me, I'll vomit," she said.

PRIVATE SYLVESTER KEITH

I came out sullen and resentful, determined that such a thing should never happen again. I felt that if people were made to understand the senseless horror of war, and could be shown the brutal and stupid facts, they would refuse to kill each other when a roomful of politicians decided for them that their honor had been violated. So I organized "The Society for the Prevention of War" and gathered around me fifty young and intelligent men, whose influence, I thought, would be important in the years to come. "People are not basically stupid or vicious," I thought, "they are only ignorant or ill informed. It's all a matter of enlightenment."

Every Thursday the group gathered at our meeting place. They asked innumerable questions concerning the proper way to hold a bayonet, and the best way to throw hand grenades. They were shocked at the idea of gas attacks on an extended front, and the brutality of liquid fire left them indignant and profane.

I was pleased with myself and proud of my pupils. I said: "I am planting in these fine young men such hatred of war that when the proper time comes they will stand up and tell the truth without fear or shame." But some one began organizing a company of National Guard in our town about that time and my disciples, anxious to protect their country from the horrors I had described, deserted my society and joined in a body.

PRIVATE LESLIE JOURDAN

After the war was over I moved to Birmingham, Alabama, and invested in a paint factory the money that my father had left for the completion of my musical education. I met Grace Ellis and she married me. We own our own home and we have three fine, healthy children. We have enough money laid by in safe bonds to keep us comfortably for the remainder of our lives. All in all I have prospered beyond the average and Grace, who really loves me, has been happy.

I had almost forgotten that I had ever played the piano at all when one day I ran across Henry Olsen in the lobby of the Tutweiler Hotel. He told me that he was touring the principal cities of the South in a series of concerts, and that the critics had given him fine notices wherever he had been. Olsen and I had studied together in Paris, under Olivarria, back in 1916, when we were both kids.

Henry couldn't get over the fact that I'd given up playing the piano. I tried to get him off the subject but he kept coming back to it and reminding me how Olivarria (he's dead now) used to say that I had more ability than all his other pupils combined, and to predict that I was going to be the great virtuoso of my day.

I laughed and tried to change the subject again. I commenced telling him about the way I had prospered in the paint business, but he kept cross-examining me closely and bawling me out for having given up my music until finally I had to do it. I took my hands from my pockets and rested them quietly on his knee. My right hand is as good as it ever was, but shrapnel has wrecked the other one. Nothing remains of my left hand except an elongated thumb and two ragged teats of boneless flesh.

After that Henry and I talked about the paint business, and how I had prospered in it, until it was time for him to leave for his concert.

PRIVATE FREDERICK TERWILLIGER

One night when we were in a quiet sector near Verdun, Pig Iron Riggin broke me out to go on watch until daylight. When I got to my post, I stood on a firestep and stuck my head above the trench to get a breath of fresh air. I was still grumbling sleepily to myself, I remember, and I yawned just when I stuck my head up. At that moment I felt a sharp pain and my mouth was full of blood. A stray bullet had gone through both my cheeks without hitting my tongue or touching a single tooth.

The doctor back at Base One was certainly a fine man. I told him how it happened and he laughed and slapped his leg. "You know what I'm going to do for you, kid? I'm going to give you the prettiest pair of dimples in the army!" he said.

I got married not long after getting out of service. My wife likes a lot of company, so once or twice a week she asks in some of the neighbors to play bridge or just sit around and listen to the radio. One night she had Ernie and Flossie Brecker over and

Flossie said: "It's a shame the Lord didn't give *me* those beautiful dimples, instead of Mr. Terwilliger."

Flossie Brecker has a long neck and pale blue eyes that pop out at you like a frog's, and suddenly I had a picture of her head coming up slowly out of a trench. Well, sir, I laughed so hearty I lost count of the cards and had to deal over. My wife said, "Don't pay any attention to Fred; you'll only make him act sillier! I wish I had dimples like that too."

PRIVATE COLIN WILTSEE

Now if you boys will gather around closer so that we won't disturb the other classes, I'll tell you a very beautiful experience which was brought into my mind by today's golden text. . . . Herman Gladstone and Vincent Toof were "pals out there," as we used to say on the line. Herman, or "Hermie," as everybody called him affectionately, was very different from Vinnie Toof! Hermie, while having "a heart of gold," used bad words, and did a number of things that he should not have done, while Vinnie was deeply religious, and had the fine qualities which I have tried to implant in you boys. Hermie scoffed at patriotism or religion or any of the things we consider sacred: But Vinnie, suspecting a finer side to his "pal," determined to win him for God, in spite of himself. . . .

One day when we were in the trenches near St. Etienne, a shell fell where a group of soldiers were playing cards for money, among them being Hermie Gladstone. A fragment of the shell hit Hermie squarely, and it was easy to see that he would soon "stand before his Maker." Vinnie came at once, when he heard the news. He had a testament in his hand, and when he reached his pal, he knelt down beside him, and began to pray and plead with him to accept Christ for his personal savior. At first Hermie would not listen to him: there was only bitterness in his heart. He cursed and reviled and begged his comrades to make Vinnie go away; but as Vinnie continued to talk to him and to describe the unending torment of Hell fire into which God casts all sinners, Hermie's attitude changed, and he saw he should not regret giving his life for his country: he realized that he could make no nobler sacrifice. A feeling of peace came over Hermie. He repeated the words that Vinnie told him to say and accepted Christ there on the field of battle, dying a few minutes later in his mercy and love. . . . The other men stood with their hats off, and their heads bowed, watching the miracle of Herman Gladstone's conversion. There was not a dry eye among them; but it was fine, manly emotion, and they were not ashamed of their tears!

And now I see the superintendent has given the signal that the other classes are all through, but before we go into the Sunday-school room, I want you boys to think about the beautiful death of Hermie Gladstone. Some day *you* may be called upon to defend your country and your God! When that day comes, remember our lives belong not to ourselves, but to the Creator of the Universe and President Hoover, and that we must always obey their will without asking questions! . . .

PRIVATE ROY HOWARD

I MET Sadie when I was on leave in Baltimore, and Christ, how I fell for her! She had the sweetest way of doing things I ever seen, like kissing a man when he wasn't expecting it, or holding his face against her breast and running her fingers through his hair. She would laugh and say: "Can you hear my little heart beating all for you, Mr. Soldier Man?"

She didn't really expect me to marry her, but I done it just the same. It didn't seem right, otherwise; and besides I couldn't bear to think of her alone and unprotected. When I got back to camp, I made her an allotment of every nickel of my pay. I done it gladly; I loved her and wanted her to have it. The boys used to say I was tight, and that hurt more than not having any money to spend for cigarettes or pinard, but I took it all good-natured.

I wrote Sadie as regular as I could, and I heard once or twice from her, but when I was discharged I didn't know where she was. I tried to trace her through the allotment, but she had moved and I couldn't find her. All I could learn was what the landlady told me, and she said that Sadie had been living with a taxi driver and that she had spent my allotment money on him. She said Sadie was on the turf now, she thought. So I went back to my old job as a riveter, and tried to forget her.

Of course I'm human, just like the next man, so after a time I met a little Italian girl whose folks had thrown her out and who was up against it, good and plenty; and before long we were living together down on Bleecker Street. She wasn't sweet, the way Sadie was, but I liked her, and we got along without any quarreling. But I didn't like the idea of living with her that way: it made me feel sneaky, so I suggested one day that we get married. Well, Mary (her name was Mary) cried and kissed me and we got married.

We lived together three years as man and wife, and had two kids in that time, all open and above board, and then one day I met Sadie on Fourteenth Street. She was just as sweet and dainty as she used to be, although anybody could tell that she was a strumpet now. She recognized me at once and tried to beat it, but I stopped her and told her that there wasn't any hard feelings as far as I was concerned. We went in a drug store for a soda. I said: "I remember you don't like anything but chocolate," and she said, "Do you remember that, after all these years?" I laughed and said, "Oh, yes, I remember that."

Sadie told me where she was living, and asked me to come around and see her some night. "Nothing like that," I said. "I'm married and living happily with my wife. It wouldn't be right to have anything to do with street walkers now." Sadie reached out and patted my hand in her old sweet way. There were tears in her eyes. "That's right," she said. Then she asked me about Mary. She hoped that I'd married a good girl who would make me happy. She wanted to know where I was living, and I told her, and she wrote down the address on the inside of a match box. Then she squeezed my hand and wiped her eyes. I felt sorry for her; she looked so helpless and lonely as she walked away. I ran and caught up with her again and took her hand in mine. "If I can ever do anything for you, just let me know," I said. She shook her head.

That was Wednesday. On Friday morning when I was eating breakfast, two policemen came around and arrested me for bigamy; and Sadie sat on the witness stand crying into her handkerchief and sending me to prison for five years.

PRIVATE THEODORE IRVINE

It seemed an unimportant flesh wound at first, but it wouldn't heal, and finally an infection of the bone set in. So they amputated my foot, hoping that would stop the infection, and for a time it seemed that it had. Then, when I had begun to hope, the bone began decaying again, and another operation was necessary. It went on and on that way; nothing could stop the rotting bone. By the end of the sixth year they had sawed my leg off in small pieces as far as the knee. I said: "When they unjoint the kneecap, the decay will stop!" But it broke out again, above the joint, and as the rot crept upward toward my thigh, the doctors kept sawing behind it. . . .

For ten years I have been like a side of beef on a butcher's block. I cannot remember, now, what freedom from pain is like. Everybody wonders at my willingness to stand the agony that I suffer every minute of the day and night. My mother and my wife cannot bear the sight of my suffering any more. Even the doctors cannot bear it: they leave overdoses of morphine near me, a mute hint which I shall not take.

I cannot get well, but I'm going to live as long as I can. Just to lie here, breathing, conscious of life around me, is enough. Just to move my hands and look at them, thinking: "See, I am alive—I move my hands about," is enough. I'm going to live as long as I can and fight for my last breath. . . . Better to suffer the ultimate pains of hell than to achieve freedom in nothingness!

PRIVATE HOWARD VIRTUE

For a week I heard shells falling . . . nothing but shells falling . . . and exploding with blasts that rocked the walls of the dugout. Rocking the walls of the dugout . . . rattling the frosty duckboards. I became afraid that I would die before the meaning of my life was made clear. I thought: "If I use my head, I can get out of this!" I remembered a joke about a man who ran around picking up scraps of paper. After examining each scrap he would discard it quickly, and say, "No, that's not it!" So the doctors pronounced him mentally incompetent, and discharged him from the service. As they handed him his discharge paper, he looked it over carefully, to see that everything was in order. Then he smiled at the doctor triumphantly, and said, *"That's* it, all right!" "I'll do the same thing," I said; "my life is too valuable to be wasted on a battle-field." I crawled out over the side of the trench and commenced picking up dead leaves, talking rapidly to myself all the time. Sergeant Donohoe came out after me and coaxed me back to our lines again.

Back at the hospital, I was afraid those smart doctors would see through my ruse, but I fooled them, too. I was transferred to the United States, and later committed to this madhouse. Here's the irony of the situation: I cannot obtain my freedom, although I'm as sane as any man alive.

You are a fair man, let me ask you a question: How can I spread the glory of my cousin, Jesus, and how can I baptize him in the River Jordan from this place where my limbs are shackled? How can I thunder the incestuousness of Herodias, or how submit, at last, when that wanton, Salome, completes my destiny . . . shaking her loins for the gift of my head? How can I do these things when my words die flatly against the padding of my cell?

Cymbals clashing and spears and soldiers cursing and casting lots and blood running in rivers from the poles destroying life and creating life. . . . Rocking! . . . Rocking! . . . And white breasts rosy tipped walking beautifully over ruin and always shells falling . . . nothing but shells falling . . . and exploding with blasts that rock the walls of the dugout. . . . And me crying in the wilderness. . . . Crying with nobody to heed me. . . .

I have told them over and over why it is necessary that I be released from this place, but the guards only stare at me and chew gum rhythmically with slow, maddening jaws.

PRIVATE LESLIE YAWFITZ

AFTER supper I clear the table and wash the dishes, while my sister sits in a chair and tells me about her work at the office, or reads the morning paper out loud. One night she came on an item about the French Academy honoring the German scientist, Einstein, and conferring some sort of an honorary degree upon him. There were a lot of speeches made about the healing of old wounds, hands across the border, mutual trust and confidence, misunderstanding, etc. There was a picture of the ceremony, and my sister described that also.

"If it was a mistake and a misunderstanding all the way round, what was the sense of fighting at all?" I asked. I put down the dish cloth and felt my way to the table.

My sister sighed, as if she were very tired, but she did not answer me.

"Since they're all apologizing and being so God-damned polite to each other," I continued, "I think somebody should write me a note on pink stationery as follows: 'Dear Mr. Yawfitz: Please pardon us for having shot out your eyes. It was all a mistake. Do you mind, awfully?' "

"Don't get bitter again, Leslie," said my sister.

"I know," I said. "I know."

"Don't get bitter again, Leslie. Please don't get bitter."

Then I went back to the sink and finished wiping the dishes.

PRIVATE MANUEL BURT

I REMEMBER it as clearly as if it had happened yesterday, and not three years ago. The date was October 2nd, 1918, and my company was lying in reserve, not far from a shelled town, having come up to the line the night before, and dug in. A little before daybreak Sergeant Howie came over to the hole where Clarence Foster and I were sleeping, and began hitting my feet with the butt of his rifle. I turned over and sat up, and when the sergeant saw who I was, he seemed disappointed.

"I'm looking for O'Brien," he said; "Lieutenant Fairbrother wants to send some reports back to Regimental." Then he added: "By God! you can never find that bugler when you want him. . . ."

The sky was still dark, but toward the east it was getting a little gray. Corporal Foster woke up, then, and began to rub his eyes. He started to speak, but changed his mind. He turned on his belly, folded his arms under him for a pillow, and went back to sleep. I lay back, too, but a few seconds later the sergeant began tapping my hobnails again. "Come on, get out of there!" he said. . . . "Come on! You'll do!"

I stood up and began to curse the outfit, but Howie did not pay any attention to me. "Come on, Burt!" he said again. "The Lieutenant's waiting. . . . Come on: get going!" I got up, then, and followed the sergeant back to an old barn where Lieutenant Fairbrother and Pat Boss, the top sergeant, were waiting. The top handed me the reports and told me what to do. "You better have your rifle loaded and unlocked," he said; "there's not any line through the woods, and you might run into a German patrol."

"All right," I said.

"You'd better fix your bayonet, too," said Lieutenant Fairbrother. Then he said: "I've told you men time and time again to keep bayonets fixed when you're on the line. . . . I've told you over and over! . . ." His voice was high and nervous, as if he were going to beat in the field desk with his open palms.

I took out my bayonet and fixed it. "Yes, sir," I said.

When I came out, the sky was getting grayer, but it was still not light enough to be seen, so I walked through an old field, pitted with shell holes and grown over with weeds, until I reached the Somme-Py road, but I kept my eyes and ears open. Later on I cut off from the road, and through the woods, and I walked more cautiously. I was beginning to feel better. I remember thinking that if I had a cup of hot coffee, I'd be all right. It was light before I knew it; even among the trees a dim, gray light filtered. It was lonely and quiet in the wood and I felt cut off from everything and entirely alone. Pretty soon I found a path which ran in the direction I was going, and was following it, thinking about a good many things, when I turned a bend, and there, to one side of the path, was a young German soldier. He was sitting with his back to a tree, eating a piece of brown bread. I stood for a few minutes watching him. The bread kept crumbling in his hands, and he would lean forward and pick up the pieces which had fallen onto the ground. I noticed that he didn't have a rifle with him, but he carried side arms. I stood there, not knowing what to do. At first I thought I'd tiptoe back around the bend, and cut through the woods to the right, but that looked as if I were yellow.

While I stood there fingering my rifle, the German turned and saw me watching him. He sat staring at me, as if paralyzed, his hand, with a crumb of bread in it, half raised to his lips. He had brown eyes, I noticed, and golden brown skin, almost the color of an orange. His lips were full, and very red, and he was trying to grow a mustache. It was dark brown, as fine as corn-silk, but it hadn't come out evenly on his lip. Presently he got up and we stood looking at each other for what seemed a long time, as if neither of us could make up our minds what to do.

Then I remembered what they had told us in training camp about Germans, and I began to get sore at him. I could see that he was getting sore, too. Suddenly he dropped his bread among the leaves and reached for his pistol, and at the same moment I raised my rifle he raised his pistol, but I was the one who fired first. I kept thinking: "Does he think he owns this path? Does he think he can make me sneak off through the woods, as if I were afraid of him? . . ."

The German had jumped behind a tree and was emptying his clip at me. His bullets were coming close, knocking off bark above my head. Then, when he had no more bullets left, he turned and tried to run through the woods, and I dropped to my knees, took careful aim and got him between the shoulder blades. He fell on his face and lay flat, got up and staggered, and turned his face toward me. His face was frightened and his eyes were twitching. I gave him the last bullet I had and he fell once more. He tried to get up again, and rush me with a trench knife, but I ran over to him and when he raised his chin up, I let him have my bayonet. I caught him under the chin and the bayonet went through the roof of his mouth and into his brain. He grunted once, and was dead before he touched the ground again.

I stood there pulling at the bayonet, but it wouldn't come out of him. I put my hobnailed shoe in his face and tugged at the bayonet, but my foot kept slipping across his face, scraping the flesh away. Finally I unsnapped the bayonet from my rifle. When I got it off, I began to run down the path as fast as I could. I reached the edge of the wood and hid in some underbrush until I quit trembling. When I was quieter, I delivered the reports to Regimental and told the runners sitting there about the German I had killed in the woods. Everybody got excited and they made me tell it over and over. Coming back I didn't want to pass him where he lay across the path, but I thought: "I'm in no way to blame for this. He'd have killed me, if I hadn't got him first."

Again I tried to pull my bayonet out of him, but I couldn't put my foot in his face any more. As I stood there, I began to feel exhilarated and to laugh. "Well, there's one Heinie who won't do any more harm," I said. Then I took a ring off his finger for a souvenir. I put it on my own finger and kept turning it around. . . . "This is a ring off the first man I ever killed," I said, as if I were speaking to an audience. . . . But before I got back to the line, I took the ring off and threw it into the underbrush. . . . "I shouldn't have put on his ring," I thought; "that will tie us together forever."

I remember all this happened on October 2nd, because we attacked the next day, and that was October 3rd, according to the official records. I kept thinking about that soldier lying across the path with my bayonet in him, and I talked it over one day with Rufe Yeomans. He said there was no reason to blame myself. All the boys I talked to about it said the same thing. And so I forgot all about that German boy. It was only after the war was over, and I was demobilized, that I began thinking of him again. He came very gradually. At first I had a feeling that the ring I had taken was still on my finger, and I couldn't get it off. I would wake up at night tugging at my finger. Then I would feel ashamed because I was frightened, and I would lie back again and try to go to sleep. I had dreams about him, finally, in which I saw his face. And then one night, when I was fully awake, I knew that he was in the room with me, although I could not see him. I lay in the room knowing that he was there. "He'll go away again, if I'm quiet," I thought; "I've nothing to reproach myself with. He'll go away of his own accord." But the German wouldn't go away. It got so that he was with me in the daytime, too. He was with me when I woke in the morning. He went with me to work. He followed me everywhere. I couldn't do my work any more, and I lost my job. Then I rented a small room on Front Street where nobody knew me. I changed my name, thinking I could hide from him, but I couldn't. He found me that first night, and came into the small room when I opened the door.

When I knew that he was there, I lay back in my bed and cried. I knew it was no use fighting him any longer. There was no use running away. Until then I had not seen him, when I was awake, but I saw him that night. He came suddenly out of space and stood at the foot of my bed, and looked at me. I could see the marks on his face which my hobnails had made. My bayonet was still sticking under his chin, driven in so far that the hilt hardly touched his chest. Then he spoke to me: "Take this bayonet out of my brain."

I said: "I would take it out, if I could, but I cannot: It is driven in too deeply." Then he handed me the ring that I had thrown away. "Wear my ring!" he said. "Put it on your finger." I held out my hand and he slipped the ring on my finger. "Wear it forever," he said; "wear it forever and ever!"

My throat was dry and my heart was pumping rapidly. I put trembling hands over my eyes and closed them tight, but I could not shut him out. He stood waiting beside my bed, and would not go away. He spoke again, finally, his voice puzzled and gentle:

"When I looked up that morning and saw you standing in the path, my first thought was to come over to you and offer you a piece of my bread. I wanted to ask you questions about America. There were many things we could have talked about. You could have told me about your home, and I could have told you about mine. We could have gone through the woods looking for birds' nests, laughing and talking together. Then, when we knew each other better, I would have shown you a picture of my sweetheart and read you sentences from her letters." He stopped talking and looked at me: "Why didn't I do what I wanted to?" he asked slowly . . .

"I don't know!" I said.

I sat up against the back of my bed, but I could not look into his eyes. He stood silent and presently I began to speak again: "I saw you eating your bread before you saw me. Before you turned around, I smiled at you, because you reminded me so much of a boy from my home town who used to laugh a lot and tell jokes. His name was Arthur Cronin and we played together in our high school orchestra. He was trying to grow a mustache, too, but it wouldn't come out very well, and the girls kidded him about it. . . . At first I wanted to laugh and sit beside you and tell you that. . . ."

"Why didn't you do it?" he asked.

"I don't know," I said.

"Why did you kill me?" he asked sadly. "Why did you want to do that?"

"I wouldn't do it again!" I whispered. "Before God, I wouldn't!"

The German boy rolled his head from side to side; then he raised his arms and held them outward. . . . "All we know is that life is sweet and that it does not last long. Why should people be envious of each other? Why do we hate each other? Why can't we live at peace in a world that is so beautiful and so wide?"

I lay on my back and pressed my pillow over my mouth and beat at the bed with my weak hands. I could feel ice flowing from my heart toward my head and toward my feet. My hands were cold, too, and dripping with sweat, but my lips were parched and clung together. When I could stand it no longer, I jumped out of bed and stood in the dark room trembling, my body pressed against the wall. . . . "I don't know," I whispered; "I can't answer your questions. . . ."

Then somebody, who was not myself, came into my body and began to shout with my voice, beating upon the door with my hands. "I don't know! I don't know! I don't know!" he said over and over, his voice getting steadily louder.

PRIVATE COLIN URQUHART

I SAW much during my thirty years as a professional soldier, and I have watched the reactions of many men to pain, hunger and death, but all I have learned is that no two men react alike, and that no one man comes through the experience unchanged. I have never ceased to wonder at the thing we call human nature, with its times of beauty and its times of filthiness, or at the level of calm stupidity that lies in between the two.

I have no theories and no remedies to offer. All I know, surely, is that there should be a law, in the name of humanity, making mandatory the execution of every soldier who has served on the front and managed to escape death there. The passage of such a law is impossible, of course: For Christian people who pray in their churches for the destruction of their enemies, and glorify the barbarity of their soldiers in bronze—those very people would call the measure cruel and uncivilized, and rush to the polls to defeat it.

LIEUTENANT JAMES FAIRBROTHER

I WOULD BE the last man in the world to deny the right of free speech, but these pacifist propagandists are making our nation a nation of cowards and milk-sops. They should be muzzled and placed where they belong. Let me tell you something, and I want you to think carefully over my words: Just so long as the United States continues to lead the world in intelligence, wealth and culture, just so long will other nations envy our happiness and fear our prosperity. . . . You've got to look at it that way, whether you want to, or not! . . .

Why do you think Italy is training an army and preaching militarism? Open your eyes and look around you! Look at Japan! They're ready to spring at our throats at the drop of a hat! And England hates us! I repeat it, my friends: Our "cousins over the sea" hate us! . . . I tell you I know what I'm talking about! . . . "Brotherhood of man," indeed.—I'd laugh if the situation were not so fraught with danger.—Germany is not to be ignored, either.—How shortsighted we were to let them get on their feet again.—And France hasn't any love for us: anybody who saw her attitude toward our own soldier boys—your sons and mine, gentlemen—knows that! . . .

And I tell you my knowledge is not hearsay. I know first hand what I'm talking about. I did my bit in the last war. I enlisted when I might have stayed at home and claimed exemption because of my wife and my little children. But no man with a spark of patriotism or an ounce of manhood would do a thing of that sort! . . . And I say, again, my friends: I do not regret the foot I lost crossing the Meuse on that terrible night of November 10th: I feel that I offered that foot on the altar of my country's honor; and I am proud that you, my constituents, have shown your confidence in me by reelecting me to represent your interests in the House of Representatives. . . .

PRIVATE RUFUS YEOMANS

Come up some night and have dinner with us, the wife would be tickled to death to have the captain of my old company for dinner. She says that she feels she knows you already. No fooling!—She really does.—Let me know when you can come, so she can have a good dinner cooked up. You know how women are about those things, I guess. . . . Say, let's make a date right now. Let's make it next Thursday. Marlene Dietrich is on at the Bijou Theatre that night and we can take that in later, if we get tired of talking about the war. All right. Fine. Bring Mrs. Matlock, too, if she'll come. . . .

Now here's the way you get there: Take the ferry at Cortlandt Street that leaves at 5:04. That puts you in Jersey City in time to get the 5:18. Be sure to get the 5:18 instead of the 5:15 because the 5:18 is an express and don't stop this side of Westfield. Get off at Durwood, walk three blocks to the . . . Oh, never mind about that. You come as far as the station and I'll meet you in the Ford. Christ! but this is a break—running into you on the street this way!—Don't fail me now. I'll be looking for you. . . . Never mind! Let's talk about that Thursday. We'll have a long talk about old times.

PRIVATE SAM ZIEGLER

I was taking an automobile trip through the East with my wife and kids, that summer, when I decided to go see the old training camp again. My wife kicked like a steer, when I told her my plans, but finally we decided that she and the kids could visit her sister in Washington, and I would join them there the following Wednesday.

When I reached the camp, I went up to the commanding officer and told him who I was, and the name of my old outfit. He was very nice to me. He showed me a roster of the post and I looked it over, to see if any of the men I used to soldier with were stationed there. Finally I came to the name, Michael Riggin. . . . "Old Pig Iron Riggin!" I said.—"Well, what do you know about that?"

"Would you like to see him?" the commanding officer asked.

"Yes, sir," I said, "I surely would.—I'd like to talk to him about old times."

So the commanding officer sent out for Pig Iron and a little later we were walking about the camp together. I had an idea that I'd like to see the old bunk house we used to occupy before we went across, so Pig Iron got the keys and we went in. On the walls were a number of small silver plates, which marked where each man's bunk had been.

"That's a very good idea," I said. Then I stood there thinking. "As I remember it now, my bunk used to be over near the stove," I said. So we went over and looked at the wall, and sure enough there was a silver plate with my name on it. It gave me a funny feeling to be standing there looking at it. Then Pig Iron and I began to look at the other plates. . . .

"Frank Halligan," I said. . . . "Why, I hadn't thought of that old hard tail for years!—What's become of him, Pig Iron?"

"He's in the service, somewhere," said Riggin. "I don't know just where, though."

Pig Iron was also looking at the plates. "Rowland Geers, . . . was that the fellow who swam the Meuse when the bridge blew up?"

"Maybe so," I said; "I don't remember."

"I remember Carter Atlas," said Pig Iron, laughing. "He was the boy who threw his mess-gear away one night when we had rice again."

"I don't remember him," I said. "I don't seem to place him."

"John Cosley lost an arm," said Pig Iron, "or was that Ollie Teclaw?—Anyway, I remember putting a tourniquet on one of them, and whoever it was, he kept saying I was putting it on too tight.—You remember John Cosley, don't you?—A tall fellow with red hair . . ."

I stood there thinking, trying to bring up the faces of the men I used to soldier with, but I couldn't do it. I realized then, that I would not have remembered the face of Riggin, himself, if I hadn't known who he was beforehand. I began to feel sad because it had all happened so long ago, and because I had forgotten so much. I was sorry that I had come to the camp at all. Pig Iron and I stood there looking at each other. We didn't have anything to talk about, after all. Then we locked the old building and went outside.

FABLES

*

The Crow and the Parrot[*]

A PARROT, much prized by his mistress, struck up a friendship with a crow. One day the parrot's mistress came to the window to see how her pet was getting along, and the crow hid behind some vines. "Does my pretty polly like the nice sun?" she asked in a mincing voice.

"Does my pretty polly like the nice sun?" echoed the parrot in the same tone his mistress had used.

The woman pursed her lips, and made a kissing noise. Instantly the parrot duplicated the sound so perfectly that it would have been impossible to tell which had been made by the mistress and which by her pet. The woman laughed with pleasure, and said, "Oh, you are so clever, my dear! You are so *clever!*"

The parrot's mood changed with her own. He, too, laughed and said, "Oh, you are so clever, my dear! You are so *clever!*"

When the mistress had gone, the crow said, "You have no opinions of your own, my friend. All you do is duplicate what your mistress says."

The parrot said, "That's correct; I can't deny it."

"It seems to me she'd be so sick of hearing her words echoed all day that she'd long since have pulled out your feathers in boredom, or wrung your neck in a rage," said the crow.

The parrot said, "No bird that lives gets the love and honor that I get. And where can you find another who's reached the ripe old age of fifty without hearing a single cross word?"

* Reproduced by permission of the New York *Post*.

The Polecat and His Friends

A POLECAT was indignant at the way the other animals treated him. He told his grievances to the old tortoise, and as he recalled the slights he suffered, his voice trembled. He said, "Do they ask me to their parties? Do they come when I invite them to mine? That never happens, I assure you. They even back off into the bushes when they see me on the road. . . . They think they're better than I am, that's what! They're all undemocratic snobs!"

The old tortoise listened for a time and then said, "Perhaps so, but there could be another reason for their conduct, you know."

"What?" asked the polecat. "What other explanation is there?"

"Well, after all, you do stink a little," said the old tortoise mildly.

*The Wild Horses**

A HERD of wild horses who had roamed the plains found themselves trapped and captured and led away to serve the purposes of men. While they had been free to go where they chose, to do what suited them best at all times, they had not thought about themselves, or the happiness of their lot, accepting their blessings as things to be expected; but when they found themselves in a corral with bits in their mouths and hobbles on their legs, they were alarmed, and huddled together. "We will not submit to this injustice," they said. "Liberty is a beautiful and a precious thing, and we must not lose it."

An old field horse stood beside the corral, and said, "I was caught young. I've seen many wild horses brought to the corral you're in now. I've heard them all say the things you're saying, but if you'll lift your heads and look about you, you'll see them all working for the comfort of our master." He sighed, shook out his mane and continued, "When we realize how precious our liberty is, and swear to preserve it, it is too late, for already we have lost it."

* Reproduced by permission of the New York *Post*.

The Woodchuck and the Old Bones

A WOODCHUCK made his home in a cemetery, between two ancient graves, and after he had dug his burrow, he came above ground and examined the inscription on the headstone to the right of his doorway. He read:

"A warrior brave, he did not yield,
Nor put aside his ashen bow.
With flashing eye he won each field,
And conquered every foe."

The woodchuck stared in surprise, then he went below to see which was correct—his own eye, or the poet's illusion. When he came back, he turned to the headstone on the left, and read:

"A perfumed lily sent by God,
She sweetened plain and dell,
Till jealous Death did seal her up,
That he alone might smell."

At that the woodchuck lay in the sunlight; but all he could think of to say was, "Well!"

The Fat Woman and the Terrier

A TERRIER was often taken for a walk by his mistress, a large woman, and as they went down the street, with the terrier tugging at his leash, and the fat woman panting a few steps behind, the dog got the idea that he was pulling his mistress along. Sometimes she would stop and talk with a friend, and the terrier, thinking she had broken down on the sidewalk, would pull with such force that his leash was as taut as a violin string. "I declare," said the woman laughing a little. "I never saw such a dog for pulling a body along."

One day as the terrier lay on the window ledge, some other dogs came up. They wanted him to play with them in the street, but he refused. "I'd like to, but I can't," he said. "I've got to take her walking in a few minutes."

"She doesn't need you when she goes walking," said the other dogs. "Where did you get such an idea?"

The terrier said, "Oh, yes she does need me! She gets stuck, and there's nobody who can pull her along like I can."

The other dogs said, "Slip out of your collar the next time you two go walking, and you'll see that your mistress can get along better without you than with you." The terrier did what the others suggested, and to his surprise he saw that they were right. Afterwards he wouldn't go out at all, but lay all day with his nose between his paws. "Why did they show me how unimportant I am," he asked. "Why did they destroy my one reason for living?"

The King and the Bright Young Men

EACH SPRING the King of the Bretts examined a score of the country's brightest young men, fitting them into that profession or branch of public life where their peculiar talents could be used to the best advantage. One year, to vary the monotony of question and answer, he thought of another way to achieve his end, and when the first candidate came into the room, he said, "A man is traveling down a road. He is stopped by a giant who is sitting on a stone. What happened afterwards?"

The first candidate said: "The traveler, knowing the giant meant to kill him, worked out a plan of defense: He walked up to the giant boldly and kicked him; then he ran in ever narrowing circles, while the giant pursued him. In this way, the giant approached the stone unawares, being intent on his capture, stumbled over it and sprawled on his face. Then, while he was helpless on the ground, the traveler picked up the stone and killed him with it."

"You belong in the army," said the king. "The army, of course."

The next candidate came in, and when given the story he smiled and said: "The giant told the traveler he had a bottle of wine, and had been sitting on the stone waiting for a merry companion to share it with. Then it turned out the traveler had cheese and bread in his sack, which he spread out on the stone, and when the giant and the traveler had eaten and drunk their fill, they sang such jolly songs, and were so happy and gay, that the whole countryside echoed with their laughter."

The king looked quizzically at this powerful, simple young man. "But wasn't the traveler afraid of the giant?" he asked.

"No," said the candidate. "Why should he be afraid? You see, the traveler was as strong as the giant, or stronger, and knew it from the beginning." The king touched the hand of this young man. "Would you like to be the bodyguard who goes with me everywhere?" he asked; and when the young man laughed and nodded, it was arranged that way.

The third candidate said: "The giant was sitting on the stone because he'd stuck a thorn in his toe and couldn't walk farther; so the traveler removed the thorn and bound up the wound with a bandage he happened to have in his pocket at the time."

The king said, "You're almost too easy. Report to the royal hospital for training."

The fourth man was more complex. He said: "When the traveler knew the giant meant to rob him, he said he was on a mission for his king, and that he'd been told to fetch a bag of jewels which were hidden in the woods nearby. The giant was taken in by the story, and thinking to exploit the man's stupidity, he said he'd accompany the traveler to the place where the jewels were hidden, to see that no harm came to him on the way. The traveler thanked the giant for this courtesy, and they started inland, but as they walked, the traveler pulled up reeds and plaited them into a strong rope; then, when they reached the side of a hill, the traveler said the jewels were hidden beneath the ledge on which they were standing, and as the giant lay flat and stretched his arms downward to reach them, the traveler tied him up with the rope he had made and left him there, after taking for himself the fine gold chain the giant was wearing."

"The diplomatic corps," said the king.

And so things went until the last man was called. When he had heard the situation, he shook his head sadly, and said: "This story can have but one true ending, and it's this: The giant seized the poor, helpless traveler and carried him off to his den in the mountains. There he tossed him into a pit where the other unfortunates he had captured awaited their dooms."

At this moment the candidate was overcome with such strong emotion that he could not continue. He beat his breast and cried bitterly. "I can't bear this," he said in a suffering voice. "The traveler's end is too terrible to think about!"

The king rang at that moment and his guards came in. "Have this man's head cut off," he said; and continued in explanation, when the captain murmured at his harsh and uncharacteristic conduct, "I can understand a cruel man, and find a place for him; I can understand a compassionate man, and find a place for him as well, but when one man inflicts cruelty and weeps for his victims in the same breath, he is a monster, and if we let him live he will someday destroy us all."

The Cock and the Capon

A cock in charge of a barnyard of hens lifted his neck, crowed, and said to his friend the capon: "Why do you complain that because of the injustice done you, you can never know love? Love is a monotonous matter of little importance. Be glad you're not mixed up in it."

One morning the farmer penned up the cock with a flock of geese, who didn't interest him in the least, and the capon came to visit him after a time; but the cock had changed his tune a little, and sticking his neck through a knothole in the fence, he said, "I want to amend what I said, and restate the matter this way: Love is of no importance so long as you can have the particular thing you want."

The Doctor and the Hippopotamus

A YOUNG orangutan was ambitious to cure the ills of others, and when he saw how often his friends died because a bone or some other object was lodged in their throats, he decided to specialize in that branch of healing. Gradually stories of his skill were told all over the jungle, and when the hippopotamus yawned one morning and got a log crosswise in his gullet, he sent for the orangutan as a matter of course.

The doctor came promptly, but although he tried all his instruments, and even stretched his arm forward as far as it would reach, he couldn't touch the log, much less remove it. As a last resort, he asked the hippopotamus to raise his neck and stretch his jaws even wider, and when he did so, the doctor walked into his mouth, braced himself, and tugged with all his might at the obstruction.

The log came loose unexpectedly, and at the same instant the hippopotamus flinched and swallowed. Then, when he had got his breath again, he began smelling about for his benefactor, not realizing he had swallowed his doctor when he swallowed the log, nor knowing, at that time, that it is the fate of specialists to perish of their own specialities.

The Fisherman and the Hen

WHEN he reached the brook where he intended to fish, an angler found he had left his bait at home, but after considering matters, he thought he might be able to catch grasshoppers and use them instead. He got down on his hands and knees, but try as he would, he wasn't successful. He had about abandoned the idea of getting bait that way, when he saw an old hen in the grass seeking her breakfast. As he watched, he realized the old hen, despite her infirmities, was a better grasshopper-catcher than himself, for almost at once she pounced on a large, lively one and held it in her bill.

The fisherman crept toward the old hen, hoping to take the grasshopper from her before she could swallow it, but the hen, guessing his intention, flushed her wings and ran through the grass. She might have escaped if the fisherman had not thrown a stick at her. He caught her squarely, and she fell in the weeds, her tail feathers twitching from side to side.

He pulled the half-swallowed grasshopper from her throat, put it in his pocket, and turned away; but noticing how pathetic the old hen looked there in the grass, he picked her up and stroked her head. "Poor old thing!" he said. "I'm sorry for what I did just now!" He lifted her higher and rubbed his cheek against her wings. "I was a brute to hit you so hard," he said.

It was the first time the old hen had had any affection in years, and she lay back in the fisherman's arms making a clucking sound in her throat, until he put her down and went back to his fishing. Shortly thereafter, he dismissed the incident from his mind, being engaged with his own pleasures, so he was somewhat puzzled when he heard a soft, seductive noise behind him. He turned, and there was the old hen with another grasshopper in her beak. When she saw she had his attention, she moved away slowly, glancing back at him over her shoulder, awaiting his blow with resignation, since an old hen will put up with any indignity if you'll give her a little affection now and then.

The Unspeakable Words

THERE were words in the Brett language considered so corrupting in their effect on others that if anyone wrote them, or was heard to speak them aloud, he was fined and thrown into prison. The King of the Bretts was of opinion that the words were of no importance one way or the other, and besides, everybody in the country knew them anyway; but his advisers disagreed, and at last, to determine who was right, a committee was appointed to examine the people separately.

At length, everyone in the kingdom had been examined, and found to know the words quite well, without the slightest damage to themselves. There was then left only one little girl, a five-year-old who lived in the mountains with her deaf and dumb parents. The committee hoped that this little girl, at least, had never heard the corrupting words, and on the morning they visited her, they said solemnly: "Do you know the meaning of Poost, Gist, Duss, and Feng?"

The little girl admitted that she did not, and then, smiling happily, she said, "Oh, you must mean Feek Kusk, Dalu, and Liben!"

Those who don't know the words must make them up for themselves.

The Unique Quality of Truth

WHEN the old scholar heard that Truth was in the country, he decided to find her, as he had devoted his life to studying her in all her forms. He set out immediately, and at last he came upon the cottage in the mountains where Truth lived alone. He knocked on the door, and Truth asked what he wanted. The scholar explained who he was, adding that he had always wanted to know her, and had wondered a thousand times what she really was like.

Truth came to the door soon afterwards, and the scholar saw that the pictures he had formed of her in his imagination were wrong: He had thought of Truth as a gigantic woman with flowing hair who sat nobly on a white horse, or, at the very least, as a sculptured, heroic figure with a wide, white brow and untroubled eyes. In reality, Truth was nothing at all like that; instead, she was merely a small, shapeless old woman who seemed made of some quivering substance that resembled india rubber.

"All right," said the old lady in a resigned voice. "What do you want to know?"

"I want to know what you are."

The old lady thought, shook her head, and answered, "That I don't know. I couldn't tell you to save my life."

"Then have you any special quality that makes you individual?" asked the scholar. "Surely you must have some characteristic that is uniquely yours."

"As a matter of fact, I have," said the old lady; then, seeing the question on the scholar's lips, she added, "I'll show you what I mean. It's easier than trying to explain."

The shapeless old woman began to bounce like a rubber ball, up and down on her doorstep, getting a little higher each time she struck the floor. When she was high enough for her purpose, she seized the woodwork above her door and held on; then she said, "Take hold of my legs and walk back the way you came, and when you know what my unique quality is, shout and let me know."

The old scholar did as he was told, racking his brains in an effort to determine what quality it was that distinguished Truth. When he reached the road, he turned around, and there in the distance was Truth still clinging to the woodwork above her door.

"Don't you see by this time?" she shouted. "Don't you understand now what my particular quality is?"

"Yes," said the old scholar. "Yes, I do."

"Then turn my legs loose and go on home," said Truth in a small, petulant voice.

Aesop's Last Fable

Aesop, the messenger of King Croesus, finished his business with the Delphians and went back to the tavern where he had taken lodgings. Later, he came into the taproom where a group of Delphians were drinking. When they realized who he was, they crowded about him. "Tell us," they began, "is Croesus as rich as people say?"

Aesop, since the habit of speaking in fables was so strongly fixed in him, said, "I can best answer your question with a parable, and it is this: The animals gathered together to crown their richest member king. Each animal in turn stated what he possessed, and it was soon apparent that the lion had the largest hunting preserves, the bee the most honey, the squirrel the largest supply of acorns, and so on; but when the voting began, the difficulty of arriving at a decision was plain to all, for to the bee, the nuts that represented the wealth of the squirrel were of no consequence; to the lion, the hay that the zebra and the buffalo owned was worthless; and the panther and the tiger set no value at all on the river that the crane and crocodile prized so highly."

Then Aesop called for his drink, looking into the faces of the Delphians with good-natured amusement. He said, "The moral of the fable is this: Wealth is an intangible thing, and its meaning is not the same to all alike." The stolid Delphians looked at one another, and when the silence was becoming noticeable, one of them tried again: "How was the weather in Lydia when you left home?"

"I can best answer that question with another fable," said Aesop, "and it is this: During a rain storm, when the ditches were flooded and the ponds had overflowed their banks, a cat and a duck met on the road, and, wanting to make conversation, they spoke at the same instant. 'What a beautiful day this is,' said the delighted duck. 'What terrible weather we're having,' said the disgusted cat."

Again the Delphians looked at one another, and again there was silence. "The moral of that tale," said Aesop, "is this: What pleases a duck, distresses a cat." He poured wine into his glass and leaned against the wall, well satisfied with the start he had made in instructing the barbarous Delphians. The Delphians moved uneasily in their seats, and after a long time, one of them said, "How long are you going to be here?"

"That," said Aesop, "can best be answered in the Fable of the Tortoise, the Pelican, and the Wolf. You see, the pelican went to visit his friend the tortoise, and promised to remain as long as the latter was building his new house. Then one day as they were working together, with the tortoise burrowing and the pelican carrying away the dirt in his pouch, the wolf came on them unexpectedly, and—"

But Aesop got no farther, for the Delphians had surrounded him and were, an instant later, carrying him toward the edge of the cliff on which the tavern was built. When they reached it, they swung him outward and turned him loose, and Aesop was hurled to the rocks below, where he died. "The moral of what we have done," they explained later, "is so obvious that it needs no elaboration."

SHORT STORIES

*

THE LITTLE WIFE

Joe Hinckley selected a seat on the shady side of the train and carefully stowed away his traveling bag and his heavy, black catalogue case. It was unusually hot for early June. Outside, the heat waves shimmered and danced above the hot slag roadbed, and the muddy river that ran by the station was low between its red banks. "If it's as hot as this in June, it sure will be awful in August," he thought. He looked at his watch: two twenty-eight —the train was five minutes late in getting out. If he had known the two twenty-three was going to be late he might have had time to pack his sample trunk and get it to the station, but he couldn't have anticipated that, of course. He had had so little time after getting that telegram from Mrs. Thompkins—barely time to pack his bag and check out of the hotel. Joe loosened his belt and swabbed his neck with a limp handkerchief. "It don't matter so much about the trunk," he thought. "One of the boys at the hotel can express it to me, or I can pick it up on my way back."

Joe noticed that one end of his catalogue case protruded slightly. With his foot he shoved it farther under the seat. It was a battered black case, made strongly to withstand constant traveling and reinforced at its corners with heavy copper cleats. One of the handles had been broken and mended with newer leather. On the front of the case there had once been stamped in gilt the firm name of "Boykin & Rosen, Wholesale Hardware, Chattanooga, Tenn.," but time had long since worn away the gold lettering.

The telegram had upset Joe: it had come so suddenly, so unexpectedly. He felt vaguely that somebody was playing a joke on him. He felt confused and helpless. It was difficult to believe that Bessie was so desperately sick. He sat for a time staring at his finger nails. Suddenly he remembered an appointment for four o'clock with the buyer for Snowdoun and Sims, and he rose quickly from his seat with some vague idea of telephoning or sending a message to explain his absence. Then he realized that the train was in motion. "I'll write him a letter when I get to Mobile," said Joe to himself; "he'll understand all right when I explain the circumstances. He won't blame me for breaking that date when I tell him about my wife being so sick." Joe sat down heavily in his seat and again looked at his hands.

Ahead of him two young girls were leaning out of the window and waving to their friends. Their eyes were shining and their cheeks were flushed and they were laughing with excitement at the prospect of going away.

Across the aisle sat a gaunt farm-woman. Her red-veined eyes protruded. Her neck was swollen with a goiter. In her arms she held a bouquet of red crêpe-myrtle, which was already wilting in the heat. Beside her she had placed her straw suitcase and several bulky paper-wrapped parcels. She gazed steadily out of the window as if afraid that someone would catch her eye and try to talk to her.

It was very hot in the coach. The small electric fan at the end of the car droned and wheezed sleepily but succeeded only in stirring up the hot air.

Joe took from his pocket the telegram that he had received from his mother-in-law and read it again: "J. G. Hinckley, American Hotel, Montgomery, Ala. Come home at once. Doctor says Bessie not expected live through day. Will wire again if necessary. It was a boy. Mother."

Joe's hands clenched suddenly and then relaxed. It had all happened so suddenly; he couldn't quite get it through his head, even yet. He had taken a buyer to lunch that day and they had laughed and talked and told each other stories. Then at two o'clock he had gone back to the hotel to freshen up and the clerk had reached into his box and taken out the key to his room and the telegram. The telegram had been waiting for him for two hours, the clerk said. Joe read it through twice and then looked at the address to make sure that the message was really for him. He hadn't understood: Bessie was getting along so nicely—she had had no trouble at all—and the baby was not expected for a month. He had arranged his itinerary so that he would be with her when the baby was born. They had gone over all that and had arranged everything. And now everything was upset . . . Then he thought: "I was out talking and laughing with that buyer and the telegram was waiting here all the time." That thought hurt him. He stood repeating stupidly: "I was out laughing and telling smutty stories and that telegram was here all the time."

Joe leaned his head against the red plush of the seat. He felt numb and very tired. At first the signature "Mother" had puzzled him. He couldn't understand what his mother would be doing in Mobile with Bessie; then he realized that it was Bessie's mother who had sent the telegram. He had never thought of Bessie's mother by any name except Mrs. Thompkins.

When he had married Bessie her mother had come to live with them as a matter of course. He was rather glad of that arrangement: he was really fond of the old lady in an impersonal sort of way. Then, too, it was pleasant for Bessie to have someone with her while he was on the road. His work made it impossible for him to get home oftener than every other week end; and many times it was difficult for him to get home that often, but he had always managed to make it, one way or another. He couldn't disappoint Bessie, no matter what happened. Their year of married life had been the happiest that he had ever known. And Bessie had been happy too. Suddenly he had a clear picture of her lying on their bed, her face white with suffering, and a quick panic gripped his heart. To reassure himself he whispered: "Those doctors don't know everything. She'll be all right. Mrs. Thompkins was just excited and frightened. Everything's going to be all right!"

Ahead of him a white-haired old gentleman opened his bag

and took out a traveling cap. He had some difficulty in fastening the catch while holding his straw hat in his hand; but his wife, sitting with him, took the bag and fastened it at once. Then she took his hat and held it on her lap. The wife was reading a magazine. She did not look up from the magazine when she fastened the bag.

Down the aisle came the Negro porter. He had a telegram in his hand. When he reached the center of the coach he stopped and called out: "Telegram for Mr. J. G. Hinckley!" Joe let him call the name three times before he claimed the message. The porter explained that the telegram had been delivered to the train by a messenger from the American Hotel just as the train was getting under way. Joe gave the porter twenty-five cents for a tip and went back to his seat.

The country woman looked up for an instant and then turned her eyes away. The young girls giggled and whispered and looked boldly at Joe; and the old gentleman, after settling his cap firmly on his head, took a cigar from his case and went to the smoking-room.

Joe's throat felt tight, and he noticed that his hands were shaking. He wanted to put his head on the window sill, but he was afraid that people would think him sick and try to talk to him. He placed the unopened telegram on the seat beside him and stared at it for a long time. Then he re-read the first telegram very slowly. "It must be from Mrs. Thompkins, all right," he thought; "she said she'd wire again if—" Then he thought: "It may not be from Mrs. Thompkins at all; it may be from somebody else; it may be from Boykin and Rosen about that cancellation in Meridian. That's who it's from: it's from the House; it's not from Mrs. Thompkins at all!" He looked up quickly and saw that the two young girls had turned around and were watching him, making laughing remarks to each other behind their hands.

He arose from his seat feeling weak and slightly nauseated, the unopened telegram in his hand. He passed through several coaches until he reached the end of the train, and went out on the rear vestibule. He had a sudden wish to jump from the end of the train and run off into the woods, but a brakeman was there tinkering with a red lantern and Joe realized that such an act would look very strange. When the brakeman looked up and saw Joe's face, he put down his lantern and asked: "Are you feeling all right, mister?" Joe said, "Yes, I'm feeling all right; but it's a little hot, though." Finally the brakeman finished his job and left, and Joe was very glad of that. He wanted to be alone. He didn't want anybody around him.

The rails clicked rhythmically and the wilted countryside flew past. A little Negro girl . . . in a patched pink dress . . . ran down to the track . . . and waved her hand. A lame old country man . . . plowing in his stumpy field . . . pulled up his lazy mule . . . to stare at the passing train. The rails clattered and clicked and the train flew over the hot slag roadbed. "There's no need of going so fast," thought Joe, "we've got all the time in the world." He felt sick. In the polished metal of the car he caught a distorted glimpse of his face. It was white and terrified. He thought: "No wonder that brakeman asked me how I was feeling." Then he thought: "Do I look so bad that people can tell it?" That worried him. He didn't want people to notice him or to talk to him. There was nothing that anybody could say, after all.

He kept turning the telegram over in his hand, thinking: "I've got to open it now; I've got to open it and read it." Finally he said aloud: "It's not true! I don't believe it!" He repeated these words a number of times and then he said: "It's from the House about that cancellation in Meridian—it isn't from Mrs. Thompkins at all." Then he tore the unopened telegram into tiny bits and threw the pieces from the end of the train. A wind fluttered and shimmered the yellow fragments before they settled down lightly on the hard hot roadbed. He thought: "They look like a cloud of yellow butterflies dancing and settling that way." Immediately he felt better. He drew back his shoulders and sucked in lungsful of the country air. "Everything's all right!" he said. "I'm going home to see the little wife and everything's all right!" He laughed happily. He felt like a man who has just escaped some terrible calamity. When he could no longer see the scraps of paper on the track he went back to his seat humming a tune. He felt very gay and immensely relieved.

Joe reached his seat just as the conductor came through the train. He nodded pleasantly as he gave up his ticket.

"Don't let nobody talk you out of a free ride," he said.

"No chance of that, Cap," said the conductor.

Joe laughed with ringing heartiness and the conductor looked at him in surprise. Then he laughed a little himself. "You sure are in a good humor, considering how hot it is," he said.

"And why shouldn't I be in a good humor?" asked Joe. "I'm going home to see the little wife." Then he whispered, as if it were a great secret, "It's a boy!"

"That's fine; that's simply fine!" said the conductor. He put his papers and his tickets on the seat and shook Joe's hand heartily. Joe blushed and laughed again. Then, as the conductor moved off, he nudged Joe's ribs and said: "Give my regards to the madam."

"I sure will," said Joe happily.

Joe was sorry that the conductor couldn't stay longer. He felt an imperative need of talking to someone. He felt that he must talk about Bessie to someone. He looked around the car to see if there was anyone he knew. The two young girls smiled at him. Joe understood perfectly; they were just two nice kids going on a trip. Either one, alone, would never think of smiling at a strange man, but being together changed things entirely. That made it an exciting adventure—something to be laughed over and discussed later with their friends. Joe decided that he would go over and talk to them. He walked over casually and seated himself.

"Where are you girls going?" he asked.

"Don't you think that you have a great deal of nerve?" asked the black-eyed girl.

"Sure I have. I wouldn't be the best hardware salesman on the road if I didn't have lots of nerve," said Joe pleasantly.

Both of the girls laughed at that and Joe knew that everything was all right. He decided that the blue-eyed girl was the prettier of the two but the black-eyed girl had more snap.

"We're getting off at Flomaton," said the blue-eyed girl.

"We've been in school in Montgomery," said the black-eyed girl.

"We're going home for the summer vacation."

"And we want the world to know we're glad of it!"

Joe looked at them gravely. "Don't make a mistake, young ladies; get all the education you can—you'll regret it later on if you don't."

Both the girls started laughing. They put their arms around each other and laughed until tears came into their eyes. Joe laughed too, although he wondered what the joke was. After awhile the girls stopped laughing, but a sudden giggle from the blue-eyed girl set them off again, worse than before.

"This is awfully silly!" said the black-eyed girl.

"Please don't think us rude," gasped the blue-eyed girl.

"What's the joke?" asked Joe, who was really laughing as much as either of the girls.

"You sounded so—so—" explained the blue-eyed girl.

"So damned *fatherly!*" finished the black-eyed girl.

Then they went off into another whirlwind of mirth, laughing and hugging each other. The old lady across the aisle put down her magazine and started laughing too, but the woman with the goiter held her bouquet of crêpe-myrtle rigidly and stared out of the window.

Joe waited until the girls had exhausted themselves. Finally they wiped their eyes and opened their vanity cases to look at themselves in their mirrors and to repowder their noses. Then he said:

"Well, I guess I ought to sound fatherly; I just got a telegram saying that I was a proud parent."

That interested the young girls and they crowded him with questions; they wanted to know all about it. Joe felt very happy. As he started to talk he noticed that the old lady had been listening and that she had moved over in her seat in order to hear better.

Joe felt friendly toward everybody. "Won't you come over and join us?" he asked.

"Yes, indeed," said the nice old lady, and Joe moved over and made a place for her.

"Now tell us all about it!" demanded the blue-eyed girl.

"You must be very happy," said the nice old lady.

"I sure am happy," said Joe. Then he added: "There's not a whole lot to tell except that I got a telegram from Mrs. Thompkins—Mrs. Thompkins is my mother-in-law—saying that Bessie had given birth to a fine boy and that both of them were doing splendidly; the doctor said that he'd never seen anybody so well before, but of course my wife wanted me to be with her, and so I just dropped everything and here I am. You see Bessie and I have only been married for a year. We've been very happy. The only bad thing is that I don't get home very often; but it wouldn't do to have everything perfect in the world, would it? She sure is the finest little wife a man ever had. She don't complain at all about my being away so much. But some day we hope to have things different."

"There isn't anything nicer than a baby," said the blue-eyed girl.

"What are you going to name him?" asked the nice old lady.

"Well, Bessie wants to name him for me, but I can't see much sense in that. My first name's Joe and I think that's a little common, don't you? But I'll leave the naming part up to Bessie. She can name him anything she wants to. She sure has been a fine little wife to me."

Then Joe started talking rapidly. He told in detail of the first time he had met Bessie. It had been in the home of Jack Barnes, one of the boys he had met on the road, and he had been invited over for dinner and a little stud poker later. Mrs. Barnes didn't play poker, so Bessie, who lived across the street, had been invited over to keep Mrs. Barnes company while the men played. He had liked Bessie at once, and the boys had kidded him about not keeping his mind on the game. He had never told anybody this before, but when the boys started kidding him he made up his mind not to look at Bessie again, as he didn't want her to think that he was fresh; but he couldn't stop looking at her, and every time he caught her eye she would smile in a sweet, friendly sort of way. Finally everybody noticed it and they started joking Bessie too, but she hadn't minded at all. He had lost fourteen dollars and fifty cents that night, but he had met Bessie. You couldn't call Bessie exactly beautiful but she was sweet and nice. Bessie was the sort of girl that any man would want to marry.

He told of their courtship. He quoted whole paragraphs from letters that she had written, to prove a particular point which he had brought up. Bessie hadn't liked him especially, not right at first, at any rate; of course she had liked him as a friend from the first but not in any serious way. There were one or two other fellows hanging around, too. Bessie had a great deal of attention; she could have gone out every night with a different man if she had wanted to. Being on the road all the time had been pretty much of a disadvantage. He didn't have an opportunity to see her often. Or maybe that was an advantage—anyway, he wrote her every day. Then, finally, they had become engaged. She hadn't even let him kiss her until then. He knew from the first that she would make a wonderful little wife, but he was still puzzled why a girl as superior as Bessie would want to marry him.

He talked on and on, rapidly—feverishly. He told how he had once determined not to get married at all, but that was before he had met Bessie. She had changed all that. . . . Two hours passed before he knew it. His audience was getting bored, but Joe didn't realize it.

Finally the old gentleman with the cap came back from the smoking room; and his wife, glad of a chance to get away, made her excuses and went over to sit with him. Joe smiled and nodded, but paused only a moment in his story. He was in the midst of a long description of Mrs. Thompkins. Mrs. Thompkins wasn't at all like the comic-supplement mother-in-law. Quite the contrary. He didn't see how he and Bessie would get along without her. To show you the sort of woman she really was, she always took his side in any dispute—not that he and Bessie ever quarreled! Oh, no! But occasionally they had little friendly discussions, like all other married couples, and Mrs. Thompkins always took his side of the argument. That was unusual, wasn't it? Joe talked and talked and talked, totally unconscious of the passing of time.

Finally the train reached Flomaton, and the porter came to help the girls off with their bags. They were very glad to get away. They were getting a little nervous. There was something about Joe they couldn't understand. At first they had thought him just jolly and high spirited, but after a time they came to the conclusion that he must be a little drunk or, possibly, slightly demented. For the past hour they had been nudging each other significantly.

Joe helped them off the train and onto the station platform. Just as the train pulled out, the black-eyed girl waved her hand and said: "Give my love to Bessie and the son and heir," and the blue-eyed girl said: "Be sure and kiss the baby for me."

"I sure will," said Joe.

After the train had passed the girls looked at each other for a moment. Then they started laughing. Finally the black-eyed girl said: "Well, Bessie certainly has him roped and tied." The blue-eyed girl said: "Did you ever see anything like that in your life before?"

Joe went back to the coach. "Just a couple of nice kids," he thought to himself. He looked at his watch. It was five twenty-five. He was surprised. The time had passed very quickly. "It won't be long now before I'm in Mobile," he thought.

He went back to his seat, but he was restless. He decided that he would have a cigarette. He found three men in the smoker. One of them was an old man with a tuft of gray whiskers. His face was yellow and sunken, and blue veins stood out on his hands. He was chewing tobacco gravely and spitting into the brass cuspidor. The second man was large and flabby. When he laughed, his eyes disappeared entirely and his fat belly shook. His fingernails were swollen and his under lip hung down in a petulant droop. The third man was dark and nervous-looking. He had on his little finger a ring with a diamond much too large.

They were telling jokes and laughing when Joe came in. Joe wanted to talk to them about Bessie, but he couldn't bring her name up in such an atmosphere. Suddenly he thought: "I was laughing and telling smutty stories with that buyer in Montgomery, and the telegram was there all the time." His face contracted with pain. He crushed the thought from his mind. Quickly he threw away his cigarette and went back to his seat.

A bright-skinned waiter came through the train announcing the first call to dinner. At first Joe thought that he would have his dinner on the train, as that would break the monotony of the trip and help pass the time; but immediately he remembered that Mrs. Thompkins would have dinner for him at home—a specially prepared dinner with all of the things that he liked. "I'll wait till I get home," thought Joe. "I wouldn't disappoint Mrs. Thompkins and the little wife for the world after they went to all that trouble for me."

Again he felt that curious, compulsive need of talking about Bessie to someone. He had a feeling that as long as he talked about her, she would remain safe. He saw the old lady and her husband in their seat eating a lunch which they had brought with them and he decided to go over and talk with them. "Can I come over and talk to you folks?" asked Joe.

"Certainly, sir," said the old gentleman with the cap. Then, in order to make conversation he said: "My wife has been telling me that you are going home to see your new son."

"That's right," said Joe, "that's right." He started talking rapidly, hardly pausing for breath. The old lady looked at her husband reproachfully. "Now see what you started!" her glance seemed to say.

Joe talked of his wedding. It had been very quiet: Bessie was the sort of girl who didn't go in for a lot of show. There had been present only a few members of the family and one or two close friends. George Orcutt, who traveled with a line of rugs out of New York, had been his best man. Bessie was afraid that someone would try to play a joke on them: something like tying tin cans to the automobile that was to take them to the station, or marking their baggage with chalk. But everything had gone off smoothly. The Barneses had been at the wedding, of course: he had met Bessie in their home and they were such close neighbors that they couldn't overlook them; but almost nobody else, outside the family, was there.

Then he told of the honeymoon they had spent in New Orleans—all the places they had visited there and just what Bessie had thought and said about each one. He talked on and on and on. He told of the first weeks of their married life and how happy they were. He told what a splendid cook Bessie was and what an excellent housekeeper, how much she had loved the home he had bought for her, and her delight when she knew that she was going to have a baby.

The old gentleman was staring at Joe in a puzzled manner. He was wondering if he hadn't better call the conductor, as it was his private opinion that Joe had a shot of cocaine in him. The old lady had folded her hands like a martyr. She continued to look at her husband with an I-told-you-so expression.

Joe had lost all idea of time. He talked on and on—rapidly, excitedly. He had gotten as far as Bessie's plans for the child's education when the porter touched him on the arm and told him that they were pulling into the station at Mobile. He came to himself with a start and looked at his watch: seven thirty-five! He didn't believe it possible that two hours had passed so quickly.

"It sure has been a pleasure talking to you folks," said Joe.

"Oh, that's all right," said the man with the cap.

Joe gave the porter a tip and stepped off the train jauntily. As he turned to pick up his bag, he saw that the woman with the goiter was staring at him. He walked over to the window that framed her gaunt face. "Good-bye, lady; I hope you have a nice trip." The woman answered: "The doctors said it wasn't no use operating on me. I waited too late." "Well, that's fine!—That sure is fine!" said Joe. He laughed gaily and waved his hand. Then he picked up his bag and his catalogue case and followed the people through the gate. The woman with the goiter stared at him until he was out of sight.

On the other side of the iron fence Joe saw Mrs. Thompkins. She was dressed all in black and she wore a black veil. Joe went over to her briskly, and Mrs. Thompkins put her arms around him and kissed him twice. "Poor Joe!" she said. Then she looked at his smiling, excited face with amazement. Joe noticed that her eyes were red and swollen.

"Didn't you get my telegram?" she asked. Joe wrinkled his brow in an effort to remember. Finally he said: "Oh, sure, I got it at the hotel."

"Did you get my second telegram?" insisted Mrs. Thompkins. She looked steadily into Joe's eyes. A feeling of terror swept over him. He knew that he could no longer lie to himself. He could no longer keep Bessie alive by talking about her. His face was suddenly twisted with pain and his jaw trembled like a child's. He leaned against the iron fence for support, and Mrs. Thompkins held his hand and said: "You can't give in. You got to be a man. You can't give in like that, Joe!"

Finally he said: "I didn't read your telegram. I didn't want to know that she was dead. I wanted to keep her alive a little longer." He sat down suddenly on an empty baggage truck and hid his face in his hands. He sat there for a long time while Mrs. Thompkins stood guard over him, her black veil trailing across his shoulder. Finally he asked: "What time did Bessie die?" His voice was tight and hard. It seemed to come from behind his teeth. Mrs. Thompkins answered, "She was dead when I sent the second telegram." Then, as if her own grief were of little importance, she pressed her hands together and said, "Poor Joe! Poor Joe!"

A man in a dirty uniform came up. "I'm sorry, mister, but you'll have to move. We got to use that truck."

Joe picked up his catalogue case and his bag and followed Mrs. Thompkins out of the station.

1928

MIST ON THE MEADOW

WHEN Brother Hightower came at last from the twilight of the pine grove he saw before him a meadowland, filled with flowers —saffron and pink, bell-shaped and shaped like stars—lying damp and cool in the late afternoon and flowing richly to meet a line of cypresses that fringed the lagoon and marked where the marsh began. It had been dark among the trees, but the meadowland swam in a light fluid and amber that blurred the outline of the cabin before him and softened the harshness of the clay plastered against its sides. The cabin was built of hewn logs that had weathered brown, and was set squarely in the midst of the meadow. At its back, a sagged chimney of sticks and red mud threw smoke into the air in a thin, curving stream.

Brother Hightower reined up his pony and removed his feet from the stirrups. "That must be the Gentry place," he thought. Before him stretched the meadow and the marsh, but to his left the land rose to irregular bluffs of red clay which hung like a shelf above the eastern edge of the lagoon.

He stretched his bony legs and turned to survey the cabin more carefully. Then he settled again to the saddle and began to think of himself and his mission. He thought of the sinfulness of the world, of the viciousness of men and of the souls he had somehow saved in his itinerant preaching years, and his heart flooded with a feeling of humility and power. He raised his arms to heaven and his eyes rolled upward. "Lord! Lord!" he moaned. "Make me worthy to serve in Thy vineyard!" His face became distorted and he twisted with pain.

As he prayed, there came from across the meadow the voice of a man calling his pigs, and the answering sound of swine welcoming and disputing their supper. Hightower had dropped his reins, and the pony, with lowered mouth, wandered at will and cropped the grass eagerly. Presently the preacher removed his clerical hat and wiped the moisture from his forehead and his hands. Then he took up the reins again and guided his pony toward the cabin.

As he drew nearer, the squeals of the swine came louder to his ears, and he could distinguish easily the words the man was using: "Hey, there—Emma! Git outen that trough! Whoever learnt you manners? What would folks say, now, if they seen you actin' thataway?" Brother Hightower frowned at the joyousness in the man's voice. He halted his pony and dismounted stiffly. Before him was a sty, in which milled a dozen fat pigs, and a man who was feeding them slops and mash from a tin bucket. The man was dressed in a brown shirt and faded overalls, grotesquely patched with colored scraps which had also faded. His sparse red beard curled upward at the ends, and his head was entirely bald. He wore no shoes. His voice was affectionate, and he laughed continuously at the antics of his pigs.

"Git away, Emma, I tell you—give old Charley a chance. He ain't had a mouthful!" With his bare foot he shoved her away from the trough with a tolerant, loving gesture. "I declare: that Emma's the *hongriest* sow ever I seen!" Again he laughed happily.

Brother Hightower cleared his throat sharply and said: "Good evening, and God be with you all." His voice was deep, with a rich, trembling intensity.

"Good evenin', preacher," the man said mildly.

"Is this the Gentry place?"

"Yes, preacher. I'm Jim Gentry."

"I allowed you was Jim Gentry. I'm the Reverend Hightower, the humblest of God's servants, and I'm on my way to hold a revival for the folks on Pigeon River."

Gentry walked to the edge of the pen and held out his hand. "I'm glad to make your acquaintance, preacher. I've heerd folks a-talking 'bout you. I've heerd it said Christ Jesus stood before you one time, honorin' and raisin' you up above all men."

Hightower bowed his head. "You have heard truly, brother. It was Him that gave me the wrath to make sinners quail and forsake their lusts. It was Him that gave me the power to heal the sick and a hand to cast out devils." Jim shifted his weight nervously and drew back, and with his bare, horny feet he stroked the backs of his swine.

Suddenly he turned and faced the cabin. "Exa!" he called loudly.

A woman appeared in the door. She was a tall woman, taller than her husband and almost of a height with Hightower himself. Between her decaying teeth was a sweet-gum brush which she chewed with a thoughtful, automatic insistence. Her eyes were pale under their bleached brows and blue veins stood out in her wrists. When she saw the stranger she drew back suspiciously, but her husband's voice reassured her.

"This here's the Reverend Hightower on his way to preach a revival at Pigeon River."

The name had a magic effect on Exa. She came down the steps quickly and approached the two men. "You don't come none too soon. The folks at Pigeon River are ungodly, I've heerd it said." She gazed at Hightower fiercely with her pale eyes, and Hightower stared back, his own eyes dark and dilated with emotion. "Ungodly and sinful, Sister Gentry," he whispered. "Singing songs and dancing and lusting after flesh."

Exa spoke to her husband: "This is a holy man, Jim." But Gentry laughed foolishly and turned to finish feeding his pigs. Exa spoke again to the preacher: "We'll be proud to have you stay with us a spell. We hain't got much, but what we have is yours withouten even askin'."

"You are kind thoughted, Sister Gentry, but I aim to pass on my way at daybreak. There's work in the Vineyard of the Lord and the reapers are few." Exa nodded her head in complete understanding. "Come into the house, preacher; supper'll be ready right soon. Jim'll take care of your pony." Hightower turned then and followed her into the house.

The cabin consisted of two rooms and a lean-to. There were no lamps, but a blaze of pine knots lighted the room and cast great shadows against the walls. Hightower removed his hat and his black, tight-fitting coat, and Exa brought him water from the stove and poured it into a basin. When he had finished his wash and had combed out his damp, black hair, supper was being placed on the table. He seated himself at once and commenced a blessing, but almost immediately he was interrupted by sudden laughter and the sound of chains being shaken. He uncovered his eyes and gazed at the burlap curtains which screened the entrance to the lean-to, but he did not pause in his prayer. As he watched, there came to his ears a sound like the popping of a cork and a hiss such as some fabulous snake might make.

Exa half turned in her chair, but her eyes remained downcast and devout. Again there came the rattling of a chain, angry and more insistent, and presently the hissing changed into an irritable and impotent chatter. Brother Hightower brought to an end his blessing and raised his head. He looked enquiringly at Jim.

"That's *Tolly,"* said Jim proudly; "that's my boy, Tolly!"

Exa was on her feet instantly. "Oh, my po' baby—did its ma go and forget it? Did its ma clean forget little Tolly's supper? Now that's a shame; that's what I call a mean shame!" As she talked, she piled victuals on a tin plate, and presently she brushed the curtains aside and went to her son. The querulous chattering ceased at once. There was now the sound of lips being smacked and food swallowed sensuously. Occasionally Exa's voice was heard whispering some endearing phrase: "Eat it all, honey —greens is *good* for Mamma's baby."

Gentry dragged one foot across the floor slowly. Then he looked down at his plate, as if to hide the pride in his eyes: "Tolly's the beatenest boy you ever seen," he said. "There ain't nobody like him in the country. They just lost the pattern after they finished makin' old Tolly!" Then he leaned back in his chair and chuckled at some old recollection.

Brother Hightower frowned and shook his head. "But chains,

Brother Gentry . . ." he began; "to put one of God's creatures in chains . . ." His voice thinned out into silence.

"Oh, pshaw!" said Gentry; "that don't mean nothing; Exa don't mean no harm by chainin' him up, but she can't be a-watchin' him every minute, after she done put clean clothes onto him, and iffen she didn't chain him up, Tolly'd just liable as not go get in the pen and wallow with the hogs."

Hightower looked up in surprise. "Will he do a thing like that?" he asked in an uncertain voice. Then an expression of distaste came over his face. "Wallowing with hogs!" he repeated; "wallow in filth with hogs!"

"Sholy," said Jim; "sholy. Now what all's wrong with that?" Then he began to speak earnestly. "They're good clean hogs; them hogs is the best in this county; they're registered stock; I guess them hogs is better blooded by a whole passel than you or me, preacher. It's their nature to wallow, and Tolly's nature to wallow, and I always say to Exa, if they don't mind Tolly in their pen, then Tolly ain't got no call to mind them."

Hightower shoved his plate away with a sudden gesture of disgust. He rose from his seat and walked to the fire, kicking at a log that protruded from the hearth and giving life suddenly to the shadows that seemed painted against the wall. But Jim continued talking in his soft, contented voice.

"He looks right cute there in the pen with them pigs, and him so covered with mud that nobody could say for sure what was hog and what was Tolly. That boy Tolly," he continued, "he sure is one case, now! He sure is the very beatenest one! But he's a real good boy and nobody can say different. He never meddled nobody's business and he never caused sorrow in his life. Sometimes of a morning he picks flowers in the medder or watches a humming bird all day, but then sometimes he goes to sleep against a cypress knee in the cool of the lagoon." Then Jim began to laugh louder and slap his leg. "That boy Tolly!" he repeated proudly, "he sure is one case!"

The curtains parted and Exa came again into the room and seated herself at the table. Hightower made a deep, sympathetic noise in his throat. "I'm sorry for you, Sister Gentry, in your trouble." Exa bowed her head and looked down at her hands. There was a long silence and then Jim glanced at his wife timidly, turning at length to the preacher for support. "There was a young fellow through here last fall, come to teach school at Liveoak. He said we ought to send Tolly to the 'sylum. Said he might get cured iffen we done that."

Exa's eyes narrowed and her bleached brows became dangerous, as if the subject were a sore one. She rose from the table and walked backward slowly. "Nobody can take Tolly and lock him in a dungeon for a lunatic!" she said. She stretched her arms across the opening to the lean-to, and stared fiercely at the two men, as if her husband's words had somehow put in motion forces which would take the boy away. Brother Hightower walked toward her, his voice sweet with sympathy. "There, now, Sister Gentry! Nobody's going to take the boy away. Brother Jim spoke without thinking. He's an earthy man and he knows not the yearning of the spirit nor the ways of God; but no man could be heartless enough to put God's own handiwork in an evil place of atheists and infidels where prayers are never heard and where His sacred word is flouted and scorned." He placed his arms protectingly around Exa's shoulders and guided her back to the table. "Sister Gentry, God has placed a heavy cross on you and yours, but rejoice and be exceedingly glad! For He punishes them that He cherishes, and you are His very dearly loved. Rejoice, sister, and kiss the hand that chastens you! Rejoice and be glad!"

Exa looked up pleadingly. "Preacher, what ails Tolly?"

Hightower walked across the room rapidly, his black hair tossing excitedly to his stride. Then he turned and faced the woman. His eyes were dilated and his hands were trembling. "Your son is possessed of a devil!" he whispered. There was a note of exultation in his voice. "Your son is possessed of a very terrible devil!" he repeated.

"Aw, shucks, preacher," said Jim mildly.

When the meal was finished at length and Exa had cleared the table, a sweet mist was rising off the lagoon and a moon rode high above the trees. The pine grove lay quiet and dark to the north and the meadowland was an enchanted and a lovely place. The men had walked onto the porch and sat smoking their pipes. Hightower was talking of his conversion and Exa, washing her dishes, could hear his deep voice plainly.

"It happened nigh to dark, when I was plowing in the field. There come a sound of wings about my ears and I seen the air was filled with angels. They roosted in the trees and sat white on the rails of the fence, singing a hymn of praise. I fell to my knees, knowing well the sinful life I had led. 'Lord! Lord!' I said. 'Wash me with blood, and make me as white as wool.' I buried my face in the dirt and waited for death to take me, but something lifted me up, and Christ Jesus stood before me. I put my hands over my eyes, being unable to bear the sight of His glory, and swayed my head from side to side, moaning. 'Spread My glory to all men, and preach My gospel to every nation!' He said. 'Halleluiah! Halleluiah!' sang the angels in voices as sweet and as high as a trumpet note.

" 'How can I preach for You?' I cried out; 'I, an unlettered man who cannot read Thy holy word!' 'Doubt not, for thou canst really do these things!' He said in a voice of thunder. 'No, Lord,' I answered, 'I never had no schooling and not one word can I read.'

"Christ Jesus raised His loving arm and I seen that He had a whip of scorpions. He brought it down across my shoulders time and time again. 'It is written that My house shall be a house of prayer, and ye doubt that I am the Son of God come to save the world from sin!' . . . And me crouching between the rows of young corn, baring my breast to the whip and saying: 'Do with me what you will, gentle Lord. Beat me! Make me the lowliest of Thy slaves and I shall love Thee dearly! Rend me limb from limb, if that be Thy sweet wish!' And when they found me my mouth was cut and bleeding and my teeth was broke and there were great bruises on my back and chest to show where the whip had been."

For a moment there was silence, oppressive and brooding, and then Hightower began speaking again: "That night when I returned, word passed amongst the neighbor folk and they come to look at me, and to marvel, and I told them what they longed to hear. When a great crowd had collected, we walked down the road until we come to the settlement, and there, in the presence of them all, I called for a Bible and read aloud the Gospel according to St. Mark. And when the people who had known me all their lives seen that I could really read, they fell upon their knees, fearing, and I baptized them in the river and received them into the church of God. Then when it was dawn we walked down the road again, singing hymns of praise and waving green branches."

Exa put down her dishcloth and stood silent in the room. The fire was dying into embers but the moonlight streamed brightly through the open window and the door. Her husband's voice, soft and apologetic, came to her ears. "I can't read none, neither."

"Praise God for that, Brother Gentry! When God wants to give a man the gift of tongues or the gift of print He will signify His wish, as He done with me. And every book except God's sacred Word should be burnt in flames." There was another long silence, so long that Exa feared the preacher would not speak again, but presently he continued.

"That morning as I walked the road with my disciples praising God and waving branches, I worked a miracle. A nigger come running down from his cabin by the creek, toting a little black girl whose legs were twisted and withered away. I put my hand on the child, who had never walked a step, and commanded that she rise up. And right away she rose up from the road and ran skipping and laughing through the fields. And when my disciples seen that they fell on their knees and kissed my dusty feet, but I said: 'Verily, verily, praise not me, but render thanks to my Father in Heaven, for I am not as mighty as He.' "

There was a silence between the two men. Jim Gentry pulled upon his pipe with a faint hissing sound, but Brother Hightower stared across the meadowland, his eyes dreaming and drawn upward. "For I am not as mighty as He," he repeated sadly.

Exa's voice sounded suddenly from the doorway. "Can you

cast the devil out of Tolly, preacher?" Her nostrils were quivering with excitement and her white eyebrows were drawn together. Hightower drew on his pipe deeply while Exa waited with clenched fists for his answer. "I have cast out devils," he said warily; "I have cast out many devils, Sister Gentry."

Jim Gentry got up from the steps and stood with his toes pressed into the soft loam of a flower bed. "Now, Exa—you all let Tolly alone, can't you?"

But Exa continued to stare at the preacher. "Can you cast the devil out of Tolly?" Her fists were pressed against her breasts and she was breathing heavily.

Brother Hightower stretched out his hands and bowed his head. "I can if it be the will of God, Sister Exa."

"Now you all let Tolly alone, I tell you. He's not a-botherin' nobody."

But Exa and Brother Hightower paid no attention to Gentry. They were staring at each other again with parted lips and furious, exalted eyes; and presently Exa went into the house and unchained her son.

Tolly was undersized and sallow and no thought held his features together or gave his face significance. His forehead bulged above his eyes and his jaw lay relaxed and toneless beneath his parted lips. He walked to the edge of the porch and held out his arms. "Fire! Fire!" he said eagerly.

"No, honey, that ain't fire—that's just the *moon!*"

"Tolly's got as much sense as you or me," said Jim; "Tolly's got as much sense as anybody, iffen he wanted to use it." Hightower shook his head vigorously. "It's the devils in him that call out for the fire!" he said.

Jim looked helplessly from the exalted face of his wife to the more exalted face of the preacher. A feeling of resentment came over him, but it passed almost immediately. He could never defy anyone as powerful as Brother Hightower and he knew it. "Po' little Tolly!" he said sadly; "po' little Tolly!"

Exa seated herself and Tolly sat beside her, resting his meaningless face against her shoulder. Hightower regarded them carefully. "How old is the boy?" he asked. "He's going on twenty, preacher, but small for his age, as you see." Exa smoothed back her son's coarse, hemp-like hair and stroked his cheek with her hand.

Suddenly Hightower spoke directly to the boy. "Tolly, look at me, son!" But Tolly paid no attention. "Tolly! Listen to Brother Hightower; he's going to make you well again." Exa had risen to her feet, lifting the boy in her strong arms. Hightower had also risen, and presently he came over to the boy and placed his hands upon his forehead. Tolly hissed and spat and his face wrinkled with terror. "Tolly, ain't you 'shamed!" said Exa reproachfully.

"Don't blame the boy, sister; it's the devils in him that done that." He caught Tolly by the arms and held him firmly, and Tolly became very excited. He struggled and spat and tried to free himself. He began to chatter excitedly and later to make low, pleading noises; but Hightower held him tightly. "This is going to be an uncommon hard devil to rout, Sister Gentry," he said; "it might be best to chain the boy up while I pray."

"What makes you all keep a-pesterin' Tolly so?" asked Jim querulously. "He ain't done nuthin' to you."

Exa gave her husband a glance of scorn. Then she picked up the loose ends of the chain that circled her son's waist and snapped them through two bent spikes driven into the logs of the cabin. Tolly looked from one face to the other quickly. He drew close to the wall and clung there in terror, but Hightower pursued him relentlessly. He lifted the boy's face and gazed at him with deep, yearning eyes.

"Devil, come forth!" he whispered. Tolly began to laugh foolishly and to shuffle his feet, but he could not draw his eyes away from the preacher's eyes. Hightower swayed his head back and forth with a slow, steady motion and Tolly's head swayed with him. "Come forth, devil, from this soul! . . ."

For a moment there was silence. Then a crane called shrilly from over the marsh and the swine, dreaming in their wallow, grunted twice and turned nervously.

Presently Hightower fell to his knees and began to pray in a deep, rich voice. He lay on the floor praying, his eyes distended and his hands splayed widely. Finally he rose to his full height and placed his palms against Tolly's cheeks. Tolly did not resist him now. He lay passive against the logs of the cabin, glancing from his mother to the preacher in terror. Hightower lifted his eyes to heaven. The muscles of his face twitched, his jaw was set and he talked cloudily through locked teeth. "Grant me this miracle, Lord!" he whispered. "This miracle you done once with your own sweet hands!" Then he forced back the boy's head until their eyes almost met and cried in a loud voice: "Come forth, devils, and depart from this boy!" Tolly began to tremble more violently. He rattled his chains and beat his head against the wall.

At that moment the pigs awoke and made a low, worried sound. They rose heavily and huddled together against the farthest wall of the sty, grunting in uncertain protest. Then they broke their grouping and trotted apprehensively around the pen, coming together, at last, in the center of the sty, to stand there, waiting, making a vague grunting noise.

Jim touched the preacher on his arm in mild protest. "Why don't you all go inside and shet the door?" he asked. "My pigs is getting upset with all this racket a-goin' on. Them's blooded, high-strung pigs, preacher, and they can't stand this to-do."

But Brother Hightower did not even hear him. His voice was becoming stronger and more exultant. Again he lifted Tolly's head, and again he gazed deeply into his shrinking eyes. "Come forth, devils!" he demanded. "Come forth and enter yon filthy swine!" A strange echoing sound came from Tolly's throat. He clutched the side of the cabin for support, clung for a moment, and fell sharply to the floor.

Instantly the pigs began to squeal in terror, lunging furiously against the sides of the pen. At the sound of their distress, Jim Gentry sprang from the porch and ran to the pen and stood trying to quiet his pigs with soft, loving words, but they paid no heed to him at all; they continued to squeal and hurl themselves against the sides of the sty until at last its walls gave way against their weight. Then the released swine ran across the meadow to the east, in the direction of the bluffs, milling and whirling in broken, furious circles and tearing each other with their teeth; and when they reached the bluffs they continued to whirl, and a moment later their bodies were silhouetted against the moon as they pitched over the edge and into the water below.

Brother Hightower stood in silence, his body rigid, his eyes flaming. Then he turned and faced Exa, praying rapidly, and Tolly rolling on the floor. "I have performed the miracle of the swine," he whispered, as if awed by his own power. "Bear ye witness," he said; "bear ye witness to my holiness!"

At the preacher's words, Tolly crept eagerly to him, kissing his hands and embracing his long legs. His face, which had once been meaningless and content, was now meaningless and frightened. "Save me!" he screamed over and over. "Save me from eternal torment!" Then his face began to twitch and his body jerked spasmodically as Jim Gentry unsnapped the chains that held him to the wall, and carried him into the house. "Po' little Tolly," he said; "po' little boy! If ere a man can show me where you're bettered withouten your devils, I'll give that man a pretty." Then he looked sadly across the meadow and closed the door to the cabin.

For the wind was changing and the mist that had hung above the marsh began to thrust furtive arms between the trunks of the trees, and to spread over the surface of the lagoon. From the lagoon the mist moved across the meadow with a slow, imperceptible motion, obliterating bushes and outhouses and familiar landmarks. Soon the pine grove and the bluffs would be lost under a covering overwhelming and impalpable; soon the horizon would be wiped away and the land blotted up completely, and nothing in all the world would remain except Tolly rattling his chains and Brother Hightower, with raised, enigmatic arms, praying harshly before the cabin.

1930

MISS DAISY

THAT afternoon Mrs. McArthur, my Sunday school teacher, came to see Aunt Juliet. I was getting too big to be in her class any longer, and she thought I should be promoted to the Intermediate Section. "I surely will hate to lose Harry," she said; "he's a good boy, Miss Piggott, in a lot of ways, and he don't give me near so much trouble as some of the others; I'll sure hate to lose him, and that's a fact; but he's just getting too big."

I was out in the backyard, playing with Leo, when Mrs. McArthur came to see Aunt Juliet, but they called me in after a little while. Aunt Juliet must have been expecting company that afternoon, for she had on her black silk shirtwaist and skirt, and her hair was parted so that the gray streak didn't show at all. She had a gold chain around her neck, with my grandmother's watch on the end of it. You could hear the watch ticking, but you couldn't see it, because it was tucked behind a leather belt that she always wore. From where I was sitting, I could see my hands in the glittering belt; they were fat and blown up, and not like my hands at all. I began to move about and try to see how much of myself I could make the belt show at one time, but Aunt Juliet stopped me.

"For pity sake, Harry! Can't you sit still more than two minutes without twisting all over the place? You're worse than a worm in hot ashes."

"If you think *Harry's* bad, you ought to see *some* of them!" said Mrs. McArthur, but she laughed when she said it, though.

I sat up straight in the chair again, but I didn't say anything. Mrs. McArthur had a square flat face. She always wore gold earrings that went all the way through her ears and fastened with a screw on the other side. The earrings were very heavy, and they pulled the bottoms of her ears down. I thought her face looked like a map of the United States with Florida on both sides.

"Don't you want to be promoted to the Intermediate Section?" asked Mrs. McArthur after a while.

"No, ma'am," I said.

"Why, I'd be ashamed," said Aunt Juliet, "a big boy like you, going on nine years old and still in the Infant Section."

"Now, Harry," said Mrs. McArthur, "you'll like it better in the Intermediate Section."

When Aunt Juliet called me in, Leo and I had been playing Indians on the warpath and we were just getting ready to attack the settlers' wagons. Leo thought he'd better go on home, but I begged him to wait and he said he would, if I didn't stay inside too long.

"All right, Mrs. McArthur," I said; "I don't mind going in the Intermediate Section."

Mrs. McArthur thought a moment and then she spoke to Aunt Juliet. "Maybe he'd like it in Miss Burton's class. Don't you think you'd like it in Miss Burton's class, Harry?"

"I don't care," I said.

"All right, then," said Mrs. McArthur. "If it suits you, Miss Piggott, I'll speak to Miss Burton on my way home and see if she's got room for Harry."

"Is it *Daisy* Burton you're speaking of?" asked Aunt Juliet.

"Yes," said Mrs. McArthur. "She lives with the widow Findley on Cherokee Street."

"I used to know her," said Aunt Juliet, "and I'll be proud to have Harry in her class. She's a fine type of Christian woman."

Mrs. McArthur nodded her head. "She's all of that and more. Mr. McArthur and I were talking just the other night about whom we considered the best practicing Christian we knew, and we both agreed it was Daisy Burton."

"Well, she's a fine woman," said Aunt Juliet, "and I don't know anybody who's had a harder life than she has, either."

After a while Mrs. McArthur got up to leave, but when I went back to look for Leo I found that he had gone home.

A lot of people thought it funny that Aunt Juliet sent me to the Presbyterian Sunday school, when all the other Piggotts were Methodists, but before I came to Reedyville to live, my mother had taken me to the Presbyterian church, that being her church, and Aunt Juliet didn't think it right for me to change, now that my mother was dead. So on Sundays Uncle Carter used to hitch up the surrey and drive me to the Presbyterian church first; then he would go back and get Aunt Juliet and Aunt Emmaline, and drive them to the Methodist church.

I liked living with my uncle and aunts. They were very good to me. Aunt Juliet was the oldest, Uncle Carter was next, then came my father, and Aunt Emmaline was the youngest of the Piggotts. My father's name was Herbert, but I could never get used to hearing my kin people call him that, as my mother had always called him Mr. Piggott. When Aunt Juliet would say to Uncle Carter: "Do you remember the time Herbert bought a goat from a little colored boy and Papa made him take it right back?" or, "It's not surprising Harry don't like okra: Herbert wouldn't eat it either, no matter how Mamma fixed it!" I always thought they were talking about somebody else.

That afternoon I kept thinking maybe Leo had got mad because Aunt Juliet had called me in, and after supper I said: "Aunt Juliet, can I go over and see Leo Zerback for a little while?"

Aunt Juliet said yes, she guessed so, but to be back before eight o'clock, because she intended going to bed early.

Mrs. Zerback had had snow pudding for dessert that night, and she gave Leo and me what was left over, and we went out on the back porch to eat it. After a while Mrs. Zerback came out and sat with us. She was a big fat woman and she wore calico wrappers all the time. She laughed in a loud way and slapped her leg like a man.

"Well, Harry," she said, "I saw old Mrs. McArthur going to

visit your house today; I'll bet you've been misbehaving in Sunday school."

"Oh, no, ma'am, I haven't!" I said. "But she's going to promote me to Miss Daisy Burton's class in the Intermediate Section."

"Well, you couldn't find a better teacher than Daisy Burton," said Mrs. Zerback seriously. "A finer woman never lived—I've always said it, and I'll say it again. Why, when my washerwoman's daughter was sick last winter, it was Daisy who sat up with her night after night, like she was her own sister, instead of a stranger, and if anybody should ask me, Daisy was the sickest of the two."

Mr. Zerback came out on the porch in his stocking-feet and brought a pitcher of lemonade and a plate of oatmeal cookies with pecans in them. "How do, Harry," he said. "Everybody well at home?"

"Yes, sir," I said. "Everybody's all right."

Mrs. Zerback was still thinking about Miss Burton. She nodded her head a couple of times. "She's what I call a real, earnest Christian, and this would be a better town if there were more like her in it."

"Who are you talking about, Lorena?" asked Mr. Zerback.

"I'm talking about Daisy Burton, that's who."

"Oh, sure," he said, as if he ought to have known all along whom she was talking about.

"When Leo grows up, I hope he marries a girl one half as sweet and good as Daisy," said Mrs. Zerback.

"I'm not going to marry anybody," said Leo.

Mrs. Zerback began to laugh and slap her leg. "I'll bet you do, though," she said. "I'll bet you marry the first little snip that comes switching down Oak Street."

The next day was Sunday, and Mrs. McArthur took me in and introduced me to my new teacher. "This is Harry Piggott, the boy I was telling you about," she said.

"Welcome to our class, Harry!" said Miss Burton in a cheerful voice. Miss Daisy was a dried-up, little, gray-headed woman, about fifty years old. One of her legs was shorter than the other, and she had to use crutches to walk. Her eyes were light blue and they looked like they were going to water any minute. Her lips were always turned up at the corners in a gentle smile. As she stood there talking to me, she balanced herself on one crutch and kept patting my head and rubbing my cheeks and hugging me around the neck. Her voice was very soft and sweet. It sounded like pigeons under the eaves of a barn.

That Sunday the lesson was about God telling Abraham to take his son Isaac and sacrifice him as a burnt offering, but Miss Daisy stopped when she came to the place where Abraham raises the knife to slay his son, which is just before the Voice of God comes in. She said she didn't like such subjects, and she didn't think they should be taught in Sunday school. So instead of the regular lesson that day, she gave us a talk. It was almost like a sermon, except that she kept looking into our eyes, squeezing our hands and patting our cheeks as she talked. "Hate is *de*-structive," said Miss Daisy; "but love is *con*-structive." She told us how terrible it was to hurt dumb animals and how badly the mother bird felt when she came to the nest and found it robbed. "Oh, if we could only love things, instead of hating them, what a better world it would be!" she said. I made up my mind that I would never shoot at cats with my air rifle or rob another bird's nest as long as I lived. When Miss Daisy's talk was over, we all stood up and recited the class pledge: "I will love God and my fellow men with all my heart and with all my soul, and I will do no act that will bring pain to others."

I thought to myself: "Miss Daisy certainly is the best woman in the world."

"Well, Harry," she said, when the lesson was over, "do you think you're going to like it with us?"

"Yes, ma'am," I said.

A boy named Albert Gran spoke up: "Harry got in the class just in time to go to the picnic."

"Oh, so he did!" said Miss Daisy; "we're having it a week from next Wednesday at James' Lake, and we extend you a very hearty invitation to attend, don't we, boys?" The boys in the class said yes, they did.

When Sunday school was over and we were waiting for church to begin, I asked a boy named Tommy Van Bergen about the picnic. He said Miss Daisy had one every July. She hired a wagon and a driver from Moore's Livery Stable and had the wagon filled with straw. Then the class drove out into the country somewhere and spent the day. Tommy had been the year before and he said everybody had had a fine time.

Tommy was the biggest boy in the class. He was almost thirteen. We sat down on the church steps and he told me a lot about Miss Daisy. She took in sewing for a living and was very poor. Mrs. Findley gave her a room free for helping with the housework, but Miss Daisy had to pay her own board. Mrs. Findley had a daughter named Sadie who was only twelve years old, but was already in the third class in High School. Everybody said she knew more than any teacher in town. I had never met Sadie Findley, but I had heard a lot about her. Leo Zerback's mother was always saying to him: "I'd be ashamed not to know the multiplication tables farther than the fours when little Sadie Findley is almost through geometry . . ."

"What makes Miss Daisy lame, Tommy?" I asked.

Tommy said he thought everybody in town knew that: When Miss Daisy was a young girl her sweetheart got her in trouble and then ran away with a beautiful bareback rider; so Miss Daisy had tried to hide her shame by throwing herself under the hoofs of a runaway horse. I wanted to ask Tommy what sort of trouble it was her sweetheart got her in, but I didn't say anything at all.

We always had fried chicken and charlotte russe for dinner on Sundays. It was hot in the dining room, but nobody seemed to care much. We had company to dinner: Cousin Katie and Cousin Ella Kendrick, who ran a truck farm near Morgantown, had driven over to spend the afternoon. They were big, sunburned women with rough hands, and they never talked about anything except tomato worms and how dear fertilizers were getting to be. Aunt Juliet made a great fuss over them, but I knew that she was really ashamed of them and that was the reason she invited them so often. Of course Mr. Charlie Hemmes was present too. He and Aunt Emmaline had been keeping company for five years, and he was like one of the family. He came every Sunday for dinner and spent the day.

Mr. Hemmes was tall and pale. He wore high starched collars and eyeglasses that hooked around one ear with a fine gold chain. I always had an idea that his head wasn't fastened on his neck at all, but was only balanced on top of his collar like an egg in an egg cup. That Sunday I got to thinking how funny it would be if his head should roll off his collar and break on the floor, and I started laughing.

"For Heaven's sake, what is Harry always giggling about?" asked Aunt Emmaline.

"Don't notice him," said Aunt Juliet. "If you notice him, you'll encourage him to act worse."

Uncle Carter reached under the table and patted my knee. He winked at me so that nobody else saw it. Everything was quiet for a little while and then Mr. Hemmes spoke to me: "Well, young man, I trust you liked your new Sunday school teacher."

"Yes, sir," I said. "Yes, sir, I did like her."

"Miss Burton is a most remarkable lady, I understand," said Mr. Hemmes.

Uncle Carter put down his knife and spoke to us all. "Dr. Atwood gave a talk to the Big Brothers' Council last week. His subject was 'Fortitude in Facing Life's Problems,' and he used Miss Daisy Burton as an example. Of course, he didn't mention her by name; he referred to her as a 'courageous little saint who lives on Cherokee Street,' but everybody knew who he was talking about. He said he had operated on her twelve times altogether, and he just didn't see how she kept going. She was in constant pain, day and night, he said; but people didn't realize that because she was always so sweet and cheerful. Every time he operated on her he was sure she would never come out of it alive, but she always did; and she came out smiling and without a word of complaint. He said he just didn't see how she stood the pain and that she should be an example to us all in meeting Life's adversities."

I had never heard Uncle Carter speak so much at one time. He had finished serving the plates and everybody began to eat.

"What complaint is Miss Burton afflicted with?" asked Mr. Hemmes. Mr. Hemmes taught English in High School.

I spoke up then: "Her sweetheart got her in trouble and then ran away with a circus rider, and Miss Daisy threw herself under the hoofs of a runaway horse to hide her shame."

Aunt Juliet put down her fork and looked at me with her mouth open, but Aunt Emmaline rolled her eyes at Mr. Hemmes and they both blushed and laughed a little.

"Harry Piggott!" said Aunt Juliet; "where did you hear such a thing?"

"One of the boys told me," I said.

"Who was it?" asked Aunt Juliet. It was Tommy Van Bergen, of course, but I pretended I couldn't remember. "Well, whoever it was, he ought to have his mouth washed out with soap," said Aunt Juliet. It was then that I found out what Tommy had told me was a lie, and that Miss Daisy really had tuberculosis of the hip. She had had it since she was a little girl.

When dinner was over, I told Aunt Juliet about the picnic and she said, "Well, I don't know whether a boy who talks like you do should go or not."

"Where are you going to have the picnic?" asked Cousin Ella. So I told them all about it. We had all eaten too much dinner and everybody was feeling drowsy. Cousin Katie kept talking about how a new kind of cutworm was killing her cabbages right and left, and Cousin Ella would say, whenever she stopped for a moment: "It just looks like it's one thing or another all the time!" Aunt Juliet was listening politely, but I knew she wanted to go back to her room and take off her corsets and put her wrapper on. "Tsch! Tsch!" she kept saying absently.

Aunt Emmaline and Mr. Hemmes had gone into the parlor and she was playing the piano while he sang. "Charlie Hemmes's got a real sweet tenor voice," said Cousin Katie sleepily. Aunt Juliet put her hand under her patent leather belt and loosened it a little. "He's a good, steady young man, too," she said.

"Mr. Hemmes ought to make a good match for Emmaline,"

said Cousin Ella. Aunt Juliet smiled and nodded her head. "We all think so," she said in a whisper.

"Aunt Juliet, can I go over and play with Leo?" I asked.

"Not on Sunday, Harry."

"Aunt Juliet—please!"

"Oh, let him go," said Cousin Katie, laughingly; "little boys don't like to stay indoors."

"Well, I don't know . . ." said Aunt Juliet. "I'm as broad-minded as the next one, but the Zerbacks are Catholics, and it don't seem right for Harry to be over there on a Sunday. If it was a weekday, I wouldn't say a word."

On the morning of the picnic Aunt Juliet woke me early, and at half past seven the wagon came by and I got in. Miss Daisy was sitting in the middle of the straw, with the boys grouped around her, and she seemed very gay. The lunch baskets were all piled up on the seat beside Zilk, the colored man who drove for the livery stable. Sitting next to Miss Daisy was a little girl with a long neck and teeth that stuck out. Miss Daisy said: "This is little Sadie Findley. She's going to help with the lunch and share our day." Sadie said: "Oh, how do you do?" in a drawling way and Ed Barron mocked her behind her back. Sadie turned to see what the boys were laughing at, but Ed's face was straight by then. Sadie Findley looked like she was always expecting somebody to ask her to bound Kentucky or to tell them the capital of Vermont.

I started to crawl in the back of the wagon, but Miss Daisy said for me to come sit by her. Everybody laughed at that, and so did Miss Daisy, and then she waved her hand and said in a gay voice: "Don't anybody listen—I've got a secret to tell Harry!" This is what she whispered in my ear: "I wanted you to sit by me because I like you better than the others!" A warm feeling that kept getting warmer came over me. "I like you, too, Miss Daisy!" I whispered back.

We had a fine time at the picnic. We went swimming in the morning, but Miss Daisy made Zilk sit on the bank and watch the whole time. Sadie sat under a tree, reading a book, and Miss Daisy hopped about on her crutches, fixing lunch. After lunch, Tommy Van Bergen jumped a half-grown rabbit, and all of us ran after him, but the rabbit went into a hollow log. Albert Gran said the best way to get him out was to make a fire inside the log, but Zilk said he knew a better way than that. He cut a forked stick from a willow tree and trimmed off the leaves and branches. Then he sharpened the forks until the points were like needles. He said the way to do it was to stick the sharp forks into the rabbit's hide and then twist it around and pull him out. Miss Daisy saw us dancing around the log and begging Zilk to let us be the one to pull out the rabbit, and she came hopping toward us on her crutches as fast as she could. "I'd be ashamed to torture a poor defenseless animal!" she said. "Oh, I'd be ashamed . . ." Then her crutch slipped and she fell down to the ground. Zilk helped her up again and Sadie handed her her crutches.

"You are a nasty lot of little boys," said Sadie, "and you ought to be—" But Miss Daisy reached out and put her finger on Sadie's lips, not letting her finish. "Don't say such things, Sadie!" she said gently. "Don't say such terrible things!"

We all helped Miss Daisy back to the spot where she had placed her pillows. A little later Zilk hitched up the team, and it was time to start home. Miss Daisy didn't say anything at all coming home. She had hurt her hip when she fell and her face was white. She lay stretched out on the straw, with her eyes closed, and she tried to smile. I kept wishing that she wouldn't try to smile that way. I sat close to her and she rested her head in my lap. The warm feeling kept coming over me and all at once I got very tight inside. I leaned over and pretended to tie my shoe, and when nobody was looking, I kissed Miss Daisy without her asking me to do it. Miss Daisy opened her eyes and smiled at me. Then she put her hand under the straw and held my hand and I knew that I loved her more than anybody in the world.

Mrs. Findley taught our class that next Sunday. She said Miss Daisy had been feverish ever since she got back from the picnic, but she hoped to be out again by next week. Dr. Atwood had been to see her several times, and he had decided another operation was necessary, but it could wait until the weather got cooler. So I told Aunt Juliet about Miss Daisy being sick and asked if I could go see her that afternoon and take her some flowers. Aunt Juliet said she thought that would be a nice thing to do. She also said I could take Miss Daisy a bottle of her best scuppernong wine. "Be sure and remember, now," she said; "a small glass before meals and a small glass upon retiring."

I knocked at Mrs. Findley's door and Sadie opened it. She took the flowers and put them in water. Mrs. Findley came in and thanked me for the wine; she was sure it would do Miss Daisy a world of good.

"Would you like to go up to Miss Daisy's room and see her?" she asked. Then, without waiting for me to say anything she spoke to Sadie: "Take Harry up to see Miss Daisy."

The room was bare except for a washstand and a bowl and pitcher painted with purple morning-glories, and some religious pictures on the wall. Miss Daisy was lying in bed when we came in. Her lids were closed and I thought she was asleep. She looked very weak and helpless. I wanted to put my arms around her, the way I used to put them around my mother when she was sick, and tell her not to worry, because she was sure to be well again before long. I felt a peculiar feeling in my throat, and I was afraid I was going to cry. I hadn't cried where anybody could see me for a long time. I walked over to the window and turned my back. "Please get well again, Miss Daisy," I whispered.

After awhile she turned on her back and opened her eyes. "This is Harry Piggott," said Sadie in a loud voice; "he brought you these pretty flowers." At first Miss Daisy didn't say anything, then she began to laugh and talk to herself. "She's out of her head again," said Sadie; "she doesn't even recognize us."

We drew our chairs close to the bed and listened to what Miss Daisy was saying. "They're going to operate on me again, and I can't stand it! I can't go through that pain again!" Her voice got so low we couldn't hear what she was saying, but tears kept running down her cheeks, and Sadie wiped them away with her handkerchief. Then she opened her eyes wide and looked about her, making a motion to show that she wanted to sit up. Sadie and I fixed the pillows behind her back and she seemed to realize for the first time that we were there.

She began to laugh sweetly. "Oh, you pathetic little fools," she said, "to sit there and feel sorry for me! You think you'll escape, don't you?" She turned her head away and closed her eyes. "Go away!" she said. "Go away! I hate the sight of you both!"

Then her voice became stronger and suddenly she began to curse and revile the Scriptures. She said she didn't believe in a future life, and the only thing that made her believe in God was the fact that He had tortured His own son on a cross. She talked that way for a long time. I felt my blood getting cold and my scalp began to prickle. If she had been screaming or making a loud noise, it wouldn't have been so bad, but she wasn't. She was talking in the low, sweet voice she used when she spoke to her class. Her lips were turned up in a gentle smile and if you were not listening carefully you would have thought she was reciting the class pledge instead of the words she was saying.

Sadie sat in a chair by the window and turned the leaves of a book. "Miss Daisy's delirious," she said.

Miss Daisy continued to talk. She said she hated everybody in town, but people were too stupid to know that. She wished a big fire would burn up the world or that a tornado would come and wipe out the whole human race. She said that only Nero could understand how she really felt because she, too, wished that the world had but one neck and that she could sever it with an ax.

"Nero didn't wish that," said Sadie in triumph. "That remark is generally attributed to the Emperor Caligula."

I got up from my chair and backed out of the room. I ran down the stairs and stood trying to open the latch on the door. Mrs. Findley came up and opened it for me. "Why, what's the matter, Harry?" she asked. "You're as white as a sheet." I didn't say anything at all. I just ran down the walk.

When I got to the old Porterfield place, I crawled behind the hedge and lay there for a long time. I kept thinking of the things Miss Daisy had said, but I thought most about her wishing the world had only one neck. I thought of the neck of the world as being the size of the molasses barrel in Mr. McArthur's store, and every time I closed my eyes, I could see Miss Daisy smiling sweetly and talking about love while she chopped at the neck with a bloody ax. Then I started to tremble. I tried to stop but I couldn't.

Old Mrs. Porterfield and her son Mr. Edward were coming across the lawn. I hoped they wouldn't see me, but they did, and they came over to where I was lying. "What's the matter, sonny?" asked Mr. Edward. "You got a chill?" I didn't say anything at all.

Old Mrs. Porterfield got down on her knees and lifted me up. "Now! Now!" she said. "You tell me all about it." She put her arms about me and tried to draw me to her, but before I knew what I was doing, I pulled away so hard that her glasses came off and she sat down in a flower-bed. Then I backed away from them, under the hedge.

"Nobody will ever fool me again!" I thought. "Nobody will fool me again as long as I live!"

1930

A SHOP IN ST. LOUIS, MISSOURI

OLD MRS. TATUM was often secretly amused at her daughter's lack of either imagination or humor, and she was, as often, pained at the contemplation of her barren, plodding life. "Mattie's the most curious girl ever you seen," she would confide to the widow Findley, across the intervening fence. "It's just work, work, work, with Mattie, all the time."

She had wanted Mattie to marry, like other girls, and have a family of her own, but Mattie had other and very definite plans for her future; or, rather, she had a single plan, a single idea, and everything she thought, said or did centered about it. The idea had come to her during her second year at the Beehive Store, after she had overheard a conversation between Mrs. Dunwoody and old Mrs. Wentworth, both of whom had traveled widely, and seen the world. Mrs. Dunwoody had said: "Mattie Tatum is too good to be working in a little town like Reedyville; she ought to have her own shop in New York or Chicago." And Mrs. Wentworth had answered: "I've never seen anybody with such an instinct for clothes. It sounds like an exaggeration, I know, but in my opinion there isn't a designer in Paris with half her natural ability."

And Mattie had knelt concealed, silent behind the counter, a smudge of dirt on her cheeks, her dull eyes suddenly bright. All that day she remembered the conversation she had overheard, and then she came to a decision. "I *will* have a shop of my own!" she said suddenly. "I'll save my money, and open a shop in St. Louis, Missouri!" (When she was a little girl her parents had taken her to St. Louis on a visit. It was the only large city she had ever seen.)

Mattie Tatum was a calm, unimaginative woman with an oily face and teeth that were never entirely covered by her lips. It was strange that one who did so much to make others beautiful should take no interest in her own appearance, but she was satisfied to remain a frumpish old maid who looked even older than her thirty-one years. She lived with her mother in a cottage on Cherokee Street, and her life was a narrow one with few companions and few pleasures. Occasionally she went to a movie, or a church social, with Katie Prestwood, her assistant at the store, but mostly she spent her evenings working on extra sewing or reading the current fashion magazines. She would pore over these magazines for a long time, examining photographs of actresses and society women in the rotogravure sections of the Sunday newspapers, stopping, occasionally, to speak to her mother. "That model ought to look good on Clarine Palmiller," she would say critically; "that is, with the waist-line raised an inch, and the skirt not quite so full."

Old Mrs. Tatum would agree hastily, and then there would be silence again. She was awed by her daughter's prominence in the community, and she would never, under any conditions, have disputed her. Then, too, she had not been well for the past year and she found it difficult to concentrate on anything that did not concern her ailments.

After Mattie had made up her mind, she thought of nothing except her shop and how to make it possible. She had only to close her eyes to see the shop plainly, her name, "Madame Tatum—Gowns," in bold gold-leaf on the window. With her usual thoroughness, she went into the matter from every angle, and she decided that she could not venture from Reedyville until she had at least three thousand dollars at her disposal.

And so she began saving her money with a methodical ferocity which startled her easy-going mother. She begrudged herself everything except the barest necessities of life. She took extra sewing at night: pleated shirts and fine, hand-made underwear for Mr. Kenworthy, Mr. Edward and Mr. Joseph Porterfield, and other gentlemen of the town. She even discharged the family washerwoman and did the work herself, bending over her tubs until two or three o'clock in the morning. But in spite of her thrift, her ceaseless pinching, the accumulation of her capital had not been an easy task. Then, after five years of working and planning, she saw a possibility of fulfilling her wish, and as her shop drew closer to reality, she could think of nothing else. Behind her calm, bulging forehead, her brain raced with excitement. At night she would lie awake for hours planning her shop, settling this or that detail. "Just think," she would whisper, "only a few months more and I'll leave this place forever." She would hug herself with excitement, and her tongue would make a caressing noise against the roof of her mouth.

She was thinking of her shop one night in October as she walked quickly down Cherokee Street toward her home, and ran up the steps. The house was dark. The kitchen stove was cold, and there was no sign of supper. She lit a lamp and looked about her. Then, suddenly she discovered her mother lying sprawled on the back porch, her head resting on the doorsill, the armful of wood she had been carrying scattered about her. She was groaning feebly, apparently in great pain. Mattie lifted her mother and carried her into the house. She said: "I'm going to call Dr. Lawrence this time, no matter what you say."

"I don't need a doctor, baby. I'll be all right."

Mattie became provoked. "I'm not going to have you suffering like this any longer. There's not any sense in it." She went into the hall, where the telephone hung, and picked up the receiver. Mrs. Tatum, who could hear her through the open door, began to groan and twist her head about. When Mattie returned to her mother's bedroom, she had taken off her hat and her coat. "Dr. Lawrence wants you to come to his office tomorrow morning. He's going to make a full examination," she said.

"There ain't no sense in that, Mattie; it's just wasting time and money." But Mattie did not bother to answer. She was busy removing her mother's clothes and slipping a nightgown over her shoulders. Mrs. Tatum began to whimper. "Suppose he says there's something real bad the matter with me. Suppose he says that." She pressed her face against her daughter and began to cry softly. "If there's something real *bad* the matter, I don't want to know it!" Then she added: "Don't make me go see that doctor! Please don't make me go!"

"Now, Mamma," said Mattie patiently. "Now, Mamma."

Dr. Lawrence had been in Reedyville only a short time. His methods were modern and impersonal, and he brought with him a considerable amount of laboratory equipment. When the examination was over, he called Mattie on the telephone, and she came to take her mother home. "Is Mamma bad off?" she asked. Dr. Lawrence nodded his head. "Yes," he said. "Very bad indeed, Miss Tatum."

Mattie stood, removing her shabby gloves. "Oh, I see," she said. "I see what you mean." Then, after a long time, she spoke quietly: "But there must be something you can do. There must be something you can do to *help* Mamma." And Dr. Lawrence answered: "An operation might prolong her life for a few months, but even that's doubtful, now." He glanced appraisingly at Mattie's run-down shoes, her worn coat and her faded hat. Mattie noted his glance and understood the thought back of it. A suspicious, defensive expression came over her face. "How much would it cost to have an operation?" she asked in a frightened voice.

"It would be expensive, I'm afraid, in the long run," said Dr. Lawrence. "You'd have to take her to New Orleans or Mobile."

Mattie sat down quickly, and linked her fingers together. So this was the way it was going to be. "Oh, I might have known something like this would happen," she thought bitterly. "I might have known." The muscles in her cheeks began to twitch, and her lips drew back suddenly from her long teeth.

"Would three thousand dollars be enough?" she asked.

"Yes," said Dr. Lawrence; "yes, I think so."

That night Mattie could not sleep. As she lay in bed, she tried to think of her mother's suffering and that she was soon to die, but that seemed relatively unimportant compared with the fact that her plans were now hopelessly disarranged. She would never be able to leave Reedyville! She would never have a shop in St. Louis! She adjusted her pillow, and lay there staring into the dark. Then a feeling of resentment came over her. "It's not right for me to go on sacrificing myself all the time," she thought. "I worked harder than a nigger for that money, and now I'm right back where I started from!" She lay awake for a long time, turning her problems over and over in her mind, but at last she got up and went to her mother.

"Mamma . . ." she began.

"What is it, baby?"

"I want you to have an operation."

An unaccustomed feeling of tenderness came over her. She put her arms around her mother and kissed her time and time again. Mrs. Tatum, unused to any show of affection, looked up at her daughter, flattered and somewhat embarrassed, and smoothed her limp, finely spun hair. "We haven't got money for operations, Mattie."

"We have, too; we got that money I saved."

"No, daughter," said Mrs. Tatum. "You got your heart set on a shop in St. Louis, Missouri, and I want you to go on with your plans."

Mattie bent down and kissed her mother. "It's sweet of you to be always thinking about me, but that money is yours, if you want it."

Mrs. Tatum sighed. "Just do whatever you think is right, Mattie," she said.

"No! No!" said Mattie in a frightened voice. *"You* say, Mamma! *You* say what to do!"

But Mrs. Tatum lay back on her pillow, her hands patient and waiting, her face tired with her monotonous years. She said: "I don't care. It don't make no difference to me one way or the other."

Mattie went back and lay on her bed. Toward daylight she fell into a troubled sleep in which she dreamed that she ran down a field, flying with outstretched arms over hedges and rivers and ravines. But when she reached the railroad station, her trunk came open and all her belongings spilled onto the floor. Everybody laughed at her shoddy equipment and pointed their fingers, and afterwards she could never make her things fit back into the trunk, try as she would. Mattie felt nervous and apprehensive because the train was approaching and she was not ready. The wheels of the train made a strange, rushing sound that steadily got louder. "Mattie Tatum! Mattie Tatum!" they said. "Oh, help me! Help me!" said Mattie to the people. "The train's coming and I'll be left." But nobody would help her. They stood there laughing and making remarks behind their hands until a waiter in a white jacket came out of the station ringing a bell.

Mattie got up and looked at her watch. It was six o'clock and somebody was ringing the doorbell. She tiptoed to the door and opened it. Miss Amelia Upchurch, one of their neighbors, stood before her. "I heard your ma was sick," she said. "I thought I'd better come over and help out. I said to myself right away, 'Poor Mattie can't work all day and take care of her ma too!' "

She was a wrinkled, heavy-lidded old woman who was never known to visit the well or the happy. Tragedy arrived and there at her elbow was Miss Amelia, a sour, snuffling old creature with a talent for sorrow. She stepped over the doorsill and walked into the room on her stiff, half-flexed legs. She took off her hat with its stuffed, moulting old bird, and hung her coat carefully on the hall tree. "You go get dressed before you take cold, Mattie. I know what to do for the old lady."

Mattie went back to her room. She unbraided her long hair and brushed it slowly. For a moment she had forgotten her problem but it came back to her intensified. Twice she stopped and the brush hung limply by her side. She thought: "This is a hard, mean world, and if you want to get anywhere you've got to be hard, too. Why should I give that money to Mamma for an operation?"

Outside she heard Miss Amelia rattling the lid of the stove as she went about preparing breakfast. Her mother was now awake. She coughed and called to Mattie in a frightened, querulous voice. "Look at Mr. Palmiller and Mr. Hardaway. Look at the two Howard boys, or anybody else who ever amounted to anything. They wouldn't hesitate a minute!"

At that instant Mattie put down her brush. The line of her jaw set defensively and a harsh light came into her eyes. "Well, I'm going to be as hard as the next one!" she said. "I'm going to St. Louis, Missouri, just like I planned to do."

Mrs. Tatum's death came earlier than the doctor had expected. It happened on a cold, rainy afternoon, six weeks exactly from the day Dr. Lawrence had made his examination. Everybody commented on how well Mattie was taking her mother's death. She went about the house putting things in order, neither helping nor hindering Miss Amelia in her plans for the funeral. Her calmness continued while she was being driven to Magnolia Cemetery, and through the sermon which Brother Saul Butler offered at the grave-side. She stood there quietly, aware only of the acid smell of new cloth that clung to her hastily sewn mourning dress and the black veil that draped her shoulders. Her mother's death and burial seemed an impersonal thing which concerned her not at all. But when the last prayer had been said, and the quartette commenced their song in slow, reverent voices, a strange change came over Mattie. "Why that's Mamma's favorite hymn!" she thought. Suddenly she seemed unable to breathe. She lifted her veil and fixed it over the brim of her hat. Her face was white, and she noticed that her hands were trembling. She began to move her feet about nervously. She clutched her fists together. "I won't give in!" she said. "I won't think about Mamma. I'll think about something else! I'm going to be just as hard as the next one!" She wished that the quartette would stop singing, but they went on and on. She lowered her veil again and clutched her hands together. "I *won't!*" she said between her teeth. "I won't give in!"

But something inside her, over which she had no control, seemed to lift her and push her forward. She fell to her knees in the wet clay and swayed her head from side to side. "Mamma! Mamma!" she cried in terror. "Mamma! Don't hold it against me!"

A group of neighbors came over and lifted her up and Mrs. Willis Overton held her protectingly. But Mattie pulled away from them, flinging her arms about. "Don't touch me!" she said in a shrill voice; "I'm not fit for decent people to touch." Without warning, she rushed forward and would have thrown herself into the open grave with her mother. She said over and over: "Take it, Mamma! Take it! I don't want it! Honestly, I don't want a penny of it!"

Later she had a recollection of being driven home seated between the Reverend Butler and Mrs. Overton; of Dr. Lawrence bending over her bed, giving her medicine to quiet her, and of the excited hum of neighbors in the room adjoining. Then she slept.

She awoke in the night. Her heart was pounding against her breast and there was a feeling of suffocation in her throat. She sat up in bed and lit the lamp beside her. She got up, unaware of the cold, and walked to her dressing-table, examining herself in the mirror; but the sight of her long, sallow face terrified her. "You're the meanest woman in the world," she said. "You really are." Then she covered her face with her hands and cried.

She lay on her bed again, her face pressed deep into a pillow. When she thought of her mother lying out in the cold rain, a sense of pain which was almost unbearable came over her, and she thought that she, herself, was going to die. She remembered the hard life her mother had led, and how nobody had really appreciated her. And now that life was over, and she would be forgotten. "Oh! Oh!" said Mattie. "Oh! Oh! Oh!" Her mind was in a turmoil. She was unable to think coherently, but she was sure of two things: She would never leave Reedyville as long as she lived, and she would not use for herself one penny of the money she had saved. The idea of a shop in St. Louis seemed unbelievable to her now.

At first she thought that she would take her money from the bank and burn it. (She felt that only after the money was destroyed could she free herself from guilt.) But as she lay on her bed thinking of Magnolia Cemetery and its poor, undignified graves decorated with shells and bits of colored glass, another idea came to her: She would erect a monument to her mother's memory with the money. She sat up in bed quickly, surprised that the idea had not come to her before. She looked at her watch and saw that it was a little past five o'clock. She would go to Mobile on the 6:22 and select the monument herself. She began to dress rapidly, putting on her mourning robe and pinning the black veil to her hat.

The monument arrived at last and was set up in the cemetery. It was made of white marble, and on it were carved two angels with expressionless faces. One of the angels stood upright and held a lily in her hand, as if undecided where to put it down, while the other figure, the bottoms of her feet upturned, knelt in an attitude of prayer. The monument dominated with its magnificence one entire corner of the cemetery, and made more trivial the graves that surrounded it. When it was new and bright, the people of Reedyville often came, merely to admire its perfection, but before the year was out it had become blackened by smoke from the Porterfield Foundry and Pattern Company, and fouled by the droppings of sparrows. Every Sunday and every holiday Mattie Tatum comes to sit by the monument. She is a middle-aged woman now. Her hair is thinning and has become gray, and her cheeks have pulled away from the bones of her face and droop downward in long triangles of puckered flesh. When she thinks how happy she used to be, sitting quietly in the lamplight with her mother, a feeling of despair which is almost unbearable comes over her. Her lips draw back in pain, the muscles in her throat twitch and tighten and her hands flutter upward and rest against her cheeks. Then she lowers her veil and wills not to remember, and after a time her face is expressionless again and her hands quiet.

She sits by the grave a long time. Occasionally she destroys a weed which has found foothold on the mound, and occasionally she gets up without reason and bends above her mother, picking up in her trembling hands the dead leaves which drift in eternally from the oaks of Wentworth Grove. "Don't hold it against me, Mamma! Don't hold it against me!" she whispers over and over, her stringy old neck bending low above her mother, her hands pressed tightly against her dry and shriveled breasts.

1931

HAPPY JACK

THE MERCHANTS PRINTING COMPANY faced Court House Square, and when work was slack, Jack Sutton, the proprietor, would sit back in a chair, his feet upon his littered desk, and smile at the people who passed his window. He was a small man with nervous hands, a jutting, deeply curved nose, and a round chin, delicately modeled, which did not seem to fit the rest of his face. After awhile, his friends would drop in, one by one, to talk. Jack was fond of people and he set great store by his friends. Secretly, he was pleased at his popularity in the town. Not even his peculiar views affected his standing. Everybody liked him, and joked with him, in spite of the fact that they thought him somewhat impractical, if not actually eccentric.

For example, a group would be discussing an actress or a society woman mentioned in the papers as having smoked a cigarette in a public place, and Jack would become excited and lean forward eagerly. "What's wrong with that, if she *wanted* to do it? I can't for the life of me see how smoking cigarettes has anything to do with her morals."

Mr. Palmiller spoke then, in his quick, waspish voice. "Would you want *your* wife, or daughter, to smoke a cigarette?" "Why, sure," said Jack; "that is if I had a wife or daughter."

"I'd hate to think what would become of the world if everybody felt like you do," said Ira Cunningham, shaking his head.

Then Jack would begin to laugh, the lines in his cheeks deepening. "Now, Ira, I'm not as bad as all that!" he would protest good-naturedly. After a moment, he would say more seriously: "Of course I can see your viewpoint, too, but I think you're wrong; you're looking at this thing the wrong way."

Then Willis Overton would speak up. "Jack doesn't really mean what he says; he's just talking to be different."

"But I do mean it!" said Jack earnestly. "I do mean it, Willis!"

Then everybody would laugh, and shake their heads. "Folks may think that way where you came from," said Ira Cunningham heavily, "but people here wouldn't stand for such things. No, sir, they wouldn't stand for such goings-on a minute!"

Later, when Jack had gone to Mrs. Findley's boarding-house, where he lived, he would think of these conversations. Then he would smile tolerantly. "These people are all right," he would think. "They pretend to be hard, and all that, but down underneath they are kind and charitable. I'm not fooled by what they say."

And so several years passed. The printing shop was prospering, and Jack felt that he was now a definite part of the town. Then one night a shocking thing happened.

Three miles from town, on the Valley City Road, a widow named Pierce ran a small farm. Her husband had been dead for some years, and, since that time, she had living on the place a Negro man called "Driver," who took care of the heavy farm work. The farm was isolated, and nobody paid much attention to the widow Pierce and her farm-hand until Mrs. Joe Cotton, in the course of her home missionary work, discovered that Driver and Mrs. Pierce were living together as man and wife.

There was considerable excitement when Mrs. Cotton made her report public, and the next night a committee of masked men called at the Pierce farm. There were eight men in the party, but they selected Ira Cunningham their spokesman, and the other men hid behind trees and bushes.

Ira walked up the steps and knocked on the door. Mrs. Pierce opened it a little. "I want to see your nigger, Driver," he said.

"What do you want to see him about?"

"I want to see him about training me a bird-dog for next fall."

"He ain't in here," said Mrs. Pierce.

"He's here, all right," said Ira. Then he turned and spoke to the men concealed outside. "Come on in; he's here all right."

The eight men pushed into the room and Driver stood there leaning against the back door, too frightened to run. His clean overalls were patched at both knees with squares of a darker material. The patches were crudely sewn, with no two of the stitches the same length, as if done by someone whose sight was failing. His shoulders were jerking and his jaw trembled. Sam Whittemore walked over and hit him in the face. Driver's head banged against the wall, but he made no effort to protect himself.

Mrs. Pierce began to throw herself about, but Bob Jowder and a man named Ellis shoved her into a closet and turned the key. She thrashed about on the floor and beat the partition with her fists. "I know the names of every one of you!" she screamed. "If you hurt Driver, I'll have you all arrested! I will! I'll have you all arrested, so help me God!" But the men paid no attention to her. They closed in on Driver, dragging him down the steps in the direction of the barn; and there, by the light of a lantern, a sack stuffed in his mouth to muffle his cries, the man named Ellis castrated him with a bone-handled pocket knife.

Before the eight men returned, late that night, the town somehow knew what had happened, and were talking about it in excited groups. But Jack Sutton did not hear of it until breakfast the next morning. One of his fellow boarders, Creary Berdine, had the exact details. Finally Mrs. Findley spoke up: "It's too bad that the law couldn't have taken its course, but Driver got just what was coming to him, I suppose." Then she spoke loudly so that the colored cook could hear her: "I hope this will be a lesson to the other Negroes in this town."

Jack sat there with a puzzled look on his face. "But why?" he asked. "Whose business was it? What difference did it make?"

Old Mrs. D'Alembert got up and threw down her napkin. "I won't stay to hear American womanhood insulted," she said. "I won't listen to it!" She looked at Jack furiously, tears of rage in her eyes.

"But I don't see?" said Jack. "I'm not insulting anybody." But

Mrs. D'Alembert withdrew from the room, banging the door behind her.

Then everybody laughed, but Mrs. Findley spoke to Jack, gravely. "We know you're only talking in fun, but you shouldn't tease poor old Mrs. D'Alembert that way, Mr. Sutton. You owe her an apology. You really do!"

Jack shook his head helplessly but he did not say anything. All that morning the matter remained in his mind, troubling him. At noon he went over to the Farmers National Bank to talk to Willis Overton, whom he considered his closest friend. "I'll admit it sounds pretty bad to an outsider," said Willis, "but what else could people do, in a case of this sort? You can't let a white woman live with a nigger that way!" "Why not, if it's what they both want?" asked Jack. "Well," said Willis, "it sets a bad example, I suppose." Jack's face became red with anger. He got up suddenly and overturned a chair. Then he sat down again, and looked at the floor.

Willis Overton was folding paper into squares, a distressed expression on his face. "You don't belong to the town, Jack, and you can't understand our viewpoint," he said. Then, as Jack Sutton rose to go, he came over to him and caught him by the arm. "Listen, Jack," he said, "you can say anything to me that you want to, but don't talk the way you have before other people. You can't do any good, and you'll only get yourself in trouble."

But Jack paid little attention to his friend's advice. All that day and for days following he talked of nothing except the affair at the Pierce farm. The more he talked about it, the more it seemed to oppress him. He stopped strangers on the street, going over his arguments again and again. Finally he wrote an article reviewing the affair, in which he defended the right of Mrs. Pierce and Driver to live together as man and wife, if they, as individuals, chose to do so. They hurt nobody, he declared, and nobody had a right to interfere or sit in judgment.

"The fact that Driver was a Negro, and Mrs. Pierce a white woman, has nothing to do with the situation," he wrote. "I am not going into that phase of the matter at all. I would feel as strongly about it if they were both white or if they were both black. That is not my point. But I do claim that they, as individuals, have a right to lead any moral life that suits them. If you people do not approve of the life they lead, then you, as individuals, have an equal right to have nothing to do with them. That is sound and simple. That, at least, is understandable. But for a mob to go out there and mutilate a human being who could not even defend himself, is unbelievable among people who call themselves civilized."

Sutton took considerable pains with his article, and when it was finished, he read it with a feeling of triumph. "When people read my arguments, they'll see the matter in a different light," he thought. "They'll be ashamed of themselves, then. You may be sure of that." Later Jack printed the article on his press and sent a copy of it to every resident in the county.

At the end of the week a farmer named Jim Prouty came to see Jack. Jim was about fifty years old. He wore high starched collars without a necktie, and when he was a boy his left eye had been blinded by a blow from a stone. Jim sat down and took from his pocket a copy of Jack's pamphlet, tapping it, for emphasis, against his knee. He came to the point at once: "I wanted to come by and shake hands with you, Mr. Sutton," he said, "because I believe you're a straight thinker, and I wanted to tell you I believe what you say is right."

Jack leaned forward impulsively, in his old manner. His eyes were interested and eager again. To himself he kept saying: "I knew it! I knew people would see this thing, once they had it put before them in the right way!"

"Yes, sir," continued Jim, "you've got the right slant. I've knowed Driver for more than twenty-five years, and there wasn't a better nigger in Pearl County. He wasn't to blame. I guess any nigger would have done the same thing, if a white woman give him the chance."

Jim blinked his blind eye, over which a dirty, phlegm-like film had formed. "Yes, sir, any nigger would have acted the same way, I guess, and, like you said, that mob shouldn't have harmed him none." For a moment Jim sat silent. Then he nodded his head a couple of times. "What the boys *should* of done," he added, "what they *should* of done, when they went to the farm that night, was to take a big needle and a piece of copper wire and sew up that sorry Pierce woman. That's what they *should* of done, I guess!" Then, before Jack could say anything in reply, Jim walked out of the office, mounted his saddle mule and rode off down the road, the sun beating on his white collar, the hooves of his mule kicking sand into the air.

When he had gone, Jack Sutton sat motionless; then, on a sudden impulse, he went to his door and bolted it, as if the town frightened him, and he wanted to shut it out. After that he lowered the shades in his office and sat in semi-darkness for a long time.

Later he got up and walked away from the town. When he had gone about three miles, he turned off from the road, through an abandoned field, and went toward the creek that fed James Lake. It was late in June and the air was very still; the sunlight beat down on the old field, leaving a shimmer above it. Beside him the creek moved quietly, and in the bay trees that grew thickly, birds chirped. Jack lay on his side and held his hand in the water, feeling its coolness. His head felt hot and tight and he trembled at quick intervals. Then, for some reason, he remembered why he had come to Reedyville to live, why he had picked it above all places. Suddenly he felt foolish, and he began to laugh at himself mockingly. He was glad now that he had never told the story to anybody, not even to Willis Overton; but when he had been a young man, during the Spanish American War, he had found himself, along with many other soldiers, on a troop-train bound for New Orleans. On the third day of the trip he had awakened to realize that the train was no longer in motion. He sat up and rubbed his eyes. All about him were men sleeping heavily, their arms and legs thrown wide, and there was, in the coach, an odor of cigarette smoke, breath, and perspiration so sharp that he could almost taste the stale odor on his tongue.

In disgust, he put on his clothes, walked to the end of the

train, and looked about him. To the left of the siding was a cottage flanked by crêpe-myrtles cut back to make a hedge, now in full bloom, with blossoms scattered on the grass. In the night, spiders had spun webs over the hedge, which had caught and held dew, and as Jack watched, the sun came up between two trees, slanting the cabin with its light and turning the drenched webs into fire. Then a cow bell sounded from a field a long way off and a bird repeated, three times, a single note that was incredibly liquid and moving.

At that instant the place had taken on a meaning beyond the scattered blossoms, the blazing cobwebs or the slow note of the bird. An eager look came into his eyes. "Everything is so quiet," he had whispered; "everything is so quiet, newly washed and beautiful." Then he had stretched his arms wide and held them out to something which he did not understand and had thought: "Some day I'm coming back to this place. This is where I want to spend my life."

As Jack remembered his gesture, he began to curse and to laugh harshly. Before him, at the edge of the old field, two mice came and looked at him, twitching their whiskers. Then he stood upright, but the sense of terror which had made him walk into the country came over him again more sharply. His knees felt weak, suddenly, and he lay down again by the stream, breaking up twigs and throwing them into the current.

But when the sun was low in the sky, he got up, feeling stronger, and more calm, and bathed his face in the stream. Then he brushed off his clothes, turned and walked toward Mrs. Findley's boarding-house. It was late when he reached it, and supper was almost over, but he seated himself, with the other boarders, and began to eat. Then immediately he put down his fork and laughed loudly, his eyes crinkled into a tight line.

"Well," said Mrs. Findley, "tell us the joke, so we can laugh too." But Jack did not answer. His nose was drawn down and white, and his round chin began to tremble. "Tell us the joke," Mrs. Findley urged. "Tell us the joke, Mr. Sutton." Jack did not hear them. His voice had become hysterical and shrill, and tears ran down his cheeks.

Mrs. Findley became alarmed. "Mr. Sutton!" she said sharply; and then, again: "Mr. Sutton!" Creary Berdine and Harry D'Alembert came over and shook Jack's shoulders. At their touch, he slid from his seat and fell to the floor, and lay with his face pressed into Mrs. Findley's red and green rug.

An hour later they had undressed him and put him to bed. They tied his arms and legs with clothes-line and bound him to the bed with trunk straps. All that night and all the following day Jack continued to laugh. "I see what you mean!" he shouted, over and over, "but I'm the only one who really understands what you're driving at! You've got the right slant on things, and I'm glad to make your acquaintance!" Then he would fling himself upward, trying to free his hands and legs, the iron bed making a thumping noise against the floor. At length he would lie back and begin laughing again. "A needle and a piece of wire was all you needed!" he would say. Then he would start laughing again.

A crowd of people gathered in front of Mrs. Findley's gate, and she went out and asked them to move on. "It's Mr. Jack Sutton," she explained. "We don't know what it is, yet, but it's some sort of fever. You'd better not stop. It may be catching."

Bob Kirkland listened to the unending laughter for a moment and spoke up: "I don't care if I do catch it, if it makes me feel as happy as Jack!" he said. Later on his answer was repeated many times, and the nickname caught on at once. The whole town discussed Happy Jack Sutton and his strange sickness. Then, three days later, he stopped laughing as suddenly as he had begun. But he seemed to have shriveled during his sickness. His face was pasty, his lips were drawn back from his teeth and the lines in his cheeks had deepened. On the afternoon he returned to his shop, a committee of his old friends dropped in to congratulate him on his recovery, but Jack would not see them. He stood locked in his office and spoke through the door. "Get out of here!" he said, "get out and don't ever come back—any of you!" Then his lips drew tight, and he bared his teeth. His head shook back and forth in a caricature of mirth, but no sound came.

That week he moved from Mrs. Findley's boarding-house, and slept on a cot in the back of the shop, eating his meals at the Deerhorn Cafe when it occurred to him that he was hungry. He began to avoid everyone he had known, and he would even stare at people with such a look of cold contempt that they were uneasy. Soon the people of the town began, in turn, to avoid him, and they would draw away, apprehensively, at his approach. His business fell away rapidly, and soon there was no work for him at all. Six months after his sickness his equipment was seized under an attachment and sold at sheriff's sale. Jack stood there indifferently. He was penniless. He had no place to turn and no way to earn a living for himself.

An old friend of his, Adolph Moore, came over to him. "Where are you going to live, Jack?" he asked. Jack did not answer. He shrugged his shoulders and turned away. Something about his frail, drooping figure touched Adolph. "I tell you what, Jack," he said. "I got a room fixed up over my livery stable. It ain't much to look at, but you can stay there, if you want to. I can pay you a little," continued Adolph, "for helping with the horses and watching the place at night. It won't be much, but it'll be better than nothing, I guess, until you get on your feet again." Jack did not look up. He stood thinking. Then he nodded his head, turned, and followed Adolph Moore.

The room was dark, and during rainy weather it leaked. At one end was a small iron stove, its legs resting on four cans of packed sand. Above the stove was a pine shelf containing a can of condensed milk, a sugar bowl with a tin spoon protruding, and a bottle of catsup which had begun to ferment.

And so a new life began for Jack. He would work for hours, drawing a curry-comb across the flanks of the horses until they were like satin, watching the wrinkles of delight that ran behind his stroke. In time each horse came to have for him a distinct individuality, and when nobody was around, he would sit on a box facing the stalls and talk to them. Often he would tell them about the time he stood at the end of the troop-train and watched the sunrise and the blazing cobwebs. "As the train moved away," he would say, "an old man with a hoe on his shoulder was crossing the tracks, making a swishing noise as he brushed through the grass. I stood there waving my arms and shouting at him; but the old man was deaf, and at first he did not understand what I wanted to know. Then the train began to move faster, but the old man ran after it, his hoe jerking up and down, his hand cupped to his ear. 'Hey? Hey?' he kept saying in a cracked voice. At last he understood what I wanted to know. 'Reedyville!' he shouted. 'This town is *Reedyville!'* Then he sat down on the track and wiped his face and neck with a handkerchief."

Jack would laugh his soundless laugh, his eyes shut, his face twisted. He would rock back and forth on the box while his whole body trembled to his silent mirth. When he had finished, he would begin to cry angrily. "One of these days I'm going to tell this town what I think of it!" he would say. "You just wait. I'll tell them yet. You'll see!" But the horses would make a whinnying sound and look at him with their soft eyes, nuzzling his cheeks with their lips.

Occasionally, when the regular drivers were busy, Jack would be called to take a traveling salesman to Morgan City or Hodgetown, but this happened rarely. His sullen manner and scowling face alarmed such strangers, and they generally preferred waiting until one of the regular drivers returned. Then, too, he had grown incredibly tattered with the years. His finger nails and ears were caked with dirt and there was about him a strong odor of the stables. He was never asked to drive any of the local people; they would not have risked their lives with him. They considered him a madman, and were of the opinion that he should be locked up.

"I saw that Happy Jack on Oak Street today," Mrs. George Wheeler would say to her Wednesday afternoon Rook Club. "I had to hold my nose, he smelled so bad! He was walking along with his lips moving, but when he saw me, he stopped and looked at me in a way that made my blood run cold! Then he stopped, and began to laugh without making any sound. His face was twisted up until he looked like a monkey."

"Something ought to be done about him," said Emmaline

Hemmes; "I don't know what this town is coming to. He ought to be put in an institution!" Then the ladies would put down their cards and discuss Happy Jack for a long time.

But Jack cared little what people thought of him. As the years passed, he went into town less and less, and finally he did not leave the stable at all, except when he had to buy food for himself. He would come into McArthur's grocery regularly at five o'clock of an afternoon, holding in his hand a slip on which was written his list of groceries, and wait silently until Mr. McArthur, or his clerk, Chester Penny, took the order. He always spent his money in unusual amounts, such as eleven cents' worth of flour, eight cents' worth of molasses, or six cents' worth of kerosene. If there were other customers present when he entered the store, they would move away and glance at him out of the corners of their eyes.

Then, later, as he walked down the street, his purchases clasped to his breast, people would step to one side of the narrow, wooden sidewalk, giving him the right of way. Often he was pointed out to strangers: "That's Happy Jack Sutton," they would say. "He had a fever fifteen years ago, and he hasn't been right since."

And so the years passed, and there was Jack Sutton, an old man with a stooped back, spindling legs and gray hair that hung soiled and matted to his shoulders. It would have been hard to recognize in this feeble creature the young soldier who stood at the end of a train, more than thirty years before, with eager eyes and uplifted arms. A new generation had grown up in the town since that time. They knew nothing of his early life. They remembered him only as a village character, a furious old man with bleary eyes and teeth rotted and broken with decay. Indeed, Jack's teeth had troubled him for a long time. Often at night they ached so badly that he could not sleep. At such times he lay in bed making a sound that resembled the whinnying of the horses in their stalls below. At last an old Negro man named Zilk, who hung around the stables, offered to pull Jack's teeth, and one night, when he was in special pain, he consented. Afterwards he lay on his bed, a soiled rag pressed against his gums. Then, on the second afternoon, he went to McArthur's grocery, to buy corn meal and milk to make gruel.

It had rained steadily that day and a misty rain was still falling as Jack walked down Lipscomb Street, stepping over puddles of water that stood undrained in the street, the few coins he possessed clutched in his palm. Then he turned into Oak Street and approached the store. When he entered, the other customers drew back in fear. But almost immediately a gasp of surprise went up, and everybody began to nudge his neighbor and whisper behind his hand. They looked at each other in a puzzled manner, uncertain if this man were really Happy Jack. For the loss of his teeth had made a startling change in Sutton's appearance. His nose was pinched at its roots and bent downward, and his face foreshortened and folded back, and as he stood there, grasping the counter for support, his body weak and breathless, even the dullest person could see that Happy Jack was not a dark figure to be feared; he was only an old man with vacant gums and a deflated face who could harm no one.

Chester Penny, Mr. McArthur's red-headed clerk, wrapped up Jack's parcels, and placed them before him. Then, from a bin behind the counter, he scooped a handful of Brazil nuts and placed them in Jack's open palm, along with his change. He winked knowingly at his other customers. "Hey, Happy Jack," he said, "crack these nuts, and you can have 'em!" Chet held his sides and laughed explosively at his joke, and everybody laughed with him. Jack stood looking from face to face, surprised, unprepared for this new attitude. Then, quickly, he flung the nuts at the clerk's head. But everybody laughed more than ever at that. They doubled up with laughter, shaking their fingers at him and clucking their lips as if they were talking to a child. "Tsch! Tsch! That's no way to act, Happy!" they said. "That's no way to act!"

Jack picked up his purchases and walked from the store. A crowd of half-grown boys and men had formed outside. "Hey! What's your rush, Happy!" they said. "Where you think you're going, anyway?" Then the crowd blocked his path, surrounding him, and began pushing him about and pulling his beard and his long, matted hair. One of the boys kicked his heels in the air and began to bleat like a goat. "H-a-a-ppy J-a-a-ck!" he said. "H-a-a-ppy J-a-a-ck!"

"Look out!" said Chet Penny from the doorway, "look out he don't *bite* you!"

Jack stood with his back to the store, examining each face as if he wanted to fix it in his mind forever. The crowd became larger and the sidewalk was blocked. People from adjoining stores peered from their windows, or stood in the street, to watch the fun, as Jack, his body shaking, his jaws working, backed slowly away. But when he reached the edge of the wooden walk, somebody stuck out a foot, and somebody gave him a push, and Jack tripped and fell into a puddle of water. He lay on his back in the mud, his purchases scattered about him, the meal sack broken and spilling slowly, the milk mixing with the mud and giving it a rich coloring.

Then he stood on his unsteady legs and faced his tormentors. His wet clothing adhered to his body, outlining its frailty, and particles of mud smeared his face and clung to his beard.

"And so I says, 'Crack these nuts,'" repeated Chet Penny from the doorway, laughing again at his joke. "I says, 'Crack these nuts and you can have 'em!'"

Willis Overton, an old man with a neat white beard, was pushing his way through the crowd. "Don't!" he said in a kindly, protesting voice. "Don't tease him! Don't tease the crazy old man!"

Jack turned then and stared incuriously at Willis, as if he had never seen him before, at the yapping, excited faces that surrounded him, at the town itself. Suddenly his lips began to move. "I'm not crazy," he said; "I wish to God I was crazy!" Then he stood erect, squared his bent shoulders. "Now is the time," he thought; "now is the time to tell these people what I think of them!" He opened his jaws and began to talk rapidly, but with his teeth gone, and his cheeks sucked in, his voice came out of his throat cracked and reedy, like a cheap whistle, hissing against his gums with a lisping sound, and the things he was saying, which he had thought profound as he lay in the dark room over the stable, seemed absurd now, even to himself.

He quit talking as suddenly as he had begun and stood there in silence, his chin working patiently to touch the tip of his nose, his arms hanging limply from his shoulders. He raised his arms and pushed at the air, as if to repudiate the town and what it stood for; then his face twisted up and his eyes closed; his lips trembled, sucked in, and puckered out slowly, and if he awaited a kiss.

The boy who could bleat like a goat began again to kick his heels in the air. Then everybody began to laugh and bleat like a goat, their voices rolling in confused volume over the roof tops, toward the sky. "H-a-a-ppy Jack!" they shouted. "H-a-a-a-ppy J-a-a-ck!"

1931

THIS HEAVY LOAD

IT WAS a dilapidated brick house, with sagging balconies and rusty, iron grill-work. Mrs. Southworth, the landlady, who was intended by nature to be a bos'n on some sailing vessel, but who, by mistake, had become a woman instead, showed me her vacant room and stood with her hands folded under her apron, her iron jaw clamped down. "All right, find fault with it, and see what happens to you, my fine sailor man!" I imagined her thinking. But when I told her the room would suit very well, and paid her for a week in advance, she became more cordial.

Later she invited me downstairs for a drink. We had three together, and by that time we were excellent friends. She began to tell me about the other people in the house: Across the hall from my room lived a man named Downey, and Mrs. Southworth didn't quite know what to do about him. He hadn't paid her a cent of rent for the past two weeks, since he lost his job, and why she let him stay on was a mystery to her! Only there was something about him, something she couldn't quite understand. But what he ate, or how he managed to keep alive, was something she couldn't figure out. He spent all his time sitting by his window, carving on a block of wood, or looking at the river, deep in thought. "If it was *you,* now," she continued, "I'd have you out in the street, bag and baggage, before you knew it, but *this* fellow . . ." She paused and shook her head, as if puzzled.

That night I saw Downey for the first time. He came out of his room as I was coming up the stairs, a paper parcel in his hand from which minute shavings were spilling. His skin was porcelain-like in its dry brittleness, and his eyes were sunken. The lines in his cheeks and in his forehead were so deep they seemed cut there with a knife. When I passed him on the stairs, he stopped and held on to the banisters for support. Then I spoke to him, and he looked up quickly and stared into my eyes; and I understood why even a realist as hard and as unimaginative as Mrs. Southworth couldn't throw him out. There was the same eagerness in his eyes that you see occasionally in the eyes of a dog mourning for his lost master. I looked at the lined face and his full, sensuous mouth for a moment. I said: "I understand we are neighbors. I've just taken the room across the hall until my ship is ready. I'll be glad to have you come in and talk to me sometime."

"Thanks very much," he said gravely. That's all there was; he didn't commit himself one way or the other. As I went to my room, I saw him still standing there by the banisters watching me. A few nights later he did come to my room. He sat in my one chair, without movement. He seemed even frailer and more exhausted than when I first saw him. I took out a bottle of whiskey from my bag and offered him a drink. He shook his head. "There's no answer in that," he said; "there's no comfort there."

"Well, maybe not," I replied; "but it'll warm up your belly nicely."

Then, somehow, I began to talk to him about my early life. I talked simply, without pose or affectation. For some reason I put myself out to please him. He listened gravely, sympathetically. When I had finished, he in turn began to talk about himself. He came of well-to-do people, I think. At any rate he had gone to college and had got his degree. The next year he returned to his hometown and married the girl he had loved since boyhood. Then war had been declared and he wanted to enlist. There had been a scene with his wife when he signed up at the recruiting station: He was married with a wife and two babies to look out for; there was no reason for him going to France. Leave that to men without obligations! But he had gone anyway. He didn't know why; he simply knew that he must go. He had come through the fighting without injury; or rather he came through without bodily injury, but what he had experienced and what he had seen shocked him profoundly. He must have been an idealistic, highly emotional man with little actual knowledge of the world.

He did not tell me all this in its proper sequence, of course. It came out by fragments which I pieced together in my mind later on. As he talked I kept looking at his strange face and tried to find a word or a phrase which would describe it, but I could not. "Austerely sensual," was as close as I could come, but that, I realized, was pompous and high-flown; and it was not quite what I wanted, anyway. But Downey was talking again in his somewhat hoarse and somewhat hesitant voice.

"When I got back home, I felt that the end of the world had come, and that I was left alive by accident," he was saying. "I kept thinking that all the time. I had been sure, once, of what was evil and what was good, but I knew, now, that those things were only words, meaningless in themselves and taking significance from other words equally meaningless and equally subject to change. I was lost in a strange world that frightened me."

As Downey talked, I could imagine his efforts to readjust himself. He had hoped when he was discharged that a return to normal life would solve his problems, but he found very soon that that was impossible. He had nothing in common with his wife any more; the deep sense of understanding which had existed between them was gone. He began actually to hate her for what he considered her smug sense of right and wrong, her constant talk of religion. He got so he couldn't stand the sight of his children either. An overpowering feeling of restlessness came over him.

One night his wife got him to go to church with her. It was the first time he had been in a church since he had enlisted. He sat in his pew, slightly sickened, not believing any man could be as harsh and as stupid as the minister seemed. Then he got up, walked out of the church and went back home. When his wife arrived half an hour later she found him in their living-room swinging an ax, smashing the furniture to bits. That same night Downey went to a friend of his, a lawyer, deeded everything he owned to his wife and children and left town.

As Downey told me his story, all jumbled up and not in its proper order, as I'm telling it to you, his voice was without emotion, and his body was quiet. Occasionally he moved his hand backward and forward on the arm of the chair, and occasionally he wet his full, sensual lips. Then suddenly he lowered his eyes. We sat there in silence, neither looking at the other. I offered him a cigarette, which he took. From the way he sucked it into his lungs I knew it was the first smoke he had had for a long time. I thought it better neither to offer comment on what he had told me, nor to ask him to continue. A few minutes later he got up and went back to his room.

After that, Downey came to see me often. He never talked so freely as he had the first time, but in the next week he did tell me a great deal about himself: After he had left his wife (he had never seen her since, and he had no wish to see either her or his children), he had gone to Chicago and had got a job as motorman on a streetcar. At night he went to the public libraries and took out books, books on philosophy and religion mostly, but he could find nothing in them that he wanted. Then —Downey thought this himself—he became slightly insane. He began writing obscene pamphlets in which he proved that there was no God; that there could be no God. Later on, he went to New York and worked in a restaurant as a dishwasher. At night he read or wrote his rambling, profane pamphlets. Occasionally he would talk to late-comers in the restaurant, trying to convince them, as he had convinced himself, that the skies were empty. But the taxi-drivers or the workmen to whom he talked laughed at him and tapped their foreheads.

From New York he drifted to Philadelphia, where he remained for a few weeks. But his restlessness came over him again. He had been in Omaha, New Orleans, Detroit, Denver, St. Louis, Kansas City and Seattle within a short time, but he remembered nothing of those places except the various furnished rooms he had lived in, and even they, because of their lack of individuality, had gradually merged in his mind into one composite room. Many times he could not find work, and more often than not he was hungry, but something inside him impelled him constantly forward. He did not know what he was seeking, or even that he was seeking anything. He simply knew when the impulse came over him that he must get away.

As he talked in my room, he could not remember the names of some of the cities where he had been. He would refer, often, to places as "where the man in the United Cigar store had a gold tooth in front," or, "where the landlady was in mourning for her daughter," identifying an entire community with one of its members.

As the years went by, he found it more and more difficult to get work. Then, too, he had started to drink pretty heavily. In Cleveland, Ohio, he met a waitress and they lived together for a time—not more than a month or so, I gathered—but he had left her, too. She had really loved him, he was sure, and he might have been happy with her, but when the urge to run away came over him he could not resist it.

Later, in Detroit, a man in a rooming-house started him using drugs, and after that his descent had been swift. He had quit reading. He had quit thinking. He worked when he could get work and stole or begged when he couldn't. There was nothing that he hadn't done, he told me, no degradation that he hadn't experienced. He told me these things quietly, without self-consciousness and without shame, as if he were speaking clinically about another person whom we both understood.

The drugs-and-drinking period had lasted about three years, he thought, and then one morning in Frisco, in an agony of disgust with himself, he had signed as a seaman on a sailing vessel. His going to sea was not premeditated. He did it on impulse, without thought. He felt, dimly, that he might find in a foreign country what he had looked for and been unable to find in America. He did not find it, of course, but the trip improved his health, and when he returned to the United States, six months later, his desire for drugs had left him. After that he had gone to sea regularly for a few years, but he rarely made two voyages in the same steamer.

Then, finally, he had been unable to get a ship at all, but he managed to keep himself alive by doing odd jobs around the docks. Later he got a job as delivery boy for a grocery store. It was while he was so employed that he came to live in Mrs. Southworth's dingy rooming-house, about a month before I met him.

He told me all this over a period of days.

"What is it you want?" I asked. "What are you looking for?"

"I don't know," he said. "I wish to God I did know. If I knew that, I could lay down this heavy load and rest."

We sat smoking quietly. We had come to the point where we would sit quiet together for long periods. "Where did you learn wood-carving?" I asked casually. He looked at me, but he did not answer. "Mrs. Southworth told me that you were carving a block of wood," I continued, "and of course I saw you taking out those shavings that night."

His lips opened and he seemed on the point of telling me something, but he changed his mind. "I'll be going now," he said. When he reached the door he turned and came back to me: "You're not offended, are you?"

"Of course, I'm not," I answered; "why, of course, I'm not." Then he went out. "He'll tell me about the carving later, when he is ready to do it," I decided. I was correct, for sure enough he did tell me. My ship was out of drydock by that time and was going on loading-berth the next day. It was my last night in Mrs. Southworth's establishment, and my bag was almost packed when Downey rapped on my door. It was January, and the weather was cold. Outside a mist-like rain was falling. The wind flung the chill rain against my window in intermittent rushes, like the brushing of leaves.

I opened the door and Downey entered. I stood gaping, amazed at the change that had come over him. His step was brisk and his eyes were shining. He seemed to have dropped his sickness, his hunger and his despair like a shabby coat. There was a buoyancy, a joyousness about him that I could not understand, and which I was not prepared for. When he came into my room, his shoulders were straight and there was color in his lined, haggard face. He kept moving about and touching things with a surprised delight. His clothes were soaked, and I could see the raindrops clinging to his frail neck and chest, but he seemed unaware of the cold, as if there were something within that warmed him. He sat back in my chair and laughed deeply, the contented laugh of a happy man—it was the most restful sound I have ever heard—and began to talk slowly, trying to find words simple enough to describe his happiness. He raised his hands and brought the blunt tips of his fingers together.

"I have found what I have been seeking!" he said. "I have put down my load!"

For awhile he talked incoherently, but gradually I began to follow his sentences, and piece out his story. It was while working as a delivery boy for the grocery store, before I met him, that he had picked up a block of wood. He had been taking a walk along the bay front that Sunday afternoon, and he saw the block on the dirty beach, just out of reach of the tide. The wood was a golden brown color, and unlike any wood he had ever seen. Apparently it had grown in a far country and had been thrown overboard from some ship by a sailor. When Downey picked up the block and turned it over and over in his hands, he saw that the wood was strangely grained, and, as he examined it, he thought he could detect in its looped and whirled surface the outline of a head. When he discovered that, he sat down and began to trace with the blade of his pocketknife the figure in the wood.

He sat flat on the dirty sand, the block resting between his legs, and worked slowly. Before him was the bay and a small beach littered with driftwood, tin cans and grapefruit rinds, while behind him, somewhere in the distance, a switch engine was spotting cars of freight for a steamer working overtime. The rhythmical bumping of the cars, as the engine hit them and shoved them forward, came muffled and uncertain, and more and more indistinct, until, at last, the sound lost its meaning for

Downey and became the booming of surf a long way off. And as he continued to work, the dirty beach disappeared also, and another and an older scene superimposed itself. This is the way Downey described the change to me:

"As I sat there carving on the block, I thought of myself not as a middle-aged delivery boy for a cheap grocery store, but as a naked brown man who had crawled out of the protection of his jungle for the first time to stare in amazement at the sea. Behind me stretched hot, misty swamps with purple and red flowers, larger than a man's head, swinging like bells from the trees. Birds, colored unbelievably, were screaming always on one persistent note, flapping back and forth between the ancient trees, or resting, balanced on the swinging lianas, their wings half flushed and ready for flight. Ferns grew as tall as cliffs, and there was a rich mist hanging over everything. And as I sat there looking into that jungle, a strange thing happened to me. I lost all sense of time and space and even of my own identity. I seemed so completely a part of the background I visioned. I could see my own body sitting there—a little, patient, brown man, making a god from a piece of curiously grained wood.

"Later, when it became dark, I returned to my room, carrying the block with me, stroking it with my hands. I had become obsessed with the block; so much so that on the following morning, when it was time to go to the grocery store, I found that I could not. I really made an effort to go out of the room and leave the figure which was taking shape under my hands, but it was impossible."

That had been three weeks ago and since then Downey had worked patiently. He knew nothing of wood-carving, he told me, and he had no tools to work with except his knife and a crude scraper which he had made out of a safety razor blade.

At first Downey had been somewhat ashamed of what he was doing, but as he continued to work the idea gradually took a firm hold on him. "Why shouldn't I make a god of my own?" he asked. "Why not? I could not accept the gods of other people." His eyes closed and his lips pressed forward with a faint quiver, as if recently touched, in love, by other and unseen lips.

"What was there absurd about that?" he asked. He sat in his dark room hour after hour carving and whispering to himself. "I am creating a god of compassion and tenderness. I am not making him all-wise or all-just or all-powerful. I am creating an eager god who loves joy, laughter and dancing; not cruelty, not bloodshed. 'Sing!' he says. 'Sing and love and dance, for the world is a beautiful place and life is something strange which passes quickly!' "

Downey continued to talk, a slight, self-deprecatory smile on his lips. I did not interrupt him. There was nothing that I could say, after all. Suddenly he got up and raised his arms above his head in a gesture of complete adoration.

"Today I completed the figure and polished it with oil until it shone like a rich lamp in my room. I stood there looking at it. It was not a very good carving, but I had made it, I alone, and I loved it! Then I began to feel half ashamed because it had taken such a hold on my thoughts. I put the figure on the table in my room, and stood aside to examine it critically, with half-closed eyes; but before I understood what was happening, I found myself on my knees before it, my head thrown back, my hands pressed together, rocking from side to side. Words came tumbling out of me, words which I had not used for a long time: 'Lord! Lord!' I prayed. 'Heal me! Save me! Make me whole!'

"Then an essence flowed through my body. I could feel it moving about in my veins, washing me clean. I could feel tight things, buried in my body for a long time, being loosened and untied by the essence and smoothed flat again. My flesh tingled with a new life. Then, as the essence surged back and forth through me, like a river, all grief, disgust and shame were washed away, and a feeling of rest such as I had never before known came over me. I knelt before the figure for a long time, at peace, my heart swelling with joy and love as if it would burst through my side."

Downey got up and walked to my window and stared for a time at the river, seen indistinctly through the rain. It was still blowing, and gusts of wind swept the rain against my window with a faint sound, like thrown sand. He stood there, silent, watching the rain swirling over the river, watching the lines of black smoke from factories breaking under the force of the wind and coming together again. Then, after awhile, he began to talk in his joyous, new voice:

"A long time afterwards, I got up from my knees and went out and walked in the rain. I had forgotten how beautiful red brick could be, or the way wet asphalt reflected in a shallower world the things that surrounded it. I wanted to touch everything with my hands: the red bricks, the iron posts, the rough bark of trees. I wanted to feel everything, see everything, and hear everything again. And so I walked in the streets for hours, surprised that the world was so much lovelier than I had thought it; watching the way a tree bent against the wind, the shape of a cloud scurrying across the sky, or raindrops congealing and dripping slowly from the end of a green blind. Somewhere during my walk a woman came to a window and said to someone else within: 'Get the blue; blue wears longer.'

"As I walked the streets, I kept turning those words over and over in my mind. To me they possessed a beauty not of this world, a significance beyond the stretch of our dull senses." Downey laughed joyously and pressed his hands together. "Do you understand what I'm trying to tell you?" he asked.

"Yes," I said.

He was silent for a moment and then he continued: "Later on, I saw a man walking toward me. He was an old Negro, and he carried a sack filled with junk slung across his shoulders. I went over to him, to help him with his load, but he pulled away, as if I meant to rob him. I had wanted to tell him about my new happiness, and to share it with him, but when he pulled away, I saw how wrong I was. That was the mistake people had always made. I knew, then, that I must never show my god to anybody or even speak his name to another."

Again Downey walked in my small room. "I'm so happy," he said; "so perfectly happy. Nothing can ever touch me again. Nothing! Pain, hunger, old age, death—they're meaningless words, now! They're nothing to me at all!" Then he lifted his enraptured eyes and stared into the sky at a vision which I could not follow.

I got up and began to finish my packing, looking occasionally at Downey standing by the window, watching his exalted face. And I knew, then, for the first time that man is not yet a completed thing; that he is only part of other things which he cannot name and which he but dimly understands. He must have a master if he is to have peace, and if he loses one, he will not rest until he has found another. He talks eternally about freedom, but he can never be free, for he is a frail, lost creature, too weak as yet to walk unaided.

I closed my seabag and snapped the lock, saddened all at once because these things were true.

1931

THE ARROGANT SHOAT

WHEN Rancey Catonhead was a fine, strapping girl of eighteen, her Aunt Lucy Hargrove, who lived in a brick house in Reedyville, came down with a spell of break-bone fever. Aunt Lucy had no children of her own. She lived alone with Uncle Henry, a good man, in many ways, but one totally incapable of taking care of a sick wife. What was more natural, then, than the letter he wrote his sister-in-law asking if Rancey could visit them during her aunt's convalescence?

Rancey was very excited over the letter. She wanted very much to go to Reedyville, of which she had often heard. She danced about in her thick-soled, man's shoes, her sunbonnet thrown back and hanging down her shoulders. "Let me go, Ma!" she pleaded. "I'll take the best keer in the world of Aunt Lucy. I never yet been nowheres, and you know it!"

Mrs. Catonhead was rinsing a mess of collard greens when Rancey read the letter to her. She lifted a leaf in her hand, against the sunlight, and pinched off a damaged spot with her stained thumb and forefinger. "We'll see," she answered. "We'll see what your poppa says."

And so, a few days later, Rancey's few possessions were washed, starched, and carefully mended. Len Williams, her father's farmhand, made a chest of seasoned poplar for the journey. Since the chest was for Rancey, he took considerable pride in his work. He planed and tinted the wood, and then studded the chest with an intricate design in brass and copper nails.

Mrs. Catonhead packed the box, kissed her daughter quickly, and off Rancey went to Reedyville.

It was the first time in her life that she had been more than a mile or two from the farm on which she had been born. Len Williams had hitched up the farm wagon. He drove her to the railhead, and saw her safely on the train. He brushed off a seat for her and arranged the box as a foot rest; then he stood in silence. Rancey had hardly spoken during the drive to the railhead. She did not speak now, but continued to look at her folded hands, as became a young girl embarking on a journey. But when the conductor called "All aboard!" she glanced up shyly and smiled at Len; and Len bent forward and kissed her ineptly on the chin. Then he ran out of the coach and stood red and embarrassed on the platform. Rancey saw him through her window. "The nerve of Len insultin' me that-a-way!" she thought happily.

Aunt Lucy was much better than Rancey's mother had expected, but the fever had left her weak. Uncle Henry said it was only a question of keeping her cheered up until she got her strength back.

Aunt Lucy was a huge woman with the unbelievable breasts that sculptors carve on heroic figures. She lay propped with pillows, a lace cap covering her thin, grayish hair.

"Well," she said. "So you're Debby's oldest girl?"

"Yes'm," said Rancey; "guess I am."

"Land sakes!" said Aunt Lucy, laughing in spite of herself, "don't you know for certain?"

Rancey laughed too, and after that she and her aunt were good friends.

Aunt Lucy had married well. Her brick house, with its fine furnishings, was a constant wonder to Rancey. On an easel in the parlor was a picture of a church set upon a lonely moor. Lying all over the moor was snow, which the artist had represented by bits of mother-of-pearl glued to the canvas; and above the church was a round moon, many times the size of what a moon should be. Back of the picture, on a shelf, rested a small kerosene lamp. One night as a surprise Aunt Lucy lighted the lamp for Rancey, and in the darkened room the moon shone out brightly from the canvas; peaceful light streamed through the church windows. The snow in the foreground sparkled and gleamed like opals. Rancey thought the picture was the most marvelous thing she had ever seen. "Oh!" she said in a rapt unbelieving voice. "Oh! . . . Aunt Lucy!"

"It's a real nice picture," said Aunt Lucy, striving to hide the pride in her voice. "There's not another one like it in Reedyville, I guess."

But as wonderful as Aunt Lucy's house was, Rancey marveled even more at the eccentricities of the fine ladies of Reedyville. She had never before seen anything like them. There was one proud lady in particular who carried a long-haired dog, and who had a nigger boy to walk behind her carrying a red sunshade. Rancey had never imagined anything so impressive.

Before Rancey came to Reedyville, a circus had been there; its posters were still clinging to fences and barns. Rancey, from her aunt's shuttered windows, could see these posters plastered to the fences opposite. She could see men and women dressed in tights flying through the air and grasping one another's hands. Then there were lines of elephants walking sedately behind each other, with strange, dark men astride their necks. There were striped tigers with mouths like red caves. But the picture that interested Rancey most of all was posted against Moore's Livery Stable. It showed a tall, stout lady with yellow bangs, before whom waltzed a young pig. The pig waltzed solemnly, elegantly, as if aware of his importance and proud of the gold chain around his neck. Below the picture were the words: "Mlle. Marie and her pet: The world's most intelligent pig."

Rancey would stand before Moore's Stable and look at that picture by the hour. Even when she thought about it at night, she would become excited. "I bet I could train me a pig, too, iffen I put my mind to it, and iffen I had ere a pig to train," she would think.

She talked about the lady with her accomplished pet so much that one day Uncle Henry brought home a tiny Berkshire pig for her. When he had seen it in a farmer's wagon before Court

House Square, he had thought immediately of Rancey, and what she had said about wanting a pig of her own to train, and the farmer had sold him the pig at once.

And so the weeks passed pleasantly. Aunt Lucy was almost well once more. She was walking about her house now, and commencing to take an interest in things again. Rancey had grown fond of her. Then there came a letter from her mother saying they needed her at home on the farm to help with the younger children. Rancey hated to leave Reedyville, but, as Aunt Lucy said, she could come to see them again sometime; so Rancey again starched and ironed her belongings, and packed them neatly into the poplar chest.

She slipped back into her old life without effort. Cotton picking was coming on, and she had little time to remember the things she had seen in Reedyville. The little Berkshire pig throve with Rancey's devotion, and grew quickly into a fine, arrogant shoat. He was so tame that he followed Rancey everywhere, and it was almost impossible to keep him out of the house. She taught him to stand on his hind legs and turn around clumsily. Rancey called it round-dancing, and even her mother laughed at that. Often she tried to tell her mother about the picture with the lamp behind it and about Mlle. Marie, and her trained friend, but her mother never had time to listen to any story to its end.

But if her mother was too busy to listen, Cliff Catonhead was always an audience. He was still in checked-aprons, the youngest of the children, and he was Rancey's especial care. She would walk with him, during the hazy fall afternoons, to the footbridge that spanned the *bogue,* the shoat trotting behind them. Then Cliff would sit wide-eyed while Rancey made the pig stand up on his hind legs, his forefeet bending delicately at their joints, and turn round and round, as if he never meant to stop.

"I'm a-goin' to get me a job in a circus," she would say; "and I'll wear spangles. I'll wear me some pink tights, too! Let them that don't like it say their say; what do I keer!" And Cliff, always silent, would stare at her with his solemn, sweet eyes, and thrust his thumb into his mouth.

Sometimes Len Williams, who never let her out of his sight for very long, would come down to the footbridge and peer under at them. Often he would see Rancey sitting quietly sewing, the shoat uprooting the earth at her feet, with Cliff asleep against her breast. One day he too sat down beside her. He bent his lips until they rested against her strong, young neck, and before Rancey knew it, she threw her arms around him. "I don't keer whether I travel with a circus or not," she said; "I don't keer ere a bit about travelin' with a circus!" At her words the shoat turned and squealed. Then, from force of habit, he rose on his legs and circled time after time; but Rancey could not see her shoat, because her face was pressed against Len Williams' overalls.

That night Len asked Mr. Catonhead for Rancey. Len was a good man; he saved his money and he was buying a place of his own in the north end of the county. Nobody could rightfully object to him, so old man Catonhead said they could marry in October, after the cotton had been ginned, for all of him; but the trouble was, he didn't have any money for wedding dresses, and Rancey would have to get along with what she wore for Sunday. He would give his consent to the wedding, and throw in his blessing to boot, but that was about all he could do with things the way they were. This shamed Rancey a great deal. She thought over the matter for several days, trying to solve her difficulties, and then she came to a conclusion. The shoat had grown enormously fat and sleek under her care. She would sell him at market and buy a proper wedding dress with the money. She had to get rid of the shoat anyway; she couldn't keep him forever. A married woman would have a house to look after.

That fall she and Len married, and for a few years she was too busy in her new home, helping Len with the farm, and taking care of the Williams children, which came, for a time, as regularly as the years themselves, to think much about her old home, or to grieve over leaving it. She thought of herself as a matron, settled for life. But when she was thirty years old, her father died. Rancey went back to the farm for the funeral. She thought her mother looked old and peaked, and the place had changed.

She, herself, felt changed also, and out of place, and she was anxious the whole time to get back to her own family.

Then, a few years afterward, her mother also died. Both she and Len went that time. They left the children at home. That same year her brother Cliff married one of the Cornells girls. Just think of little Cliff married! It made Rancey want to laugh. Why, Cliff was only a baby when she left home, and now little Cliff was a man, getting married! Well! The thought of Cliff's marriage brought back, somehow, memories of her shoat, and she got out the pink ribbon which he had worn when he was small, and which she had carefully folded away at the bottom of her poplar chest. "Oh, well," she thought, "he brought a good price at market, anyway!"

And so the years slipped by. It was surprising how quickly they passed. Here is Rancey Williams with grown children, with a boy old enough to be wanting to enlist in the army and fight Germans. That struck Rancey as funny. There were several German families in the county, now. She remembered one old man in particular who wore a pair of light blue pants and who played on a horn. And little Len wanted to go shoot Germans! She had to laugh at the absurdity of people.

The next year Millie, her oldest daughter, wanted to marry. She had picked out a man named Jim McLeod. He wasn't the sort of man Rancey would pick to marry, but if Millie had her mind set on it—

Millie had her mind set on that one thing. "But, Millie, you're so young to be a-gettin' married!" said Rancey.

"I'm older than you were when you got married," said Millie.

There was no getting around that. There wasn't anything more for Rancey to say. A few days later she opened the poplar chest and took out her wedding dress. She went to Millie with a smile, the dress across her arm. "I'm a-goin' to wear my wedding dress at *your* wedding, Millie," she said proudly.

"Oh," said Millie. Then, after a moment, she added reproachfully, "But Mamma . . ."

The smile left Rancey's lips. She felt her spirits droop. "What's the matter with it, Millie?" she asked.

Millie sought for words: "But, Mamma, don't you see? It's all out of style. People don't wear clothes like that any more."

So that was it. Millie was only worrying about her old mother. She wanted her mother to look as well as anyone else at the wedding. But little Rancey cared what folks thought, or whether or not they laughed at her. Let them laugh! There was little enough fun in the world anyway! "Don't you worry, Millie," she said. "I won't keer ere a bit if folks laugh fit to bust."

Millie looked at her in silence, irritated at her stupidity. "But, Mamma! Be sensible! Of course I don't care what you wear, but Jim's folks will be there, too, and they're particular."

Rancey thought a moment before nodding her head. "All right, Millie; it won't make no difference to me. I want you to have your wedding like you want it, honey." She went back to the porch and looked at the dress in the morning light. It was out of style, there was no getting around that, and the silk had lost some of its luster, and was beginning to crack where it had been folded so long. Then, for some reason, Millie and her earnestness struck her as funny. She began to laugh. She folded the dress back into the box and wrapped tissue paper around it.

After Millie and Jim married, they went to live in Morgantown, but twenty-five miles didn't seem such a distance any more. People got about quicker. There were automobiles everywhere, now.

More years passed. Things were easier on the farm. There wasn't so much work to be done. Rancey started putting on weight about that time. She had once been proud of her small waist and her fine body, but somehow it didn't matter now how fat she got. She would stand before her mirror and look at herself. Her neck was thick and reddened and there were rolls of fat across her shoulders. Her throat flowed to her breast in great corrugated ridges. "If Millie Marie had a-looked like me, nobody could a-told which was the *pig,*" she thought. Then she would go sit on the porch and rock and watch the road. The country was getting more densely settled. New people were coming in all the time, and the old settlers were dying off or moving out. It was surprising how many people passed up and down the road in a day.

Millie, to her mother's surprise, seemed bent on carrying on the family tradition for fecundity. There was always a baby at the McLeod house. They were prospering, too. Rancey would rock and rock and think of them, a tender smile on her lips. At night she tried to spend her time sewing, but she discovered that her eyes were not so good as they used to be. She had to call Marie, her second daughter, to stop her housework and come thread the needle. When she made a dressing-sacque for herself one night out of the wrong side of the flowered goods, she was very provoked. The children laughed at her for her mistake, and she was hurt. That night she cried for the first time in years. It wasn't the way she had cried when they told her about little Len being killed in a foreign land—that time people heard her crying as far away as Tarleton's store—but quietly and hopelessly. It was all so senseless. There was no reason for her crying that way.

The next week Len took her to Morgantown to visit Millie and Jim, and while there an oculist fitted her with glasses. Her teeth were getting bad; they hurt her a great deal. But Rancey had made up her mind that she would never sit in a dentist's chair, no matter what happened. The idea terrified her. Len had all his teeth pulled out and a plate fitted that trip. Both Millie and Jim spoke to each other about how stubborn Rancey was getting as she grew older.

It was about that time that Rancey began talking to the children about her wonderful trip to Reedyville, and what a fine house Aunt Lucy and Uncle Henry had lived in. She talked of the strange ways of the city ladies, with their white hands and their fine manners, and of a ruby ring which Aunt Lucy had worn on her finger. She mentioned the wonderful picture her Aunt Lucy had had, with snow made out of pearls; but mostly she talked of the shoat that she had raised on a bottle and taught to round-dance.

"I sold my shoat, though," she said. "Yes, sir, I sold him! When they taken him away, he tried to stand up in the crate and do the steps I'd learned him, a-squealing all the time, but the crate was too small for him and he kept bumping his head and falling down. He kept squealing and waltzing and knocking his head until the man had drove out of sight down the road. Then I run behind the branch and hid in a thicket of gall berries until your gramper come down and made me go up to the house." Suddenly Rancey began to laugh. "Law," she said. "Law! What a skittery girl I must a-been!"

But somehow the children didn't seem interested in her trip. They would listen politely enough, but when she had finished talking, they would go away quietly. It wasn't any fun telling about things if folks didn't ask questions! But Rancey excused them: They were young, and there were so many other things to occupy their minds.

One spring day Rancey complained of a pain in her stomach. She had felt the pain off and on for some months, but she hadn't said anything about it. A woman of her age couldn't expect to be without some sort of ailment; it would pass off. But the pain got worse as the weeks went on, and that spring day she told Len about it. Len insisted on taking her to Morgantown to see a doctor. She resisted, ridiculing the idea that anything serious could be wrong with her, but in the end she gave in.

The doctor was young and brisk. There was about him a clean smell of scented soap and carbolic acid. She was suddenly ashamed of her fat old belly. She wanted to tell him that she had once had a fine figure and had been considered pretty, but she realized the doctor wouldn't care one way or the other. After the doctor had finished his examination he stood thinking for a time. He prescribed some medicine which stopped most of the pain. So Rancey went back home with Len, but she couldn't get out of bed any more. Everybody was very kind. The neighbors used to send in little things for her to eat, or stop Marie or one of the other children and ask about her, but often Rancey did not know this, because the medicine the doctor had given her made her drowsy. Sometimes, however, in spite of the drugs her mind was alert and she would sit up and look about her, completely conscious, completely aware of her surroundings. She was in such a condition one Sunday afternoon when Sarah Tarleton, a friend of many years, called.

"You must hurry and get well, Rancey. You got so much to live for."

"I'm a sour and a disappointed woman," said Rancey. "Death can't come too soon for me."

"You must think of Len and the children," continued Sarah in her exact, stilted voice. "Len is a good, steady man, and your children all turned out a credit."

"Len's a man like any other; and as far as the children go, I don't see where it makes ere a bit of difference whether they were born or not. My whole life was throwed away."

"No woman who has made a home and brought up eight children has wasted her life," observed Miss Sarah sententiously.

"Janie Barrascale raised fourteen. Who cares? I wish now I'd a-taken my shoat and run off to a circus, like I started to."

One night Rancey died in her sleep. Millie and Jim came as quickly as they could. Len sat on the front porch the next morning smoking his pipe and feeling lost and uncomfortable. The fact that he wasn't working made it seem like a Sunday. Rancey's death wasn't exactly a shock. They had all been expecting it for a long time. Millie came out on the steps and sat down beside her younger brothers and sisters. Her father and Marie were talking about Rancey's good traits. Marie started crying again, and Millie couldn't help crying too, try as she would not to.

All that morning Len rocked back and forth on the porch in his chair, his mottled, sparse neck stretched forward like the neck of a guinea cock. "She made me a good, contented wife," he kept saying to the people who came on the porch to sit beside him and offer comfort. "We had a sweet, full life together."

1932

PERSONAL LETTER

Hamburg, Germany,
December 17th, 1932.

DEAR MR. TYLER:

I wrote you a long, official letter last week and forwarded same via the S.S. *Manhattan*. That letter, which should be in your hands by the time you receive this, contained information you wanted regarding berthing facilities, pilotage in and out, tug hire, stevedoring costs, etc., etc. If I failed to cover any point that you had in mind, or if any part of my report is not detailed enough, please let me know, and I'll remedy the situation promptly.

As you will remember, you also asked me to drop you a line under private cover regarding my personal impression of this country, and that is what I would like to do in this letter. I have thought a good deal about the best way to accomplish this, and have come to the conclusion that the easiest way to do it is to simply recount a little incident which happened the other night in a cafe.

First, let me say again that the agents you have in mind for representing us here are very efficient and have co-operated with me at all times. Herr Voelker, director of the agency, has been especially helpful. He is an intelligent and highly educated man. A few nights ago, he asked me to have dinner with him and attend the opera later, which I did. After that, he suggested we take in a beer cafe that he knew of, and so we went there, too. This place was pretty well filled up when we arrived, mostly with men in storm trooper uniforms. I won't explain who they are, as I covered that point in my first letter under the heading of Political Situation and Future Outlook, to which I refer you.

Well, Herr Voelker and I went to the basement bar and ordered our drinks, talking together all the time. We were speaking in English and discussing business matters and things in general, and at first I didn't notice that a group of these storm troopers had closed around us, shutting us off from the others at the bar.

To make a long story short, the leader of the group touched me on the shoulder and told me that I was in Germany now, and that while I was in Germany I would speak German or nothing at all. Most of these North Germans speak English very well indeed, since they have eight years of it in school, and so, naturally, this fellow spoke English, too.

I twisted around and looked these boys over, but they only held their backs stiffer, threw out their chests and frowned, just like something out of the opera I'd just seen. I still couldn't believe I'd heard correctly, and so I said, "Were you speaking to me?" And this leader answered in a voice which trembled with anger, "I repeat for the last time. When you are in Germany, you are to speak German. If you cannot speak German, you are to remain silent. Is that clear? We will endure no further insults from foreigners."

By that time I was sure it was some sort of a gag which Herr Voelker and the boys had cooked up for me. You know the sort of thing I mean, don't you? Like the time at the Traffic Association dinner when they played that joke on Oscar Wilcoxon. If you remember now, a girl with a baby in her arms burst into the dining-room just before the speeches began. She asked if there was a man present named Oscar Wilcoxon, and when the master of ceremonies said that there was, she demanded that he marry her, like he had promised to do, and give a name to his child.

Everybody was in on the stunt except Oscar himself, and it got a lot of laughs. Oscar kept trying to explain that somebody else must have been using his name illegally, because he'd never seen the young lady before in his life; but this girl had been carefully coached in her part, and the more Oscar tried to explain matters, the worse things got. I kept thinking to myself at the time that if anybody pulled a trick like that on me, I'd fall right in with the gag and say yes, I was the father of the baby all right, but I couldn't be sure about the mother because it was always so dark in the alley back of the pickle works where we met.

Well, when the storm trooper said what he did about not speaking English in Germany, I wanted to laugh, it struck me as so comical, but I didn't. I'd already decided to play it their way and pretend to take the whole thing seriously. So I kept a straight face and said, "You gentlemen would like others to believe that you are real Germans, but you are not real Germans at all. If a real German heard what you have just said, he'd cover his face with shame."

I waited a moment and then added, "If you were real Germans, like you pretend to be, you'd realize that since I'm not a German, but an American, that I'm not as bright as you are. You'd know that Americans haven't got your culture, and that we haven't had your natural advantages. Americans think slowly," I said. "They don't master languages the way you do." Then I sighed and turned back to Herr Voelker, as if the subject was ended, as far as I was concerned.

The storm troopers seemed nonplused at my attitude, and they went into a huddle at one end of the bar. My German isn't the best in the world, but I could understand most of what they said without any trouble. The gist of it was that I was right, and that they were wrong; that even though I was a foreigner, I had the true philosophy. Well, I let them talk it over for a while, and then suddenly I wheeled around and gave them the other barrel. "A true German doesn't expect the same perfection from inferior people that he expects from himself," I said. "I thought that was something everybody knew by this time."

I said all this in a quick, stern voice, Mr. Tyler, and the troopers straightened up and stood at attention while I gave them a thorough dressing down. At the end of my speech, I said, "So you see? If you were true Germans, and believed in your mission, you wouldn't humiliate me before my friends. Oh, no, you wouldn't do that at all! Instead, you'd come to me as a teacher and say, 'Let me instruct you in our beautiful language! Let me explain to you our wonderful way of life!' " I waited a moment and then said sadly, "No. No, you are not true Germans. You only pretend to be. And now go away please before I lose the last of my illusions."

I nudged Herr Voelker with my elbow and winked behind my hand, but he only raised his eyes and stared at me over the edge of his glass. By that time there were tears in the eyes of the leader of the troopers. He apologized to me in great detail. He wanted to buy me a drink, to prove that everything was all right, but I thought I'd keep the thing going a little longer, and played hard to butter up. Finally, I did let him buy me a drink, and then I bought him one in return. I thought, then, that the joke would break, and the laughter and the explanations come, but that didn't happen, and I began to feel a little uneasy.

Not long afterwards, Herr Voelker and I got up to leave. When we were outside, Herr Voelker said he was sorry such an unpleasant incident had occurred, and that he would have prevented it if he had been able to do so. He said he thought I had acted with rare presence of mind in being frank and aboveboard with the storm troopers, instead of trying to lie my way out of the situation. I was so astonished that I stood still on the pavement and said, "Did you think I meant what I said? An intelligent, educated man like yourself? Did you really believe I was in earnest?"

And, before God, Mr. Tyler, Herr Voelker drew himself up haughtily and said, "Why shouldn't I think you meant it? Every point you made was logical and entirely true."

Mr. Tyler, I've often read in books about an icy hand which clutched at somebody-or-other's heart. I never before took the words seriously, thinking it was just a phrase that writers used, but now I know that it's a true expression. That's exactly the way I felt as I walked along with Herr Voelker until we reached the taxi rank on the corner, and I got into a cab alone, and went back to my hotel.

Now, maybe there isn't anything important in the incident, but I think there is. There's something going on beneath the surface here as sure as you're a foot high. I don't quite know what it is so far, but I do know that it's something horrible.

This turned out to be a long letter, didn't it? I suppose you'll be receiving it during the Christmas holidays, so let me take this opportunity of wishing you a happy Christmas and a prosperous New Year. People here celebrate Christmas in a big way. They gather together in groups, sing songs about the Christ child, and weep over the loved ones who are far away. It is the season of love, goodwill, and the renewal of old affections, or so Herr Voelker tells me. He invited me, as a special compliment, to spend the day in the bosom of his own family, so I could see first hand what a German Christmas is really like; but I expressed my regrets, and said that business obligations made it necessary for me to be in Paris on that day. To tell you the truth, Mr. Tyler, everybody here frightens me a little—they are all so full of sentiment and fury.

With best regards, and again wishing you the compliments of the season, I remain,

Sincerely yours,

ROBERT B. MCINTOSH.

1932

THE TOY BANK

ARTHUR'S birthdays were exciting events largely because his grandfather sent him a present on that day, something unusual, and not to be anticipated like the toy his mother bought for him, or the single handkerchief, with his name, Arthur Kent, worked in one corner, which came each year from Aunt Lida in Tennessee; but this year the gift from his grandfather had not arrived, and it was already afternoon and he had been six years old for almost a whole day.

It was spring and he went into the back yard and sat under the china-berry tree that grew there like a giant umbrella. Even if Grandfather had forgotten him, or thought him too big for presents any more, it was something which he must accept, as he accepted all the incomprehensible doings of grown folks. Before him, on the beaten, grassless earth which lay like a circle in the tree's shade, Argentine ants were crawling in an implacable circle, their heads lowered as if smelling the earth for guidance, their long bodies sucked sharply at the waist, as if drawn taut, with thread, into two exact ovals.

Arthur leaned against the tree and closed his eyes. His birthday this year had been unsatisfactory as a whole, for his father had been away for almost a year, and there had been no toys at all from his mother, only sensible things which he needed, such as stockings and a new cap. Above him the china-berry tree was loaded with tiny, lavender flowers, but they were already a little past their full bloom, already shriveled a little and crisped at the tips of their minute petals; and bees flew in and out making a drowsy, comforting sound. From the house came his mother's voice, summoning him:

"Arthur? . . . You, Arthur?"

Her voice, when she called him this way, was always uncertain, rising on the last syllable of his name as if she asked a question, as if she pondered his reality. He got up and went to her.

"I want you to run down to the grocery for me," she said. "Here! I've written out a list of things to get. Then go to the butcher shop and ask Mr. Long to give you a pound of stew-meat." All at once she became gay. "When you've done that, you may stop at the drugstore and ask them to send a pint of ice cream at six o'clock."

Arthur's eyes opened wide. "Chocolate or strawberry?"

"Whichever you decide. It's your birthday and we'll have a celebration."

She laughed and touched his head, but almost at once her laughter died, her gaiety vanished. She was counting the coins again and frowning, annoyed and helpless before their inadequacy. "We won't have the ice cream after all," she said. "We'll have it another time."

"But you promised," said Arthur. "You promised; you know you did!"

"We'll have it another time, Arthur. There'll be lots of other times."

Arthur put on his new cap and went out of the door, a puzzled look on his round face. Why had his mother promised the treat and then gone back on her word? He sighed. It was incomprehensible, and there was no sense in trying to figure it out. He must simply accept it as a thing which grown people did, a thing which he could not understand.

He was busy with these thoughts when he returned to the house. His mother saw him and came out to the gate to meet him. She said that the postman had called during his absence and that the present from his grandfather had arrived, after all. It was a toy bank made of iron and trimmed with nickel. It was shaped like an old-fashioned safe and rested solidly on four small legs. Arthur held the present in his hands feeling its weight, excited and slightly disappointed.

"What is it?" he asked. "What is it good for?"

"Why, it's a bank. It's for saving money. I think it's very nice, don't you?" She laughed bitterly. "Very nice, and in extremely good taste, too. Oh, very appropriate!"

The front of the bank could be opened like the door of a vault, and the key which unlocked it was looped through one of the bank's handles with a pink ribbon. Arthur inserted the key and turned the lock. The door swung open and two crisp, one-dollar bills, folded with a piece of notepaper, dropped to the floor. His mother picked up the note and read the message which his grandfather had written:

MY DEAR GRANDSON:

You are getting old enough to learn thrift and about the value of money. You will find soon enough that it is the only thing you can rely upon in this world, and if you have it you will be independent of everything and everybody. I hope this small gift will be the nucleus of your future fortune, and I wish you a very happy birthday.

Your obedient servant,

JOHN M. KENT.

At that instant the bank became very precious to Arthur. He had not understood the letter entirely, but he felt that his grandfather had given him a talisman against his uncertainty and terror. There were so many things to be afraid of: his father's long and mysterious absence from home, his mother's shabbiness, her worry and her sudden fits of crying. But most of all the toy bank was a thing to protect himself and his mother against the world which lay all about them, the menacing world that his mother knew but of which she did not speak.

Arthur locked the two bills inside his bank and carried the key on its ribbon around his neck. When he shook the bank and listened he could hear the rustling the notes made as they brushed against the iron sides of the cage; and then, one day, he had an idea: he would take the bills and change them into small coins, and each night before he went to bed he would drop one of the coins through the slit in the bank's top. When he told his mother of the plan, she smiled and nodded, and that afternoon the grocer changed the money for him. He went later to the butcher and the druggist, reducing the coins to smaller and smaller amounts, and by nightfall he had forty nickels in his pocket. One of these he dropped into the bank immediately; the others he put into a tobacco tin and hid them under his shirts and underwear.

Each night after he had said his prayers and his mother had gone away, he took a single coin from the tobacco tin and dropped it into the metal bank, listening to the clinking sound it made as it struck the side of the cage. Gradually the bank became heavier and heavier, until, at last, the final coin was deposited. It was then that Arthur gave the key to his mother to keep, as if he feared that he would lose it, or that he might be tempted to open the door and spend the money he had saved; and every night before he went to bed he would lift the bank from its position on the mantelpiece and feel its weight, listening to the sliding sound the coins made as they shifted from side to side at his whim.

Sometimes he would take the bank in his hands and hold it for comfort as he sat in the shade of the china-berry tree. It was late June now and the sun was hot. The tree was covered with small, hard berries, greener than young grass and as lustrous and as polished as emeralds. At his feet the unresting ants passed patiently in their unending circle, or radiated at angles toward the weeds that smothered the garden. Arthur turned the bank over and over in his hot hands. He closed his eyes. He would start school next fall; then, in no time at all, he too would get a job like the grocer's boy; but he would put all the money he earned in his bank, and when it was full he would ask his grandfather to send him another and a larger one.

One day it seemed to him that the bank was lighter. He told his fear to his mother. She smiled and kissed him.

Arthur said: "But it *is* lighter. Here, take it yourself, and you'll see!"

His mother answered, "I think it's just the same. You're six months older than you were when the bank came and you are getting to be such a big, strong boy that it only *seems* lighter."

Then Arthur went away, not quite satisfied, but accepting what his mother told him as something beyond his reason; and when a few days later the bank was alarmingly lighter, so much so that anybody could tell the difference at once, he said nothing at all. That night he lay in bed thinking, and all the terrors which the bank had quieted came back to him. The next day the bank did not shake at all, no coins rattled against the sides or slid with a comforting, rustling sound over each other when he tilted the bank sidewise.

His mother said: "The coins are stuck together, that's why they don't clink any more. It often happens." She smiled and bent down to kiss him, but Arthur pulled away from her and went outside. He watched his mother from the porch until he saw her go into the kitchen, make a fire in the wood-stove and start preparations for supper; then he tiptoed into the house and entered his mother's bedroom. He found her purse where she kept it hidden in her bureau drawer, and in a pocket was the key to his bank, the pink ribbon, a little soiled and faded now, still dangling. He walked into his own room and lifted the bank from the mantel; but even before the miniature, vault-like door had swung all the way back, he saw that the bank was empty. He stood there for a while holding the bank in his hands. He had known all the time that he would find the bank empty and that his mother had lied to him, but there had been an unreasoning hope that the actual opening of the bank would prove him wrong. He stood holding the bank stupidly, his mouth slightly opened, his eyes frowning; then he made a quick, shrill sound and hurled the bank against the wall.

Almost at once his mother stood in the doorway watching him. She had been wiping a cup, and she still held it half concealed in a dishcloth. When she saw the opened bank a shamed look came over her face.

"Arthur," she said pleadingly. "Arthur, listen to me!"

Arthur said, "You took it! You took it! I trusted you and you took it!" He threw himself upon the floor and pressed his face against the uncarpeted boards. He repeated over and over: "You took it! You know you took it!" He turned on his back and held his hands over his eyes. "Why didn't you ask me for it? I would have given it to you."

His mother put down the cup carefully as if, in her poverty, she was afraid, even at this moment, that a thing as precious as a cup might be broken. She got down upon her knees and tried to comfort him, but he would not let her touch him. She sat back on her haunches and regarded him, and when she spoke at last her voice was unexpectedly bitter:

"Who are you to condemn me? How can you know what I've been through?"

She cried harshly, her thin hands pressed against her cheeks. "Do you think I *wanted* to take your money? Do you think I'd have done it if I hadn't been at the end of my rope? Do you think that badly of me?"

But she saw that he was too preoccupied with his own grief to hear her or to understand what she was saying. She got up, picked up the cup and the dishrag and went out of the room, closing the door behind her. A long time later, after he had exhausted himself, Arthur, too, went out. He sat again under his tree and stared at the familiar and toiling ants. He broke a stick from the tree and held it across the circle in which the ants ceaselessly moved, and the line halted in dismay, touching with their feelers this uncalculated impediment to industry. One large ant, bolder than the rest, began to crawl over the stick, but Arthur lifted the twig and held the ant suspended vertically in mid-air. The ant climbed slowly to the top, and when it found nothing further to grasp it reared upward and explored the vacancy of space with its forefeet, balanced exactly at its black, wasp-like waist; then Arthur reversed the stick and the ant drew the two smooth cylinders of its body together, turned, and finding new purchase, patiently began the ascent again. He was still playing with the twig and the ant when his mother came to the back door and called in her timid, questioning voice:

"Arthur? . . . You, Arthur? Come eat your supper."

But Arthur would not answer his mother at first. He sat rigidly under the tree, his eyes fixed on the earth. "She took it," he repeated over and over. "I trusted her, and she took it." His mind could go no farther than that.

"Arthur?" she called again. "Arthur, where are you?"

Her voice was anxious and she waited for his reply. Suddenly the boy got up in terror and ran toward his mother through the thick weeds. She met him at the steps. She sat down and took him in her arms, smoothing his hair while he cried against her breast. He had accepted what his mother had done although he did not understand it, and he had forgiven her, but he knew, dimly, that while neither of them would ever mention the toy bank again, it would lie between them like a barrier as long as they both lived.

1934

BILL'S EYES

The nurse came into the room where Bill sat and glanced around to assure herself that everything was in readiness for the doctor. They weren't used to such famous men in hospitals of this sort, and she was afraid each time he came to see Bill that the doctor would ask some question which she could not answer, some technical thing which she had learned in her probationary days and had promptly forgotten, such as, "Define lymph, Miss Connors, and state briefly the purpose it serves in the economy of the body."

She dragged her forefinger over the table, examined it critically for smudges, and looked briskly about her for a dustcloth. Since there was none, she lifted her uniform above her knees and held it away from her body while she wiped the table clean with her underskirt. She was conscious of the exposure of her thighs, and she turned her head slowly and looked at Bill. He was a strong, thickset man with a muscular neck and a chest so solid that it seemed molded from the metals with which he had once worked. He was, she judged, about twenty-five. The fact that such a young, full-blooded man could neither see the charms that she exhibited nor react to them, because of his blindness, as a man should, excited her and she began to talk nervously:

"Well, I guess you'll be glad to get this all over with. I guess you'll be glad to know for certain, one way or the other."

"I know now," said Bill. "I'm not worrying. There's no doubt in my mind now, and there never was."

"I must say you've been a good patient. You haven't been upset like most of them are."

"Why should I worry?" asked Bill. "I got the breaks this time, if ever a man did. If there ever was a lucky man it's me, if you know what I mean. I was lucky to have that big-time doctor operate on me for nothing just because my wife wrote and asked him to." He laughed contentedly. "Christ! Christ, but I got the breaks! From the way he's treated me, you'd think I was a millionaire or the President of the United States or something."

"That's a fact," said Miss Connors thoughtfully. "He's a fine man." She noticed that she still held her uniform above her knees and dropped it suddenly, smoothing her skirt with her palms.

"What's he like?" asked Bill.

"Wait!" she said. "You've waited a long time now, and if you wait a little longer maybe you'll be able to see what he looks like for yourself."

"I'll be able to see all right, when he takes these bandages off," said Bill. "Don't make any mistake about that. There's no question of maybe. I'll be able to see all right."

"You're optimistic," said the nurse. "You're not downhearted. I'll say that for you."

Bill said: "What have I got to worry about? This sort of operation made him famous, didn't it? If he can't make me see again, who can?"

"That's right," said the nurse. "What you say is true."

Bill laughed tolerantly at her doubts. "They bring people to him from all over the world, don't they? You told me that yourself, sister! Well, what do you think they do it for? For the sea voyage?"

"That's right," said the nurse. "You got me there. I don't want to be a wet blanket. I just said *maybe*."

"You didn't have to tell me what a fine man he is," said Bill after a long silence. He chuckled, reached out and tried to catch hold of Miss Connors' hand, but she laughed and stepped aside. "Don't you think I knew that myself?" he continued. "I knew he was a fine man the minute he came into the hospital and spoke to me. I knew—" Then he stopped, leaned back in his chair and rubbed the back of one hand with the fingers of the other. He had stopped speaking, he felt, just in time to prevent his sounding ridiculous. There was no point in explaining to Miss Connors, or anybody else, just how he felt in his heart about the doctor, or of his gratitude to him. There was no sense in talking about those things.

Miss Connors went to the table and rearranged the bouquet of asters which Bill's wife had brought for him the day before, narrowing her eyes and holding her face away from the flowers critically. She stopped all at once and straightened up.

"Listen!" she said. "That's him now."

"Yes," said Bill.

Miss Connors went to the door and opened it. "Well, doctor, your patient is all ready and waiting for you." She backed away, thinking of the questions that a man of such eminence could ask if he really put his mind to it. "I'll be outside in the corridor," she went on. "If you want me, I'll be waiting."

The doctor came to where Bill sat and looked at him professionally, but he did not speak at once. He went to the window and drew the dark, heavy curtains. He was a small, plump man with a high, domed forehead whose hands were so limp, so undecided in their movements that it seemed impossible for them to perform the delicate operations that they did. His eyes were mild, dark blue and deeply compassionate.

"We were just talking about you before you came in," said Bill. "The nurse and me, I mean. I was trying to get her to tell me what you look like."

The doctor pulled up a chair and sat facing his patient. "I hope she gave a good report. I hope she wasn't too hard on me."

"She didn't say," said Bill. "It wasn't necessary. I know what you look like without being told."

"Tell me your idea and I'll tell you how right you are." He moved to the table, switched on a light and twisted the bulb until it was shaded to his satisfaction.

"That's easy," said Bill. "You're a dignified man with snow-white hair, and I see you about a head taller than any man I ever met. Then you've got deep brown eyes that are kind most of the time but can blaze up and look all the way through a man if you think he's got any meanness in him, because meanness is the one thing you can't stand, not having any of it in you."

The doctor touched his mild, compassionate eyes with the tips of his fingers. "You're a long way off," he said laughingly. "You're miles off this time, Bill." He switched off the shaded light on the table, adjusted a reflector about his neck and turned back to his patient, entirely professional again.

"The room is in complete darkness now," he said. "Later on, I'll let the light in gradually until your eyes get used to it. I generally explain that to my patients so they won't be afraid at first."

"Christ!" said Bill scornfully, "did you think I didn't trust you? Christ! I've got too much faith in you to be afraid."

"I'm going to take off the bandages now, if you're ready."

"Okay!" said Bill. "I'm not worrying any."

"Suppose you tell me about your accident while I work," said the doctor after a pause. "It'll keep your mind occupied and besides I never did understand the straight of it."

"There's not much to tell," said Bill. "I'm married and I've got three kids, like my wife told you in her letter, so I knew I had to work hard to keep my job. They were laying off men at the plant every day, but I said it mustn't happen to me. I kept saying to myself that I had to work hard and take chances, being a man with responsibilities. I kept saying that I mustn't get laid off, no matter what happened."

"Keep your hands down, Bill," said the doctor mildly. "Talk as much as you want to, but keep your hands in your lap."

"I guess I overdone it," continued Bill. "I guess I took too many chances after all. Then that drill broke into about a dozen pieces and blinded me, but I didn't know what had happened to me at first. Well, you know the rest, Doc."

"That was tough," said the doctor. He sighed soundlessly and shook his head. "That was tough luck."

"What I am going to say may sound silly," said Bill; "but I want to say it once and get it off my chest, because there's nothing I'm not willing to do for a man like you, and I've thought about it a lot. Now here's what I want to say just one time: If you ever want me for anything, all you got to do is to say the word and I'll drop everything and come running, no matter where I am. And when I say anything, I mean *anything*, including my life. I just wanted to say it one time."

"I appreciate that," said the doctor, "and I know you really mean it."

"I just wanted to say it once," said Bill.

There was a moment's silence and then the doctor spoke cautiously: "Everything that could be done for a man was done for you, Bill, and there's no reason to think the operation was unsuccessful. But sometimes it doesn't work, no matter how hard we try."

"I'm not worrying about that," said Bill quietly, "because I've got faith. I know, just as sure as I know I'm sitting here, that when you take off the bandages I'll be looking into your face."

"You might be disappointed," said the doctor slowly. "You'd better take that possibility into consideration. Don't get your hopes too high."

"I was only kidding," said Bill. "It don't make any real difference to me what you look like. I was kidding about what I said." He laughed again. "Forget it," he said. "Forget it."

The doctor's small, delicate hands rested against his knees. He leaned forward a little and peered into his patient's face. His eyes had become accustomed to the darkness and he could distinguish Bill's individual features plainly. He turned on the small, shaded light, shielding it with his palm. He sighed, shook his head and rubbed his hands against his forehead with a thoughtful movement.

"Have you got some kids at home, too?" asked Bill.

The doctor went to the window. He pulled gently on the cord and the thick curtains parted and slid back soundlessly. "I have three little girls," he said.

The autumn sunlight came strongly into the room and lay in a bright wedge across the floor, touching Bill's hands, his rough, uplifted face, and the wall beyond.

"Well, now, that's funny. I've got three little boys. Can you beat that?"

"It's what they call a coincidence," said the doctor.

He came back to the chair and stood between Bill and the sunlight. "You can raise your hands now, if you want to," he said wearily.

Bill lifted his hairy, oil-stained hands and rested them against his temples. He spoke with surprise.

"The bandages are off now, ain't they, Doc?"

"Yes."

The doctor shook his head and moved to one side, and again the strong sunlight fell on Bill's broad, good-natured Slavic face. "I don't mind telling you, now that I got my eyesight back," said Bill, "that I've been kidding about not being afraid. I've been scared to death most of the time, Doc, but I guess you knew that too. That's why I'm acting like a kid today, I guess. It's the relief of having it over and knowing that I can see again. . . . You can turn on the lights any time you want to. I'm ready."

The doctor did not answer.

"My old lady was in to see me yesterday," continued Bill. "She said they're holding my job for me at the plant. I said to tell 'em I'd be there to claim it on Monday morning. I'll be glad to get back to work again."

The doctor was still silent and Bill, fearing that he had sounded ungrateful, added quickly: "I've had a fine rest these last weeks, and everybody has been damned good to me, but I want to get back to work now, Doc. I'm a family man and I've got responsibilities. My wife and kids would starve to death without me there to take care of them, and I can't afford to waste too much time. You know how it is with your own work, I guess."

The doctor went to the door, and spoke gently. "Nurse! Nurse, you'd better come in now."

She entered at once, went to the table, and stood beside the vase of asters. She looked up after a moment and examined Bill's face. He seemed entirely different with the bandages removed, and younger, even, than she had thought. His eyes were round, incorruptibly innocent and of an odd shade of clear, childlike hazel. They softened, somehow, his blunt hands, his massive chin and his thick, upstanding hair. They changed his entire face, she thought, and she realized that if she had not seen them she would never have really understood his character, nor would she have had the least idea of how he appeared to the people who knew him before his accident. As she watched him, thinking these things, he smiled again, pursed out his lips and turned his head in the doctor's direction.

"What's the matter with you?" he asked jokingly. "What are you waiting for? You're not looking for a tin cup and a bundle of pencils to hand me, are you?" He laughed again. "Come on, Doc," he said. "Don't keep me in suspense. You can't expect me to know what you look like until you turn on the lights, now can you?"

The doctor did not answer.

Bill threw out his arms and yawned contentedly, moved in his chair and almost succeeded in facing the nurse who still stood beside the table. He smiled and winked humorously at the vacant wall, a yard to the left of where Miss Connors waited.

The doctor spoke. "I'm about five feet, eight inches tall," he began in his hesitant, compassionate voice. "I weigh around a hundred and seventy-five pounds, so you can imagine how paunchy I'm getting to be. I'll be fifty-two years old next spring, and I'm getting bald. I've got on a gray suit and tan shoes." He paused a moment, as if to verify his next statement. "I'm wearing a blue necktie today," he continued; "a dark blue necktie with white dots in it."

1936

NOT WORTHY OF A WENTWORTH

I HAD fallen into the habit of visiting Mrs. Kent on Wednesday afternoons, and it soon became an established fact that I was expected on that day. She received me on the wide porch which opened onto her garden, and while she fixed my tea and offered me the small, pecan cakes I liked so well, she told me of the town and its people.

On this particular Wednesday I looked idly at the garden while she talked, my eyes fixed on the fig trees banked against the whitewashed back fence. She followed my glance and nodded. "Figs will be ripe in another week at most," she said. "The trees are loaded this year." She put sugar in her own tea, then leaned back and said: "I'm glad the crop is going to be good, because Carrie Wentworth and her mother are so fond of them." She paused, then added in explanation, "You see, it's always been understood that the Wentworths have the figs from the branches on their side of the fence."

"The Wentworths?" I asked. "Who are the Wentworths? I don't think you've told me about them yet."

She stared at me with disbelief. "Do you mean to tell me that you've been in Reedyville for two whole months and haven't heard of the *Wentworths* yet?" She bent forward and patted my cheek gratefully. "You're such a comfort!" she said. "Imagine having somebody all to yourself who doesn't know the first thing about this place!"

"When I think of it," she continued after a moment, "I'm not surprised, after all, that you haven't heard of the Wentworths.

They've lost their money and they've gone down a lot since my day. . . . Just ask your mother, when you write her, about old Mrs. Cora Wentworth and her daughter Caroline! She'll remember them all right. . . . When we were girls, your mother and I used to be awed pretty thoroughly at the Wentworth magnificence, and to wonder if we'd ever grow up to be as dainty and accomplished as Carrie." She stopped again, nodded her head and went on with her story, her voice cool and brisk.

The Wentworths, it appeared, had once been a numerous family with their relatives and their connections, but they had died off or moved out of the state until there were left now only the two women next door. Old Mrs. Wentworth before her marriage had been Cora Reedy, so her daughter Caroline was closely related by blood to the Porterfields, the Gowers, and the Claytons. On her father's side there were, beside the powerful Wentworths, the Howards, the Eades, and the Lankesters. It was thus obvious, if I would permit my hostess to be a trifle lush, that Carrie Wentworth was, in a manner of speaking, the unique vessel in which the most aristocratic blood of Alabama met and blended.

This fact was first pointed out by her great-uncle, old Mr. George Gower, during the family celebration which followed Carrie's christening, and the Wentworths, with his words, realized the gravity of their responsibility. When she was old enough to begin her education, Carrie had had a special governess for languages and painting, while her grandmother, old Mrs. Reedy herself, had taught her needlework and deportment. But Carrie had been in no way precocious, in spite of her distinguished ancestry. She learned what was expected of her as well as the average girl, and that was all.

My hostess gave me these preliminary facts with the offhand efficiency of a property manager arranging his set. She was silent for a few moments, recapitulating her facts to determine if anything essential had been left out. "Oh, yes," she said. "Carrie developed a nice soprano voice as a young girl and she took lessons on the harp." It seemed, during these years, that Carrie often played for family guests in the gilded, Wentworth drawing-room, but people were impressed less by her skill as a musician than by the fact that anybody as tiny as Carrie could play an instrument as formidable as the harp at all.

To summarize, Carrie as a young lady had been dainty, pretty and quite accomplished with her music, her water colors, her needlework and her languages, but then so had many of the other girls. It was her laugh more than anything else which made her so attractive. The laugh was clear and tinkling and it differed from the flat laughs of most people in that it leapt upward from note to note with the clear certainty of a coloratura soprano practicing a passage. "Everybody in Reedyville, but her family in particular, took it for granted that Carrie would make a brilliant marriage," said Mrs. Kent. "The only problem was, Where could a man be found who was worthy of her?"

When Carrie was about sixteen she was sent to a finishing school, where she specialized in voice and the harp. She came home that summer and the first thing she did was to fall in love. The boy's name was Herbert Thompson and he worked in a bank. Carrie used to meet him when she could at the old pavilion near James Lake, and Herbert told her all about himself and his plans for the future. He was ambitious, and he didn't expect to be a bookkeeper all his life. He was studying every night at home, and one day he expected to be an accountant or a bank examiner.

It was then Carrie realized that she didn't even know the multiplication tables very accurately, but she went to work at once and before the month was out she was halfway through the arithmetic Herbert had lent her. It was due to Carrie's sudden interest in mathematics that the Wentworths learned about the affair.

When questioned by her family, Carrie admitted that she and Herbert were going to marry just as soon as he was able to support a wife in *any* sort of style; and she thought her interest in arithmetic should be plain enough to anybody with ordinary, common sense. Her future husband was going to be an accountant, and she meant to help him achieve that ambition. It was true his more intricate problems would always be beyond her small, feminine mind, but in time she hoped to become so proficient under his guidance that she could handle most of the lesser, routine matters by herself, thus leaving him free for the important deals when they came up. Naturally they would have little to live on, particularly at first, but, when you came right down to it, who cared?

The Wentworths were shocked at Carrie's attitude, but they were sure nothing would come of the affair, since Carrie and her sweetheart were both so young. Anyway, old Mrs. Wentworth took her daughter abroad in the fall. They returned three years later, when Carrie was about nineteen or twenty. She spoke French, Italian and German fluently now, and she had picked up a working knowledge of Spanish. She made her formal debut in New Orleans that year and she was a great success, but the men she liked didn't come up to the standard the Wentworths had set for themselves, and the one or two that the family regarded as eligible made Carrie, as she expressed it, "sick."

"Carrie and her mother came back to Reedyville the following spring," continued Mrs. Kent. "I'll always remember Carrie sitting in her carriage one April evening about dusk. She was going to a party with one of her admirers from New Orleans who had come to visit her, and, as I gawped, she lifted her dainty, plump shoulders and laughed her famous, tinkling laugh. She had on a white satin gown, and she was wearing a blue velvet evening cloak with a high collar of white fur. I suppose the fur was some sort of fox; at any rate, I'd never seen anything so magnificent before, and it seemed to me that Carrie was exactly like one of the porcelain figurines which my mother kept locked in her parlor."

Mrs. Kent laughed softly. "I must have been about fourteen in those days and I was a big, lummox of a girl. When I got home that night I remember I cried for a solid hour merely because Caroline Wentworth was so dainty and so charming, and I wasn't. I remember Carrie's exact age that way too, because I asked my father to get me a velvet cloak with white fur and he laughed at me. I pointed out that Carrie Wentworth had one, and my mother said, 'Of course she has. She's eight years older than you.'

"What I didn't know at the time," continued Mrs. Kent, "was the fact that the cloak was a present to Carrie for giving up Herbert Thompson the second time. You see, when she got back from her season in New Orleans, she met Herbert at a party and fell in love with him all over again. The family was provoked, but they handled the situation with what most people considered a great deal of common sense. This time they tried to ridicule Carrie out of love."

There hadn't been much the matter with Herbert personally. The greatest objection the family had to him was the unalterable fact that his father openly shaved people in a barbershop at the corner of Magnolia and Broad streets. But Carrie had a mind of her own, and she insisted that she would marry Herbert Thompson and nobody else. She would be very glad to live in a room over the barbershop, among the mugs and old razors, as her family predicted; she would even lather the faces of her father-in-law's customers, as her uncle Ralph Porterfield humorously suggested. She stuck out her firm, Wentworth jaw. She was going to marry Herbert Thompson, she said, and the family might just as well make up its mind now, as later!

She gave in finally, just as everybody knew that she must, and went to visit relatives in Louisville for the season. It looked as though her people were right when they said she would forget Herbert, once she was in different surroundings, because before the year was out she was in love once more, this time with a watch-repairer named Samuel Maneth. The affair had been under way for some weeks before the cousins in Louisville found out about it and wrote back to Reedyville in alarm. Mrs. Wentworth and her mother, old Mrs. Reedy, went immediately to the rescue.

It wasn't that the Wentworths had any prejudice against Jews or anybody else, and it was all right for Mr. Maneth to marry whom he pleased, so long as it wasn't a Wentworth. Then, too, if a Jew did actually marry out of his own faith, it was only reasonable to expect him to have a considerable sum of money. But this little man didn't have a penny to his name beside his wages. He couldn't even hold a job very long.

All the family connections got together that time. The whole thing would be funny, they thought, if it weren't so exasperating, and Carrie's talent for falling in love with the wrong people was really getting to be a problem.

The family feelings weren't helped very much when Carrie attempted to justify herself, to make her position clear. Mr. Maneth was perfectly respectable, she explained, and she had met him when she took her watch to the jeweler's to be repaired. He was so thin and nervous, his hands were so cold and damp, that it was plain to anybody that what he needed was a faithful wife who would cook nourishing meals for him at proper intervals and to see that he dressed himself warmly and took better care of his health. He was not only a watch-repairer, Carrie explained, he was interested in social problems as well, and he was always addressing meetings after his working hours. Carrie had gone to several meetings with him. His mind was so brilliant, she explained, and his theories of right and wrong, particularly with regard to real property, so abstruse, that they were beyond her for the moment, but she could at least read books and learn, and while she never expected to approach him in the intellectual field, she could, at least, give him the sympathetic understanding and companionship which he needed so badly. Certainly she could take care of him, cook for him, wash his clothes if necessary, and raise his children.

At this point Carrie burst into tears, according to Mrs. Kent, and ran out of the room, while her family sat looking at each other in complete bewilderment, wondering from what strain Carrie had inherited her innate commonness. They shook their heads, for Carrie's attitude made it difficult to handle the matter. In the end Mr. Maneth solved the problem for them. Everybody was surprised, as they hadn't thought that he might have his pride, too. He returned Carrie's letters and wrote her a note saying that marriage for them was an impossibility.

Mrs. Kent raised her eyebrows humorously and passed me another pecan cake. "It might have been better all around if Carrie had either been more yielding or independent enough to break away from her family entirely," she said. "At any rate, she didn't do either. She simply drifted along, hoping that things would somehow right themselves. But in the meantime the girls she had known, the girls of her own age, were marrying right and left and starting families of their own, and there sat Carrie with her languages and her skill on the harp waiting for a man to come along who was good enough for her to marry."

The man who suited her family in every particular appeared when Carrie was about twenty-five, and his name, with what Mrs. Kent considered "an unprecedented example of poetic appropriateness" was Rex Ayleshire. He came from Louisiana and he was a distant connection of the Claytons'. He was handsome, witty, intelligent, and he had money; and what was more important, the Wentworth and Reedy families conceded freely that his family was even better than their own.

He was a lawyer who had come to Reedyville to settle the estate of a client, and when the family saw him, they knew that here was Carrie's husband sent to them by a divine providence. They sighed with gratitude when he fell in love with Carrie almost on sight. But Carrie, to their dismay, shook her head, laughed her tinkling laugh and said no. She admitted his obviously superior qualities, but the fact remained that he simply made her "tired."

Then, as if to consolidate her position and to end the family pressure, she fell in love right under Mr. Ayleshire's nose. This time it was a man named Charlie Malloch, a machinist. The whole town was laughing by this time, and they predicted that Carrie would turn up at the machine shop the next Monday morning in overalls, handing Charlie his tools when he needed them.

The family anxiety shifted quickly. It wasn't so much a question now as to whether Carrie could be induced to marry Rex, it was rather how she could be prevented from marrying Charlie. The result was that Rex went back to Louisiana and Carrie and her mother went to London for a visit.

Mrs. Kent lit another cigarette and leaned back in her chair. "Everybody was sure that Carrie would land an earl or a duke or something equally grand. Other American girls, with far less money, family or good looks, had done the same, but when they returned to Reedyville, Mrs. Wentworth told her friends with considerable disgust that Carrie refused to interest herself in her opportunities. She was through with Carrie, she said. She gave her up as hopeless.

"Oh, yes," said Mrs. Kent thoughtfully, "I must tell you this: When Carrie came back from England that time she was wearing exaggerated earrings and she smoked openly and rouged her cheeks and lips. Her clothes were too young for her, so everybody thought. She had taken to dotted swiss dresses, sashes and pink sunshades. She went everywhere in those days and her tinkling, gay laugh was heard a great deal. Her father died about that time, too, and it was found out that while the family was well-off, they didn't have nearly so much as people had thought. . . . Afterwards, with Carrie and her mother living alone, they quarreled more than ever."

But the worst quarrel of all took place when Carrie was in her middle thirties. It seemed that a Swiss baker had come to town and opened a pastry shop. He borrowed money from the bank to get started, and after a time he was doing reasonably well. Carrie, along with the other ladies of the town, used to patronize him. The man's name was Zuckmar, and he was Carrie's age or a little older. It wasn't long after she met him before Carrie began to take up cookery and to comb the town for family recipes, and Mr. Zuckmar started baking little cakes for her with her name outlined in colored icings.

Carrie left off her earrings, her sashes and her organdies and buckled down to the work of helping Mr. Zuckmar make a success of his shop. Before the summer was out he had asked her to marry him, and Carrie had cried for an hour on his shoulder and then consented. But she had learned caution, and she was determined that nobody should thwart her plans this time. She decided to keep their engagement secret until the store was paid for and they were operating free of debt. When this happened, they would simply go to Montgomery or Selma and get married, telling nobody until afterwards.

Indeed, Carrie and Mr. Zuckmar handled their affairs with

such discretion that her family had no idea whatever of what was going on, so Mrs. Ralph Porterfield had a shock one Saturday morning when she took a short cut through the alley that ran behind the pastry shop and suddenly heard her niece's coloratura laugh on the other side of the high, board fence. She opened the gate and went in, and the thing she saw took her breath away:

There was Carrie Wentworth with her knees resting on a piece of sacking and her skirt pinned back over her waist. She had a scrubbing brush in her hand, and as she laughed and talked she scoured the kitchen of the pastry shop briskly with lye soap and water. Above her stood Mr. Zuckmar, who was also laughing. He had a spoonful of sticky cake-icing, and he was threatening to pour it down Carrie's back unless she gave him another kiss instantly. They were speaking Italian, so Mrs. Porterfield didn't know what they actually said, but their meaning was obvious enough when Carrie gave in laughingly and lifted her lips upward to his. At that moment Mrs. Porterfield backed out of the gate, not believing, even then, what she had seen.

Naturally the family was shocked at the idea of Carrie married to a pastry cook. Old Mrs. Philip Howard predicted that she would end up clerking in the store or even waiting on the tables, and Carrie forgot her caution for the moment and flared up in her old manner. She said that waiting on tables was precisely what she intended doing, because, after they were married, she and her husband were going to put in tables and sell ice cream and cold drinks. Mr. Zuckmar, she explained later in a more placating voice, was the sweetest, the most honorable and the most marvelous of men, and he was one of the very cleverest, too, once you got to know him, but he was a little helpless, like all men, and she couldn't give him up now, even if she wanted to, because she didn't know what would become of him if she wasn't there to aid him in his difficulties.

The family row that night was the worst in the history of the town, but Carrie refused to budge an inch this time, and Mr. Zuckmar couldn't be moved out of his phlegmatic, even-tempered calm. They might have succeeded, after all, except for two things: Carrie, naturally, didn't have one penny of her own, and Mr. Zuckmar was operating on borrowed money. When the family put the matter before Mr. Palmiller, of the Palmiller State Bank, he saw at once that a girl of Carrie's standing couldn't be permitted to disgrace her family the way she planned. He called his loan and forced the pastry cook out of business. A few days later a committee visited Mr. Zuckmar and suggested that he locate in some town in the West, where business conditions were better. . . . When she got Mr. Zuckmar's farewell note, Carrie began to cry shrilly. "My God!" she screamed over and over. "My God, can't you ever let me alone?"

After that Carrie didn't even bother to quarrel with her mother any more, and for a long time nobody saw her at all. But times were changing rapidly, and after a year or so nobody even thought of her very much, for already she belonged to the past. It was about this time that the Wentworth family had to sell their big house on Reedy Avenue, and move into the cottage whose back garden joined the garden of my hostess.

"And that," said Mrs. Kent, "is the monotonous history of Carrie Wentworth, on your thumbnail! I used to laugh at her, along with the rest of the town, but I don't any more. I understand her too well now." She sighed. "Poor Carrie! All she wanted was to marry a man who needed her, one she could love and serve faithfully. She was the most uncomplicated woman I ever knew." She stopped and laughed softly. "Poor Carrie," she repeated. "If she'd succeeded, she'd probably have bored her husband to death, and he'd have wanted to wring her neck a dozen times a day, but he'd never have given her up. Never as long as he lived. He would have loved her too much."

I sat silent for a moment, watching the shadow of the camphor tree touch the fence slowly and lengthen. Then, all at once, there came a sound of high, tinkling laughter from the Wentworth yard, laughter which leaped upward from note to note and died away. It was almost as if the crystals of a chandelier had been brushed unexpectedly by a passing hand.

"What is she like now?" I asked.

Mrs. Kent said, "Would you like to see her for yourself?"

and when I nodded, she got up from her chair, and we walked down the steps and across the lawn. We reached the dividing fence and peered over.

Before us, a withered little girl sat under a pear tree playing with dolls. She was wearing a frock which ended above her knees, and her gray hair hung over her shoulders in thin, exact curls. Her legs were bare except for the pink socks which reached her ankles, and anchored over her ears were old fashioned, steel rimmed spectacles.

Mrs. Kent rapped on the fence to attract her attention and called, "Carrie! Oh, Carrie! Come here a minute."

Carrie looked up with her bright, eager eyes. She picked up an armful of her dolls and skipped to the fence. She stared at me with curiosity.

"How old are you, little girl?" I asked.

"I'm sixty-two," she said, "and my name is Caroline Wentworth." She held up the dolls for me to see.

"We came out to look at the figs," said Mrs. Kent. "They'll soon be ripe again. I know you'll be glad. You and your mother must take all you want."

From inside the house there came a voice surprisingly full and vigorous. "Carrie!" said the voice hoarsely. "Carrie, who are you talking to?"

Carrie said: "I can speak five languages. I can sing quite well. I can do embroidery."

"Carrie!" called the voice in terror. "Carrie! Carrie!"

Carrie said: "Yes, Mamma, I'm coming now." She started away and then came back to the dividing fence, her eyes roguish behind her spectacles.

"My name is Caroline Wentworth," she said gaily. "I can paint in water colors. I can play the harp."

She turned, then, and skipped up the gravel path, her dolls riding before her in her spread skirt, her gray, thin curls tossing up and down to her stride. She reached the door and faced us again. She waved her hand, laughed her high, tinkling laugh and went inside.

When she had gone, we stood quietly beside the whitewashed

fence, the late sun touching our hands. It was Mrs. Kent who spoke first.

"I seem to be *bristling* with platitudes this afternoon," she said softly, "and I know how platitudes frighten young intellectuals from the city, but I never heard old Mrs. Wentworth call her daughter, nor see Carrie skip up the walk and into the house, without thinking that the Wentworth back door closes slowly on a whole generation, a period of time, an era which cannot live again." We turned from the fig trees and walked back to the wide, vine-shaded porch. "Yes," I said. "Yes."

1937

A MEMORIAL TO THE SLAIN

At least Reedyville is unusual in one way," I said. "There's no war memorial. How did you escape?"

My hostess, Mrs. Kent, leaned back in her chair and held a lace handkerchief to her eyes. Her shoulders shook with merriment. "Don't ask me to tell you *that* story, Clark," she begged. "After all, I do have my standards of reserve." She smoothed out her thin summer dress and looked at me mockingly. "Not that I wouldn't like to tell it," she continued, "because the affair of the war memorial is the most amusing thing that ever happened in this town."

For a moment she sat with her brows drawn together and then began:

"The story is a little involved, and I think I'd better tell you first about a girl named Honey Boutwell. She was run out of Reedyville by the same society that objected to the war memorial some years later, so the story ties in there, too. Anyway, Honey was our prize bad girl while she lasted, and she lived out near the canning factory. I can recall the Boutwell family very well indeed, since their mother used to do sewing for us by the day. I remember one of the boys—his name was Breckenridge—even better than I do Honey. By the way, you'd better keep Breck's name in mind, too, because he comes into the story later on. I suppose he's the hero. But let's stick to Honey Boutwell for the moment.

"Honey spent her time hanging around the Magnolia Hotel mostly, watching the drummers and waiting to be picked up;

and before she was sixteen, she had already been mixed up in a scandal or two. In those days she used to wear her hair in what we called a Psyche knot, so you can realize how long ago it was. When she wasn't picketing the hotel, she was usually standing in the alley back of the old opera house waiting to talk to the actors. . . . You see, Honey considered herself an artist too, because she danced and sang songs at stag suppers. It was said that she also took off all her clothes for the gentlemen when they paid well enough, and it was this lack of formality, more than anything else, that made Mr. Palmiller and his vice society get after her so relentlessly, coming, as it did, on top of her unfortunate affair with old Mr. Howard. Unfortunate for old Mr. *Howard,* I mean."

Mrs. Kent smoothed back her gray, neatly waved hair. "In those days," she said, "nobody ever thought that dingy, hoarse-voiced little Honey Boutwell was going to be the only famous person that Reedyville ever produced, but that's the way it worked out. After she left town that night so hurriedly, to escape going to reform school, nobody heard of Honey for a long time. Then she turned up in Boston, of all unlikely places, mixed up in a murder. She must have been twenty in those days. Next she was singing on the stage in Paris, where she still is, so far as I know. The French say that she's a great artist. Maybe she is. Anyway, she's very celebrated, I understand."

Dr. Kent, hearing our voices, came out of the house and sat with us on the porch. He spoke to his wife: "Excuse me a minute, Cordie, but one of my patients from up Pearl River way brought me a hatful of turtle eggs. I gave them to Mamie and she's fixing them for supper."

Mrs. Kent smiled and went on with her story. "Have you got Honey all straight in your mind?" And when I nodded, she said: "All right; let's get on to her brother Breck. I can place Breck more easily than the other Boutwell boys because he was the one with an inverted thumb. You see, it grew backwards, toward his wrist, instead of straight up, as a thumb should.

"When she went out to work by the day, Mrs. Boutwell used to bring each new baby with her until it was weaned. I was studying Roman history during Breck's nursing period, and the first time I saw him, I picked him up and said: 'Why, he's just like the Emperor Elagabalus, isn't he?' Then Mrs. Boutwell took off her spectacles and sat at the sewing machine while I read the passage about Elagabalus out loud. She was proud of Breck after that, but disappointed, too, since the Roman emperor had both thumbs inverted, while Breck had only one."

"I told Mamie to simmer those turtle eggs in spiced sherry," said Dr. Kent. "I hope she doesn't spoil them. She says she knows how to do it."

"Don't worry, darling," said Mrs. Kent. "Mamie's a very good cook. They'll be exactly right." She smiled absently and went on with her story:

"When Breck grew up, his love life ran true to the Boutwell tradition, and from all accounts he should have been enough to keep Mr. Palmiller's vice society working every minute of their time, but the trouble was, they couldn't get anything on him: not one of his girls ever gave him away. I understand that when he wasn't making love and getting the little canning factory girls in trouble, he hung around Rowley's Pool Parlor, shot dice and bet on race horses.

"I hadn't seen Breck for a long time," continued Mrs. Kent, "until one day just before we got into the war. I was walking down Magnolia Street and there was Breck on a bench outside the pool parlor. I knew which one of the Boutwell boys he was when I got a look at his upside-down thumb. He had on a pale, fawn-colored suit that day, and a plaid cap, and in his lapel was a button which read: 'Let's Get Acquainted.' I suppose he must have noticed me looking at him, because the next thing I knew he was walking beside me, squeezing my arm.

" 'Hello, Peaches!' he whispered, 'let me be your cream!' "

Mrs. Kent's shoulders shook once more with merriment, and once more she pressed the lace handkerchief to her eyes. "I was so surprised, I couldn't say anything at all. I just stood there backed against the window of the Beehive Store with my mouth opened like an idiot's and watched Breck chew the stub of a toothpick. He was perfectly at ease. Across the street Professor

Inman was giving a lesson in his studios. The piece being played was 'O Promise Me,' one of his favorite selections for the violin, and his pupil, I think, was little Charlie McMasters; but whoever the pupil was, he was earnest and he was putting in a lot of feeling.

" 'Why, Breck Boutwell!' I said at last. 'Aren't you ashamed of yourself?'

"He smiled good-naturedly and rolled his eyes. 'All right, Cutie,' he said. 'There wasn't no harm in *asking*, was there?' Then, since he recognized me at last to be an old patron of the family, he added in explanation: 'I didn't mean to insult you none, Mrs. Kent, but I work on averages, like a baseball pitcher. You can't beat averages.'

" 'No,' I said. 'No, I suppose you can't.' "

"I walked away to the obbligato of little Charlie McMasters' violin, trying my best not to keep step with

> O *prom*-ise me that *some*day you and I
> Will *take* our love to-*gether* to some sky . . .

but not succeeding. Well, that was the last time I ever saw Breck Boutwell."

Again Mrs. Kent leaned back in her chair and laughed deeply. "At any rate, we're getting a little closer to the war memorial," she said, "because I'm sure you guessed long ago that Breck was killed in the war. He was. It was at St. Mihiel, and to everybody's surprise he died quite heroically, with a couple of medals."

At that moment some friends went by and Mrs. Kent waved to them. When they had passed, she continued her story.

"All right! We've got all three sides sketched in. There's Honey, her brother Breck, and Mr. Palmiller's vice society. Hold on to them while I tell you about the campaign of the *Reedyville Courier;* it won't take long.

"In 1920 the editor of the *Courier* discovered that we didn't have a war memorial and it shamed him, he said. He took the matter up with the Legion Post and discovered that Breck Boutwell was the only man from our town who had been killed in the war. The editor would have preferred somebody from a good family, but Breck was better than nothing at all, and that week the *Courier* printed his picture and an account of his military career in the Marines, paying a good deal of attention to the two medals. In the same issue there was a long editorial pointing out the need for some appropriate memorial to our slain, and urging the formation of a committee.

"The next week a committee was actually organized, with Robert Porterfield as chairman, to raise money for the monument, and Mr. Palmiller and his society came out publicly as sponsors of the plan; but before the committee had a chance to get down to work in earnest, an unexpected thing happened: The *Courier* got a letter from Honey Boutwell, of all people. We learned something then that we hadn't known: Honey had never missed a single issue of the *Courier* since she left town, and she was still on its list of subscribers; so while we had often *wondered* about her, she had always *known* what we were doing from week to week.

"The letter really came from a firm of French lawyers, and it wasn't very long. Their client, the great *artiste,* Madame Honey Boutwell, had read of the plan to raise money for a monument, and she was willing to finance the whole thing herself in memory of her beloved brother, Breckenridge. She had already taken the liberty of discussing plans with the renowned sculptor, M. Paul Gagnon, and he would accept the commission because of his warm personal friendship for Madame Boutwell and because of his admiration of her as an artist. The only stipulations were, naturally, that the design be left entirely to M. Gagnon and Madame Boutwell and that the monument itself, when completed, be displayed in a dignified and prominent place in the town, a place worthy of the genius of its creator."

Mrs. Kent rubbed the arms of her chair and winked knowingly. She said: "The first thing Mr. Porterfield's committee did was to look up the sculptor, since they didn't have too much faith in Honey, and they didn't really believe that she associated with serious, substantial people. To their amazement they discovered that what the lawyers had said wasn't French exaggeration as they had suspected. It was all true. That settled it. It wiped out Honey's bad character almost overnight. If she associated with great men, they argued, men whose biographies were actually in encyclopedias in public libraries, then she had either changed for the better since she left Reedyville, or they had been mistaken about her in the first place.

"Mr. Palmiller and his society, who had objected at first to accepting anything from a woman they had been forced to run out of town, were won over one hundred per cent. They said it was plain that Honey had repented at last, that there was good in her after all, and that it would not be Christian to prevent her doing this good and generous deed. So the committee accepted the gift formally, and in due course the statue arrived."

Dr. Kent took out his pipe and filled it. "And what a ruckus it stirred up when it did arrive!" he said softly.

"At that time, anybody in town would have defined a war memorial as 'one to three doughboys in leggin's and helmets, with extended bayonets,' " said Mrs. Kent; "but on the day the statue arrived the Memorial Committee, at least, knew that it wasn't always as simple as that. They had planned to put the thing in the center of Court House Square, the busiest place in town; but after one look, they began to doubt the wisdom of that.

"The *Courier* that week carried an article by Mr. Porterfield. He said that, after reflection, it had been decided that M. Gagnon's distinguished piece of work would show up to better advantage against a background of greenery, so the date of the unveiling was postponed until a proper site in Wentworth Park could be prepared. By that time we all knew something had gone wrong, but only the Committee knew what, and they wouldn't say.

"Well," continued Mrs. Kent, "the whole town was simply crazy with excitement, particularly when it was known that Mr. Porterfield had telephoned the Metropolitan Museum of Art in New York to find out if Paul Gagnon was really a respectable and reliable man. They wondered if there hadn't been some confusion in names, after all; but the gentleman from the Metropolitan said quite firmly that there was only one Gagnon and that there was no mistake, adding that the town should be immensely proud to have a piece of his work to exhibit."

Mrs. Kent clapped her hands with delight, like a little girl. "Reedyville was simply crazy with curiosity, as I've already said, but we found out soon enough, on the day the statue was unveiled, and I'll never forget that day as long as I live."

"What was the statue like, for Heaven's sake, Miss Cordie?"

"Don't try to rush her, son," said Dr. Kent gently. "You won't make any progress that way."

"It went far beyond anything we had suspected!" said Mrs. Kent. "Oh, far beyond that! And it was plain why the Committee thought shrubbery more appropriate than the traffic of Court House Square. You see, the memorial was made of white marble, and it was quite orthodox in execution. In the background there was a female figure with draperies, scaled a little larger than reality. I suppose she represented Death or Mother Earth or something of that sort. The second figure, the one in the foreground, was male and life-size. The legs were rigid and firmly planted, and the body swayed backward a little from the hips. The arms were extended, and we saw at once that one thumb was inverted toward the wrist, instead of growing upward, and that the face was unmistakably the thin, intense face of a Boutwell."

"That sounds harmless enough," I said.

"Wait," said Mrs. Kent mockingly. "Wait until I tell you the rest." She leaned back in her chair again and pressed the handkerchief to her eyes. "You see the figure in the foreground, the figure of Breck Boutwell, which everybody had recognized at sight, was entirely naked and it was—" She stopped a moment and then went on: "It was entirely *complete!* It was the most uncompromisingly complete statue I've ever seen. M. Gagnon had been generous with both his time and his material, and nothing had been skimped."

Dr. Kent tamped his pipe lightly. "That piece of work almost wrecked this town," he said.

Mrs. Kent said: "It was something like meeting an acquaintance on the street when he didn't have his clothes on, the statue was so lifelike. Breck's eyes were half-closed and his head was inclined a little to the left, and as I peered past old Mrs. Clayton's shoulder, I could almost hear him sucking his toothpick stub and whispering, 'Hello, Peaches. Let me be your cream!' "

Mamie, the cook, appeared unexpectedly at the door. "Miss Cordie," she began, "them turtle eggs Dr. Frank brought home is swiveling round the edges and they done started to turn brown. They ain't acting right."

"That's what they're supposed to do," said Mrs. Kent. "Another half-hour on the stove won't hurt them." Then, when the cook had gone, she continued her story: "The invited audience at the unveiling took it politely enough, although I'll never forget the expression of baffled rage on Mr. Palmiller's face when he realized that he had sponsored this thing and that he had been tricked. Then everybody began to talk and to move away, leaving poor Breck Boutwell naked and abandoned in the middle of some rhododendron bushes." She sighed. "Poor Breck; I'll always remember him. He was the only man who ever insulted me."

Dr. Kent said: "It was averages, honey. Breck had three zeros and a decimal point in front of *you.*" He winked and turned to me. "Why don't you stay to supper?" he asked suddenly. "If you haven't eaten fresh-water turtle eggs, you've got something to look forward to."

"Of course he's going to stay," said Mrs. Kent. "Of course he is!" She smiled, patted her husband's hand and went on with her story.

"News about the memorial got around in no time, and that afternoon a batch of girls from the canning factory came to see for themselves. There was already a crowd when they got there, but the girls elbowed their way through, laughing and making remarks. 'That's Breck Boutwell, all right,' they said critically. 'That's Breck Boutwell, and no mistake!' They stopped beside the rhododendron bushes and slapped each other on the back, screaming with mirth and pointing. 'Hi, there, Breck!' they shouted. 'Hi, there, kid!'

"That monument divided this town for a few months," said

Dr. Kent. "I don't know what Honey expected out of it, but I, for one, think she got her money's worth."

Mrs. Kent said: "The town fell into three groups. One of them, headed by Mr. Palmiller, was determined to have the memorial removed, Paul Gagnon or no Paul Gagnon, agreement with the French lawyers or no agreement. The second group, with Ella Doremus as spokesman, thought the work very beautiful—which it was—and considered its artistic value wiped out any local inferences, accidental or otherwise. The third party thought the whole affair a joke, and good publicity for the town. Feeling got very bitter in a few weeks, particularly after Mr. Palmiller and Sister Joe Cotton began to distribute leaflets."

Mamie came once more to the side door. "Miss Cordie," she began in a worried voice, "them turtle eggs *still* ain't doing right! I baste 'em and baste 'em, but they don't firm up inside!"

Mrs. Kent said: "Turtle eggs never do. Anyway, we're coming in very soon now. Have a little patience, Mamie."

"Yassum," said Mamie doubtfully. "Yassum."

"The funniest leaflet of all was signed by Mr. Palmiller himself," said Dr. Kent, "and I've always thought his closing lines, from the standpoint of an old romantic like myself, the most disheartening I've ever read. Here they are, as nearly as I can remember them: 'And so the womanhood of Reedyville must daily view this spectacle to their detriment, our pure womanhood, many of whom are mothers!' "

Mrs. Kent said: "And so things went on until one Sunday morning when Mr. Palmiller and his society took matters into their own hands. They met about daybreak in front of Breck's statue. There was a prayer and a verse of 'Stand Up, Stand Up for Jesus,' I understand, before Sister Cotton climbed on the pedestal, pulled a cold chisel out of her bosom and held it firmly while Mr. Palmiller swung his mallet and made Reedyville safe for both maidens and ladies already married."

"Afterwards," continued Mrs. Kent, "there was nothing left for the town to do except take Breck down for repairs. They've got him in a shed back of Moore's old livery stable, they say. He's been there for the past fifteen years."

"What became of Breck's—" I began and then stopped. "In other words, what happened to—"

"You mean," prompted Dr. Kent mildly, "what became of the *detached* part of the memorial? If you do, I'll have to admit that nobody really knows. Some say the vice society has it on file with their postal cards and obscene literature; others claim that Sister Joe Cotton uses it in her office as a paperweight."

At that moment, the screen door behind us creaked slowly and the three of us turned our heads at the same instant. We saw Mamie's serious face being pushed toward us through the widening crack. She wiped her perspiring arms on her apron and rolled her eyes upward. "Miss Cordie," she began desperately, "them eggs done started *poppin'*, now! They ain't gwiner hold out much longer!"

At that instant, and without warning, the three of us began to laugh like idiots. We leaned back in our chairs and rocked from side to side, while Mamie looked from one to the other with surprise and rubbed her lip.

I went over to Dr. Kent and took him by both forearms. "I never ate turtle eggs," I gasped. "How big are they? How do you do it?"

But this set Dr. Kent off worse than before. He got up, pulled away from me and leaned against a post. "They're the size of big marbles," he said helplessly, "and they've got soft skins." He circled the post with his arms and rested his cheek against it. "You break 'em against your teeth, like grapes!" he shouted hoarsely.

Mrs. Kent bent forward, with his words, and pressed her streaming eyes against her palms. "Set another place, Mamie," she whispered as if in pain. "Mr. McBride is staying for supper."

She leaned back in her chair, relaxed and defenseless, her plump shoulders shaking.

Then Mamie, who had watched us with such perplexed dignity, doubled up suddenly against the screen door, her hands folded over her belly. She had not understood our laughter, but she was taking part in it against her will. She raised her body up and down from the waist, like a man doing exercises. "Lord God!" she cried in an ecstasy of mirth. "Lord God, have mercy on this crazy household!"

1937

THE FEMALE OF THE FRUIT FLY

HE PAID the taxi-driver and came up the steps, glad that another lecture trip was over and that he would soon see his wife again. He fumbled for his latchkey and let himself into the hall. "Edie! Edie!" he called. He whistled the three muted notes which were a signal between them. "Edie! Why didn't you meet me at the station?"

There was no answer and he put his bags down, telling himself that there was, as yet, no cause for alarm. No doubt his wife had failed to get his telegram or had mistaken his train. The door at the end of the hall opened and Mrs. Peters, the cook, came out wiping her hands.

"Mrs. Farr isn't here," she said. "She left last night after she got your telegram. There's a letter for you upstairs. It's on the mantel."

He started up the stairs while the cook stood staring at him. She said: "Supper is ready any time now. I'll put it on the table when you come down, Professor."

"I take it," he began slowly, "that my wife won't be here tonight."

"She won't be here," said Mrs. Peters. "That's right. She took the seven o'clock train last night."

He went up the stairs and into the bedroom which he had shared with his wife. He saw the note at once. It was leaning against a vase, propped by an ashtray. When he had read it twice, he folded the note slowly and put it into his pocket.

He turned after a moment and began unpacking his bags.

From the bottom of one bag he took out the present which he had brought home for his wife. It was a jade elephant with spread feet, whose neck lifted triumphantly in the air and whose trunk curved backward a little. The gift had been too expensive, really, but he knew that Edie would like it for her collection, which marched before him on the mantel; so he had bought it anyway.

Later he washed his hands and face and went downstairs again. Mrs. Peters began at once to put supper on the table.

"I suppose everybody on the campus knows by this time."

"If they don't," said Mrs. Peters, "it's only because they're all blind and haven't got ordinary sense."

He sat at the table and unfolded his napkin. "In her note, my wife said she was leaving with a man named George Reilly. Do you know who he is? Did he live here in town?"

"Oh, I know him all right," said Mrs. Peters. She put both hands on her hips and shoved downward. "George Reilly runs that bar and grill on Green River Road. You know. The place where soldiers from the training camp hang out. But how she met him in the first place is a mystery to me."

Mrs. Peters hovered beside the table, unable, in her indignation, to go away. She began to talk rapidly: She had worked for many people in her day, both here, at the university, and in town, and she had made it a point in the past to keep her mouth shut about matters which didn't concern her. She thought the professor could truthfully bear her out in this, and he nodded his head absently.

She had thought she'd learned something about people, after all these years, but apparently she hadn't. She sighed and raised her arms outward. The affair wouldn't be so baffling to her if Mrs. Farr had been another sort of woman; but she had always seemed so intelligent and refined, a woman so content with her husband, her home and her circle of friends.

Dr. Farr bent over his food but he did not answer.

Mrs. Peters picked up the used dishes and backed toward the pantry door. "You asked a minute ago if I *knew* George Reilly. Yes, I know him well, because he grew up in this town, and there's one thing sure: He won't give her the love and care that you did. He won't even take care of her proper, and when the time comes, he'll walk off an' leave her, and that'll be the end of it."

She rested her back against the pantry door and said helplessly: "I just don't understand Mrs. Farr at all. A man like George Reilly shouldn't fool a four-year-old child." She pushed suddenly against the door with her back and sidled through to her kitchen, puffing a little.

Dr. Farr lifted his spoon and turned it in his palms, remembering the time he had first met his wife, and how he had fallen in love with her almost at sight. She had been very popular, and as he had sat that first afternoon turning a cocktail glass in his palms and listening to the blurred babble of voices about him, he had calculated his chances with her. He had concluded they were not good. Later, when he knew her better, and learned that she was engaged to a man in Chicago, he had thought that he had no chance at all. But he had persisted blindly and then, suddenly, she had married him one night, to the surprise of her family and himself.

Mrs. Peters came back with coffee. "We had good weather here while you were away," she said, "except on Tuesday. It rained all day last Tuesday."

When he finished his coffee, Dr. Farr got out his typewriter and sat at his desk. His vacation was over and the new term began the next day. He flipped the pages of his desk diary until he came to the page he sought and noted the first item: "Monday, 9:30 A.M.—Class Elementary Biology." He bent above the diary, his hand shading his eyes, thinking: "Why? Why didn't I insist on her going with me? Why did I leave her alone for two whole weeks?"

As a rule he started this particular term with a lecture on the significance of mutation. He opened his desk and searched for his last year's notes. When he found them, he started to type, but before he had finished a page he tore the sheet from the machine and inserted another. He had changed his mind. He rearranged his margins and began again, typing in capitals at the top of the new page: "Notes on the Theory of Sexual Selection."

Farther down the page he continued: "For a long time there has been a theory that the females of certain species tend to select as mates only the most active, the most brilliantly colored or the strongest males of their kind. This principle was first comprehensively stated by Charles Darwin, but it was disputed, even in Darwin's own day, and for a time it fell into disrepute. At the moment, the trend seems to favor it once more. Then let us examine briefly the facts on which this theory was built and see how consonant they are with facts which the investigations of our more brilliant, present-day scientists have brought to light."

He wrote methodically, his mind concentrated on the task before him. He could hear Mrs. Peters in the kitchen washing the dishes, still mumbling to herself. She came into the room at length, folded a cloth and put it away. Dr. Farr stopped his work and turned in his chair. "Would you say that George Reilly is better looking than I am?" he asked.

Mrs. Peters seemed a little surprised. "Why, no," she said after a moment. "No, I would not say that."

"Is he more intelligent, or stronger than I am? Is he better able to protect her?"

Mrs. Peters smiled for the first time that night. "Now, Dr. Farr," she began. "I've already told you the kind of man George is, and you know it."

He sat quietly for a time, his hands clasped around his knees. "You're a woman, the same as my wife," he said. "Maybe a woman's viewpoint is different from mine. Can you think of any reason she might have had for leaving me?"

Mrs. Peters pondered the question. "Maybe you're a little too sobersided for a young man," she said at length, "but that don't seem like reason enough to me." She shut the drawer and came closer to the desk. She seemed a little embarrassed. "You always seemed affectionate enough with her, Dr. Farr, and I, for one, would never take you for a cold man with anybody you really cared about, but sometimes—" she stopped, apparently unable to shape her words delicately enough . . . "but sometimes things are not right between a couple, if you know what I mean, no matter how loving they look to outsiders."

"Everything was all right between us," he said. "It was nothing like that."

Mrs. Peters sighed and went back to her work. A moment later Dr. Farr began to type rapidly: "Now that we have discussed the evidence on which this theory rested originally, let us examine as impartially the evidence against it, taking first for our purpose, the newt.

"In its breeding season the male, ordinarily a dull brown color, acquires stripes of yellow, orange or orange-red, and an imposing crest whose purpose seems to be entirely decorative often grows upon his back. With this equipment he goes in search of a female, and when he has found one, he deposits near her a small sack which contains his sperms. Then, wildly, he swims around his female, displaying his crest, his coloration and his antic charms to the best possible advantage; and if he succeeds in interesting her, she will go to his bundle and pick it up, thus ensuring the continuation of her kind.

"Superficially this appears to support the theory that the female through her sexual preferences determines the characteristics of some species, in that she will select as a partner only a male handsome enough or vigorous enough to put her into a receptive state; but let us look at things a little more closely.

"As scientists far more able than myself have pointed out, it must often happen that several males come upon the same unstimulated female at the same time, and that they find themselves all competing for her favor. Let us assume for the purpose of this lecture that one of the males is of normal vigor but of exceptionally beautiful coloration; that another is vigorous enough in his antics but is of ordinary coloration, and even lacks the characteristic crest, while the third competitor has no mating coloration at all and is so lethargic as hardly to be interested in the female at all.

"Under these conditions it is reasonable to assume that after the female has been put into a receptive state by one male, she has no means whatever of distinguishing his sperm sack from the sacks of his rivals. Thus it is likely that the brilliantly colored male will be the one who stimulated her sufficiently, and as a result of such stimulation that she will pick up the sack of the dun-colored male who did not interest her at all.

"It is therefore apparent that the newt who succeeds through his courtship in putting the female of his kind into a willing state and the male with whose sperms she eventually fertilizes her eggs, are not necessarily the same."

He broke off and stared at the wall before him. He closed his eyes, trying to blot from his mind the face of his wife and her lover. There was little that he could do now, and there was no point in thinking too much. He lit a cigarette, his hands trembling. To him there had always been something childlike and appealing in his wife's sweet helplessness and he spoke aloud, as if already he defended her to the world. "It isn't as if she were a depraved woman," he said. "It isn't as if there were anything immoral about her. People will say that about her, but if they understood her as well as I do, they would know at once that it was not true."

The telephone rang, and he got up at once and went into the hall. He stood with his fingers beating on the surface of the small table, listening to the insistent ring which seemed, now, to fill the house with sound; then, without lifting the receiver, he came back to his desk, and after a moment the ringing ceased. Mrs. Peters came through the connecting door. "It's been ringing like that all day," she said. "I told them I didn't know where Mrs. Farr was, or what her plans were."

All at once Dr. Farr wanted to talk to somebody. He began slowly, his voice hesitant, while Mrs. Peters stood across the room and nodded her head at intervals.

This was not the first time his wife had left him. It had happened once before, three years ago. He had been teaching in another college at the time, and that was the reason he had left and come to this place. They hadn't exactly asked for his resignation, but after his wife returned to him, a few months later, he had found it necessary to leave, just the same. He closed his eyes again and lifted his hands, making a small, beating gesture against the air.

He must start looking for another job, he supposed, and the sooner the better, but he dreaded going through all that again. It was a pity, in a way, because he liked his work here and he liked the friends he had made.

Mrs. Peters gathered up the loose strands of her hair and tucked them under her hat. "Will you take her back this time, too?"

"I don't know."

"Then you'll take her back," she said. She went to the door and opened it. "I haven't told anybody what I know, and I don't intend to," she continued. "There'll be a lot said this time, too, but none of it will come from me." She closed the door, and after a moment Dr. Farr turned back to his typewriter.

He wrote: "In conclusion, there are those experiments which have been made with the common fruit fly. The male of this species, when courting the female, does so by alternately stretching out each of his wings, and after a short time union takes place. It has been demonstrated, in cases where the wings have been completely removed from the males, or only partially removed, that a longer period of courtship is necessary before the female responds, so it would seem incontestable that the male with an efficient wing spread is more attractive to the female of the fruit fly than one whose wings have been modified or removed entirely.

"But let us examine what happens, in actuality, when a female is given the opportunity to choose, after she has been stimulated, between a fully winged male, a partially winged male, and a male with no wings at all. In such cases, it has been found after repeated tests that the female shows no selective faculty whatever, that she will choose the partially winged male, or the male with no wings at all, just as often as she will choose the superior one, and that she will accept any male at all after the lapse of time characteristic of courtship with a fully winged male.

"It is thus obvious that when the female of the fruit fly has the opportunity to discriminate she cannot do so. She can only be stimulated by one male until she reaches her instinctive, willing state, and when she has reached that state she will submit to copulation, but the male of the fruit fly with whom she copulates is merely a matter of propinquity and chance."

Dr. Farr got up from his typewriter and walked about the room, his hands touching the objects about him nervously. Another sort of man, he felt, would get drunk, or curse, or even go after his wife and her lover with a gun, but he knew that he, himself, would never be able to achieve relief so simply.

He came back to his desk after a time and read his notes through, redrafting a sentence or changing a word here and there. He looked at his schedule for the next day. He was down for another lecture at eleven, but he would have time to prepare that in the morning. He shoved back his chair, feeling tired all at once; then he locked and bolted the door and went to his bedroom.

At once he saw the jade elephant, still resting on Edie's dressing-table where he had put it. He picked it up, and as he stood with his thumb caressing the smooth jade, he had an impulse to throw the ornament through the open window, into the shrubbery below. Instead, he went to the mantel and shifted the procession of elephants until the new statue was fitted into its proper place in the long, graduated line. He thought: "I am what I am, and Edie is what she is, and it isn't likely that either of us will ever change. That is unfortunate. That is really unfortunate."

Later, he undressed and lay in bed. He found his cigarettes after a moment and lit one, watching its tip brighten and die away against the darkness. He knew, then, that no matter what Edie did, or how greatly he despised her, as he did at this moment, when George tired of her, as the other man had, he would be waiting to take her back, just as Mrs. Peters had predicted.

He wondered bitterly why this should be, why he denied himself those luxuries of indignation which others knew. Another man would have considered himself irreparably wronged. He would have thought only of himself, feeling no responsibility toward her at all; and since he could comprehend no viewpoint except his own, he would have cursed her and washed his hands of her as a simple matter of principle, sure of the world's approval and of the expressed sympathy of his kind.

Then, slowly, he saw the basis of his bondage and acknowledged it to himself. "Yes, yes!" he said wearily. "But how could I do such things? How could I defend such a position for myself? . . . I understand her too deeply."

He crushed out his cigarette and turned on his back, his head pressed against the cup of his laced fingers, his eyes looking straight into darkness. . . . You were taught that understanding was an enriching thing, that it brought contentment and happiness to those who possessed it, and yet this was not always true. As often as not, understanding was a most cruel bond which tied the strong to the weak forever, and without pity.

He turned again, settling his pillow, staring at the line of elephants seen dimly on the mantel. At that moment he knew clearly what the remainder of his life was going to be, and he shuddered.

1937

THE FUNERAL

When her little niece died, Mrs. Kirby went at once to her brother's house on Madison Street and took charge of things. She had made all the arrangements for the funeral herself, she had even selected the small, satin casket, and she stood, now, receiving late floral offerings and greeting the friends who came to offer their sympathy.

"It's very sad," she kept saying. "I can't believe it, even yet. Only a week ago and she was as well and strong as you or I. She took sick two days after her seventh birthday."

The bell rang again and she turned from her friends and opened the front door. It was then that she saw Reba, the cook's little girl. Reba stood beside the fence, a look of amazement on her scarred, black face. Her nappy hair had been plaited by her mother and tied with thread the Sunday before, but the thread was coming loose and the plaits, unraveled a little now, stood up on her skull like tiny lengths of frayed, black hemp. She was wearing a faded, print dress which the dead child had outgrown; but the dress was too small for Reba, as well, and beneath it her bare legs and a stretch of her lathlike, black thighs were visible.

Mrs. Kirby opened her mouth, as if to speak to the child, but she did not. She merely took the wreath from the delivery boy and went into the parlor where the coffin was. She put the flowers down, and when she came back to the hall, she saw that other friends had come. The new arrivals went at once and stood above the small, white casket. They were early, and after whispering together, they seated themselves at the far end of the room and waited for the funeral service to begin.

Mrs. Kirby came onto the porch once more, stopping beside the cypress vines. "Reba," she said, "you can't stand out here staring at people. Go play in the back yard."

"Yassum," said Reba. "Yassum." She moved from the fence regretfully, looking back over her shoulder. At that moment the florist's wagon turned the corner and stopped again, and the delivery boy came up the walk with another design. It was from the schoolchildren of the little girl's class this time. The design was almost as tall as Reba herself, and it showed two gates swinging outward, gates made of dampened moss into which flowers had been stuck. Above the opening gates, and supported by a rod, there floated a stuffed, white dove with outspread wings.

"Reba," said Mrs. Kirby patiently. "Reba, don't you hear me talking to you? Go back to the kitchen and stay with your mother."

Reba looked at her imploringly. "Yassum," she said meekly. "Yassum." But it was not possible for her to move from the fence. She turned her neck and her black, bullet-shaped head slowly, following the floral offering up the steps with her eyes and sighing when the door shut away its magnificence. Mrs. Kirby started to speak again, but changed her mind. She went to the kitchen where Cora, the cook, bent over her sink, scrubbing pots.

"You must tell your little girl to go away from the fence," she said. "She's standing there staring at everybody who comes in. I've told her to go away, but she won't mind me."

Cora looked up and wiped her lips on her sleeve. "Reba ain't got good sense," she said reproachfully. "You knows that. You knows Reba never did have good sense." She turned ponderously and reached for the thick switch which lay on the shelf above the woodbox. She went into the side yard and stood half screened by shrubbery. "Come away from that fence, gal!" she whispered fiercely. "Come away from that fence befo' I put another knot on your haid!"

"Yassum," said Reba meekly. "Yassum."

She backed warily away from her mother, making a wide half-circle, but when the clump of cypress trees and small crêpe-myrtles were between them, she turned and ran, throwing her legs out.

"Let me ketch you by that fence agin," said Cora. "Jes' let me hear one mo' word about how you doin'!" She followed her daughter, shaking her switch, but Reba ran into the kitchen, picked up the scouring cloth and began washing the pots still left in the sink.

When the dishes were done, she went onto the back porch and stood beside the steps, remembering once more the remarkable things she had seen that day. She sat down by the window on an upturned scrubbing bucket and began plaiting the strands of an old mop with her black fingers. Then she got up quickly, having forgotten her mother's wrath, and went again to the side yard, but this time she did not go near the gate; instead, she sat in the swing that hung from the limb of a small sycamore tree.

The swing and the tree were partly surrounded by the half-circle of crêpe-myrtles and cypress saplings, and it would be difficult for Mrs. Kirby to see her there. She gripped the two ropes of the swing and propelled herself backward and forward, her head nodding rhythmically to the creaking of the ropes, one bare, skinny leg dragging in the dust.

Between gaps in the shrubbery, she caught occasional glimpses of the sidewalk. Many people were coming to the funeral now, and when she twisted sideways, and craned her neck, she could see them open the gate and walk on tiptoes up the gravel path. At length the minister turned in at the gate, and the funeral service was about to begin. The minister was dressed in black, and he was tall and solemn. His eyes, at once stern and forgiving, looked searchingly at the congregated people before he inclined his head a little, as if he gave his blessing to all alike.

Reba began swinging wildly, her head higher than the limb to which the swing was fastened, her black, out-thrust legs agitating the tops of the crêpe-myrtles. It was then she saw, above the tops of the shrubbery, that there was no longer room for visitors inside the house, and that latecomers stood on the porch outside. Beyond the gate, on the sidewalk, the classmates of the dead child waited, their backs pressed against the picket fence.

She swung back and forth furiously and laughed with a strange excitement which she did not understand. Then all at once she became quiet. She brought the swing to a standstill as quickly as she could, trailing one leg in the dust as a brake, and glanced fearfully from Mrs. Kirby to her mother.

Mrs. Kirby said: "You can't hear anything inside except that swing creaking back and forth, and it looks from the windows like a hurricane had hit the tops of those crêpe-myrtle bushes."

"Come away from that swing, gal!" said Cora angrily. "Come away, like I tell you!"

"Yassum," said Reba in her soft, meek voice. "Yassum."

She sidled cautiously away, and when she had the shrubbery between herself and her mother, she began to run. She ran as far as the old carriage-house; but she stopped there, grinning foolishly. "You see, Mrs. Kirby?" said Cora. "You see?"

When Mrs. Kirby had gone, Cora walked toward the carriage-house, but she stopped when she was almost there. "What make you pick a day like this to act so crazy?" she asked. "If it wasn't disrespectful to the daid, I'd whup you within an inch of your life." She went back to her work, pretending that she had forgotten about the swing, and a few moments later Reba came trotting up the path.

Cora seized her by the neck when she came in the door. "Now, Miss," she said triumphantly. "I got you now, and I ain't gwiner let you get away from me agin." She shoved her down onto the stool beside the stove and thrust a bowl into her hands. "Here, gal," she said. "Finish shelling them peas." She went into the pantry and began sifting flour on her breadboard. "Say something, Reba," she said. "Keep saying something so I'll know you ain't run off agin."

"I don't know nothing to say."

"Say yassum. Keep saying yassum."

"Yassum," said Reba meekly.

She picked up the bowl and began shelling the peas, thinking once more of the funeral. It was the first time she had seen a funeral for white folks, and she had not imagined that anything could be so magnificent; but there was much that she did not understand, and as her mother walked from pantry to kitchen and back again, she considered these puzzling matters with her slow mind. A week ago the little girl who had died had merely been another child, like any other, but with death she had taken on a strange sort of importance; and people who had hardly known her, now crowded the house for the privilege of looking at her; they wept openly for her; they wore black in her honor; they sent her flowers.

It was then that Mrs. Kirby came into the kitchen and asked Cora if she wanted to see the little girl for the last time. Cora began to cry, wiping her eyes on her skirt. She rolled down her sleeves, put on a clean apron, and followed Mrs. Kirby into the hall; but she stopped in the doorway and spoke warningly: "Keep sitting on that stool until I get back, Reba," she said. "You move one inch off that stool and I'm going to put a knot on your haid. See if I don't!"

"Yassum," said Reba meekly. "Yassum."

She sat quietly for a time, trying to concentrate on the peas before her, but when somebody began to play on a fiddle, and somebody began to sing a white-folks' hymn which was both sad and comforting, she could hold out no longer. She put down the bowl and twisted her raveling plaits, rolling her black, bullet-shaped head from side to side. Then she got up from the stool and went through the back door. "Yassum," she said pleadingly in the direction her mother had taken. "Yassum."

When she turned the corner of the house, she saw that the hearse and the carriages for people to ride in to the cemetery had come. The hearse was drawn by white horses and they stood, now, shaking out their manes and biting at each other's necks. Reba took in these details quickly and then dropped to her hands and knees, following the line of shrubbery that circled the house. She crawled carefully, and when she reached the parlor window, she stretched her thin neck upward and peered in.

The first thing she saw was the coffin. It was set in the middle of the room. It was pure white and beautiful, and it was piled high with flowers. There were silver handles to the coffin, and streamers of white ribbons hung from its sides. She caught her breath with amazement. She stared with her mouth half open, her eyes wide with wonder.

The preacher stood beside the casket and comforted the weeping people. Then he turned and spoke to the parents of the dead child: The ways of God were not our ways, and it was not given to mortals to understand them. We could only bear our losses with fortitude, and this mother and this father must comfort themselves in the knowledge that their child was not dead in the real sense of the word, but that she awaited them in heaven.

Reba sighed and shifted her weight. She craned forward a little, and she saw her mother standing against the far wall. Cora's shoulders shook with her grief, and at intervals she lifted her apron and pressed it flat against her streaming eyes. All at once Reba sank back on her haunches, her face cupped in her palms. "Yassum," she said softly, drawing the word out interminably. "Yassum."

The service was over at last and men carried the coffin down the steps and put it into the waiting hearse, piling the flowers around it. Then, when the carriages were filled and the hearse moved away, Reba could remain hidden no longer. She went again to the fence and stared openly, dragging her feet in the dust. The procession was under way now, and as it moved off, the schoolchildren, who had waited so patiently, fell in behind the last carriage and marched solemnly.

The last carriage had disappeared around the corner when Reba felt her head jerked backward and heard her mother's voice. "Now, then!" Cora said. "Now, then, I'll settle with you, Miss!" She shoved her daughter forward until they reached the old carriage-house. Reba fell down and pressed her face into the dust. "Don't whup me," she begged. "I won't do it no more.

Don't whup me, please, ma'am." But her mother brought the stick down over her cringing head and shoulders. "You gwiner mind me," she said. "From now on, you gwiner do what I tell you!"

The whipping was over at last and Cora started back to the house, but she stopped in the path. "They'll be back from the graveyard in a little while, and they'll be hongry. I got to get supper going," she said. Then she sighed despairingly and raised her arms outward. "What make you *do* the way you do, Reba?" she asked. "What make you provoke me the way you do?" She rolled down her sleeves. "I ain't a mean woman. Ever'body knows I ain't a mean woman."

"Yassum," said Reba.

"Go wash that blood off'n your haid," said Cora, "and then bring me in some stove-wood."

"Yassum," said Reba meekly. "Yassum."

She waited until her mother was in the kitchen and then she stood up, leaning against the door. She unbuttoned her dress and turned her head sideways, examining the bruises on her scarred back. She touched the bleeding place on her head and began to cry again. "Yassum," she said. "Yassum." She sank to the ground once more, her hands, with fingers interlocked, clutched between her thin, black knees. She rocked back and forth and made her foolish, intaken sound. "Yassum!" she said over and over. "Yassum! Yassum! Yassum!"

She got up after a while and carried in the wood for her mother, but when the box was filled, she went again to the side yard and stood at the gate. It was beginning to get dark, and already the small cypresses and the crêpe-myrtle bushes cast shadows against the house. Before her, on the gravel walk, were the heads of flowers, fixed by florist's wire to toothpicks, which had fallen from the mossy designs in which they had originally rested. Reba picked up the flowers and stuck them into her tightly plaited, nappy hair, until it looked, after a moment, as if she wore a white wreath on her head.

Afterwards she went to the swing and shoved herself backwards and forwards, thinking once more of the little white girl's funeral. At first it had seemed to her that the funeral could not have been more magnificent, but familiarity with its details made her, now, more critical; and as she swung back and forth, one leg dragging in the dust like a brake, she talked to herself:

"When I have *my* funeral," she said, "I'm gwiner have me a band, too. Gwiner have *all* white horses at my funeral, and folks gwiner send up sky rockets that night."

Then, slowly, she let the swing come to rest and sat quietly. Something important had occurred to her and she was motionless for a time, her hands gripping the ropes of the swing. "Why, I can have a funeral, too, if I feel like it," she said in surprise. "Nothing to stop me from having a funeral as good as *anybody,* if I want to."

She swung back and forth slowly, pondering this idea, her toes almost reaching to the edge of the crêpe-myrtle bushes. It seemed to her at that moment that she had found out, unaided, a fact of great importance, a thing which should be known to everybody, but was not. She opened her eyes very wide. She threw back her bullet-shaped head, stretched her mouth and made her foolish, intaken sound. The thing she had discovered seemed so simple, so easy to arrange, that she wondered why everybody else didn't think of it too.

"Why, there ain't nothing to having a funeral," she said contemptuously. "I can have a funeral if *I* want to; ever'body can have a funeral if *they* want to." She swung more rapidly, her legs shooting up above the tops of the crêpe-myrtles. When she remembered again the words the preacher had spoken as he stood beside the white child's coffin that very afternoon, it did not seem sensible that anybody would want to live in a world as harsh as this one was when they could have, so easily, not only eternal happiness in heaven, but a magnificent funeral as well. She brought the swing to a stop and got up. She took the wooden seat from the swing and stood it carefully against the trunk of the tree.

She hesitated a moment, then, having made up her mind, she climbed the sycamore like a small, excited monkey, anxious to put her plan through before her mother or Mrs. Kirby found out what she was up to and stopped her. She straddled the limb to which the swing was fixed and unfastened the knots in the rope; she wound the rope around the limb until she had shortened it expertly to the length she needed, laughing all the time with pleasure and nodding her head in anticipation of her triumph.

Cora came onto the porch and called, "Reba? Reba, where you at? I want you to go to the meat market for me."

But Reba flattened against the tree. She held her breath while her mother continued to call, seeing again, in her mind's eye, the triumphant details of her approaching funeral. First, there were the white horses and the brass bands. The bands played slow, sad music continuously, and the proud horses, as if conscious of the importance of such an occasion, pawed at the ground and shook out their white, silken manes. Mrs. Kirby was dressed in black silk, and she pressed a lace handkerchief to her eyes. She stood at the front door to take the floral designs, explaining the details of Reba's death to the mayor of the town, the minister of the Baptist church and the unending stream of lesser people who crowded behind them.

"It's little Reba, this time," said Mrs. Kirby. "Yes, sir, it's little Reba, and we're all so upsot we just don't know *what* to do!" She began to cry again. "Looks like we don't get shut of one funeral in this house till we have another one, now does it?" She bowed her head submissively. "Yassum," she continued, as if answering a particular question, "Reba was a sweet child, and no two ways about it. I tell you *ever'*body gwiner miss Reba, and that's a fact!"

Cora called from the porch: "Reba! Reba, where you at? You better answer me, gal, if you know what's good for you!" She stood a moment on the steps as if debating a point, then she went toward the old carriage-house mumbling to herself angrily. When she was out of earshot, Reba spoke: "Yassum," she said in her small, meek voice. "Yassum, I hears you."

She stretched her neck and peered around the trunk of the tree, but when her mother reached the carriage-house and went inside, she bent down and caught up the dangling rope. Then she straddled the limb and inched forward cautiously. She stopped when she reached the middle of the limb and looked about her. She lifted the rope and wrapped it around her throat, tying a knot solidly at the side. "Yassum," she said, drawing the word out interminably. "Yassum."

Cora came away from the carriage-house and stopped beside the canna bed. "I knows you're hiding out some place," she said. "I knows as well as I'm standing here that you hear every word I'm a-saying." She went back onto the porch and took a drink of water, throwing what was left in the dipper onto the ground with a faint splash.

But Reba sat quietly for a time, her black knees gripping the sycamore limb, looking about her slowly and listening to her mother's voice. At that instant she had a clear picture of Cora weeping over her coffin, just as she had wept over the coffin of the white child. "Reba! Reba, come back to us!" she said over and over, her face twisted with the force of her grief. "Don't leave us here to mourn, sweet little Reba! Don't leave us this-a-way, honey!"

Then Reba drew back her head and made her foolish, intaken sound. "Yassum," she said softly. "Yassum." Suddenly she lifted her arms and swayed forward. She unlocked her knees from the limb and fell eagerly, the rope pulling her up and jerking her head sideways. At once she lifted her lathlike arms and tried to grasp the limb above her head, but she could not; then she jerked her body convulsively and made a shrill, strangled noise while the rope spun outward in a circle.

Cora said: "I hear you, Miss. I hear you laughing and acting silly and provoking me!" She shook her shoulders angrily. "All right, stay where you is! You'll get hongry befo' long, and then I'll catch you!" She went inside and rattled the stove-lid, throwing in firewood. A few minutes later she came back to the porch and looked about her again.

"There ain't no way to get away from me, gal," she said. "You'd know that by now, if you had any sense." She looked straight at the clump of crêpe-myrtles which screened the swing from the house and raised her voice a little, as if she addressed personally the bundle which hung limp and strangled at the end of the still-vibrating rope. She said: "When I get supper cooked I'm gwiner come look for you; and when I look for you, I'm gwiner *find* you; and when I find you, I'm gwiner give you a whupping you'll *remember!*"

1937

CINDERELLA'S SLIPPER

He was the Mr. Hollings of the law firm of Wetherall, Byrne, Hollings and Lipman; not yet so experienced, politically, as his immediate senior, C. Ralph Byrne, nor so well connected as old Mr. Wetherall with his endless settlements of estates and his trusteeships for rich old women, but he had gone a long way for a man thirty-five years old who had started without influence or money. He had succeeded through the force of his determined ability, and as he came into the outer office and saw again his name, Mr. Vernon L. Hollings, in gold lettering on his private door, he felt a sense of satisfaction, knowing that this reality marked one of the goals he had set for himself.

He stood at the switchboard, inside the railed-off enclosure, and took off his gloves. Before him was the stenographers' room, and he saw at once that Miss Cavallo's place had been filled. He drew his gloves through his palms three times and went to the drinking fountain, bent over, and pressed the button that threw a small stream of water into his mouth. From the drinking fountain, he could see the new girl more plainly, and the first thing he noticed about her were her feet. She was wearing, probably for the first time, a pair of black, patent-leather slippers whose gleaming newness stood out all the more against the background of her general shabbiness. Her shabbiness was not a thing that you could identify definitely, it was more generalized; but you knew at once, no matter how unimaginative you were, that she had had no new clothes, with the exception of the bright slippers, for a long time.

He turned from the fountain and went toward his private offices. His secretary, Miss Link, was on the 'phone when he came in. She covered the mouthpiece with her palm. "It's the executive council of the Non-Partisan Church League," she said. "They want you to speak at their dinner tonight. Senator Swathmore was to have done it, but he got sick at the last minute."

He smiled and nodded, and Miss Link turned back to the 'phone. "Mr. Hollings just came in," she said, "and he'll be very happy to be with you. Let me have the address and the time, please."

Hollings went into his inner office. He was about to push the button for Miss Link when old Mr. Wetherall, the senior partner, came in and sat down in the wide chair by the window.

"Well, Verne," he began genially, "I got the goods on you this time. I saw you admiring the little number who took over Miss Cavallo's job." He laughed heartily. "When you went to get a drink of water, you weren't fooling *me,* my lad! I knew it wasn't a drink of water you had on your mind."

He was a man in his middle sixties with white hair and a full, sensual mouth. He had been famous for his love affairs in his day, and he still treated the jet-trimmed old ladies, who were both his clients and his contemporaries, with heavy, male coquettishness.

Hollings took off his reading glasses and leaned back in his chair. He smiled and nodded his head. He had learned, long ago, that falling at once into the mood of others was the surest method of having your own way in the long run. "You caught me this time, Mr. Wetherall," he said amiably, "so I won't try to fix up an alibi."

Mr. Wetherall laughed again, pleased with himself, and pulled at his white waistcoat. He rolled his eyes suggestively. "You didn't know it, Verne, but I was behind you all the time, and I thought: 'Verne always was a sly dog with women, one of the sly ones, and keeps them all guessing; but this time I've got the goods on him.' "

Verne sat looking at his senior, smiling ruefully and nodding, but his mind was far away. He thought again of the new girl, of the patent leather slippers which seemed so out of place in her generalized, genteel shabbiness, and he wanted to laugh. Possibly she had bought the slippers with her last money when she got this job, her old ones being too far gone to serve any more.

When Mr. Wetherall got up and went back to his own office, Hollings rang for Miss Link. She came at once with her book, and she made a slight face at the door through which Mr. Wetherall had passed. She turned back to Mr. Hollings and they both shook their heads and laughed. She was in love with him and she had been for a long time, but then so were all the other girls in the office. She had no hope of having him for her own. She had given that up long ago. He was a man, she felt, who would belong to no particular woman, but to the world. There was something about him at times that made her think of a character in history, and underneath his courteous, smiling tolerance she felt a fierce driving force which made him alien and a little terrifying.

He picked up the pile of letters and went through them, his mind working with the sureness and the rapidity which Miss Link had always admired. Between letters he stopped, looked into Miss Link's eyes and smiled his slow, ingratiating smile.

"Mr. Wetherall," he said lightly, as if answering the question which had been in her mind when she came in, "seems quite smitten with the new girl who took Miss Cavallo's place."

Miss Link put down her pencil. "At his age!" she began indignantly; then seeing the faint, ironic smile about his eyes, she too had smiled.

"Who is she, anyway?" he asked.

And Miss Link told him what she knew. She was a Miss Purdy and the managing clerk had just hired her. This was her first job, but she had good recommendations and the shorthand school said she was going to be expert with a little more experience.

"Poor kid," said Verne. "She looks frightened to death, doesn't she?"

When Mr. Hollings was in this sort of mood, when he showed the tenderer side of his character, Miss Link found it difficult to hide her devotion.

She got up when the dictation was over. She stopped by the door, her hand on the knob. "Oh, by the way," she began suddenly. "We were talking yesterday about that new reform party. Well, I told them you'd see their committee this afternoon at 3:15."

He nodded, thanked her, and turned back to his work, but his mind was no longer on it, and he kept thinking against his will of Miss Purdy. He wondered what her first name was, and for a moment he was tempted to call Miss Link back and ask her, but he realized that that would be too revealing. He would find out in time, anyway. He could wait.

He met Charlie Byrne, one of the other partners, when he was returning from lunch. They got out of the elevator together and came down the corridor.

"Say, what's all this about your running for office?" Byrne asked. Then, without waiting for a reply, he went on: "I'll say one thing, and it's this: You're a wonder. You're one in a million. One of the organizers of the party lived next door to me out in Sandford Hills, and he told me that they'd been checking up on you for a month. They even talked to maids and elevator boys at your place, but they didn't turn up a thing. They've just about come to the conclusion that you're God's gift to the party." He became more serious. "Say, fellow," he said, "do you know that half the women in this town cut your pictures out of the papers and frame them?"

They paused inside the door, beside the switchboard. To the left the stenographers were busily at work and Hollings looked again at Miss Purdy, his eyes focused on her trim ankles and her glistening, new slippers. Her feet were so dainty, he thought, so ridiculously small for this clumsy age.

Then he went into his office and plunged once more into his work. He was still busy when the committee called. They explained the purposes of their party and the support that was behind them. A good many people were sick of the conditions in town, they said, and if Mr. Hollings would consent to run on an independent ticket, he could depend on their organization 100 per cent. They had looked him up and had come to the conclusion that he was the one man who could be put in. His speech-making, his wide social life, and his public stand against vice in the past had made him more prominent, possibly, than he realized.

Hollings listened politely. He was quite aware of his growing political importance. Did these people take him for a fool? Did they think he wasted his evenings addressing silly clubs because he liked doing it?

"Of course we realize that your law practice is important," said one of the gentlemen. "It's asking a great deal of you when we ask you to give it up. But then you can do so much good."

Mr. Hollings inclined his head, but he did not speak. It was true his law practice was very profitable, more so, possibly, than these people imagined, but it was not an end in itself; it was merely a stepping-stone to the thing that he wanted more, and that was power. He would have what he wanted some day, but he knew it was not yet time. He said finally: "I'd be defeated this year, and so would anybody else you supported; but two years from now it should be a different story."

He went to the door with the committee and stood chatting with them beside the drinking fountain. Over their heads he could see Miss Purdy still typing away, her blonde hair brushed out of her eyes and anchored back of her ears with clips. She looked very tender and very young. He followed the line of her body with his eyes and saw, then, that she had taken off one of her shoes. He wanted to smile. She was probably quite conscious of the daintiness of her feet, and, in her vanity, she had bought the new shoes a size too small. He wondered what she had done with the missing shoe. He shifted his position a little and moved his head slowly. He saw after a moment that she had hidden it behind her wastebasket. No doubt she thought that the basket hid both the shoe and her stockinged foot from the outer office.

When the committee had gone, Mr. Hollings went over to Miss Purdy and spoke casually. "Take a memorandum for me, please," he began. "I'm afraid I'll forget it if I don't make a record now."

She looked up at the sound of his voice, and when she saw who it was, she became a little confused. She picked up her book, moved her chair back, and, in her nervousness, she brushed her pencils onto the floor. He bent over and picked them up, smiling reassuringly at her. "Just take it onto the machine," he said quietly. "It's very short."

He began to dictate slowly, and when he had finished, Miss Purdy took the typed note from her machine and handed it to him. He thanked her and smiled his slow, ingratiating smile; but when he was seated again at his desk, he rolled the memorandum into a ball and stuck it into his pocket. His throat was dry with excitement. His hands felt cold all at once, and he pressed them together. He noticed that his hands were trembling a little.

Miss Link brought him his letters at half past four, reminding him that he must leave earlier than usual if he expected to change his clothes and get to dinner on time. There was nothing else for the day, she explained, except routine matters which she could handle herself. If anything important came up before closing time, she'd call him at his apartment.

He put on his coat and hat and went with Miss Link into her smaller, adjoining office. He opened her door, and as he stood there drawing on his gloves, he noticed that there was a slight commotion in the stenographers' room. Miss Link went at once to see what it was, and he stood beside the door watching her. When she came back she was shaking her head at the absurdity of the situation she had discovered.

"It's about Miss Purdy's shoe," she said. "One of Mr. Wetherall's old ladies was in to see him about an hour ago, and she brought a terrier puppy with her. The puppy was running about the office like mad. Well, one of Miss Purdy's shoes is missing—she said she took it off for a minute to ease her foot—and it seems the dog must have picked it up and hid it somewhere about the office, or took it home with him."

Mr. Hollings buttoned his overcoat slowly. "Well," he said laughingly, "that *is* a crisis, isn't it?"

"It's more serious than you think," said Miss Link. "Miss

Purdy hasn't got another pair of shoes to her name, probably. And how is she going to get home tonight? She can't go down the street with one shoe off and one on."

Mr. Hollings thought once more of Miss Purdy and again he had that warm, tender sense of beauty which made him feel as if he were going to start trembling again. He took out his wallet quickly. "Poor child!" he said softly; and then, "Find out what size she wears and get her another pair before closing time." He handed Miss Link a ten-dollar note. "Don't let her know where the money came from," he said. "It would probably embarrass her."

Miss Link said: "I'll tell her that Mr. Wetherall's client found the shoe in her automobile and called up to ask me to replace it." She took the money and stood watching him as he passed through the office and out of the door. There were not many men in the world as fine as Mr. Hollings, she thought. If there were more like him, this would be a happy place to live in, indeed.

He took a taxi downstairs and was driven to his apartment. He stepped into the elevator and looked at his watch. It was only a quarter past five, and he had plenty of time to take his bath and dress. His valet, hearing a key in the lock, came into the living-room as Mr. Hollings entered. Miss Link had 'phoned earlier in the afternoon, he said, and he had already laid out Mr. Hollings' evening clothes. He came a step closer, as if to take his employer's hat and coat, but Mr. Hollings shook his head and went into the small room which served as a study, and which he kept locked. He stood for a moment listening at the door while the valet moved about the living-room outside, and when everything was quiet once more, he put his hand into his coat pocket and took out Miss Purdy's lost shoe.

He sat beside his desk and held the shoe in his hand, stroking its glazed, black surface with his fingers; then, after a moment, he went to the closet, which he also kept locked, and opened it; and there, on a shelf before his eyes, were the other shoes that he had loved, the shoes which had preceded Miss Purdy's.

They were all women's shoes except one, and all black, as Miss

Purdy's shoe was black, except one. The single, masculine shoe, the alien one, was light tan, and it sat, like some great shoe of shoes, guarding the small, feminine flock about it.

He had seen the tan shoe and its mate, freshly polished, outside the door of a hotel room early one morning, and he had taken it. He did not know why, because he had never before been interested in men's shoes; but this particular shoe had taken his fancy anyway, possibly because of its newness, its old-fashioned last, and the glazed brightness of its almost lemon color. It was a high-topped, countryman's shoe with wide toes. There were eyelets half way up, and beyond that were a series of metal hasps into which the crossed strings fit neatly. He hadn't seen a shoe like that in years, and he had picked it up upon impulse, stuck it under his coat, and hurried back to his own room. Later he had put a twenty-dollar bill in an envelope and stuck it into the remaining shoe. He was not a thief.

He heard his valet coming back to tell him that his bath was ready, and he shut the closet quickly and locked it. He came into his bedroom and undressed, thinking again of the committee who had called upon him that day. They knew very little about him, indeed, if they thought that he would be content with an office as trivial as the one they had offered him. He had considered it at all only because the office would serve as an entering wedge to his larger ambitions. Naturally, he had not told this to the committee, but his interest was not so much in enforcing the inadequate laws already in existence, as in passing other and more drastic laws, laws which would protect people more completely from their own disgusting and inherent desires.

When he had finished his bath and had dressed, he came into his study once more, and once more he unlocked the closet. He took Miss Purdy's shoe tenderly in his two hands, as if it were some small, terrified bird, and bent above it, rubbing his cheek against its gleaming surface.

It seemed incomprehensible to him, at that moment, that another man would embrace a mass of flesh, stuffed with digesting food, when there were shoes to be loved, shoes as impersonal and as beautiful as the one he now held against his lips; and yet there were: in fact, you couldn't go to the theater or to the movies, or even walk in a public park, without seeing men and women locked in each other's arms, their lips pressed together.

He lifted his head, his eyes burning with the pure, fierce light of a crusader. A shoe was also flesh, in a way, he thought; but it was flesh with the disgusting things taken out. He drew his lips down quickly. There was something terrifying and something pathetic in the intensity of his disgust. He resembled, at that moment, nothing so much as one of the handsomer, early Christian martyrs.

He put the shoe back on the shelf at last and turned from the closet. It was unfortunate that he had to go to the dinner, but he would get away as quickly as possible; he would spend a long, happy evening with the shoe, after all.

He went to the door and stood there regretfully with one hand on the knob. In his mind's eye he saw the slipper sitting with a sweet placidity on its shelf, awaiting his return like a faithful wife. Again he had a feeling of quick, warm excitement and he felt for a moment as if his flesh had somehow liquefied and was dripping slowly from his bones. He leaned against the door for support, his blood pounding in his ears, his breath coming with difficulty through his half-open mouth. He recovered in a moment, turned and blew a kiss to the slipper.

"Good-bye, my love! . . . My love!" he said passionately. "Good-bye, my love! . . . Good-bye for a little while!"

1937

THE FIRST SUNSET

WHEN Albert Evans was six years old, his mother took him to spend the afternoon with Mrs. Langkabel, a school friend of hers. Mrs. Langkabel, a widow, ran a truck farm about ten miles from Reedyville. She was on the lookout for her guests, and when she saw their automobile turn in from the road that day, she hurried to the gate to meet them. A tall man with a brown, wrinkled face walked behind her.

After she had greeted her friend, Mrs. Langkabel introduced the old man. "Katie," she said, "I want you to meet my cousin from the old country. He wasn't here the last time you came out for a visit."

The old man said: "I am Dr. Albert Ehrlich. Emma forgot to tell you my name, didn't she?" His English was perfect, but he spoke it with a slight foreign accent.

Mrs. Evans laughed gaily. "Well, now that *I've* just met an Albert," she said, "let me introduce one to you, Dr. Ehrlich." She indicated the boy who stood beside her. "I mean by that, I want you to meet my *son* Albert."

The old man and the boy looked at each other and then shook hands. The fact that they both had the same first name made them friends at once, and while the two women laughed and talked together about old times, the doctor showed his namesake around the farm. Late in the afternoon they went to gather eggs, and coming back, they sat on the kitchen steps and watched the sun go down behind an oak thicket.

Inside the house Mrs. Langkabel and Mrs. Evans were still

talking, and Albert could hear their voices plainly. "Mamma was born in the old country, too," said Mrs. Langkabel. "You remember her, don't you, Katie? How we used to laugh behind her back at the way she spoke English? Well, Dr. Ehrlich is her first cousin, and she was always talking about him when she was still alive. She was so proud of him later on, and they used to write to each other. So I asked him to come live with me because of Mamma."

Albert looked curiously at the old man, but he realized that his friend had not even heard Mrs. Langkabel's words. His mind was far away, and his eyes were fixed on the setting sun. Then, suddenly, he spoke:

"Did you ever hear the story of the first sunset?"

"No, sir," said Albert. "No, sir, I never did."

"Dr. Ehrlich is well known in his own country, I imagine," said Mrs. Evans. "Such a distinguished-looking man. Such nice manners."

"He's well known the world over," said Mrs. Langkabel. "It's more than you think, Katie. And why shouldn't he be? He devoted his whole life to the good of others."

The doctor lifted his chin a little, nodded thoughtfully and began his story: "All this happened a long time ago, Albert—long before Christ was born, and even before our own God was known about—but once upon a time there was a land something like our own, except that it wasn't round the way our world is, but was shaped more like a big mill wheel with two flat sides.

"The underside of the wheel was on the ocean," continued the old man, "so of course the upper side faced the sky; and it was here, in this region, that the old, pagan gods lived. The gods had many fine palaces to live in, but the most magnificent of all was on the sun. Early in the morning the sun-palace would come up over the eastern edge of the wheel, just as it does over our world today, my little Albert, and would begin its trip across the sky. It was the source of all light and all heat, and the wheel-people knew this quite well; so when they saw that the palace had appeared again, they would come out of their holes in the rocks, stare upward and make their cruel, bloody sacrifices.

"All day long the wheel-people had the sun to warm them and give them light, but when it had traveled all the way across the sky and had reached the western rim of the wheel, it went off into unknown lands, and the wheel was dark and cold again until it returned."

Dr. Ehrlich paused a moment, smiled and looked down at his namesake, who sat on the step just below him. Then he bent forward timidly, as if he wanted to put his arm about the boy, but, as if remembering something, he sat up straight again and continued his story:

"Life on the earth-wheel was a terrible experience," he said. "The people there were cold and miserable all the time, and there was never enough to eat. It was a bleak, rocky land that they lived on, and there was not much around them except the ocean, the sky and the wide salt marshes.

"It would seem that the common misery of the wheel-people would draw them together, wouldn't it, Albert? . . . Sadly, it did not work out that way, because they were unforgiving and cruel to one another and they were forever fighting among themselves. It was the only thing they knew."

"What did the wheel-people look like, Dr. Ehrlich?"

The old doctor thought a moment, his lips pursed slightly. "They had thick, clumsy bodies," he began, "and their backs didn't straighten all the way up, as ours do. They had long arms and short, twisted legs; they had coarse, yellow hair and their mouths were half-open all the time.

"And so things went on like this for ages and ages, and then a strange little boy was born among the wheel-people, and our story really begins. At first the boy seemed like the rest of his kind, but there was something inside him that made him very different from them. You see, Albert, this peculiar little boy didn't believe in the cruelty and bloodshed which he saw every day, and he said so when he was old enough to express himself; but when he tried to talk about the things which he *did* believe in, such as justice and kindness and mercy, the people didn't know what he meant. They had never even heard of those things before.

"If he had been only a little different," continued the old man, "they would have killed him outright, no doubt, and forgotten all about him; but as it was, they were afraid of him, and they thought that he was the servant of some powerful devil, so they only drove him out of the tribe with rocks and clubs and left him back of the marshes to die of cold and hunger."

Albert moved up to the step beside the doctor and looked steadily into his eyes. "What was the boy's name?" he asked.

"It was Surd. Do you think it fits the story all right?"

"Yes, sir," said Albert.

Dr. Ehrlich got up and went to the shelf where a bucket of water stood. He drank slowly, as if pondering his next words, his sunburned throat rising and falling as he swallowed. In the silence Albert heard his mother and Mrs. Langkabel talking again:

"Cousin Albert looks real well now; yes, Katie. It's being out in the sun and the open air so much. But you should have seen him when he first came. So pale and sick-looking then. So thin and peaked. I guess, though, that came from being in prison so long."

"My heavens!" said Mrs. Evans in a shocked voice. "Did they really put him in prison?"

"Yes," said Mrs. Langkabel. "They did. They really did, Katie."

When Dr. Ehrlich had finished his drink, he turned to the boy and began to talk again, gesturing with the empty dipper:

"No wonder the wheel-people didn't know what to make of Surd," he said. "They had a right to be puzzled, because a great thing had happened, and the first human being had been born. I doubt if even Surd realized it, but if he really *was* the first human being, as many scholars think to this day, then it was a great moment in the history of mankind, indeed, wasn't it, Albert?"

"Yes, sir," said Albert. Then he added: "I'll bet Surd didn't die, though, like they all thought he would."

Dr. Ehrlich laughed and put his hand on the boy's head. "Oh, no, Albert; that didn't happen. No, indeed. Surd managed to live somehow and to grow up to be a man."

"What did Surd look like then, Dr. Ehrlich?"

"Well," said Dr. Ehrlich slowly, "at a glance he looked a great deal like the other wheel-people. Certainly his back wasn't quite straight, and he walked on short twisted legs, just as they did. His long yellow hair fell down to his shoulders, the same as theirs did. But his blue eyes weren't cold and cruel the way theirs were, and I imagine if anybody could have told the great difference between him and the other wheel-people, it would have been that way.

"The thing which would have puzzled the wheel-people the most, if they had known about it," said Dr. Ehrlich, "was this: Surd didn't have any hard feelings against them at all, even though they had treated him so badly. All he wanted was to make them believe in his new ideas, and he would lie for hours on the rocks wondering how he could ever manage it. Things must have seemed hopeless to him in those days, because if he even tried to come near one of his people, they would either run away in terror or pick up stones and throw them at him. The whole thing looked impossible, didn't it, Albert? But he didn't give up; and then one day as he looked about him and saw how drab and gray the sky and the earth-wheel were, how little color there was, he thought of a way to do what he wanted to do so badly."

To the left a neighbor walked down the lane. He stopped when he saw the old man and waved his hand. "Howdy, Dr. Ehrlich," he called out. "How's Miss Emma getting along?" The old doctor waved back. "Very well," he said. "Very well, indeed, thank you."

When the neighbor had passed, Dr. Ehrlich turned his head and looked once more at the sunset, which seemed to grow in brilliance each minute. "That was one of Cousin Emma's friends," he said. He smiled and shook his head humorously. "I've already met him three times, but I still have no idea what his name is, because Emma never tells a name when she introduces people." He smiled again, sat beside the boy on the top step and clasped his hands around his upraised knee.

But the boy was not interested in these details. "What was it Surd thought of?" he asked.

Dr. Ehrlich said: "It was a crazy sort of an idea, I suppose, or some people would think so, anyway; but to me it's always been the most wonderful thing I've ever heard of." The boy moved closer to him on the step, looking earnestly into his eyes.

"What Surd wanted to do," said the doctor after a moment, "was simple, really, as all wonderful things are, and it was this: He wanted to paint the gray, cheerless sky with colors." The old man paused, smiled and stroked his white beard. He nodded his head slowly, a faraway look in his eyes.

Inside the house Mrs. Evans spoke again: "Poor man! He's certainly had his troubles! I hope Albert doesn't plague him too much. If I had known what I know now, I'd have kept him here with us."

"Albert won't plague him," said Mrs. Langkabel. "Don't think that for a minute. Why, Cousin Albert's talked more to him today than he has the whole three months that he's been here with me."

"From the moment he had his great thought," continued Dr. Ehrlich, "Surd didn't think of anything else, and the first thing he did was to pick out the best place in the sky for his work. It was the spot where the sun-palace passed over the rim of the wheel, just before night came. There was a high mountain there, with a shelf which stuck out a long way over the ocean.

"So Surd made himself some brushes and put them away. Then he looked about for colors to work with, but all he could find were a few dull-colored berries. They didn't look very promising, but they were the best he could do, so he gathered them up, and one morning he set out to do his work. It was well into the afternoon before he got to the top of the mountain and walked across the shelf. It was just as he had thought: the sky was so close at this place that he could stretch out his arms and touch it.

"Then Surd put his berries into hollows in the shelf, each

according to its color. He crushed the berries and poured water into the vats. He dipped in his brushes and began to paint the sky, but his colors faded as fast as he put them on. He painted for a long time, not willing to give up even then, but when he had used up all his colors, there was nothing to show for his work. The sky had closed over it and wiped it all out."

The doctor paused in his story and looked at the boy beside him. Albert smiled and moved closer, and the old doctor lifted his arm suddenly and put it about the boy. They sat that way for a few minutes and then the doctor went on with his story:

"When Surd's colors failed him, he knew what it was he had to do next; so he filled his vats with water again and then he pulled out his long, yellow hair. He put the hair into one of the vats, and all at once the water there turned a bright yellow. Then Surd dipped in his brushes and began to paint again, and this time his colors held fast. The yellow streamed across the sky in long, trembling lines that spread out to pale lemon at their edges. Surd looked with joy at what he had done, but almost immediately he began to shake his head, because he wasn't entirely satisfied with his work. 'It needs some red in it,' he said critically. 'It needs a little red.'

"So Surd ripped his body open with a stone and reached upward for his heart. He held it in his hands for a little while and then he put it gently into the second vat. Instantly the water there turned the deepest and most beautiful red you ever saw, my little Albert, and when Surd touched the red with his brushes there came a soft, humming sound. Then Surd painted the sky with red, and again his color held fast. He mixed the red and the yellow together so well that it looked, after a moment, as if they would never be separated again." Dr. Ehrlich was silent for a while, leaning back against the steps with his eyes closed, and during the silence Albert heard his mother's voice once more:

"Did Dr. Ehrlich have a family in the old country, Emma?"

"That's the most terrible part of all!" said Mrs. Langkabel. "I said to myself, 'I won't tell Katie *that* part of the story even if she asks me to!' . . . It was all so senseless. Cousin Albert and his family never hurt anybody in their whole lives." She sighed deeply. "Well, anyway, it's all over now; and I for one can't understand how Cousin Albert has stood it as well as he has. If it was me, I'd have given up and gone crazy long ago."

The old man opened his eyes, sat upright and continued his story: "And so Surd stood there on the rocky shelf looking at what he had made. 'Who would have thought that all that bright color was in me?' he said in surprise. He lifted his arms high above his head and began to sing, and he had a right to, if ever a man did, but after a little while he stopped singing and shook his head stubbornly. The picture still was not quite right, and he knew it. 'What it needs now, is blue,' he said. 'It would be perfect if it had some blue in it.'

"He sat down on the rocky shelf and began to cry in a weak voice, because he knew very well that if he did what he *must* do to make his sunset perfect, he would never be able to see his work in all its beauty. He would not even have that pleasure before he died. Then he looked up and saw that the sun-palace was directly over his head. Soon it would pass over the rim of the wheel, soon the earth would be dark and cold again, and he must hurry.

"It was then that Surd found the courage he needed. He got up, walked over to his third vat, and took out his mild, blue eyes. He dropped his eyes into the water, picked up his brushes and began to paint the sky with a color which was bluer than any sapphire you ever saw; and again his color held fast. The blue mixed with the red and the yellow in rich and delicate shades never seen before. Color flooded the sky from north to south and upward and downward. Surd painted quickly, and when the blue was all used up, he fell down exhausted, his blind eye-sockets turned eagerly toward the first sunset."

The old man's voice became very gentle. "After awhile the great, pagan gods looked down from the sky, and they were very much upset when they saw that somebody had defaced their property and left it alive and flaming with colors, just as it is at this instant, my little Albert."

Dr. Ehrlich and the boy turned their heads at the same moment and looked at the sunset before them. It had reached its greatest brilliance, and across the western sky there were long lines of purple, gold and crimson. The sunset seemed to reach up with its lavenders and greens as high as the very top of space itself, and even the clouds which were in the east were pearl-like and rosy from beneath.

It was the doctor who first lowered his eyes. He smiled, touched the boy's head and spoke softly. "Oh, yes, little Albert, there was a great commotion when the gods looked down and saw what Surd had done. They were furious and puzzled at the same time, but when they saw Surd lying on the rocky shelf, they realized what had taken place, and they sent a messenger for him. That is how Surd happened to be brought into the presence of the great pagan gods themselves, if we are to believe the stories that his followers on the earth-wheel told their grandchildren and great-grandchildren later on."

The old doctor stretched out his legs and sighed. "I often think," he continued, "how small and helpless Surd must have seemed in such a company; but he wasn't afraid of them in the least, my little Albert, and he wouldn't wipe his sunset off the sky no matter how much they threatened him. He only shook his head at their threats and answered, 'What pain can you think of that I haven't already known?' Then he raised himself upward and spoke again: 'It may be, when the people on the earth-wheel understand my sunset, that they will repudiate their hate and cruelty and injustice, as I have done; it may be that they will understand at last what I wanted to tell them, and that they will believe in mercy and kindness and love, as I believe in those things.'

"So when the gods saw they couldn't do anything with him, they killed him, thinking to be rid of him and his sunset that way. To be on the safe side, they ground his body between two stones and scattered his dust to the winds, so that it wouldn't defile the sun-palace again, and we come to the end of our story."

Dr. Ehrlich laughed in a tender, half-ashamed way. He took out his pipe and filled it, packing the tobacco in with his thin, brown fingers, catching up the shreds which hung over the bowl and tapping them in lightly. When he had lighted his pipe he smiled, put his arm closer about the boy and looked at the sky once more.

"Well, little Albert," he said at length, "those are the bare facts, but the story doesn't really end at this place after all. This is the kind of story which only begins when all the facts are known." The doctor narrowed his eyes thoughtfully. "It's true the story might have ended at this place if the pagan gods, instead of scattering Surd's dust, had sealed it up somewhere in space, but they didn't think of that, as we have already seen."

Dr. Ehrlich drew on his pipe, making a faint, sucking sound. "Oh, yes," he said, "the pagan gods made a mistake when they scattered Surd's dust, because his dust was blown about by the winds and some of it settled on the earth-wheel again. Some of it settled on our own earth, too, although it was only the tiniest pinpoint in space in those old days. . . . You see, Albert, the gods didn't realize that Surd's spirit was a thing which would not pass away when he died. His spirit was in his dust, too, and since that time, whenever a grain of it touches a man, there is always something inside him which is a little like the first sunset. These are Surd's true followers. They are the beautiful people of the earth and they confirm with their lives or their works, each according to his particular talent, Surd's message of beauty and mercy and love."

The old doctor bent forward and rested his face in his cupped hands. When he spoke again, he spoke slowly, as if he were putting into words for the first time things which he had long pondered in secret. "Sometimes," he began after a moment, "it happens that a man is so worthy of the trust or is touched so deeply with Surd's dust that he becomes as great as Surd himself was. These, the great ones, are not alone Surd's followers; they are his children, and their mission is to lead the world from brutality and hate back to peace and dignity again."

The boy was quiet for a time, turning these matters over in his mind. "Are you one of Surd's children?" he asked.

"No," said the old man sadly. "I wasn't selected. I wasn't honored so highly. I am only one of those who believe."

Mrs. Langkabel and Mrs. Evans came onto the porch at that

moment. Mrs. Evans had her son's cap and coat in her hands. It was time for them to go home. Dr. Ehrlich got up from the steps when he saw them. He said that he would get their automobile from behind the barn, where he had parked it, and would drive it through the lane and leave it in front of the house for their greater convenience.

Mrs. Evans stood looking at his retreating figure. She shook her head sadly. "The things you've told me today don't seem believable, do they? Why, they're enough to make you lose faith in everything and simply give up in despair. Personally, I don't see how he's stood what he has. I couldn't. I know that."

"That part's a mystery to me, too," said Mrs. Langkabel. "Sometimes I think he draws comfort and hope from things we don't know anything about."

The boy pulled away from his mother suddenly and ran toward the barn, in the direction the old man had taken. He was so young that the fissures in his mind had not as yet closed up, and the deep, primitive parts of his being were not shut off from his consciousness. He understood the story the old man had told him that afternoon with his whole body, and he accepted its inconsistencies without criticism. In some ways it seemed more real, more sensible to him than dozens of other things which he accepted every day as truth; more believable, even, than the cruelties he had heard his mother and Mrs. Langkabel talking about.

Dr. Ehrlich was standing beside the barn, as if he knew all the time that the boy would come, and was waiting for him. Albert spoke when he got his breath again, his eyes fixed earnestly on the old doctor's face.

"Is Surd's dust still blowing about the world?"

"Yes," said the old man. "Oh, yes. You may be sure of that."

"How do you know? How can you tell for sure?"

Dr. Ehrlich said: "I think you'll be sure, too, when I finish the story and tell you the part I saved for the end. You see, it happened this way, Albert: Before Surd died, he said a thing which the gods didn't believe at the time, but which came true. He said that the sunset was to be the symbol of the things he believed in and that it would be against the sky as long as beauty and gentleness and love lasted among men. When those things died, his sunset would die with them, and fade out of the sky."

"I'll bet they laughed at Surd for saying it," said the boy seriously. "I'll bet they thought he was trying to fool them."

"Yes," said Dr. Ehrlich, "I imagine they did; but you may be sure Surd didn't care whether they made fun of him or not, because he was thinking at that moment how hard life was in a world of intolerance and cruelty, and how unhappy he had been. He knew that his followers wouldn't have an easy time of it either, and these were the things that concerned him the most. So he was determined that his sunset should come back every day at the time the sun-palace passed over the rim of space, and shine out in the western sky, for then his children could look at it when they were feeling weak and helpless and know they weren't all alone in the world."

The boy thought a moment, shaping his next question carefully: "When we were sitting on the steps," he began, "you said sometimes a man is touched so with Surd's dust that he acts like Surd himself did, and leads the world back to what Surd believed in." He stopped speaking for a time and stood with his brows puckered a little. When he spoke again his voice came rapidly. "Is one of Surd's children living in the world now, Dr. Ehrlich? Do you believe there's a man like that in our world this very minute?"

Dr. Ehrlich rubbed his eyes as if he were very tired. "Yes," he said. "Yes, I believe that. I don't know who he is or where he is, my little Albert, but he is there. I know that in my heart. He is in the world somewhere." The old doctor lowered his hand and let it hang wearily at his side. "Yes, I believe that. If I didn't believe it, I wouldn't have courage enough to live." He stopped speaking suddenly and smiled, his lips turned up in an odd, quizzical way. "Do I sound too sentimental?" he asked. "Do you consider me a little silly? Are you ashamed of me?"

The boy shook his head.

Dr. Ehrlich leaned against the barn door, looking down at his namesake with tired eyes. "It is a strange thing," he said, "but a man may shout out his hatred without shame and feel that he is both intelligent and dignified when he does it, but if he dares to say that he has a spirit, then he must do it apologetically, in whispers, and his friends are embarrassed at the spectacle." He lifted his hands helplessly and laughed in a mild, self-deprecatory way. "It is a strange situation, indeed, but it's something you'll find out for yourself when you're older." Then his eyes wavered and he looked at the ground, turning over the littered straw with his foot.

When he raised his eyes again there was a pleading look in them. "Yes," he said softly. "Yes, I believe there is someone, somewhere in the world, who will lead us back to peace and kindness again. I believe that because I must: There are people who can live in a world from which all beauty and tenderness and hope have gone, but I am not one of them."

Then the boy held out his arms and walked toward his new friend blindly. Dr. Ehrlich dropped to his knees and took the boy in his arms, and for a few minutes they clung to each other without speaking.

Later, the doctor drove the car through the lane and left it in front of the house where Mrs. Langkabel and Mrs. Evans were waiting. At that moment the neighbor who had passed earlier in the afternoon came back from his errand. He had an old horse collar over one of his shoulders, and he turned when he saw Mrs. Langkabel, waved, and walked toward her.

Albert and the old doctor looked at each other, nodded and smiled knowingly, since the same thought was in both their minds. The doctor bent down and said, "I think I'm going to meet him again."

"Maybe she'll tell his name this time," said Albert.

The old doctor shrugged humorously. "Wait!" he whispered. "I know Cousin Emma too well. You'll see."

Mrs. Langkabel had already begun the introductions. She spoke first to Mrs. Evans. "I want you to meet a neighbor of mine," she said. "He lives on the Reedyville Road and raises the finest onions in Pearl County." Then she turned to the stranger. "This is a lady I've known for a long time. We used to go to high school together when we were girls. She and her son came out to spend Sunday afternoon with me and my cousin from the old country."

Dr. Ehrlich spoke quickly to the boy. "You see?" he whispered. "I was right about Cousin Emma." He raised his shoulders in mock despair and shook his head humorously. "Oh, well—I'm resigned now. I'll never know that gentleman's name as long as I live."

The boy took a step forward, turned and glanced at the doctor over his shoulder. He winked mysteriously and pursed out his lips as if to say: "Just wait! Just watch *me* find out his name!" Then he walked toward the stranger with his hand extended. "Howdy-do, Mr. Onions," he said gravely; "I'm glad to meet you."

The farmer's jaw dropped in surprise and he drew back so quickly that the old horse collar almost fell from his shoulders. "Now, listen, Sonny!" he began patiently. "*Onions* is what I raise for a living. It ain't my name. My name's *Barber,* like Miss Emma just told you." He shook his head sadly and turned to Dr. Ehrlich. "Chillun get more book-learnin' than they did when you and me was boys, but they don't seem to get no *apter,* do they, Doc?"

Albert and the old doctor began to laugh at the same instant, their arms about each other. Later, he and Mrs. Langkabel stood at the gate and watched while Mrs. Evans drove away down the country road, passed a bend and was suddenly lost to sight. Mrs. Evans drove slowly, guiding the car between the bumpy ruts. "Emma was telling me all about Dr. Ehrlich while you two went walking," she said. "You might not realize it, being so young, but he's one of the most famous men in the whole world. You must always remember this day, Albert, and some day you can tell your own little boy about how you met him."

She yawned, tired out from her visit and anxious to be in her own home again. "It's been a real nice visit, hasn't it, son?"

"Yes'm," he said.

The colors of the sky were fading now, soon it would be dark again. At the side of the road were tangles of blackberry vines and wild okra bushes. Bullbats were out, darting ghostlike through the air and making now and then their thin, cheeping sound. Everything was tranquil and very quiet. There was only the chirping of crickets and a scurrying of small animals among the vines.

The boy sat back in the seat and watched the puffs of red dust which rose from in front of the car and floated in long lines across the fields, toward the western sky, thinking of the story that Dr. Ehrlich had told him. He knew, then, that he loved the old doctor in some strange way which he had never known before. It was not the way that he loved his mother or his father, or even the way he felt about Mr. Vernon Baker, the milkman, who took him to ride in his cart. It was something else entirely. It was deeper and different and it was at once passionate and impersonal.

He straightened up suddenly, thinking these things, and caught his breath, his eyes wide with surprise. It seemed to him at that moment that he had stumbled upon something of the greatest importance. He stretched out his legs and looked at them for a time; then he stared curiously at his hands, as if he had never seen them before. All at once he leaned out of the automobile and tried to catch the settling dust in his hands. "Touch me, Surd!" he said under his breath. "Make me one of your children!" His eyes had a faraway look in them and they were half closed, as Dr. Ehrlich's had been, and his lips turned up with the distinctive, quizzical expression which he had seen on the old doctor's face.

His mother, seeing what he was doing, spoke quickly, her voice sharp and frightened. "Sit farther back on the seat, Albert!" she said. "You'll hurt yourself, if you aren't careful." Then she laughed with relief, softly. "Heavens and earth," she said. "I never saw a boy who could find so much trouble to get into."

The boy sat back against the seat, his legs stiff and straight before him, but his eyes were still remote and his thoughts still far away. He had not, before this moment, thought of himself as having any identity apart from the reflected identities of his father and mother, nor had he considered an existence apart from them, outside the circle of protection they provided him; but he knew, now, that he was something in his own right as well. He was individual and separate and himself, a part of time and space, just as other people were. He was a living link which joined those who had lived before him with those who would inhabit the earth long after he, too, had died, with the dependencies and the responsibilities that such a relationship inevitably brought with it. He was all these things, and yet he was different from all others. He was uniquely himself, Albert Evans, with decisions and judgments which he must make for himself alone.

After a moment he turned his head and looked again at the shadowy fields, at the red, dusty road and the fading sunset; then, suddenly he straightened his knees and leaned forward a little. "Touch me! Touch me!" he repeated stubbornly. "Touch me! Make me one of your children!"

1938

THE SLATE

GRADY had a rash on his scalp that spring, and his mother stood at the dividing fence discussing his condition with her neighbor, Mrs. Webster. She wondered unhappily if it were worthwhile to continue sending the boy to Dr. Cromwell, the doctor who handled the company business under contract, since his condition, as anybody could see for himself, was not improved.

Mrs. Webster was of the opinion that Dr. Cromwell was capable enough at simple problems in medicine, such as cutting off a leg or probing for a bullet, but that he was entirely inadequate before the more complex ailments of man. He was particularly bad when it came to rashes and eruptions, she said positively, and that was a thing which she had always told others with the completest candor.

The screen door of the Webster cottage creaked on its hinges and slammed shut with a bang and Mrs. Webster, twisting her neck sidewise, watched her daughter Mamie lumber to the end of the back porch and empty a pan of dishwater in the weeds. Mamie Webster was a strong, clumsy girl of sixteen, and her mother regarded her now with heavy and habitual disapproval.

"Fix your stockings!" she said fretfully. "And brush that loose hair out of your eyes! How do you expect to catch a fellow for yourself when you go around looking like a tinker's slut?"

The theme of her daughter's unattractiveness was one which Mrs. Webster never quite exhausted. Mamie, as usual, pretended that she did not hear. She yawned placidly and came to the fence, the wet dishpan dripping grease and water against her legs. She stood leaning against the pickets and looked into space, saying nothing.

Mrs. Webster went on with her interrupted conversation. "No, sir," she continued heatedly. "I wouldn't even send a dog I thought anything of to Dr. Cromwell for tetter, ringworm or rashes of any sort." Suddenly she moved closer to Grady and examined his scalp thoroughly. "If this boy was *mine,*" she said at length, half closing her eyes and holding him away from her as if he were a collector's item, "I'd send him right off to Dr. Eldridge, dead wife or no dead wife, slate or no slate. Personally, I never saw anything so crazy about the doctor. It looks to me like he was only grieving more than ordinary."

Grady pulled away from Mrs. Webster and glanced up at his mother, waiting for her to veto the idea; but she only raised her left hand and held it flat against her cheek. "I don't know," she said doubtfully. "I don't know what's the best thing to do."

Everybody in town knew the stories that were being told about Dr. Eldridge, except, perhaps, the doctor himself. He had married in his late forties, and his devotion to his wife, who had been a school teacher when he met her, had caused the town much amusement during the three years they lived together. Then, unexpectedly, tragedy had struck, and Mrs. Eldridge drowned while bathing with friends at Crown Point. The situation was commonplace enough, and the doctor's grief at the death of his greatly loved wife was understandable. That was all natural and to be expected, as everyone agreed; it was his behavior afterwards which gave rise to the whispered stories about him.

At first he had refused to believe that she was dead and he had worked over her without rest for a long time, trying to bring breath into her body once more. At the end of the third day he collapsed and they put him to bed, his exhausted hands lying quietly on the counterpane at last. "Do what you please with her body," he said, "but I will have no part in it." Then, turning slowly on his side, he wept.

They buried her that afternoon while he was still asleep. Afterwards he refused to discuss her death with his friends, and when the Reverend Hamber called to pray with him, to counsel him to bow in humility before the stern will of God, Dr. Eldridge said: "I find you a little presumptuous, I'm afraid. How dare you offer me sympathy? How can you possibly know what I have lost?"

These things were in the mind of Grady's mother as she stood that day listening to Mrs. Webster's advice. "I don't know," she repeated. "Anyway, I don't think Grady would go, even if I told him to."

Mamie Webster spoke for the first time. "If Grady won't go of his own free will and accord," she said, "I'll take him for you, Mrs. Dorney. I'm not scared of the doctor's wife or of his slate, either." She glanced down at the eight-year-old boy with quiet ferocity, nodding her head a couple of times. "I'll see that he gets there, all right," she said. "Don't worry about that."

"Maybe that's really the best thing to do," said Mrs. Dorney after a moment. "Nobody ever denied that Dr. Eldridge was a good *doctor,* even if he does hold traffic with spirits." Then, as if she had reached the end of her endurance, she gave her son an impatient shove and said, "Go see him! Go with Mamie right this minute! I'm tired of looking at that bothersome head!"

Mamie went toward her own house, saying over her shoulder: "Wait a minute till I change my clothes. I won't be gone no time at all." When she returned, she had on her Sunday dress and her new shoes. She had combed out the front section of her hair, but the back of her head remained as tangled and untidy as it had been originally. Her face was excessively powdered and she had sprinkled herself with cologne. She approached the dividing fence slowly, a little self-conscious in all her finery.

Mrs. Dorney said, "There, Mamie! Take his hand so he can't run away!"

"Come on!" said Mamie. "Come on, cry baby!"

"I'm not scared to go there," said Grady. "I'm not even thinking about that slate. I'm not thinking about ghosts, either."

"You're not scared," said Mamie. "Oh, no! I can see that!" She closed the gate behind them and gave him a jerk forward.

Later, on the road to the doctor's office, Grady abandoned his pose of contemptuous bravery. He spoke breathlessly now, half running to keep abreast of Mamie Webster. "Is it really true that he keeps a slate under his pillow?" he asked. "Is it, Mamie? Is it?"

"I wouldn't be surprised," said Mamie in an affected voice. "I wouldn't put anything silly past a man."

"Does his wife really come back from her grave and write messages on the slate like everybody says?" Grady insisted.

"Maybe she does," said Mamie. "Maybe she don't. How do I know?"

"People say that he looks at the slate every night and every morning, and if there's a message on it from his wife he always does what she tells him to without asking any questions. Do you believe it, Mamie? Do you?"

"If it's not true, then most of the folks in this town tell lies all day long," said Mamie. All at once she seemed annoyed at the boy and she jerked his arm roughly. "Talk! Talk!" she said. "Chatter! Chatter! . . . That's all boys or men, either, know how to do!"

They walked in silence after that and presently they came to the bungalow which served Dr. Eldridge both as an office and as a home. The Negro woman who kept house for him opened the door when they knocked, and they went into the reception room and sat down. To the left was the bedroom, and through the half-open door a chest of drawers, a mirror and a portion of the bed itself were visible. Grady tugged at Mamie's sleeve and pointed to the bed excitedly, but she pretended that she did not know what was in his mind.

"Sit up!" she said sternly. "Sit up on your chair; and don't give Dr. Eldridge no trouble, if you know what's good for you."

Dr. Eldridge, who had few patients these days, came out of his office a moment later. It would be difficult to imagine a less sinister figure. He was thin and not very tall. His hair was turning gray at the sides, and there was a patient, uncomprehending expression in his mild, gentle eyes. Seeing that the bedroom door had been left open, he went there first and closed it, and when he turned once more and faced his visitors he had managed somehow to bring himself back to the practical world of reality.

"Yes?" he asked, speaking to Mamie. "You came to consult me professionally?"

An astonishing change came over Mamie with the doctor's entrance, and Grady, staring at her in surprise, his jaws relaxed a little, was of the opinion that she had suddenly lost the last of her wits. She giggled, scraped her foot across the floor and rolled her eyes alarmingly. "It's not *me* that needs treatment," she screamed. "It's Mrs. Dorney's little boy who came for treatment."

She continued to laugh shrilly and to roll her eyes, pressing her crushed handkerchief against her mouth as if the doctor's mistake were too witty to be endured. She lowered her lids and opened them rapidly, glancing sidewise and coquettishly at the doctor, but when she had recovered sufficiently she said: "Dr. Cromwell's been treating him, but he didn't do him no good at all, so I told Mrs. Dorney that she ought to send him to you. 'Dr. Eldridge is a perfectly wonderful man in every respect,' I said to her, 'and if he can't cure Grady's rash you might as well give up and say that *nobody* can cure it!' " She spoke more softly now, looking provocatively at the doctor through half-closed eyes.

For a moment Dr. Eldridge stared thoughtfully at the girl and then he seemed to dismiss her from his mind. He came to the boy and put his arm about him. "Come in, Grady," he said. "We'll have a look at that scalp of yours in my office." He opened the door and stood aside while the boy preceded him. "There," he said. "Sit in the chair by the window where the light is better."

All his vagueness had left him now, and he seemed very thorough, very efficient. He bent above the boy and whistled softly, eager to be at work again. He patted the child reassuringly and said: "It's my guess that everybody in town except me has already prescribed for that scalp of yours. Tell me: Did your mother put on it everything the neighbors suggested?" He sat on the window ledge and lit a cigarette, shaking his head gently from side to side.

Suddenly Grady's fears were all gone. He looked straight into the doctor's eyes and smiled. "Yes, sir," he said, as if he and Dr. Eldridge shared the ultimate riddle of women. "Yes, sir, that's what she did, all right."

"You're suffering from a bad case of too much attention," said the doctor. He drew deeply on his cigarette, exhaled and continued: "Your scalp will clear up of its own accord in a few days if your mother will leave it alone that long." He turned toward his desk, saying: "Here! I'll write her a note and explain the situation." He stopped, stroked his chin and pursed out his lips humorously. "No," he went on, "I'd better prescribe something after all." He winked at the boy as if they were conspirators together, and said: "The salve I'm going to give you won't help your head in the slightest degree. Its sole purpose is to keep your mother's mind occupied. Do we understand each other, Grady?"

He came closer to the child and looked down at him affectionately. "Tell your mother that she isn't to put anything else on your head while you're using my salve—particularly no more soap and water. Tell her if she does, certain obscure chemical reactions will instantly take place, and her fine-looking young son will explode before her eyes like a cannon cracker." He laughed again and touched the boy's shoulder; and turning toward the anteroom where he compounded his own prescriptions, he added: "I'll fix the ointment for you now."

Grady waited by the desk for a time, thinking about Dr. Eldridge and staring idly out of the window; then wondering what Mamie was doing, he returned to the reception room. To his surprise, she was nowhere in sight, and he wondered if she had tired of waiting and had returned home alone; but seeing that the door to the bedroom was open once more, he approached and looked inside, and there, before his eyes, was Mamie Webster standing over the doctor's bed. She had a large, clothbound slate in her hands and when she heard the shocked, involuntary sound the boy made, she returned it quickly to its place beneath the pillow, smoothing out the sheet and counterpane. A moment later she closed the bedroom door, stuck out her heavy jaw and said: "You say one word to Dr. Eldridge or anybody else and I'll—"

She had got out of the bedroom just in time, for the doctor returned with the ointment before she could finish her sentence. He handed the jar to Mamie, saying gravely, "The directions are written on the label. They're quite simple." Inexplicably his cheerful, professional manner had deserted him, and he looked down at the floor, the lost uncomprehending expression once more in his eyes.

"Mrs. Dorney didn't send no money," said Mamie nervously; "but if you'll tell her what she owes you, she'll take care of it, she says."

"The money," repeated Dr. Eldridge vaguely. "Of course. I beg your pardon for forgetting." He reached absently into his pocket and put a fifty-cent piece in the boy's palm. "I'll try not to forget again," he said. "My wife usually handles these details for me but she went to Crown Point for the afternoon with some friends. If I didn't know what an expert swimmer she is, I'd be getting a little worried about her." He passed his hands over his eyes, bowed stiffly and turned away, having already forgotten Mamie Webster and the patient she had brought.

When they were on the road once more, Mamie spoke defensively: "All right, tattletale! Tell everybody in Williston what you saw! What do I care? I'll say I didn't do it, and everybody will believe me, because I'm grown up and you're not."

"He really keeps a slate under his pillow like they say," said Grady. "That part's the truth, isn't it, Mamie?"

"Yes," she said. "It's the God's truth. And what's more, there's a slate pencil tied to it with a string, if you've got to know."

"That makes it easier for his wife when she writes her messages," said Grady. "It saves her the trouble of looking for the pencil every time she comes."

Suddenly he stopped in the road, caught at Mamie's hand and pulled her around so that she faced him. He stared at her a moment, an odd, intent expression in his eyes. "Was there anything written on the slate?" he asked. "Was there, Mamie?"

Mamie, her alarm at being caught red-handed having abated somewhat, decided to compromise. "Listen!" she began. "If I swear to tell the truth, will you swear never to repeat what you hear?"

"Yes," said Grady, "I swear."

"All right, then," said Mamie: "There wasn't anything written on the slate when I took it from under the pillow and looked at it."

The precise phrasing of her reply puzzled the boy. He knew she was holding something back, being so familiar with her character, but he could not decide what it was; then, remembering that she had had the pencil in her hand when he discovered her bending above the slate, he understood in a moment of intuition precisely what she had done.

"You wrote something on it *yourself!*" he said. "What was it you wrote on the slate, Mamie?"

Her eyes wavered and she glanced down. She thrust her rough, manlike hands behind her and her face and neck turned red slowly. "Let me alone," she said. "Why can't people mind their own business and let me alone?"

"What did you write on the slate?" he insisted. "You better tell me, because if you don't keep your promise, I don't have to keep mine, either. I'll tell everybody in town what I saw you do, and the first one I tell will be your mother."

She turned away in confusion and hid her face in her hands. "I can't say it right out," she said after a time. "I just couldn't! I'd be too ashamed."

"Write it on the ground," said Grady. "You can rub it out as soon as I read it."

Mamie hesitated a little longer, but squatting by the roadside at last, she picked up a twig and wrote laboriously in the dust:

When loanley or looking for
good company
comunercate right away with
Miss Mamie L. Webster
here in town.

For a time the boy and the gawky, unattractive girl knelt beside the road staring at each other; then Mamie rose upward on her heavy thighs, thrust out her foot and obliterated what she had written. "Now you know as much as I do," she said sullenly. "Are you satisfied?"

The boy said: "Do you think he'll do it, Mamie? Do you?"

"Why not?" she said reasonably. "Don't he always do what his wife tells him?"

At that moment Grady had a clear picture of how Mrs. Eldridge had looked in life: She had been gay and provocative and gentle, and half the men in Williston had been in love with her at the time she married the doctor. She had been soft and gracious and lovely—the very opposite of Mamie Webster in everything. It was then he knew that Mamie had revealed herself without purpose, that she had accomplished nothing, and with the detached brutality of children, he shook his head slowly and spoke:

"He won't do it, not even if he does think his wife asked him to. You're too big and greasy-looking."

But Mamie seized his hand more firmly, jerking him along so rapidly that he was running every few steps to keep abreast of her. "Talk! Talk!" she said bitterly. "Chatter! Chatter! It's all boys or men know how to do!"

1939

THE WILLOW FIELDS

WHEN she answered the bell and saw her sister there at the door, Mrs. Niven drew back in dismay and laughed softly. "I declare, Agnes," she said; "I was just on my way to visit Nettie Rodney upstairs. A minute later and you wouldn't have found me in." Then, her hand still grasping the knob, she explained about Nettie, and why she didn't like to break the appointment with her.

Mrs. Rodney, it appeared, had been widowed only a few weeks before, so naturally she was still heartsick and lonely. Then, too, she had no people of her own to turn to in her sorrow—no children, either, and that made things harder, Mrs. Niven thought. "So I run up for a visit every afternoon about this time," she went on, "and Nettie makes tea, and we talk—or rather Nettie talks, and I listen."

The sisters stood in the small vestibule, sighing and shaking their heads. They were much alike in appearance, both of them being bony, solidly built women who seemed capable of turning even the heaviest mattress with one quick, efficient flip of their wrists.

"But why don't you come along with me?" Mrs. Niven asked suddenly. "Nettie will be glad to have somebody new to talk to. She talks about her husband mostly, and I've heard it all so many times."

And so, shoving their durable busts before them, the sisters went into the hall and ascended the fragile, uncarpeted stairs. Nettie Rodney, hearing the noise of their feet, came to her own landing and peered down the stairwell. "You're a fine one, Dora Niven," she called out gaily. "I was ready to ring up the police and get out a search warrant to find you."

She was plump and middle-aged, and as she watched the heads of her visitors rise higher and higher toward her, she jerked her body from side to side with the coquettish, sudden gestures of a robin. She was wearing a bright print dress with short sleeves, and the powdered flesh of her forearms, as she bent forward and rested her elbows on the stair-rail, had the fluted, bluish-white appearance of a plucked hen. Her hair had recently been bleached yellow and elaborately waved. Her lips, cheeks and fingernails were an indiscriminate scarlet.

Dora said, when they were inside Mrs. Rodney's apartment: "This is my sister Mrs. Agnes Nicolson. She lives in Jackson Heights, and she dropped in unexpectedly just a few minutes ago; so I brought her along with me, knowing you wouldn't mind."

"I hope it wasn't an imposition," said Agnes, "seeing that you've just sustained a loss. What I mean is, people in mourning generally want to be by themselves until—" She paused in confusion, realizing at that instant that Mrs. Rodney was most plainly not in mourning. Nettie, feeling that an explanation was expected of her, hesitated and then said, "Fred didn't believe in making a show of your feelings."

"Fred was her husband," said Dora unnecessarily.

Nettie jumped up from her chair and placed one finger against her crimson lips. "The water!" she said in a high, vivacious voice. "It's boiling away on the stove!" She hurried to her kitchen, and a moment later the sisters heard her arranging cups and saucers on a tray.

"She doesn't have to worry about money the way some widows do," said Dora solemnly, "because Fred left her comfortably off." She lowered her voice and listened, then realizing that Nettie would be busy for the next few minutes, she recited the salient facts of Mr. Rodney's past in a hollow, hushed voice. He had had a good job with an insurance company, and he had been in the same position for many years. He had been a real family man, not caring about outside company and hardly drinking at all, or throwing his money to the winds, the way many did. Nettie had always given in to him and pampered him in little ways. Maybe that was a mistake—tying yourself so close to a man, no matter what good qualities he had. Maybe it would have been better if she'd gone out and made friends of her own. Maybe if she had done that she wouldn't feel his loss so terribly now.

"Why, she seems real gay and unconcerned to me," said Agnes. "I would never call her a grief-stricken woman."

"It's all show," said Dora. "She's taking his death very hard, but of course she's got to keep going as best she can."

At that moment their hostess returned with the tea, and Agnes changed the conversation abruptly. She said: "I see they're showing 'Commandos from the Sky' in this neighborhood. I saw it last week. It's a good picture, I thought."

Nettie put down the cups and saucers and turned quickly. "Now, that's a coincidence," she said: "Your mentioning moving pictures, I mean. . . . You see, Fred was crazy about them. It was the only thing that interested him much; that and reading the papers. He read three different ones after he got home at night."

She opened her compact and examined her make-up; then, sighing inaudibly, she went back for the teapot and the sugar. When she returned, she poured tea for her guests with complete absorption, her toe tapping nervously against the rug.

"I always thought Fred missed his calling when he went into insurance," she said. "A man with so much appeal for the ladies, and with such a handsome face and fine figure, should have been on the stage. He joked about it when I brought it up, and said he'd only make a fool of himself, because he didn't know the first thing about acting. And so I used to tell him, 'But you don't have to know anything about acting. A good director could teach you all the tricks and movements in no time.' "

Agnes, who had pictured Mr. Rodney as another type of man entirely, spoke in surprise: "Was your husband as good-looking as all that? I didn't realize."

Nettie smiled and nodded toward a table which stood against the wall, a table entirely bare except for a photograph which had plainly been posed and tinted by someone who believed with his whole being in the camera as a medium of artistic expression.

Agnes straightened up and twisted her head, examining the photograph with concentrated care. The face which stared back at her from the expensive frame was that of a plump, middle-aged man whose features were small, glum and unobtrusive. His hair was thin but still dark, and it had been plastered fiercely to his skull, with two small almost circular curls on either side of the part. His eyes were fixed and somehow intolerant behind the glasses he wore, and his lips pursed slightly, as if he had contemplated making a suggestion or two to the photographer, but had thought better of it.

"You see?" said Nettie. "You see what I mean?"

Then, as if her words had evoked thoughts too near the surface, emotions too powerful to be easily controlled, she passed the sugar and cream needlessly, repeating under her breath all the things which Fred had said about showing your grief in public. Dora and her sister glanced at each other, and then, staring again at the elaborate, tinted photograph, they smiled cautiously and shook their heads.

Agnes was the first to break the silence. "Where did you find such a nice frame?" she asked. "It's real leather, isn't it?"

"I got it after he died," said Nettie. "I looked and looked until I found that shade of green. It isn't exactly right, but it was the closest I could come to what I really wanted. Green was always his favorite color. I mean that real bright shade of green—the color of grass in spring, or of willow trees coming out." She leaned forward with eagerness now, and her words came in a rush, as if she could no longer keep them bottled up in herself.

"Now, here's something I wouldn't tell just anybody, for fear they'd laugh, or think it sounded crazy, but Fred had a peculiar notion in his head, and he used to talk about it sometime. I suppose it wasn't so much a *notion* as it was a sort of *picture,* if you know what I mean. . . . Anyway, the thing that bothered him at times was whether he'd really seen the picture, or whether it was something he'd made up in his mind."

Agnes put down her cup with a small clatter. "What was it, Mrs. Rodney?" she asked excitedly. "What kind of a picture did he see?"

"It was a place out in the country," said Nettie, "and the main thing about it was the fact that it was so untroubled and silent. There was a white farmhouse and a sign which read: THE WILLOW FIELDS; and all about the house there were sloping meadows so green that you couldn't believe your eyes. There was a stream of water running through the fields, with clumps of willow trees growing along its banks. It was all so strange, and yet it was real too in a way. He could see it so plainly, and if he told me about it once, he told me about it a hundred times."

Agnes, who had expected something more dramatic, said in a vigorous, practical voice: "Maybe he really did see such a place. When he was a little boy, perhaps, before you two met."

Nettie shook her head instantly, as if she had long anticipated this solution and was prepared for it. "No," she said. "No, it couldn't have been that way. You see, Fred was born right here in New York City and his mother told him, when he asked her about it, that he'd never left the city at all when he was young—not even to go to Brooklyn."

"I think it was something he imagined in his mind," said Dora. "What else could it have been?"

Nettie leaned back in her chair and pleated her dress with her white, nervous fingers. "Anyway," she said, "Fred believed that such a place existed somewhere. He meant to go look for it some day, after he'd retired from business and had more time."

She got up suddenly and went to the kitchen. She returned with fresh cream and a pitcher of hot water, and when she had refilled the teapot and taken her seat again, Agnes said: "Your husband really fell in love with that place, didn't he? It must have made a great impression on his mind."

Nettie did not speak at once, but after she had replenished the cups, she nodded twice and answered, making her voice as casual as she could: "Yes, that's very true." She leaned back in her chair and rested her forehead against her palm. She felt herself sinking, despite her will, into the despair which seemed always to wait for her. With determination she straightened up again and forced her lips to smile. Afterwards she talked rapidly, compulsively, going over and over the trivial details of her trivial life. She talked on and on, her shallow eyes desperate and staring, her plucked, powdered forearms digging into the upholstery of her chair; but at last her guests rose to leave, and standing there on the landing once more, she watched until they were out of sight, knowing at that moment that her whole day had been lived through in anticipation of this casual visit.

When she heard Mrs. Niven's door close, she came back into her own apartment and stood before the photograph in its green frame, moving it forward a little so that the late sunlight brought out its details more clearly; then she carried the dishes out, washed them and put them away. When that task was done, there was nothing to do until she cooked her supper; afterwards there would be nothing to do until it was time for her to go to bed.

Without thought, with no definite plan in her mind, she went into her bedroom and put on the dress she had bought a few days before. It was made of some soft, clinging material; it was years too young for her, and its color was an intense, clamorous green. Her dyed yellow hair, arranged so elaborately above the green of the dress, gave her the appearance of a rumpled and ornate buttercup.

Later, she tried to read, but she could not; and pressing her palms flatly against her cheeks she went to the window and looked down at the street, watching the dense, five-o'clock crowd hurrying to their individual and unknown destinations. There were so many people in the world, she thought—so many people, and she meant nothing to any of them. "But they mean nothing to me, either," she said aloud. "Nothing at all." She found this thought too dreadful to face, and moving back into the room, she stretched out on her sofa, her hands locked and tense between her bulging knees, her bright green dress outlining the plump curve of her body.

She had not slept well since her husband's death, but now she had a feeling of drowsiness, as if she wished to escape, somehow, from the shrill, relentless thoughts which beset her mind. She turned on her back and adjusted the pillows against her head, thinking vaguely of Mrs. Niven and Agnes Nicolson. She wondered if she had been indiscreet in speaking so freely to them—if, after all, she had not made herself absurd. She was not sure, but Fred would know, if he were alive, and he would tell her at once.

She sighed and turned slowly on the couch. The sounds from the street seemed farther and farther away, and a moment later even the familiar room became blurred and remote. Then, strangely, although she was not in the least surprised, she found the farmhouse which Fred had looked for, and at once she thought: "It was not a dream after all. May God forgive me for having doubted him." She looked about her thoughtfully, speaking softly to herself. "There is the sign outside the house," she said. "There are the wide, green fields and the willows growing in clumps along the stream."

She turned slowly, staring with a sense of incredulous delight, and at that instant she saw her husband plainly. He was standing alone, at the edge of the farthest field, and he looked precisely as he had when she first met him. She started forward in her eagerness, and stretching her arms wide, she ran toward him, without effort, through all that sea of bright young green. She felt there was something both definitive and overwhelming which she should say to him, but she could not remember what it was. She could only cry out, "Fred! Fred!" in a thin, tremulous voice; but when she reached the place where he was standing, and lifted her hands to touch his face, she awoke from her dream with a nervous start, shuddered and sat up straight on the sofa, thinking that she would never be able to move again. She sat there as if dazed for a long time, her hands pressed tightly against her face.

It was then she remembered a conversation with her husband many years ago. "Even if you did find the willow fields again," she had said, "you'd probably be so old and tired out that you wouldn't care whether you went there or not. That's the way things usually work out in this world."

"I'd still want to go there," he had said, "no matter how old or tired I was at the time. I'd go there all right, no matter what the circumstances were—even if I had to come back from the grave to do it."

"No, no, Fred!" she had answered. "You mustn't say such things, even in fun. They're sacrilegious!" But he had only laughed his odd, individual laugh and continued stubbornly: "I'd do it though, just as sure as you're a foot high."

It was dark in the living-room now, but she did not turn on the lights. There were no sounds from the street at all, and even the small, intimate noises of the house itself had ceased. In this complete, waiting stillness she could hear the sound her own breath made, the tiny, scratching sound of her stockings as they pressed together. She got up from the couch, and for a time she stood in the center of the room in complete and waiting passivity; but when she could bear her thoughts no longer, she turned and went to the bedroom which she and her husband had shared for so many years, to the chest of drawers which still held his intimate belongings.

His shirts were arranged neatly in rows, just as he had left them. From one of the shirts she took a piece of rough, grayish cardboard which the launderer had put there to hold it firm; and then, her mouth tight with her desperation, she found a pencil and printed boldly on the surface of the board: THE WILLOW FIELDS.

Without pausing to consider, her eyes wide and frightened at the audacity of the thing she meant to do, she opened the door of her apartment and fixed the sign there with a thumb tack. She drew back against the wall, but she left the door open a little so that nothing would impede his progress when he came back to her. She patted her curls into place and rearranged her silly, bright green dress seductively. "Here I am," she said softly. "Here, by the door."

She waited there in the dark for a long time, her breath coming irregularly in thin, quick rushes, her puckered, dead-white hands making small, meaningless gestures. Then, realizing that her throat was dry and constricted, she started for the bathroom to get a glass of water. She recognized the stuffed chair, the smoking-stand and the big, metal lamp as she passed and fumbled them for an instant; but when her hands touched the photograph on the polished table, she trembled so that she sank slowly to the floor. In the darkness she rested her yellow, elaborately curled head against the edge of the table. "Here I am," she said. "Here."

She got up after awhile and went to the bathroom. She turned on the light above the basin, examining her rouged, harassed face in the mirror. Automatically she fumbled for her compact, but such a feeling of distaste came over her at that instant that she never completed the gesture. Instead, she leaned back against the towel rack, stared at her own reflection, and wept. "Old woman!" she cried fiercely. "Old woman! Old woman!"

She could no longer endure the sight of her own face and she walked quickly away from the mirror; but when she came into the living-room again, and stood there in indecision, as if she could no longer recall the purposes which impelled her, her knees collapsed beneath her and she fell forward against the rug, knowing clearly at that moment that no matter how senseless her husband's death seemed, nor how greatly she longed for his return, he would not come back to her.

Then, slowly, she turned on her face and gave way completely to grief, but even in that bitter moment of realization she found excuses for him, for she said to herself over and over: "But why should he? Why should he come back to a silly, impossible old woman like me?"

1943

I BROKE MY BACK ON A ROSEBUD

This is a story which Corporal Curtain tells to those who will listen, and this is the way he told it to me:

I'm talking about the last war, remember—not about this new, fancy one. . . . Say, how old do you take me to be? All right. Go on. Go on and say sixty. It won't hurt my feelings any. But you'll be wrong if you think that, because I was forty-eight years old on my last birthday.

Okay. Okay. So I'm forty-eight on my last birthday, and that makes we twenty-four in 1919, now don't it? And you want to know something else? My birthday falls on the eleventh of November—Armistice Day—remember that far back? I was luckier than most, I used to say to myself, because I went through the fighting and didn't get a scratch. Didn't get gassed, either. Didn't even get flu or trench-feet. Didn't get anything, see?

Then, after it was all over, comes this parade in New York City, up Fifth Avenue, and as we marched along, I kept thinking that my army days were about over—that it wouldn't be long before I was on the outside. And so we paraded up the avenue at attention, according to regulations. People stood on both sides of the pavement, waving flags and cheering, but I didn't pay them any mind. I was too busy checking off each landmark as we went by. "That's Fourteenth Street ahead," I'd think; or, "There's Madison Square to the right, as big as life and right on schedule." So finally we got into the public library neighborhood, and I knew we'd be passing the reviewing stand before long.

There was some sort of commotion taking place near the south side of the library steps. I looked in that direction, without really turning my head, and there, standing on a pedestal above the crowd, between the front feet of one of the stone lions, was a good-looking woman. A pink basket was hung around her neck on a wide, pink ribbon; and what's more, the pink basket was full of pink rosebuds. Not the stems and leaves, too, mind you—just the pink heads. . . . And every once in a while she'd show all her pretty teeth, blow a kiss to the troops and sing out, "Welcome home to each and every one!" Then with a little twitch which started at her ankles and ended in a shake of her yellow curls, she'd reach in her pink basket and toss a pink rosebud to the boys.

Now listen carefully to me, because here comes the pay-off. . . . When my platoon was almost flush with the stone lion and the dame standing there above the heads of everybody else, I cut my glance up and around a little—and there she was, looking straight into my eyes. So she reached in her silk basket, picked out a fat rosebud, all for me, and tossed it in my direction. "Welcome back!" she called out, while people on the sidewalk looked at her and clapped their hands. "Welcome back to the United States of America!"

I felt the rosebud hit me on the chest, and I saw it bounce off; and the next thing I knew, there was something soft and sliding under my foot, like a big, pink eyeball. I tried to get my balance back, but I couldn't; and then I was lying flat on my back, right in the middle of the street, with the men of my company detouring around me. I didn't feel pain anywhere—the only thing was, I couldn't get up when I tried. So first they carried me into a store. After that an ambulance took me to the hospital, but it wasn't until a couple of days later that I knew, for certain, my back was broke. . . . You know the rest, I imagine. Somebody must have told you already that I've been lying on a board since 1919. Figure it out for yourself. That's a quarter of a century. Well, that's the way it is, and there's nothing I can do to change it.

Pull down the shade a little, will you, fellow? The sun's in my eyes.

All right! All right, let's get on with the story. . . . Anybody would think I'd be downhearted, knowing I had a fractured spine, but I wasn't. Well, not right away. I kept saying to myself, "Look at the discoveries doctors are making these days. Somebody is sure to find out what to do for me." And so I lived on hope for ten years or more, and every time something new came up, why, I'd let 'em do it to me first, saying to myself that this time everything was going to be all right; but it never was. The Government took good care of me, and sometimes when visitors came, the doctors would point to me and say, "This is Corporal Curtain. He sets us all an example in fortitude."

Hope dies hard in a man, but it does die finally. . . . Am I telling you something new? Am I telling you something you haven't heard before? I don't know how hope died in me, but one morning I woke up wise to myself. I knew, then, what the doctors had known all along, and that was, I'd never be any better, no matter what they did for me. That's when I started to see the woman's face again. I'd close my eyes and try to shut it out, but I couldn't. I cursed her and damned her from morning to night, like a crazy man. "Why wasn't she home, where she belonged, cooking her husband some dinner?" I'd say. "Why did she have to show herself off like she did?"

I'd known from the beginning, you see, that she didn't come out that morning to look at the soldiers. She came out to have the soldiers look at her. . . . And she didn't throw me a rosebud because I was a returning hero in her eyes. Oh, no! Not that one! She did it so people could see how nice she *looked* throwing a rosebud! That was the worst thought of all, and when it came to me, I'd close my eyes and lay my head deep in the pillow.

Lift my neck up some and give me a drink of water, will you? My throat's dry. . . .

Now, here's a thing I never figured out to my satisfaction: You'd think hate would last longer than hope, but it didn't work out like that. Not with me, anyway. And so after a year or two I wasn't able to see her face any more. I didn't blame her for anything, either. I leaned over backwards to be fair and reasonable. She couldn't know that I was going to slip and fall, now could she? How could anybody anticipate such a thing? It was probably something which had never happened to a man before in the whole history of the world, so why hold her responsible? Then I had another thought, and it was this: Maybe the woman was an instrument in the hands of God. Maybe I was being punished for something I did once, but couldn't remember. So I said to myself, "If that's the way it is, that's the way it's going to be, and I've got to accept it." So you see? First I hoped, and then I hated—but at last I was resigned.

Then a year or so later I saw things in another light, and now I laugh to myself when I think back. Can you figure out what changed me? I've already given you a hint or two. You can't? Okay. I'll tell you before long, but let me lead up to it gradual. Let me tell you first about the man who wrote a piece about me in the newspapers.

It was Richard Emery Simms, the famous columnist, and the story was printed all over the country, in I don't know how many papers. A lot of people read about my case, and it wasn't long afterwards before some of the boys I knew in the old outfit, who had forgot me years ago, started writing me letters, or even coming to see me here at the hospital.

Now, hardly a day passes without somebody dropping in—strangers or otherwise. The boys from my old outfit talk about themselves for the most part. I guess they figure that since I never had a real life of my own, I'd be glad to hear about theirs. They tell me who they married, and how many kids they got. They tell me everything that's happened to them since we saw each other last—what they had hoped to get out of their lives, and what they had really got.

So one morning a fellow named Jamie Ethridge (he used to be a sergeant in the old second platoon) came to pay me a visit. He talked about his troubles even more than the others. All he had ever asked was a little peace and security, he said. Once he thought that he had it, too, and then something had gone wrong somehow. He had hoped so much, he said. He had tried so hard, and then something had happened, although he didn't know how or why. I quit listening to him about that time, and my mind went back to my own troubles.

At first, what happened to me seemed like an accident without sense, then it seemed like something planned for me alone. All at once I knew both ideas were wrong, and I've been a changed man from that minute on. This may sound silly to you. If it does, that's all right with me, too! But now I think of that woman as something made out of paper and wires. Something curled and painted pink for the people. Something that lives right there in the library, with the romances and poems. . . . And every once in awhile the authorities get her out, dust her off, and send her out for the world to see—like a beauty contest winner with Miss Universal Dream across her belly.

When that thought came into my head I started to laugh in earnest, while Sergeant Ethridge looked at me and wondered what had happened. . . . You see, I used to think that no other man was in my particular fix. That was my mistake, and I know better now. Oh, no, fellow! I'm not the only man who broke his back on a rosebud. Not by a long shot. Sometimes it seems to me that everybody in my generation done the same thing one way or another. "I'm not the only one," I say to people now. "There's many another. Oh, many and many a one."

Light me a cigarette and put it between my lips, will you, bud?

1943

DIRTY EMMA

IN WILLISTON, when I was a boy, there was a woman known to everyone by the cruel but accurate name of Dirty Emma. The expression had become so familiar with usage that even the Friendly Society—a group of ladies banded together for the fostering of kindness—were conscious of no lack of charity when they openly used it in addressing her. Often she was seen on the streets of the town, moving timidly from place to place or resting in the shade of a china-berry tree, her matted hair hanging about her eyes in confusion, her skirts fouled with burrs and caked with mud at the hems.

All agreed that she was an eyesore and a public disgrace. It was even said that she stole at times, but if she did, nobody bothered to bring her to justice, for her station in life was so low, her appearance so wild and degraded, that others felt they could not in fairness demand the same standards of her that they demanded of themselves. Thus it was that the position of Dirty Emma lay somewhere between that of the Negro, who was so innocent in outlook, so ignorant of the subtleties of good and evil, and that of the barnyard animal, to whom the laws of decency and morality did not, in the eyes of God, apply at all.

The Friendly Society often discussed her as a problem, knowing as they did that she lived miserably with a man who beat her. Mrs. Oscar Blake, perhaps, would say: "I saw Dirty Emma at the meat market this morning. She didn't speak a word—just stood there at the counter begging with her eyes and looking more than ever like an old wet sheep until the butcher filled her apron with beef bones. Her face was a sight this time. Her lip was split and one eye was so puffed out that she couldn't open it at all. After she'd gone, the butcher said with a wink, 'It looks like Tom Gunnerson's on the warpath again, now don't it?' "

Most of the ladies sighed and folded their hands, but old Mrs. Cobb said indignantly: "There's a law against wife beating in this State. People ought to see that it's enforced, if you ask me."

"The butcher told me a funny thing later on," continued Mrs. Blake. "He said that after Tom had treated her real cruel, Dirty Emma always came down the next morning to beg beef bones for soup, so that she'd have something hot and nourishing for him to sober up on. He said it looked like the worse Tom treated her, the more she did to please him."

"She's not really married to Tom Gunnerson," said Mrs. Opal Nesmith in an uncertain voice, as if knowing in advance that she would not be believed. "She lives with him in open concubinage, or so I've always been told."

The ladies pondered this familiar bit of information once more, and then they once more rejected it as absurd, persisting stubbornly in their belief that Emma's union was both regular and blessed, since, in the cynical and disenchanted minds of the pure, the distasteful and the legality of the marriage bed are so closely associated.

One clear, crisp morning in late winter, my mother decided to transplant her hyacinth bulbs from their old place near the porch to a new bed against the fence, where they could be seen to better advantage. She was proud of her hyacinths, and each spring when they were in bloom they were admired by people passing our house. In theory, at least, I was helping with the transfer; actually, all I did was to sit on the steps and watch as she dug up the bulbs and separated them, according to the color of their flowers, into small, neat piles.

Later, I looked up and saw Dirty Emma approaching our gate. That day she was wearing a pair of Tom's old shoes which were run over at the heels and which she had laced up raggedly with common twine. Her skin had that yellowish, dense look of ditch water seen in sunlight; her nails were broken and caked with grime, and even her lips and her eyeballs seemed soiled.

My mother, following my glance, turned her neck and smiled absently, as if Emma were her oldest and dearest friend, and they had parted only an hour before. Emma nodded, blinked her eyes and spoke timidly: "I seen them blossoming last year when I passed by, and I said to myself at the time that I never seen flowers set out prettier."

My mother rocked back and forth on her heels and laughed with pleasure. "Oh, did you really think so?" she asked gaily. She went on to explain that the hyacinth was her favorite flower. She didn't know why, but perhaps the old story of Apollo and Hyacinthus had a great deal to do with it. "Do you remember it from your own childhood?" she asked.

"No," said Emma thoughtfully. "No, ma'am, I never heard that story."

My mother had been a school teacher before her marriage and she had never lost her desire to impart knowledge. She put down her trowel, sat beside me on the steps, and began softly: "Long ago in ancient Greece the god Apollo worshiped a boy named Hyacinthus, the most beautiful mortal on the whole face of the earth. Now, things of this sort never run smoothly, as we all know, and so it happened that Zephyrus, who was really the West Wind, also admired Hyacinthus, and when he realized the boy preferred Apollo to himself, he planned to take his revenge.

"One day as Apollo and his friend played quoits together, Zephyrus seized the discus which Apollo had thrown and hurled it back in such a fashion that it struck Hyacinthus on the forehead. It was plain to all that the boy was going to die, and when Apollo realized it too, his grief was terrible to see. He wept, tore his robes and cried out: 'Thou diest, Hyacinthus, robbed of thy youth by me! Would I could die for thee!'

"But Apollo could not do this, for he was a god, and the gods are immortal; and so he decreed that a flower as lovely as Hyacinthus himself should spring up from the blood of his dying friend, and it happened that way. Then the great god Apollo bent in humility before the perfection of the flower and marked it with the words, 'Ai! Ai!' which mean 'Alas! Alas!' in our language. . . . And so it happens each spring when hyacinths bloom once more that the grief of Apollo and the beauty of Hyacinthus are renewed and made plain for all to see."

There was a silence, and then Emma spoke timidly: "What happened to the West Wind, Mrs. Gavin? Did he get punished for what he done to that poor boy?"

My mother laughed a little and went back to her bulbs. "Why, really, I don't know," she said. "It's a point I never considered before."

Emma put her elbows on the fence and glanced sideways at the bulbs; then, shaking back her limp, oily hair, she sighed and turned away. Somehow, my mother knew the thought in her mind, for she said quickly: "You'd like one of the bulbs for your own, wouldn't you?" Emma could not bring herself to answer; she could only hang her head, as if abashed at such presumptuousness on her part, and shuffle her feet in the dirt.

"Which color would you prefer?" continued my mother in a casual voice. "I have several shades of both pink and purple; then there's a sort of bluish color, and one that's pure white."

Emma raised her head desperately and looked into my mother's eyes for the first time that morning. She said: "I'd like one of the white ones, if you're sure it ain't putting you out none."

My mother went to the fence and placed a plump, handsome bulb in Emma's hand. She explained in detail how to plant and care for the flower. She said that if Emma put it in a pot and kept it indoors, it would bloom long before spring came. Emma said over and over, as if she were not really listening: "Yes, ma'am; yes, ma'am, I sure will"; and when the instructions were finished, she turned and walked rapidly away, her greasy old skirt pulling up sharply in front and trailing in the dirt behind.

She held the bulb lightly in her hand, as if it were alive, and as she walked past the log pond, in the direction of her house, she spoke aloud in a thin, delighted voice: "Mrs. Gavin didn't have to tell me how to plant and care for you," she said, "because I already know. You wait and see. You won't have no complaints at the treatment you get."

When she reached the sagging, unpainted old shack where she lived—a place which had long since been abandoned by others as unfit for habitation—she paused outside and listened; then, hearing no sound from within, she went below the slabpit for leaf mold and moss. She selected, sighed, and discarded, her lips puffed out thoughtfully, her eyes fixed and intense, but after she had collected what she needed for her purpose, she came back to her house, punched drainage holes in a tomato can, and prepared a bed for her flower.

She had hardly finished before she heard Tom shuffling up the path. He was a man in his early thirties, perhaps ten years younger than Emma herself. He was rapidly growing bald, but as if to counterbalance the loss, reddish hair grew in thick, tight coils on his forearms and erupted shaggily above the throat line of his undershirt. He was powerful physically and completely mature. Mentally, he was perhaps average. Emotionally, he was a child of six, with all the petulant and ingenuous cruelty of the boy and with none of his defenselessness.

Emma peered anxiously through the shack's one window, but she saw at once that he was in a good humor. He would not even mind if his dinner was a little late, for he had a new funny paper under his arm, and as she watched him, she saw him sit down on the steps and begin to spell it out. His literary ideal was the blonde member of the Katzenjammer team, and in a moment Emma heard him laughing loudly and slapping his leg at the irresistible antics of his favorite. Perhaps those boys who never grow up do, on occasion, become Peter Pan, as we have been taught; more often they become Tom Gunnerson.

Emma turned and surveyed the mean, bare shack before her. It consisted of one room and a lean-to, which served both as a kitchen and as a woodshed. It was almost bare of furniture and its walls were plastered with newspapers and patched with bits of tin. It was incredibly dirty. Suddenly she felt depressed and a little apologetic. She picked up the can which contained her bulb and put it behind the stove, where it would be both dark and warm.

"I don't know why I ever took so much trouble to plant you

right," she said, "because I'll bet you haven't got any idea whatsoever of coming up."

Nevertheless, the knowledge of the bulb lying there so close to her, gave her a sense of excitement, and she examined it once more, to see that everything was in order, before she finally called Tom to his dinner. Each morning afterwards, as soon as Tom was safely out of the shack, she went to examine her plant, not really believing that it would grow. "I want you to know I won't hold it against you, even if you don't come up," she said craftily, "so just suit yourself about it. Come up, if you want to; stay down there, if you want to. But don't come up to do me a favor, no matter what you do."

Then one day she saw the first spearhead of green thrusting upward from the dirt. At once she moved the can to a shelf beside the window, examining it with a sense of incredulous delight. She laughed, nodded her head and said: "Do you know what you look like? You look like the little green tongue of a kitten sticking out. You really do, for a fact." All at once her excitement left her. She sat down on the bed and brushed her hair out of her eyes. "But you won't bloom," she said cautiously. "I know that just as well as you do."

The plant grew steadily, and soon a tight bud formed in the center of its protective sheath of green. When she saw the hard, brilliant bud for the first time, Emma stood still in the center of the shack and spoke with a carelessness she did not feel: "All right! Maybe you really are going to blossom, but that's nothing to brag about. Anyway, I bet you won't turn out white when your time comes." She went to the door and paused, then, speaking over her shoulder, she continued indifferently, as if to mislead the jealous and evil spirits who envied her: "But if you're not white, after all, it won't matter to me in the least. To tell you the truth, I wish now I'd asked Mrs. Gavin for a purple one."

Then even this last anxiety was dissipated and the bud opened into a hyacinth as perfectly formed and as white as any she had ever seen. The miracle, or so she took it to be, left her shaken and almost at the point of tears. "Well!" she said. "Well, I never!" She raised her arms in the air and shook her head with amazement, for she felt that she had been through some revealing and shattering experience, one whose implications she did not perfectly understand; then she went outside and sat on a box in the sunlight, throwing her apron over her head.

A few nights later, having money in his pockets once more, Tom went to town and got drunk. He came home late, and Emma heard him muttering to himself as he stumbled up the path. The hyacinth was in full bloom now, and Emma glanced at it nervously, wondering if it would not be wiser to put it some place beyond the reach of his whirling, drunken fists; but she waited too long, and as she sat there in indecision, the door opened and Tom stood before her.

He was in one of his petulant moods, and when she saw his face, she approached fawningly and stroked his arm. "Come sit here by the stove," she said. "I saved your supper. I'll warm it up in no time." She hurried about the house, as if to divert with movement the direction of his thoughts, but Tom saw through her intention and sighed, following her with his eyes.

"What kind of life is this for a man?" he asked in a despairing voice. He staggered and steadied himself against the door. "Every hand is against me and always has been. Even when I was a boy at home the others got everything and I got what was left." The wrongs he had suffered itched eternally in his mind, unforgiven and forever unresolved, and his face twisted with bitterness as he remembered anew the old and unavenged insults he had endured. He sat solidly on the bed and unbuttoned his jumper coat, allowing the thick, reddish hair of his throat to boil upward stiffly like crimped and raveling rope.

"There's good blood in my veins," he continued; "blood as good as any in this here land. And what have I got to show for it? I got nothing to show for it but poverty and injustice and a filthy slut no other man would look at twice."

Emma spoke patiently: "Let me take your shoes off for you. You can't sleep all night with shoes on. It might stop the movement of your blood."

He sat tractably as she approached him, but when she was within range of his arm, he bent forward and hit her with his heavy, opened palm. "Clean this place out!" he shouted. "It's dirtier than a pigeon run!" Blood flowed from her nose and from the old split in her lip which never seemed to heal completely. She backed away from him and stood braced against the wall, her shoulders sagging, her eyes lowered abjectly.

The people of Williston predicted that some day Tom Gunnerson would kill old Emma and that he would hang for it. In this they underestimated both the prudence of his temperament and the high refinement of his skill. There was not the slightest chance that he would kill her, for he had perfected his technique over a long period, and he was as familiar with the strains her body could stand as an engineer is with the stresses of the common arch.

He beat her now with a formal and discreet fury. After he had finished, he walked to the kitchen and washed his hands and face, thinking once more of injustice and how cruelly the world had used him; then, raising his eyes, he caught sight of the hyacinth on its shelf. He went to it at once and held the pot balanced in his hands; and with a disavowing gesture, as if some tiny pocket of fretfulness remained unexpressed within him, he twisted off the flowering spike of the plant and threw it to the floor, obliterating it slowly with his sliding, brutal shoe.

Emma, from her place beside the stove, where she had fallen, drew in her breath like some tormented old animal. "You didn't have no call to do that," she said miserably. She bent forward from her haunches and trembled. "No," she said. "No, you didn't."

"Keep this place clean, like I told you to a thousand times!" said Tom. "It's dirtier than a hog wallow!"

Later, he stretched out on the bed, yawned, scratched himself, and went to sleep at once. When she heard his heavy breathing, Emma pulled a chair to the bedside and stared at him with a most minute and flattering care, as if she had never seen him before. Her mind filled slowly with sadness and with a sense of inexpressible loss. It seemed to her that the finished span of her sorry and ridiculous life opened outward before her, with finality beyond her power either to affirm or reject. It was at this instant that the thought first came into her consciousness, and she looked about her wildly, and shuddered, shaking her head in helpless denial of what she knew to be inescapable. "No!" she said. "Oh, no!"

Then, not quite believing in the actuality of her intention, she locked the kitchen door and shuttered the window so that it could not be opened from the inside. When she had completed these tasks, she lifted the lamp and held it high above her head, examining the walls, the floor, and even the ceiling of the shack with a thoughtful, impersonal glance. Later, moving backward a little, she pursed out her lips, sucked them in, and threw the lamp suddenly against the wall. She waited long enough to see the kerosene explode, catch fire and spread; then, smiling to herself, as if she knew a most charming secret, one which she could never be coaxed into telling, she locked the door and stood outside in the dark, hearing the flames as they crackled, sighed and moved steadily across the walls.

She waited beside the door for a time, a still, transfixed look on her face, before she turned and moved off down the path. Later, after the roof had fallen in, she went to the log pond and sat on a cypress stump. It was there that others found her. When she saw the crowd, she showed them her beaten face and touched her nose lightly with the back of her hand. "Tom ran me out of the house and locked the door," she said. She shivered, as if suddenly cold, and covered her ears, swaying back and forth in the glare from the burning cabin. "He was drunk at the time. I guess he upset the lamp."

Nobody doubted her story; nobody questioned her further.

She disappeared from town a few days later, and afterwards she was rarely seen in Williston. It was said that she wandered about the countryside alone, begging her food from others and sleeping wherever she could find shelter. Once she stopped at our back gate and stared at the house. My mother called to her, but she hurried to the corner, hesitated, and looked back over her shoulder. Then my mother put food in a paper bag and left it on the fence post, and after a time Emma approached and took it, like an alarmed and mistrustful old animal.

Occasionally a farmer coming to town reported having seen her. "There she was sitting alongside the road," he would usually say. "She had her hands clapped over her ears, like there was something she didn't want to hear, and when she seen me coming toward her, she jumped up and loped away across the fields."

Many months later, a half-grown Negro boy came to our house with a message for my mother. It seemed that while he and his sister were picking berries near Sour Water Swamp, they had found Dirty Emma lying sick and helpless in a clump of bushes. Not knowing what else to do with her, they had borrowed a wheelbarrow and had taken her to the Negro quarters, where she now was. "She won't let nobody fetch the doctor for her," he said, "leastways, not till she see you first. She keep saying, 'Go get me Mrs. Gavin. She the one I want to talk to.' She mighty sick, and I think, please, ma'am, you better hurry. Ever'-body say she can't last the day out." My mother asked me to come with her and we went at once.

Emma was lying on a pallet in the long shade of a cedar tree. The quarters themselves, usually so noisy, so bursting with excitement and sound, seemed completely deserted. Since this was an affair which concerned white people, and the Negroes were determined to have nothing to do with it, every shade was drawn, every door and window closed. There was not even a child or a dog outside, and after the boy had finished his errand, he, too, disappeared into one of the silent houses.

We approached the pallet and stood there, listening for a time to her harsh, labored breathing. We were startled, despite ourselves, at the changes in her appearance. Her eyes were rolled backward in their purple sockets; her body was blotched and dried out, as if mummified imperfectly in its own dirt, and her hair, which had been cropped close to her skull, was matted with grass seeds and bits of straw.

My mother spoke after a moment, and Emma, at the sound of

her voice, rolled her head from side to side. "I got a black sin on my soul," she said. "I want to tell it before I die." Then, lying back on the pallet, her face burning with fever, her voice coming weakly, as if each word that she used exhausted her more, she told us the things which I have already told you.

When she had finished, she closed her eyes and sighed, plucking feebly at her dress. "That night of the fire, I knew the very second Tom woke and jumped up," she added, "because I heard his shoes hit the planking. The next thing, he was at the door shaking the knob. 'Emma!' he kept saying. 'Emma, let me out of here!' He threw his shoulders against the door, but he couldn't break it down, so he went to the kitchen and tried the door there. He couldn't get out that way either, and I heard him stumbling about and calling to me. 'Emma!' he kept saying. 'Emma! Emma!' But I wouldn't let him out, no matter how loud he called.

"So he came back to the bedroom and tried to open the shutter. When he couldn't move it, and knew for certain what was going to happen to him, he put his mouth to the little crack between the window and the wall. And you want to know what he done then, Mrs. Gavin? . . . He screamed. 'Emma! Emma! Emma!' he kept saying over and over. That was when I covered my ears and walked down the path, but I couldn't shut out that sound, even with my ears covered up."

I went to the porch for a basin of water, and when I returned, my mother bathed Emma's hands and face with a wet cloth. "I think God has more perception than we give Him credit for," she said. "He understands why you did it. Try not to worry so. I think He will forgive you."

There was a silence, and then I spoke for the first time. "Everybody knew how mean Tom Gunnerson was, and I don't believe a soul in town would blame you for killing him, not after the brutal way he treated you."

Emma raised her hands weakly and attempted to sit up, bewildered that her motive had been so greatly misunderstood. Then, with many pauses, as if she sought from her meager vocabulary the precise words for her purpose, this dying old woman made clear to my mother and myself both her individual system of esthetics, and the peculiar standard of values by which she governed her life.

"If the people of Williston think they made up the name Dirty Emma, they're way off the track," she said, "because I been called that all my life. Now, Mamma used to wash me as much and put fresh clothes on me as often as she did the others at home. She even put my hair up in curlers a time or two, but when the papers were off, my hair wasn't crimped and pretty the way you'd expect it to be. It just hung down limp and dirty-looking, like it is now. You could wash me with hot water and soap until you were tired out, and still I looked dirty. My stockings fell down when everybody else's stayed up, and I could put on a clean dress, sit in the front room doing nothing, and still look dirty. So everybody called me Dirty Emma from the beginning, no matter whether I was really clean at the time or not. At first I used to cry and hide under the house when they said it, but afterwards, all I could think of was, 'Well, it's the truth. That's what I am, for a fact.' So finally I gave up and quit trying."

She was growing feebler, but she talked on and on, reciting for others the simple alphabet of her humility. She explained that she had neither felt resentment against Tom for the manner in which he had treated her, nor blamed him afterwards in her heart. She had accepted these things as her due, she said, since she was so clearly what she was, and could understand how greatly she had provoked him. But the hyacinth had been something else entirely, for it had not been dirty in the least. On the contrary, she had considered it as clean and pretty as anything in this world can ever expect to be. It was fully open at the time of its destruction, she explained, and it was so fragrant that you could smell it plainly as you came up the path.

"He didn't have no call to harm a thing like that, now did he, Mrs. Gavin?" she asked anxiously. "Twisting off its neck the way he did, and then tromping it to pieces with his foot. That was a cruel thing to do, and I said so at the time; and as I lay there by the stove, I kept thinking to myself, 'You ought to be punished for doing such a hateful thing. You ought to be taught a real good lesson, and that's a fact!' " She turned her head away, overcome by the things she remembered, and cried harshly against her pillow.

She had reached the end of her story. She had made the confession which she felt that she must make, and now she was no longer interested in us. There was a long silence, and then, moving one infirm and feverish arm across the pallet, she said, with no interest at all in her voice, "You can send for the doctor now, if that will comfort your mind any." My mother said, "Emma, is there anything you want? Anything special that I can do for you?" Emma said no, there was not, or if there was, she could not remember it at the moment.

She died that same afternoon, and they buried her later in the company graveyard beside the railroad tracks. Afterwards, I thought of her a great deal, and for a time I even dreamed of her now and then. I knew that my mother thought of her too, but neither of us mentioned her name for a long time; and then, months later, when we sat in the living room before the open fire one night, my mother turned to me and said softly, as if unconsciously speaking her thoughts out loud: "You know, Jamie, the classic Greeks would have understood old Emma from the beginning."

My father laughed, put down his newspaper and said: "Make for the hills, children! Your unfortunate mother is on the *Greeks* again!"

My mother laughed a little too. She was sewing on school dresses for my sisters, and for a time she worked in silence; then, biting off a thread, she spoke quietly to my sisters and myself: "There are two kinds of crimes against humanity, children, and the Greeks, who saw things so much more clearly than we do, knew this well. First, there was the obvious crime, the crime which even the dullest understood and knew how to punish."

She held the dress closer to the light, examined the buttonhole she had just completed, and then said: "The other kind of crime was more difficult to detect, and often it was so cunning in its seeming innocence that even the gods, themselves, were misled. That was why they created three terrifying old women, and assigned to them the task of rooting out and punishing these other crimes. They called these old women The Furies, and that was an appropriate name indeed, for they were without mercy in fulfilling their mission."

She searched in her sewing-box for her strawberry-shaped emery bag, and when she had found it, she continued: "When I think of Emma now, I see her with the lamp held above her head, at the instant she moved back a step and hurled it against the wall. I see her in this pose because I've come to think of her as one of The Furies themselves, a creature dedicated to the avengeance of those subtle crimes against mankind which pass unnoticed—those most terrible crimes of all, since men, as individuals, are so often unaware that they have been wronged."

She got up and put away her sewing; then, bending above my father, she laughed softly, kissed his forehead and said: "And now I think I shall go to bed, if my handsome but illiterate lord will accompany me."

1944

SHE TALKS GOOD NOW

MR. ROSEN, a methodical man, circled the path twice before he found a place which suited him: and that was a wide, flat stone beneath a willow tree, against a bank which sloped upward to the terraced walk above. Before him was a small brook; beyond that, an insipid lawn which had been a lake before the authorities filled it in. He seated himself, opened his book and leaned against the bank, his cigarettes, his spectacles-case and his other small belongings arranged beside him. Later, he was conscious of somebody standing on the path before him, of a soft, surprised voice saying: "Look-a-dere, little Ermie! A white gennelman done taken our seat! What you speck we gwiner do now, sweetheart?"

He turned and looked up, closing his book on his index finger. Before him stood a massive woman in a white, thickly starched uniform such as nurses wear; and against the texture and strength of this heavy material her confined flesh strained outward. Her black, broad face was good-natured and without guile, and as Mr. Rosen examined her, she laughed, stooped ponderously and said: "Honey, what make you hide behinst Lula's skirt? This white gennelman don't aim to bother nobody. He didn't have no way of knowin' that this was our regular restin' place, now did he? So come on out and show him how pretty you is."

A three-year-old girl, dressed in a pink, elaborate frock, peeped from behind her nurse's sheltering bulk. "This here is little Ermie," said Lula proudly. "Now, ain't she the sweetest thing in this big city of New York, New York?"

Mr. Rosen agreed, got up and began assembling his belongings.

"Oh, he fixin' to give us our seat back," said Lula with spurious surprise. "Ain't that a nice thing to do, honey? He say he druther sit on that little rock over there, 'cause that rock is sized right to fit him, but not near big enough for ole spread-out Lula." She laughed good-naturedly and raised her arms in the air, and instantly the little girl duplicated the laugh and the gesture with a fidelity which was startling. Lula bent down, as if she could no longer control her affection, and lifted the child in her arms. "My baby," she said. "She like to do ever'thing the way Lula do it."

Mr. Rosen, who had intended moving to a bench on the terrace above, found himself settling down, instead, on the small, flat stone which Lula had selected for him—drawn there, somehow, through the sheer force of the woman's genial, overwhelming personality. When he glanced up again, he saw that Lula had opened a week-end case and had taken from it a bathing cap and a pair of coveralls. She undressed the child and adjusted the coverall deftly. "Now, stand still a minute longer," she said, "till I get this ole rubber cap fixed right, 'cause I don't want your pretty curls to get muddy this time." When everything was arranged to her satisfaction, she held the child at arm's length and then said: "Now, go play in the branch and get as dirty as you want to."

The child ran eagerly toward the brook, and when she reached it, she knelt beside the sluggish, rather dirty water, clapping her hands and laughing with pleasure. "Ain't she sweet," said Lula, almost bursting with love and pride. "Ain't she the sweetest thing in this wide world."

"A most attractive child indeed. What is her name?"

"Her name's Ermintrude," said Lula; "but it was a crazy way to name my baby, so I call her Ermie."

Mr. Rosen filled his pipe, struck a match and nodded. The child was plainly not the Ermintrude type, and never would be.

"Maybe you heard tell of her mamma and papa," continued Lula, " 'cause they mighty well known people. Her papa's Professor Reginald Ainsworth, and he take an interest in the Greeks, and them ole dead people. Always goin' around diggin' up buried towns, and fumblin' with bones. He and his lady been out of town all summer long—in Mexico, some place; but they got to come home pretty soon now, and go back to teachin' at the University. Yes, *suh,* the Professor's a smart man, and no two ways about that. They tell me he was ready to go to college when he was twelve years old, and done so; and what's more, he come out first in his classes. I heard once what they called him, but I completely forgot."

"A prodigy, perhaps," said Mr. Rosen.

"That's it," said Lula. "It's the word I heard him named; but ever'body say no matter how smart he is, he ain't nowhere near as smart as his good lady. She was a little English prodigy, and come from the city of London; but they managed to meet up, one way or another, and marry. Her name's Kate Hopperly Ainsworth, and she speak ever' language there is, or nerabout. She's wrote I don't know how many books, on one subject or another. She's a great one for grammar and always talking proper, too." Lula paused and stared thoughtfully across the lawn. "The Professor and his lady are sho finicky people," she said after a moment. "With them, ever'thing got to be cut and dried, and accordin' to the way the book say do it."

"I suppose you've been the child's nurse for a long time?"

"No, suh, I haven't. Fact is, I been Ermie's nurse only 'bout three weeks now. Befo' that time they had a nurse that was trained in college. You see, ever'body figgered since the Professor and his wife was *both* so smart, any child they had was bound to be as smart as they was, if not smarter. That's why they tried so hard to make something out of Ermie, I expect.

"Why, when the Professor got home from the University, he used to go in for an hour and talk deep things to that baby lyin' there in her little cradle; then, after he done left, his lady would come in and read to her in Greek and other languages too, I expect. I was cookin' for the Ainsworths at the time, but for some reason or other, wouldn't nobody let me come *near* Ermie; and then one day that ole college nurse taken sick, and they had to ride her to the hospital for treatment. The Professor and his wife was in Mexico long before that, so it left me and Ermie alone in the house, and that's when we really got together."

Ermie had taken off her shoes and stockings and was wading in the brook, but hearing her name mentioned, she turned and waved. At once Lula shook her finger and said: "Quit spreadin' them stories about me! I didn't put no conjur on that nurse woman, and you better quit sayin' so, you ole mean Miss Ermintrude, you!" She bent forward from her bulging thighs and laughed gaily, rolling her eyes from side to side. The child laughed with her, bending forward as her nurse had done, rolling her eyes in an identical manner.

"And did the little girl become a prodigy, too, with all that training?" asked Mr. Rosen after a moment.

Lula glanced at the child and lowered her voice. "That's the trouble," she said gravely. "You put your finger on something that time. Oh, they tried hard enough to make her one, like I told you, but it wouldn't work out, 'cause my baby's got a mind of her own, and nobody can make her do nothin' she don't want to do. Fact is, the Professor and Mrs. Ainsworth got mighty scared toward the end, 'cause they thought there was something bad the matter with Ermie, and they taken her to all sorts of doctors. Trouble was, Ermie was almost three years old, and she never had spoke a word in her life. They was afraid there was somethin' bad the matter with her little brain. I was the onliest one that wasn't worried, and I knowed all along what ailed her, 'cause Ermie was just like me: You see, we ain't apt, and don't want to be!" Then, attracting the child's attention, she called out: "We ain't so bright, is we, sugar?"

Ermie shook her curls and danced up and down.

"We don't *need* to be bright," said Lula, exploding with mirth once more. "We're *pretty!*"

Then, lowering her voice, she continued: " 'Course Ermie didn't talk none! There wasn't nothin' she wanted to say! Ever'-

body used such big words around her, she didn't know what was goin' on half the time. Here I am, a grown woman forty years old, and iffen I couldn't understand that high English, how come a little girl can understand it?"

Mr. Rosen admitted that this was a point reasonably taken, and added: "And can the little girl talk now?"

"Talk!" said Lula in astonishment. "'Course she can talk now! Ermie can talk as good as anybody, when she wants to, but it's got to be somethin' she likes to hear herself sayin'."

At that moment there came a shrill, frightened sound from Ermintrude, and she ran forward blindly, her arms stretched before her. Without raising her eyes from the child, Lula said: "She's seen a policeman. It's the onliest thing she skeered of now. Somebody tole her a policeman will lock her up in jail and feed her bread and water." She bent forward, making soft, reassuring noises, and lifted the child to her lap. "Where he at?" she asked. "Where that policeman at?"

But the little girl only trembled and pressed herself closer to Lula's breast. Lula shaded her eyes and squinted across the brook. A stout, somewhat dispirited policeman was walking at the far edge of the lawn, and when he reached the path that led to an ornamental bridge to the right, he paused, scratched himself thoughtfully and looked upward. "I see him!" said Lula. "I see him now!"

Then, stroking the child's curls, she added: "That policeman ain't aimin' to bother you, baby; but if he try to, I'll bust him down so quick he'll think a truck hit him, and furthermore wish it had!" The little girl lifted her head and stared solemnly at her nurse, but she was still trembling a little. "It's exactly what I'll do," said Lula. "I'll bust him down one time right after another, and I'll step my foot on his ole fat, red neck." She pressed her lips to the child's forehead. "You ain't got nothing to be scared of, honey, because when I finish doin' all I said, I speck I'll hit him with a rock, too."

But the little girl was not entirely reassured, and Lula continued soothingly: "A little later on, I'll hold him down and you can tromple him till he so scared he don't know *what* to do. And pretty soon, when you trompled him as much as he can stand, he'll begin to cry and take on. 'Mamma! Mamma!' he keep sayin'. 'Come here quick and pull Miss Ermintrude offen me!' "

Suddenly the child laughed and scrambled from her nurse's lap. She stuck out her jaw and strode up and down, muttering to herself and making ferocious gestures; and when, a little later, she returned to the brook to play, she paused every few steps, examined the horizon for policemen, and stamped on the turf with her foot.

"That's right," said Lula. "That's the way to do it. Whup him good, so the next time he sees you in the park, he'll remember who you is, and run the other way." She closed her eyes and leaned against the bank. "My baby," she said dreamily. . . . "She's my lamb, that's what she is."

Mr. Rosen said, "When do you expect the family back?"

Lula sat up and pulled thoughtfully at her lip. "Well, sir," she began, "the Professor and lady are due next Monday morning, but that nurse woman don't get out of the hospital till Thursday of the same week." She lowered her voice, hesitated, and glanced about her cautiously. "I been thinking about that nurse," she said, "and how to keep her from takin' Ermie away from me; and so I cooked me up a scheme, and I expect it gwiner work out fine."

She paused to collect her thoughts and then said: "Now, I already told you how ever'body was worried to death because Ermie couldn't talk, and how they thought she might be deef and dumb, or worse, even, than that. Remember? Well, just as soon as I got her to myself, I learned her to talk in no time at all. She talks good now, like I told you, but her mamma and papa don't know that; and so I learned her a little welcome speech to say as a surprise when they come in the door." Then, raising her voice an octave higher, she called out: "Honey, come here a minnit. This gennelman wants to hear your welcome speech."

The child came at once and stood in the path. She put her hands on her hips and spread her legs in a manner which Lula, herself, affected, pursing her lips and rolling her eyes from side to side. When she spoke, her voice was so like that of her nurse in timbre, accent and phrasing, that, if you turned your head away, you could not be sure which of the two was speaking.

"Welcome back, dear Mommer and Popper," she began. "I hopes you had a fine time down there where you been at, 'cause Lula and me sho had us one fine time here in the city. Now, ain't you all surprised to hear me talkin' good? Well, sir, it was Lula what learned me. She done it all by herself, as sho as God made little apples. So why don't you jus' let Lula be my nurse from now on, and keep learnin' me like she started out to do?"

Lula laughed with pride and slapped her thigh, and, after the child had returned to her play, she said: "When the Professor and his lady hear Ermie jabberin' away like that, I expect they gwiner fire that other nurse, like Ermie asked them to. They gwiner say, 'Lula, you take care of Ermie from now on, 'cause we know there's a heap mo' you could learn her, iffen you had mo' time to do it in.' That's exactly what they gwiner say, and I know it just as sho as I'm settin' on this rock."

She turned with an eager gesture, her starched uniform crackling and straining at its seams, confident that Mr. Rosen would confirm her hopes. But he would not look at her immediately, fixing his gaze, instead, on the ornamental bridge and the piled boulders beyond. He was mistrustful of her plan, and, frankly, he did not think it would work at all, for in his mind's eye, at that instant, there was a clear picture of both the scientific professor and his austere English wife—the lady who spoke so many languages, who laid such stress on the essentials of grammar, the purity of diction.

"Don't you think they gwiner be surprised?" asked Lula once more. "Don't you think they gwiner let me *keep* Ermie?"

Mr. Rosen glanced at his watch, buttoned his jacket and prepared to make his departure; then, realizing that an answer was expected from him, he sighed and said that at least Lula could be certain of one thing: The Professor and his wife were going to be *surprised.*

1944

NOVELETTE

*

OCTOBER ISLAND

AFTER so long a time in residence, Sam Barnfield and his wife Irma had come to think of October Island as their own, something which they themselves had visualized and moulded into its tapering, gourd-like shape, had colored theatrically with reds and yellows and greens, and had set down, at length, in the cobalt and sapphire waters of the vast Pacific Ocean.

On that first day when they had landed from a schooner, their goods piled helter-skelter on the stone mole that ran out into the lagoon, Sam had turned to his wife and said, "Here is a field awaiting the plough of the Lord." Irma nodded absently, but she did not speak at once, for her eyes at that instant were fixed with disbelief on a delegation of natives—a welcoming group who stood with an alert and graceful unconcern among a grove of wind-curved palms and watched their visitors in silence. She saw at once that they were entirely naked, except for their jewelry and the rather inadequate breech-clouts they wore; then, since the truest function of nudity is to make the clothed aware of their own more specialized immodesty, Irma tried the buttons of her shirtwaist, to assure herself that they were securely fastened, blushed, and settled her skirts more evenly about her shoetops.

The nakedness of the men, she felt, since there was nothing to corrupt the muscular, impersonal line of their bodies, was unremarkable and in no way offensive to her; it was the more focalized nudity of the women that had made her eyes widen in astonishment, for their stuffed, satiny breasts hung arrogantly from shoulder to waist, lifting in rhythm to the breath of their owners, or vibrating and swaying from side to side as the women yawned or laughed softly among themselves. Never in all her life—never at any time, or in any of the strange places of the world, had she seen such a brazen, fleshy opulence, and she lowered her eyes in confusion, thinking, "We must get clothes on them. That is clearly our first duty."

She turned back to the mole, and to the schooner anchored

there, and in the pure, shallow water of the harbor, the fragile hull of the ship was outlined clearly. She could see the thin anchor-chain as it cut through the water, and the three flattened, brilliantly colored fish that swam untiringly around it in an exact and idiotic pattern; she saw the anchor itself as it lay, like the abandoned toy of a child, atop the yellow sand and the pink, monotonous coral. The schooner had seemed neither frail nor small while she had been aboard it, and only yesterday she had thought of the anchor and its chain as things capable of holding any object firmly, under any stress or condition; but seeing them now at this angle, in this light, she was suddenly filled with anxiety. For a moment her life seemed senseless and of no importance to herself or to others; she doubted her mission, and in that terrifying interval, she was amazed at herself for having abandoned so many things that others set store by to embark on her life of thankless sacrifice and deprivation.

She reached out to touch the familiar flesh of her husband, but he had already moved away from her in the direction of the watching natives. When he was a courteous distance from them, he paused and said: "I am the Reverend Samuel Barnfield, and this is my wife Irma. We want to live here and share your lives, if that is agreeable to you. Do not be afraid of us. We are missionaries, and we have come to bring you peace and the Word of God."

When he had finished, the natives began to laugh and chatter among themselves, finding the seriousness of this spare, graying old man both stimulating and amusing; then, recognizing some signal unheard by others, they turned and ran through the palm trees, toward the beach at the far side of the harbor; and as the women balanced themselves and moved forward, each in turn, raised her left arm in a ritualistic, supporting gesture, lifting her breasts up, and holding them outward, as if she displayed a basket of ripe, tropical fruit for others to view and admire. The men, being unimpeded, ran more easily, and with a greater grace, their splayed, prehensile toes curling a little and grasping the sand for support. They outdistanced the women easily, but at intervals, when they saw their companions were falling too far behind, they would pause on the crumbling sand, pivot, and extend their arms to the brown, laughing women.

Almost at once the headman of the island appeared among the trees. Since he considered the greeting of visitors not a public occasion, but an affair of the deepest intimacy, he wore his heavy headdress of clam shells, and his ceremonial robe of yellow and green feathers; and in a long, rather tiresome speech, he welcomed the strangers to October Island. When he had finished, one of the sailors from the schooner, a young half-breed named Hansen, who inappropriately combined the flaxen hair and gray eyes of his father with the barely modified features, the slightly diluted skin of his mother's people, stepped forward and translated the headman's words:

It appeared that the white visitors who had preceded the present ones had been scientists of one sort or another, and had spent their time spading up the dry beds of old streams, digging in the hills, or searching through the interior jungle; but whatever it was they looked for, they had not found it, and, in disappointment, they had quit the island some years before, leaving behind them the house they had built, many books, and a few broken pieces of furniture. The house was still intact, and the Reverend Barnfield and his wife were welcome to live there, if they wanted to. He would show them the way in person, and, later on, when the young people had recovered from their nervous amusement, they would see that the strangers' belongings were properly transported from the stone mole to their new home.

The house was situated on a high, green plateau. It commanded an almost perfect view of Min-Raybaat, the great, twin-coned volcano for which October Island was celebrated, and after her new house had been repaired, scoured, and decorated with bright, native mats and blue-calico cushions and curtains, Irma would often stand outside, one hand shielding her eyes from the quivering, tropical sun, and stare upward at the twin cones with a sort of rapt disapprobation.

The volcano was the first thing you saw as you approached the island, and on that memorable day when it had appeared suddenly in the distance, seemingly without support above the curving horizon of the sea, Irma had caught her breath and had moved back from the rail of the schooner, alarmed at the menace implicit in its towering, austere magnificence; but the captain of the schooner had reassured her, telling her that Min-Raybaat had not been active for hundreds of years, and that for all purposes of reality, it could be considered extinct. It was true, on occasion, that senile, echoing rumbles were heard from its depths, and at times streams of smoke and ineffectual jets of steam issued from its craters, but that was about all. In fact, she need not concern herself further about the volcano, for she would be as safe in its shadow as she was on the deck of his fragile, straining ship. . . . Now, remembering the captain's words, Irma lowered her eyes and said aloud, "I am God's creature, and I am in His hands. What he has destined for me, I will accept."

She sighed, turned and went back to her tasks, finding a certain just appropriateness in her laborious, unimaginative toil. She left the spiritual side of their mission to her husband, feeling that while he was a preacher whose eloquence could move others to repentance and repudiation, her own usefulness was that of ministering to the dull, everyday wants of the congregation. In her heart, she knew herself to be a woman of little sense and of only the slightest moral worth—a restless, aggressive old charwoman of God whose duties were the menial ones of keeping the temple sweet and unprofaned, of seeing that the long, difficult road to salvation was swept and unimpeded.

Later, when she and her husband had made friends with the islanders, and Sam had already begun his first efforts at conversion, Irma would often take walks along the seashore, picking up dry wood for her oven, or shells for the borders of the flowerbeds she was setting against her porch. Once, while deep in the interior, not far from the base of Min-Raybaat itself, she saw a plant growing from the side of one of the small, rocky hills. From a distance it seemed to be a violet, and yet, from another angle, it was plainly too large, too brightly colored for any violet she had ever seen; nevertheless, it was as close to a violet as any plant in this land of brilliance, immodesty and ridiculous size could reasonably be expected to be, and at once she wanted it for her garden.

The roots of the plant went deeper than she had thought. They were laced about a small, elliptical stone, and she dug out both stone and roots together; but when the plant was safely in her hands, the stone fell away from the dirt and lay obscenely in the sunlight, beside her feet. She stared at it in disbelief, being unable at that instant to credit its shocking, hermaphroditic frankness. She would not touch the stone with her hands again, but she turned it over with the toe of her boot, got down on her knees, and examined its flat, smooth sides; then, shrouding one hand in her skirt, she grasped the stone by the end which represented a breast, and reburied it in its original place. She dusted her hands and hurried away, saying indignantly, "Who would have thought such nastiness could be hidden behind a violet?"

The unpleasant incident, which ordinarily she would have dismissed from her mind at once, made an odd impression on her, and that night as she lay beside her sleeping husband, she saw the image again in all its lewd significance. The surfaces of the stone were even and highly polished, and they were covered with faint, but quite legible characters. She told herself that these characters were merely the accidental markings of time and erosion, or, at best, the meaningless scribbling of an ancient native; but she could not make herself believe these things, for in her heart she knew that the markings on the stone were the written words of thousands of years ago, and that they had been put there for a purpose by some patient and highly skilled hand.

There was a set of encyclopedias among the books which the archeologists had left behind, and since she knew she could not sleep that night, she got up, lit a candle, and turned to *October Island,* not really expecting to find a place as obscure as it was mentioned at all. To her surprise, the island was not only mentioned by name, but there were many columns of fine print devoted to its remote and most remarkable history.

She read on and on, discovering that the island's name, which she had taken for granted as being the identifying month of its discovery, was, in reality, a corruption of the far older title,

Ok-tur-baat, which was believed by Professor Hans Axel Hansen to mean, "Garden of the Living Breast," or, alternatively, "Garden of the Final Redemption"; or even, according to the dissenting reading of Reginald Sykes, "Place of the Beginning and Ending."

But regardless of the scientific battles which had been fought over its name, October Island was universally accepted as being the site of the world's first important culture—a sort of pagan Garden of Eden where Shurabast, that cult dedicated to the worship of the hermaphroditic god Raybaat, had originated some six to ten thousand years before the birth of Christ. At its peak, Shurabast had been world-wide in scope. Then, gradually, its power had abated, until, at length, its rituals were observed only on the island of its origin, and even there, according to Professor Hansen, who had studied the natives at first hand, in only a rudimentary and inconclusive form.

Some scientists, notably Professor Johannes Katz and Dr. Clement Higgs, were of opinion that the priests of Raybaat had perfected the first alphabet, and had passed it on to the budding civilizations of the mainland. There was little evidence to support this contention, since no example of Ok-tur-baat writing had so far come to light, although several expeditions, notably the one of Wayland Yates in 1900, had gone to October Island to seek it out; but if these claims could be supported in time, if October Island had actually possessed an alphabet, and had preserved a written record of its civilization, then it was plain that many of the sciences, and much of the history of man's eternal struggle upward, would have to be rewritten, or rejected in part.

The article ended with a description of Min-Raybaat: It was situated near the island's one harbor, a few miles back of the coastal-plain. It was once considered the home of Raybaat himself, the god occupying the larger cone, his enormous, top-heavy wife inappropriately dwelling in the smaller. . . .

When she had finished her reading, Irma went back to the bedroom and stared thoughtfully at her husband. He was deeply asleep, his mouth opened a little, his stringy, graying legs exposed as high as his thighs. She sighed patiently and pulled down his nightshirt, blew out her candle, and lay primly beside him. The article had both disturbed and frightened her, and she was glad now that she had not told her husband about the stone she had found that afternoon. His temperament was different from her own, and he would have insisted, in his patient yet stubborn voice, that the stone be sent to a museum for study, and perhaps eventual deciphering.

She turned on her side, wondering if, by any possible stretch of imagination, the stone contained matter at variance with her individual, specialized belief. She got up and walked about the room restlessly. It was not that her own faith was too weak to withstand some foolish, heathen doctrine, she thought scornfully. That was not the issue at all. She was sure of herself, and what she stood for—but were the faiths of others equally strong?

She sat by her window, her head lowered, her hands pressing against her cheeks; then, in a moment of commonplace revelation, she understood the purpose of the obscene, polished tablet she had found: It was a sort of prayer-stone, she thought—something prepared by the priests of Raybaat, and sold to their followers; and if this assumption was correct, then the hill itself was a priestly post office, a place where the worshippers had buried their petitions with the naive trust of children sending letters to Santa Claus up a chimney.

She considered these matters for a long time, wondering where her truest duty lay, and then as the land breeze freshened, and the tropical daybreak was unbearable with the clangor and screaming of the harsh-voiced, beautiful birds, she dedicated herself to the performance of new acts of faith: to the destruction of the idolatrous writing.

That morning after her housework was done she dug up the stone she had reburied, broke it, and threw its fragments into the sea. In the years that followed, she could be seen daily as she scurried about the island on her quest. She dug patiently in the hills, she balanced herself on the slippery ledges beneath waterfalls, she lowered herself through crevices in the cliffs to investigate the existence of caves. Her passion was successful, and she found many specimens of the writing she sought, although her major find did not come until the twelfth year of her search.

It consisted of a few items of religious paraphernalia, and many tablets of baked clay, each tablet being covered with legible, minute writing. The objects were wrapped in thin, beautifully worked kidskin. They rested together in a carved stone box, and while she did not understand their significance, she knew that once they had been of overwhelming importance to others, since they were concealed so cleverly, in such a remote and unexpected place. She examined the tablets for a long time, one hand resting in indecision against her cheek, but she broke them all at last, just as she had done the others.

She found the last specimen of writing during her twentieth year of residence on the island. At the end of the twenty-third, she concluded that there was no writing left to be found; but by that time the natives had been saved in a sudden, mass conversion, and both she and her husband were content, feeling their tasks were accomplished at last.

It was in the years which followed that they first began thinking of home again, and wishing they could return there. Irma would often speak of the friends she had once known, wondering which of them were living, and which were now dead, and as she moved about her house, or sat rocking on her porch, she sometimes visualized her return, and she smiled gently, seeing a great gathering of her loved ones, all those that she had once cherished and held so dear, there at the station to welcome her.

Her husband's desire for his homeland was more focused in its aim, more intense in its origin; and sometimes at night when he knelt to say his prayers, he would find his lips saying instead, "Dear Lord, if I could only be cold once more! If I could only hear sleigh bells again, or see snow!" Then, to his astonishment, he would find himself weeping, his face pressed flat against the mattress of his bed. It was almost as if he were passing through some delayed and inappropriate change-of-life, and that the object of his fading desire was not the conventional, warm-bodied young girl, but the granite contours, the cold, spinsterish charm of his native Vermont.

Their actual departure from the island came suddenly and quite simply: It happened when Samuel was sixty-four, and his wife sixty-one, and the board of missions which had supported them so long merely wrote that their treasury was in a poor condition, and that they could no longer underwrite the good work being done on October Island. The letter came on the regular, autumn trip of the *Mattie B. Powell,* and after Samuel had read it aloud to his wife, she sat quietly for a moment, nodded, and began packing their possessions with her eyes.

Samuel said: "Do you remember that helpful young half-breed in the crew of the vessel that brought us here? He's the new mate on the *Powell.* He remembers you very well, and asked how you were getting along."

"His name is Hansen," said Irma. "We had long talks together on the voyage out. His mother was a native woman, I remember, and he was born right here on the island."

Sam nodded, and then continued: "The schooner can return for us in about two weeks. I think we'd better leave on it."

"Yes," said Irma. "I suppose we must."

The words became a sort of refrain for her during the days that followed, and she moved about in a world of indecision and operatic unreality, surrounded by the lamenting friends she must leave behind her forever; but once aboard the schooner, on her way to Honolulu, her vigor returned, and she felt herself again.

But she was unhappy in her idleness, for years ago, when she was a small girl and lived in Vermont, her grandmother had once told her that each new day was like a treasure-box of hours and minutes and seconds. These powerful gifts were not granted us to be wasted, she said; instead, they were to be used thriftily, and with thoughtful kindness, and they were to be lived up with such an undeviating earnestness, that none of them was frittered away, or remained unexpended at nightfall. She had long since forgotten both her grandmother and the parable she had heard, but the effect of the story was to remain with her forever—a part of her character, a pattern in her mind—so that even now, where others might have relaxed and enjoyed a holiday at sea, she had only a feeling of uneasiness, a sense of guilt in her idolence.

And so she asked Mate Hansen to bring her his clothes and the clothes of the other members of the crew that needed repairing; and seated placidly on the small deck of the ship, she worked methodically. Often, when he was off duty, Mate Hansen would come and walk with her. Before coming aboard, she had thought of him as being young, as he had been when she saw him last, but in the twenty-six years which had passed since that time, his hair had whitened at the sides, and there were now deep lines in his pensive, dark-skinned face. He regarded people warily, his gray eyes narrowed and on guard. He was familiar with every vice; he had participated in every depravity known to man; and he had rejected them all at length; not because he considered them wrong, but because he found them tiresome, so that now, as he approached his middle-age, he had achieved not corruption, but a kind of impervious and monstrous purity.

He leaned against the rail, watching the green, running water. The day was so calm, the schooner moved so imperceptibly, that for a moment he had a sense of danger, thinking himself on land again; then Irma bit off a thread, looked up from her work, and began talking once more of the things that interested her.

On this particular morning, she said rather plaintively that since the islanders were obviously simple people, one had a right to expect them to have simple minds, simple customs, and a simple language with which to express their needs. At first, she had reasonably assumed these things to be true, and had been taken in as a result of her trusting nature, for she had soon found out that the minds of the natives were not artless at all, but quite cunning in a harmless, captivating way; that their customs, instead of being simple, were, in reality, so complex, so dictated by tradition, that one despaired of understanding them at all; and insofar as language was concerned, there was not one to master, but four: the language men used in speaking to men; the language women used in speaking to women; the language men and women used in common, and the courtesy language for public occasions and for addressing strangers.

Mate Hansen nodded, took out his pocketknife and began whittling a soft board. There was another language on October

Island—the language that the natives used in communicating with their god and his consort, but since Irma did not know of it, after her years of residence there, he felt it would be discourteous to mention it now, and he remained silent.

Later, she tried to draw him out, to induce him to discuss his religious convictions, his purpose in life, his plans for making the most of the years that remained; but he was embarrassed at her sentimental fervor, and to escape her, to divert her missionary zeal onto less personal things, he uttered the first thought that came into his mind. The one thing that he wanted now, was to own and command his own schooner, he said, although he realized there was little chance of his achieving such an ambitious goal. She chided him for his lack of faith. She would join her prayers with his, she promised, and perhaps God would see fit to grant his wish—particularly if they could convince Him that the schooner, if given, would be used somehow in a furtherance of His own Power and Glory. The mate did not answer, and, as she sewed busily, she talked on and on—affirming, defining, and arranging the articles of her belief.

He paused in his whittling at length, and glanced at her with his long, light gray eyes, impressed anew with her relentless kindness, feeling once more the shallowness of her inbred faith. He wondered, at that moment, if the identifying mark of adolescence was not the easiness of its definitions, its garrulous intimacy with concepts which awe the imaginative and mature and leave them silent. He sighed and lowered his head, since his was the melancholy of those who are neither one thing nor the other. Once, long ago, he had lived with assurance; but as the years receded, and the cleavage in his nature became more and more apparent, he saw nothing about him but sadness, as if a deep pathos, for his kind, was the assence of life itself, the background against which we are born, and struggle, and live out our lives to their ends.

He turned at the sound of footsteps, but it was only Sam Barnfield coming across the deck. He walked slowly, with little, mincing steps, putting down each foot as though it were precious to him, for this continent, saintly old man who neither drank, smoked, nor indulged in rich foods, suffered the punishments which are promised the drunkard, the glutton and the lecher as an atonement for their pleasures.

When he had seated himself on the covered hatchway beside Mate Hansen, Irma held up a pair of dungarees and examined their seams in the sunlight. She said, "There's still one question I'd like to ask you, Mate Hansen, and it's this: The women of October Island have a certain—well, a certain physical *peculiarity*, if you ever noticed what I have in mind. Both my husband and I have often wondered what the cause of it was, and if you know, perhaps you'll tell us."

Mate Hansen raised his head and stared at the unsteady rim of the sea, a far-away look in his melancholy eyes. He explained that, in the legendary past, when Shurabast had been all-powerful, the whole Pacific had been searched for young girls of such an overpowering attractiveness, that they were thought worthy to serve at the altar of Raybaat himself. When found, each novice was oiled, decked with flowers, and sent to October Island, where, in an elaborate ceremony of dedication, she became the spiritual bride of Raybaat, and the physical bride of his priests. The present people of the island were the random descendants of those voluptuous, carefully selected priestesses and their prurient, but sacred partners; and no doubt the specialized beauty, the freakish proportion which had been the sole factor in determining the vocation of the mother, had been passed on with such persistence by her, that, in time, Nature had sanctioned the variation from average, and had fixed it forever in the daughter.

Irma put down the dungarees, picked up a faded workshirt, and studied the condition of its cuffs. "Well!" she said. "Well, of all *things!*"

For a moment, Mate Hansen worked on the figure he was carving, his thin, brown fingers plying his knife with confident skill; but after a short silence, he turned his head and stared at Irma Barnfield with such thoughtful intensity that she became self-conscious, and fidgeted a little in her chair. Her hair had been admired all her life, she recalled. It was auburn, silky, and abundant; and there was no gray in it at all.—Even Samuel, although he had never been an ardent man, had once told her that it was her hair which had first attracted him to her; and so, remembering these things, this aged, wrinkled old woman arranged her scarf more modestly about her head, and tucked in the small, damp tendrils of floss which curled on the nape of her neck, as she did not want to be the instrument of Mate Hansen's undoing, or to tempt him to lust after her in his heart.

But she had misread the import of the mate's steady, inquiring glance. Actually, he was not thinking of her as a woman at all, but merely as one of the principals in the mass conversion of the people of October Island. Already the affair was famous in the neighboring ports. He had even heard of it in places as far distant as Singapore, for once, in a waterfront brothel there, a plump, sedate young woman had entertained her patrons with an interminable song about it—a song which she called, "Condensed Milk Salvation." The woman sang softly, to the swishing accompaniment of the two small, sand-filled gourds that she held in her hands, and when she finished, her audience made kissing sounds with their lips, laughed gently and leaned back against their mats once more.

Mate Hansen, recalling the scene, now wanted to determine the facts, to discover, if he could, which of the song's allegations were fanciful, and which true. Then, as if the thought had just come to mind, he tossed his carving over the side of the schooner and asked his question casually; but some unconscious delicacy, connected perhaps with a memory of the singing woman and her rustling gourds, impelled him to speak not to Irma, whom he knew well, but to her husband, who had always alarmed him a little.

Sam looked up slowly, a rather vacant expression on his face. He suffered an enlargement of the liver, but he had known that for a long time, and, in a sense, he had come to accept his affliction as average and to be expected; but of late, he had also been plagued by days of dull, almost unbearable prostatic pain. He suffered such pain at this moment, and it was difficult for him to concentrate on anything outside his own misery, but hearing himself addressed personally, he summoned his will power, pressed one hand against his side, and said:

"When we first went to October Island, my wife and I knew that many missionaries had been there before us, and that they'd accomplished nothing at all. For many years the natives resisted us too. Oh, they were courteous and considerate enough; they were kind, gentle, and unassuming on all occasions; but when I tried to preach to them, to show them the way to happiness and divine peace, they would laugh, nudge one another, and then run off through the trees.

"Now, one of the old women of the village came down with a most peculiar sickness. She wouldn't move off her mats, and she wouldn't take food, except a little coconut milk at night and in the morning. We thought she'd die in a short time—from starvation, if nothing else; and it was at this point that my wife suggested we try giving condensed milk to the unfortunate woman. It was easy to take, and it was very nourishing; and there were a number of cans left over from our last consignment of supplies from the mainland; so when my wife and I concluded that condensed milk could do the poor creature no possible harm, and might even help sustain life a little longer in her, Irma went back to the house to fetch some of it."

His voice faltered, and he passed his hands roughly across his face, as if to brush something away from him. Irma, seeing his distress, took up the story, and finished in her quick, nasal voice: "When I got home, I opened a fresh can of milk; but I didn't want to serve the sick woman out of the tin itself, as that wouldn't look very polite, I thought; so I emptied the milk into an ornamental cup which I'd found on the island one day, and went back to the place where Sam was waiting for me."

She hesitated guiltily, for she had found the cup and the clay tablets together in the same box. At first she had meant to destroy the cup too, but the practical side of her nature had prevented so petulant an act, for she felt that, divorced of its heathen associations, and washed well with soap and hot water, she could easily put it to some Christian, everyday use of her own choosing.

"It was really less a cup than a ceremonial vessel of one kind or another," she said presently. "It was made out of polished stone, and there was a milky translucence about it. Perhaps it was alabaster, perhaps a variety of white jade. . . . Anyway, there was a decorated lid for the vessel, with a piece cut out where the spoon came through." She went on talking about the cup, describing it in circumstantial detail, but when she paused for breath, Mate Hansen bent forward excitedly and said, "Will you tell me what happened next, please?"

"What happened next was sudden, and almost incredible," said Irma. "You see, when I came back to the sick woman, Sam held up her head, and I offered her a spoonful of the milk. She took it willingly enough, but when she caught sight of the cup and the spoon, she got up from her bed and ran outside shouting, "Manoa-el-rubo-aam! Manoa-el-rubo-aam!"

Mate Hansen rolled a cigarette, lit it, and stared at Mrs. Barnfield, a disbelieving look in his eyes, but he did not speak. Irma said: "Almost at once, the other residents of the village came rushing out of their houses; and when they heard the sick woman's story, and saw the cup still in my hands, they gathered in groups and talked in a language I'd never heard before. Then they approached me slowly, as if they were in awe of me all of a sudden, and when they were a little way off, they knelt down and bowed their heads. I didn't know what was expected of me, but I gave them all a taste of the milk that remained in the cup, and after each had taken the milk, he fell on his face before me and kissed my shoes. Neither Sam nor I knew why they were behaving in such an odd manner—in fact, we don't know to this very day—but we did realize that God had somehow placed a great instrument for good in our hands, and we meant to make the most of it. Afterwards, the islanders made a confession of belief, as Sam instructed them to. Later, we baptised them all, and led them finally into the Church of God."

She turned to Sam for confirmation, but he only sighed and inclined his head. He raised his face to the sunlight, and suddenly he knew that death stood there beside him. He trembled at his knowledge, closed his eyes and spoke soundlessly. "Dear

Lord!" he said. "Do not let me die at sea! Let me see my mother's grave once more! Let me be buried among the hills where I was born!" He lowered his head, wondering if the faith of Shurabast was as ridiculous as he had once thought it; that if, after all, it was not the first and the final religion of all who live. He stared outward at the serene, deceptive sea, and in that interval he experienced a moment of clarity and resignation. It seemed to him, then, that when everything else had gone, hope sometimes remained; but when hope had gone too, then dignity must somehow take its place. . . .

Irma said: "Administering the milk became a bit of a nuisance later on. There were a number of ceremonials which the natives expected me to participate in, some of them quite original indeed. For instance, the milk must be given at sunset, and then only in that little grove of trees at the base of Min-Raybaat. I must stand in just such a way at the time, and I must hold the cup and spoon in the correct hands, at the right distance from the altar. Luckily, Sam and I were never ones to bother much about religious precedent, so we agreed to all the reasonable demands our congregation made on us."

Mate Hansen excused himself and went below to think out the things he had just heard, for the vessel which Irma had described in such detail seemed identical with the legendary communion cup of Raybaat. The story, which he had heard as a boy, and which he did not now believe, was concerned with the history of thousands of years ago; with the days when October Island had been attacked by savages from the mainland, and its civilization destroyed. It seemed, on that terrible, remote day, that the high priest had hidden the emblems of the temple in a place which only he knew. Later that morning, he had died in the general slaughter without revealing the place of concealment, and the holy communion cup, which Raybaat had fashioned with his own hands from the skull of his divine, cannibal mother, had never been seen again.

The loss of the cup had inevitably meant a loss of the power of Shurabast, which had drawn its strength from the holiness of the vessel; but there was comfort in the legend too, for it was prophesied that when the prestige of Raybaat was lowest, when his religion was discredited everywhere in the outside world, then he would return his cup to the faithful through the medium of a great priestess, a priestess who would restore Ok-turbaat to its old power, and bring with her a thousand years of peace and glory.

Mate Hansen kicked off his shoes and stretched out on his bunk, his arms folded beneath his head. The words the sick woman had used when she ran out of her hut were in the fifth, or sacred language of the island. Translated freely, they were: "She is here! The Great Breast Mother of the Universe is here!" . . .

All at once he turned on his belly and laughed for the first time in months. He laughed hysterically, his mouth pressed flat against his pillow, for he wondered at that moment if the missionaries had actually converted the people of October Island to Christianity, as they imagined, or if they, themselves, had not unwittingly embraced Shurabast. Later, when he was calm once more, he washed his face and hands and went on deck about his duties.

Irma and her husband were still sitting in the sun. She had finished her mending for that morning, and as it was now close to lunch time, she folded the garments she had worked on, piled them on the deck, and patted them lightly with her hand. The gesture made her think of the islanders and the difficulties she had met with in clothing them. In a way, she felt that she had *succeeded* in her efforts; and yet, in another way, she had not succeeded at all, for although the women were now clad modestly from ankle to throat, they had cut holes in the waists of their frocks and let their long, ripe breasts hang outward against the calico. She had tried every means in her power to induce her daughters to cover themselves all over, but the women, who as a rule were so docile, so pathetically anxious to please her, had only smiled and shaken their heads, pretending that they did not understand her scoldings.

"I keep thinking about the natives and remembering how much they esteem us," said Irma after a moment. "Perhaps we were wrong to leave them, Sam." Her husband did not answer, and she went on: "We've been gone only a week, but already I miss them, and wonder if they miss us a little too." She got up from her chair, smoothed down her dress and continued quickly, "But of course they miss us too! They must miss us dreadfully, after all the things we *did* for them!"

She was correct in her surmise, for the people of October Island missed them a great deal indeed, and at the very moment she spoke, they were taking the most practical means at their command to bring their benefactors back again. They had missed them even on that first day, when the gray, dirty little schooner had receded slowly into the immensity of the Pacific Ocean, and they had stood in desolation among the palm trees, singing hymns and praying the prayers they had been taught; but to their surprise, the disappearing vessel, with only the tips of her masts now visible against the sky, did not miraculously turn in her course and speed back to them.

When there was no sign of the schooner at all, they turned and went back to their villages, but not without hope, for no matter how ineffectual the religion of the missionaries was in their unskilled hands, they still had the ceremonials of Raybaat to aid them in resolving their calamity.

Raybaat, as everyone knew, was fond of the flesh of fat young children. If such a child was delivered to him at sunrise each morning, he would in time, when his social debt became too embarrassing to be ignored further, see that the accompanying prayer of his donors was granted. . . . But the people did not want to sacrifice their greatly loved children if a milder solution could be found. They discussed the problem with sighs and shakes of their heads, and then one of the villagers pointed out that since Raybaat was so old, the chances were that he could no longer distinguish between the flesh of a child and that of any other young animal—a pig for example.

At once, the islanders began discussing this new way out of their dilemma. Pigs and children were identical both in appearance and in their disregard of all habits of ordinary daintiness, they said eagerly. Both were stubborn and unreasonable; both ate their food without manners, making loud, gulping noises as they did so; both cried all day long, and screamed with rage the instant their wishes were thwarted. They debated the question at length, coming to the conclusion that the most noticeable difference between a pig and a child was the fact that a pig was covered with hair, and a child was not—but that distinction, they said slyly, nudging one another with their elbows, was one which could be remedied.

So, early the next morning, they shaved a young pig with a sharp clam shell, and uttering their prayers for the return of the missionaries, they dropped the pig down the crater of the volcano. That day they waited nervously to see if Raybaat had been taken in by their cleverness, but just when they were convinced they had fooled him, a jet of steam and a few stones rose indignantly out of the crater, followed by grumbles from the depths of the cone, and a short, cynical belch of derision.

It was then they knew there was no hope of deceiving their god, and next morning, and each morning thereafter at sunrise, a living child, washed, oiled and perfumed with spices, was dropped into the crater; but at the end of the ninetieth day, the day when Raybaat should have granted their prayers, nothing had happened at all. Some time afterwards, when they were becoming desperate, teams of islanders would station themselves on either side of the volcano and hold pointed conversations across the crater.

One team would shout loudly: "It seems that when people do a certain favor for a person of high position, that that other person, no matter how exalted he happens to be, should, in common fairness, do something in return for the people we're speaking of at this instant."

Then the answer from the other side of the crater would be: "That's the way it seems to us, too. The laws of politeness advocate a prompt return of favors, as everybody knows; but some, whose names we would not dream of repeating, for fear they might hear us, and hold it against us, seem to be so old and discourteous that they've lost all the common decencies that others observe."

They continued these conversations through the sixth, the seventh, and the eighth months of their prayers, apparently neither arousing Raybaat, nor goading him into action; then, toward the end of the ninth month, when they had almost lost all hope, one of their number looked toward the harbor at the moment the sun freed itself from the sea, and lifted above it. He turned to the others and pointed in triumph, for there, coming toward them, was the schooner *Mattie B. Powell* under full sail.

At the sight, the people embraced one another and wept with a sort of nervous joy. Then, when their first emotions were expended, they hurried down the side of the volcano, some of them going to the home of the missionaries to clean it and decorate it with flowers and tropical fruits, others racing to the harbor, to stand there and chatter together shrilly. One of the group at the end of the mole shielded his eyes and called out suddenly, "Look! Somebody is standing at the bow of the vessel! Perhaps it's the missionary. Perhaps it's his wife!"

It was neither. It was Captain Hansen himself. He had called his passenger, Mrs. Barnfield, a little before sunrise, as she had asked him to do, and he now awaited her on deck. He lifted his binoculars and watched the natives as they waved their arms and scurried up and down the narrow beach. Listening, he could hear their voices when they shouted, and even the sound of their distant flutes and finger-drums; and he lowered his glasses and sighed, for the very warmth of this welcome, which so plainly was not for himself, reminded him inevitably of an event in his own past, and saddened him a little. . . .

His father was Professor Hans Axel Hansen, the famous antiquarian who had once lived on October Island to investigate the customs of its people, and who, obviously enough, had done so with some success. He had left the island, never to return, when his son was two years old, and, naturally, the boy had not remembered him at all. Later, when he was growing up, he thought of his father a great deal. He had visions of meeting him again, visions in which they were alone together in a quiet room. At first, they would stand looking at each other, neither quite knowing what to do next; then, at the same instant, they would raise their arms and walk toward each other blindly, and embrace, their cheeks pressed together. Perhaps the old man would weep a little, laugh with embarrassment and turn his head away so that his son could not see him; perhaps the boy himself would weep a little, too. . . . Then his father would give him his blessing, and the boy would kneel, kiss his father's hand, and walk out of the room satisfied, without looking back.

This fantasy had so haunted his youth, that, later on when he was a seaman, and in a port near his father's home, he had written him an affectionate but rather illiterate note, in which he expressed his intention of visiting him on a certain day at a certain hour. On that particular day, he walked down the quiet, European street where his father lived, stopped before the correct house, and rapped on the door. At once two policemen came out of the vestibule and confronted him. They thought it was only fair to advise him of the punishment that awaits the extortioner, they said. He must write no more threatening letters, and he must make no further effort to see Professor Hansen. If he disregarded this warning, he would be arrested and jailed immediately.

In those days, Captain Hansen had been a boy of nineteen, and he had listened to the policemen with a sort of shamed amazement. He kept saying, "But what you say is not true at all. He is my father. How could I possibly want to harm my own father?"

Then he had bowed gravely, and walked down the steps; but when he was on the sidewalk once more, something impelled him to turn and look at one of the upstairs windows. The curtain there was pulled to one side, and for a moment he stared into the cold, wary eyes of his father; then suddenly the face was gone, and the curtain had fallen back into place, and he was entirely alone once more.

The memory of that bitter day had remained with him all his life. When it was fresh, he would often stop what he was doing, stand still, and shudder; but now, so many years afterwards, he merely felt shame and a little regret as he recalled the senseless, unnecessary humiliation, and he sighed and moved his hand slowly across the rail.

Mrs. Barnfield joined him a minute or so later, and he handed her the binoculars without comment. The sounds from the island were clearer now, more definable in their purpose, and Irma, watching the natives, said quickly, "But how did they know I would be on this particular ship, at this particular time? How did they know I was coming back at all?"

Her one regret was that Sam was not present to share her triumph. Thus far, she had not been able to speak of his death, not even to Captain Hansen during the days they had spent together in Honolulu; but now, seeing the warmth of the welcome that awaited her, she felt as though she were released at last; and standing there in the early light, she explained that the Vermont winter had been too much for her husband, and that he had died a short time after their arrival.

She said: "When he was dying, and knew it, he asked me to bury him at the old Barnfield farm, where he was born. I promised I would, and did what I promised. He died when it was below zero, with the earth frozen solid. The farm was several miles from town. Nobody lived there any more, and the family burial-ground where he wanted to lie was on one side of a flinty hill. I went there with the grave diggers to see that everything was the way he wanted it. It was snowing lightly at the time, and as the men dug among the rocks, their picks struck sparks which sprang outward, and were quenched by the snow; but at last the grave was wide and deep enough, and that afternoon, we put him in it. Those in the village who remembered him stood there beside me in the cold; but during the long prayer, it began to snow once more, and before the men could fill the grave with earth, it had filled up first with snow."

She turned resolutely and smiled, knowing that this was no time for grief, but a time for joy. The schooner was nearing the lagoon itself, and the welcome from the beach was increasing in intensity. She pressed forward against the rail, waved her hand, and then blew a kiss to her worshippers. At once they began to scream louder, and to dance about the beach. Some of them plunged into the water and swam toward the vessel. When they reached it, they frolicked like welcoming porpoises, diving, turning, and coming to the surface to laugh and shake water from their hair, their teeth shining in the sunlight; but at last, when the schooner was abreast of the mole, and the people had moored it there, Irma came to the rail once more, while the natives, in an ecstasy of exhilaration, capered, cried out, and pelted her gently with flowers.

It was then she noticed that in her absence her converts had discarded the clothes she had made for them, and that they were now as naked as they had been on the day she first landed on the island. She made a mild, clucking sound of disapproval, then, collecting her thoughts, she held up her hand for silence, and began her official speech of return.

She explained that she had not once been happy after she had left the island, for it appeared that the land which she had always thought of as being her home, was not, in reality, her true home at all. October Island was her true home, she said, and not the foolish, terrifying world outside it; and now that her husband was dead, and no longer needed her, she had returned as quickly as she could to those she loved, and who loved her in return. She was deeply moved by the welcome she had received, and she promised she would never leave the island again. . . .

She paused, and at once the islanders began one of the hymns she had taught them, accompanying themselves with their pebble-gourds, their drums, and their native marimba-like instruments. Irma tilted her head and listened thoughtfully. There was something *wrong* with the hymn, she thought, although she could not say precisely what it was. The words seemed accurate enough, and the tune itself was reasonably true; but there was an excitement about it, a certain sensuousness which no hymn should have, and she shook her head in disapproval, and listened critically. When the hymn was finished, she continued her speech in her quick, positive voice saying:

"My return is the result of a miracle worked by the Lord. You see, I prayed diligently that I could somehow come back to you, and at last my prayers were answered, for a cousin of mine whom

I'd not seen since childhood—a certain Miss Amelia Goodpasture—died without making a will, and the court decided that I was her next of kin, and sole heir. I was completely astonished, particularly when I was told the net estate was substantially more than a half million dollars."

She paused significantly and then said: "Now, at the finish of my prayers to be returned to October Island, I invariably appended a prayer on Captain Hansen's behalf: a prayer that he be granted a schooner of his own, since I knew that that was his dearest wish; so, since both prayers were linked together, I concluded, naturally enough, that both had been answered, and I arranged to meet him in Honolulu three weeks ago. He demurred at first, but finally he accepted the *Mattie B. Powell,* which I assured him was not a gift from me in any sense, but a gift from the Lord."

She motioned to Captain Hansen, and when he stood beside her, she finished her speech, stating that the remainder of her inheritance had been put into a trust fund for the benefit of the island, and that her agents on the mainland had been instructed to see that quantities of condensed milk were purchased, and transported to the inhabitants there at regular intervals.

She paused, shook hands with Captain Hansen, and began descending the ladder briskly, while the natives rushed toward her shouting, "Manoa-el-rubo-aam! Manoa-el-rubo-aam!" At once they lifted her in their arms and carried her to a sort of flower-decked throne, which they had prepared in anticipation of her return. They seated her on it, took the pins from her hair, and allowed it to fall loosely about her shoulders. They put a head-dress of feathers and shells about her forehead, and anointed her brows, her lips, her hands, and her feet, with an ointment of a particular fragrance. She laughed at them with a sort of apologetic pleasure, protested the silliness of their activities, and tapped them indulgently with her fan; then, as the ceremonial neared its completion, she understood at last the real motive which had urged her to destroy the tablets: Their discovery would have meant a prompt emigration of scientists to the island, and that she did not want at all. The island was particularly her own, she felt. That was a thing she had known from the beginning, and she could do very well without the company of Mr. Reginald Sykes, Dr. Clement Higgs, Mr. Wayland Yates, or even Professor Johannes Katz, whose name had always fascinated her.

Seeing these things so clearly, she smiled, nodded her head, and looked languidly about her; and at once she knew what had bothered her since her return: There were almost no children at all in the welcoming crowd, and sitting up straight on her throne, she said in surprise: "But where are the children? What has become of all the children?" . . .

Captain Hansen, observing the last ceremonies of Mrs. Barnfield's deification—the final rites which were making her not only a goddess, but the divine concubine of Raybaat, as well, was suddenly filled with a sense of impotent horror. These goddess-concubines—although there had not been one on October Island since ancient times—were worshipped by the people for a year, and for a year only. During the period of their reign, they knew an adoration without limits; at the end of their year, they were dropped into the crater of the volcano in order that they might rejoin Raybaat, and lying intimately beside him, explain the human frailties of his followers, and intercede with him to forgive them all.

He wanted to call out to the old woman, to tell her of her danger; but he realized that she would not believe him if he warned her, or, if she did believe him, that she would only lift her chin and say in her nasal voice, "I've looked after myself all these years without your help, young man! If you'll mind your own business now, I'll continue to do so!"

When the ceremony was over, the natives made a sort of sedan chair of the throne, and riding there so high above her people, Mrs. Barnfield put the pins back in her hair, laughed easily, and called out: "But where are the children? Really, you must tell me where the children are!"

Suddenly, Captain Hansen was sick of this kind, opinionated, generous, stupid, courageous old woman; and as she disappeared with her worshippers around a curve in the beach, he knew that he never wanted to see her again, that he was through with her forever. In a short time, he must go below and see to the unloading of the condensed milk, but for the time being, he wanted only to stand here in the morning sunlight and think of Mrs. Barnfield, and her works. . . .

Once, a long time ago, when he had first left October Island, and his ship was on drydock in San Francisco, he had passed a theater at which a musical piece was playing. He had never been to the theater, and hoping that the experience would give him a better understanding of the lives and customs of others, he bought his ticket timidly, and went inside.

Even after all these years, he still remembered that wonderful evening, for the principals had been in good voice, the music tuneful, the costumes new and elaborate, and the girls beautiful. As the evening advanced, the plot of the piece became more and more involved, until, at length, there seemed no way out at all; but sitting alone in the darkened theater, in a strange land he had not seen before that morning, he accepted the play as real in every detail, until, at length, a stranger appeared in the final scene to set matters right for everyone: to clear the overseer of the forgery charge; to pay off the mortgage on the pineapple farm; to end the misunderstanding which kept the secondary lovers apart; to reveal that the handsome but penniless tenor was actually a prince, and, as such, worthy to marry an American girl.

It was at this point that he doubted the play's validity, and he had shaken his head in disbelief, saying, "Things don't happen that way. It's not true to life." But now, remembering what Mrs. Barnfield had accomplished for others, he wondered if his judgment had not been a little hasty. Certainly it was true that, through her efforts, he now owned a splendid schooner; that Sam had his cold grave on a bleak hillside, precisely as he had desired it; that the islanders had their great goddess and her cup filled with condensed milk; that Irma, herself, had the inexhaustible adoration she craved, and, later on, would have her quick unanticipated death in the volcano. . . .

When he said the play was untrue to life, did he not really

mean it was untrue to his experience, to the special logic which gave his own life consequence, and made it tolerable? He moved his hands slowly along the rail, thinking that if we desire greatly enough, if we seek with a proper diligence, everything becomes true to life at the end. Perhaps that was the meaning which the divided ones like himself, who have peace nowhere in the world, seek with such desperation, and rarely find.